BLACK MESA

BLACK MESA

SHARON BALTS

To Kathy Anderson –
Best Wishes!
Sharon Balts
1/16/08

TATE PUBLISHING & *Enterprises*

This title is also available as a Tate Out Loud product. Visit www.tatepublishing.com for more information.

Published by Tate Publishing & Enterprises, LLC
127 E. Trade Center Terrace | Mustang, Oklahoma 73064 USA
1.888.361.9473 | www.tatepublishing.com

Tate Publishing is committed to excellence in the publishing industry. The company reflects the philosophy established by the founders, based on Psalms 68:11,
"The Lord gave the word and great was the company of those who published it."

Edited by Tracy Terrell
Cover design by Jacob Crissup
Cover photograph by Gerard Kowalski
Interior design by Lindsay B. Behrens

Published in the United States of America

ISBN: 978-1-60247-587-3
1. Fiction 2. Western 3. Romance
07.08.29

Dedicated to Kennith, the newest blessing in my life.

ONE

The sound of a truck screeching to a halt at the far end of the service road did not distract Cassidy from her efforts to free the little dog's tangled leash from the bushes. But when doors slammed and voices were raised, the young woman peeked from under the guard rail to investigate the commotion. As she peered from her hidden spot, the scuffle escalated. A tall, big-boned man slammed his fist into the stomach of a much smaller, dark-haired one whose arms were being held tight by two more assailants.

Over the booming bass echoing from the nearby tavern, a string of curses filtered through Cassidy's ears along with a dire warning. A gruff voice growled, "Nobody runs away from Trent Dominic…," as another blow was dealt.

The captive spit at his attackers and cursed them, bringing a further beating until he slumped over in the arms of his enemies.

Cassidy scarcely dared to breathe as she remained kneeling behind the guard rail post. She was thankful for the long shadows being cast down from the mountain peaks by the setting sun. In the gathering darkness, hidden under the bushes as she was, it was unlikely she would be detected unless Pansy started barking. She turned her attention to the problem pup who had dashed under the rail and wound the leash into an intricate knot around the brush.

The beaten man suddenly rose up with all his might, breaking the hold of the smallest of the three attackers and knocking him to the ground. As the victim fought with the assailant, the big man drew a knife. With one quick thrust, the weapon was driven into the back of the beaten victim as he broke the grip of the one who held him. Cassidy watched in horror as the dark-haired man's knees crumpled under him, dropping him slowly into the dirt.

The little dog tussled at the leash.

"Wait, Pansy," Cassidy coached in a whisper as she freed the leash from the tangle. "Be quiet…"

Pansy ran under the guard rail and hit the end of the leash, then protested the confinement with a high-pitched yip. Cassidy's heart beat wildly. She motioned for the little dog to come to her. The five-pound terrier answered with another sharp bark. Cassidy peeked again under the rail to see if the sound had drawn the attention of the men. The big man was climbing into the driver's side of a silver, extended cab truck as the other two swung the body of his victim over the rail, then pushed it over the edge of the cliff to the darkness below. One man opened the passenger door of the vehicle while the other walked around the area, probably to ensure that no evidence of their crime remained.

Cassidy considered her options. She had no idea what lay below her and dared not try to slide out of sight into the ravine, for the deep shadows did not reveal the depth or steepness of the abyss. If Pansy drew the attention of the killers, Cassidy knew she would have to run toward the buildings. She wondered if she could get across the small open area and through the door of the gas station or restaurant before the men could traverse the length of the service road to stop her.

An explosion of yelps from the impatient little dog propelled Cassidy into action. She bolted from her position under the rail and raced toward the back of the buildings, praying that there was a back door that wasn't locked. With Pansy in tow, she ran past a loading dock and was quickly out of sight of the men, but knew by the distant shouts she'd been spotted. While footsteps crunched on the gravel, the truck engine was started and tires spun as the accelerator was punched.

A hand suddenly covered Cassidy's mouth and a strong arm enveloped her small waist. A voice whispered close to her ear, "This way!" She was pulled along the edge of the building by a man in a black cowboy hat and black leather jacket. Pausing at a dumpster, the man wrestled the leash from the young woman and looped the end over a steel bar. He grabbed Cassidy's jacket, yanked it off her, and threw it in with the trash.

Cassidy couldn't even find the words to protest as she was jerked through a narrow alley between the buildings. Just before stepping up onto the boardwalk, the stranger boldly unclipped the barrette that held Cassidy's long hair and tossed it away into the dust.

With her golden brown tresses tumbling down over her shoulders, Cassidy blindly stumbled along behind the stranger. He stopped suddenly in front of a door just as the large silver truck came into view around the corner of the far building. The stranger had his hand on the doorknob but instead of disappearing inside as Cassidy hoped, he casually turned and led her toward the parking lot.

As the silver truck approached slowly, menacingly, Cassidy tripped and nearly fell. The stranger helped her stand upright. "Easy, girl," he whispered. "Stay calm. We're going to get you out of here. Just keep walking."

The silver truck was parked nearby and the driver stepped out. The man who held Cassidy questioned in a loud voice, "How many drinks did you have while you were waitin' for me?"

Cassidy's mind could hardly focus, but the tavern came to mind. They were in front of the tavern. She realized her rescuer was pretending they had just left the place and that she was stumbling drunk.

"Ahhhh....ahhh, two?" she ventured, not knowing how many it would realistically take to make her stumble as she did.

"Two!" her rescuer laughed. "And you just had two more! You ain't drivin' yourself home, Darlin'!"

Cassidy sensed that the men were circling the buildings in search of a woman with a red jacket who witnessed their awful crime. She concentrated on putting one foot before the other. Her appearance of drunkenness wasn't hard to accomplish when raw fear made her knees shake uncontrollably. Had her companion not been holding her close, she doubted she would have been able to walk at all.

As the stranger steered her toward a white truck, Cassidy was aware that the killers had found Pansy tied to the dumpster. She desperately wanted to run to her family's motor home and hide inside before the little dog saw her. But she knew her brother, Jason, would have locked the vehicle when he moved it from the gas pumps to park it near the restaurant.

The small parking lot seemed endless as the pair strolled across it, walking arm-in-arm as though they were intimate friends with no cause to hurry anywhere. The stranger helped Cassidy step up inside the truck cab and closed the door behind her. As he walked around the vehicle and entered on the driver's side, Cassidy watched the scene behind her in the rearview mirror. The tall man with the gruff, raspy voice took Pansy from his accomplice who held her and carried the little dog into the tavern. The man who had just given up Pansy remained in front of the restaurant, while the third returned to the alley from which Cassidy and her rescuer had just come.

As the white truck slowly backed out of the parking lot and casually proceeded down the highway, the young woman allowed herself to let out a tentative sigh of relief. Though her heart still beat wildly, she felt a momentary hope of safety.

Once they were out of sight of the buildings, the stranger pushed the truck's accelerator and propelled the vehicle at high speeds along the winding mountain road. Cassidy stiffened with renewed fear and clutched the door handle as the man negotiated the road's dangerous curves.

"You're not from around here, are you?" he questioned Cassidy after several moments of silent concentration on his driving.

"No, I live in Minnesota," she answered and suddenly wondered if she should be giving such information to a stranger. Though the man appeared to be her rescuer, Cassidy decided she should be cautious.

"Were you traveling with anyone?" he asked bluntly, keeping his eyes on the road.

"My mother and brother," Cassidy replied curtly.

She recalled seeing little Pansy in the arms of a murderer. The tall man would probably take the dog to one business after the other hoping the pet would identify her owner, thereby pointing out their murder witness. Once he entered the restaurant, Cassidy's mother and brother would learn that Pansy was left alone behind the building. Then they, too, would join the desperate search for Cassidy. The young woman was glad her mother scarcely resembled her, for the killers could not possibly mistake Elaine for the witness they sought.

"We may have bought a few minutes, but it won't be long before that dog leads those men to your family," the stranger said, affirming Cassidy's fears. "Once they start asking questions, they'll probably figure out the gal that just left the parking lot is the one they're looking for."

The stranger pulled a cell phone from an inner pocket of his coat. "Do either of them have a phone?" he asked.

Cassidy brightened. "Yes, my brother will be carrying his!" she replied excitedly.

"Call him. We won't have a signal once we cross that next ridge. Tell him you witnessed a murder. Ask him to go to The Alibi Saloon and tell Joe, the bartender, to call the sheriff. Then I want to talk to Joe," the stranger instructed.

Cassidy dialed Jason's number as quickly as her shaking hands would allow. Her brother answered immediately and Cassidy blurted, "Jason, don't talk! Just listen! I witnessed a murder out behind the buildings and the killers saw me and I had to run away and I'm hiding from them. Go to the tavern! Tell Joe, the bartender, to call the sheriff. We're probably going to lose our signal as soon as we get over the next hill, so I don't have much time to talk!"

"Okay," Jason answered when Cassidy paused for a breath. "I'm on my way."

Several seconds passed in silence before Jason's voice could be heard again. "I'm outside now," the young man spoke quietly. "Some big, tall guy just brought Pansy into the restaurant and gave her to Mom."

"He's one of the killers that are after me, Jason! A tall guy with a tan hat and a vest over a striped shirt and he's got a big belly," Cassidy spoke excitedly. "And the other two were outside. A small, short guy with a dark hat, wearing a denim jacket and another one a little taller with a brown coat.

"Yeah, I saw 'em," Jason said, as loud, thumping music nearly drowned out his voice.

Cassidy listened in silence as Jason said, "Joe?"

A deeper voice asked, "What can I do for you, young man?"

"Please call the sheriff. There's been a murder."

"Jason, give the phone to Joe!" Cassidy shouted in her brother's ear.

"Joe here."

Cassidy passed the phone to the driver, who spoke hurriedly. "Joe, it's Brady! Three of Dominic's men knifed a guy and tossed the body into the gulch behind the old motel. A young lady witnessed the scuffle, and I've got her with me. Do whatever you can to delay those guys so we can get some distance between us, 'cause sure as you're born they'll chase after us. I'm gonna get out of the area and try to get…Joe?…Joe? Can you hear me?"

The stranger studied the minute lighted screen of his cell phone for a moment before folding the device and dropping it onto the console. "Well, I have no idea how much of the message he got, but they're on their own now," he said with a sigh, "and so are we."

Cassidy ventured to study the stranger beside her. His wide-brimmed cowboy hat cloaked his eyes, but the neon glow of the dash lights made visible high cheek bones and a strong jaw that sported a precisely trimmed beard and mustache. He glanced her way and caught her watching him.

"Are you scared?" he asked.

"Yes," she replied.

"Of me?"

"I don't know. I don't know you and I don't know where you're taking me and my family doesn't know where I am…" Cassidy lamented.

"My name is Brady Hollister," the man introduced himself. He glanced Cassidy's way and smiled.

"Cassidy Henderson," she returned politely.

"I'm pleased to meet you, Cassidy Henderson," Brady said with a lingering glance toward his passenger. "I sure wish our meeting was under better circumstances. If I'd known you weren't alone and had somebody who would look for you, maybe I'd have stayed put and let you run past me. But you headed straight for me, and those guys would have found me when they were looking for you."

"You saw the whole thing too?" Cassidy questioned.

"Yeah. I'm a private detective. I knew something was up when I saw those three guys together, so I went snooping around and ended up outside the back of the saloon. I couldn't believe it when I saw you hiding behind that guard rail. What in the world were you doin' under there?"

"I was walking the dog…and daydreaming, I guess. Next thing I knew, she'd gone around and around the bushes and gotten stuck," Cassidy explained.

"That dog could have gotten you killed."

"I know," she acknowledged with a shudder.

"Are you cold?" the man asked. He closed his partially opened window and adjusted buttons on the dash. "I forgot I took your jacket. I've got a blanket in the back. You're welcome to it."

Though it was the first week in July, chilly Big Horn Mountain air invaded the high desert hills when the sun dipped below the horizon. Cassidy had been so engrossed in her escape she hadn't felt chilled until now. She turned around and searched for the blanket amidst the contents of the narrow back seat of the extended cab truck. A lariat and slightly smelly boots lay on the floor next to a box that contained folders and papers. She located the blanket under a cooler and slid it out. Unfolding it, she tossed it around her shoulders.

As she settled back down in her seat, Cassidy realized the stranger had been studying her curvy figure. Detecting a faint smile on his lips, she adjusted the blanket to cover herself fully and then strapped on her seat belt and became intent on watching the dark landscape portrayed in the truck's headlights. She decided she'd better start looking at road signs and paying attention to where she was in case she had to flee from this man.

"So, you're from Minnesota, huh?" Brady questioned. "Where in Minnesota?"

"I live in a suburb of Minneapolis."

"Oohh. Big city girl," Brady said in a lightly teasing tone. "What brings you to Wyoming?"

Cassidy bristled at the remark about being a big city girl, but chose to ignore it rather than confront the man. *Let him think I'm a city girl,* she stubbornly decided. *That way he'll never know I grew up on a farm in Wisconsin. The less he knows about me, the better.*

"My brother and his wife live in Idaho. They just had their first baby. We were taking a scenic route through Wyoming on the way home from visiting them," she politely explained.

"Was that your big motor home in the parking lot?"

Irritation rose again. *He certainly is snoopy.* The thought flitted through Cassidy's mind. She quickly pushed it away. *He said he was a detective. It's just his habit to ask a lot of questions.*

"My Dad and his brothers bought the motor home together. The families take turns using it," she answered.

The stranger glanced her way and caught Cassidy blinking rapidly, trying to dispel the sudden hot tears that so often threatened at the mention of her recently deceased father. Too late, she turned away from the man to face the window.

"Your father didn't make the trip with you?" Brady questioned.

"No, he passed away," Cassidy whispered hoarsely. It was the only answer she could muster at the moment. Her loss was too recent, too painful to share with a complete stranger. She couldn't bear to discuss her father's death with such an overbearing man who too quickly pried into other people's business.

"I'm sorry," Brady apologized gently. "I didn't mean to upset you. I thought maybe if you talked about your family, you'd forget about what you saw for a while."

The man's words took Cassidy by surprise. She had been mentally criticizing him and then he made a sincere apology. His unexpected kindness and concern added to her emotional upheaval. She could no longer hold back the tears that slid silently down her cheeks. Brady drove in silence for several minutes, allowing her to release her pent-up anxiety in as much privacy as the truck cab would allow.

Cassidy jerked out of her reverie when she realized the truck was slowing and the blinker was on. They were turning off the main road onto a dirt one. She hadn't been paying attention as she planned and had no idea where they were.

"Where are you taking me!?" she demanded.

Brady answered patiently, "We're going to try to get help from a relative of mine. He's an old duffer that lives back here in the hills. I'm thinking maybe we can swap trucks with him to confuse anyone who might be following us. And he's probably got some food he can spare. Are you hungry?"

"Yes, I'm famished!" Cassidy admitted.

"I'm hungry, too, but don't start lickin' your chops yet," Brady warned his passenger. "We're still a long way from Jubel's place." He motioned to the back seat. "You can check the cooler back there. There might be a couple candy bars and cans of pop left."

Cassidy unfastened her seat belt and stretched over the seat once again. This time, she made sure she was draped with the blanket to prevent unwanted attention. Brady snapped on the overhead light as she lifted the lid of the small cooler.

"What kind of diet are you on?" she asked her companion. "All you've got in here are sweets!"

"Yeah, well," Brady answered, "I pack my lunch off the convenience store shelves."

Cassidy returned to her seat with two cans of cola and two candy bars. She opened one can and secured it in the circular holder on the console within the driver's reach, then tore open a candy bar and passed it to him.

"Thanks," Brady nodded and looked fully at her. With the truck cab lights on, Cassidy was able to really see her companion for the first time. She briefly returned the man's gaze, noting his light blue eyes, sculptured features, and sun-darkened face. He peered back at the road as Cassidy turned her attention to opening her candy bar.

As Brady flipped the switch to turn off the cab lights, Cassidy detected a slight grin that twitched the corner of his mouth. She wondered again if this man could be trusted.

TWO

Elaine Henderson stood outside the door of the women's restroom with Pansy nestled tightly in her arms. She had been searching for Cassidy since a stranger brought her pet and told her he had found the little dog tied to a dumpster. Elaine had checked the motor home and the restrooms in the gas station and restaurant. *Surely Cassidy understood that we were going to meet in the restaurant,* she thought. With growing alarm, she whispered a prayer to her Heavenly Father for her daughter's safety, even as her mind imagined the type of clientele that might lurk at the nearby tavern. She sensed that something was terribly wrong.

Through tear-filled eyes, Elaine watched as Jason approached her, making his way past several dining room tables. "I can't find Cassidy anywhere," she sobbed quietly.

"Mom," Jason put his long arm around the shoulders of his much-shorter mother. He leaned slightly and whispered in her ear, "I got a call from Cassidy, and I want to tell you what she said. Let's sit down a minute."

Jason led the way to a table in the far corner of the diner, as far from the other customers as possible. It was clear as patrons and staff watched the scene in silence that everyone sensed something was amiss.

"Mom, Cassie says she's okay. That's what she told me over the phone."

"Where is she?" Mrs. Henderson whispered.

"She didn't say. She only had a few minutes to talk. She said she witnessed a murder behind the buildings when she was walking Pansy. The killers saw her and ran after her, and she's hiding from them."

"Oh, Lord!" Elaine breathed the words.

"Mom, we've put in a call to the sheriff and alerted him about the murder. When he gets here, I'll go talk to him."

"But where can she be?" Jason's mother asked tearfully. "She's been gone so long."

"She's with someone, Mom. And she was calling from a cell phone, but not her own."

"I'm going to the motor home. She'll come there if she can," Elaine resolved as she scurried out of the booth and headed for the door.

As the pair walked across the parking lot, a police car pulled into the drive and parked in front of the tavern.

"Come with me to talk to him, Mom," Jason ordered. "I don't want you staying in the motor home alone. Not even for a few minutes. Cassidy described the men involved in the killing and the one that was carrying Pansy is one of them."

Elaine shuddered to think that she had brushed hands with such a violent man just a few minutes before. She quickly unlocked the camper and shoved Pansy inside before following her twenty-one-year-old son toward the tavern.

The officer was questioning the husky man behind the bar about the call he had made when Elaine and Jason entered the unfamiliar, smoky blue atmosphere. As the patrons of the place eyed the officer, the bartender turned the music down to allow for easier conversation.

"All I know," Joe insisted as he pointed out the approaching Jason to the deputy, "is that I had a phone handed to me by this young man and the voice at the other end said 'Call the sheriff. There was a murder out behind the motel.' Apparently some guy got knifed and his body was thrown into the ravine."

"Who called you?" the deputy asked Jason.

"My sister," Jason stated.

"And where is your sister?" the officer asked.

"She's hiding. The killers saw her and were coming after her so she ran away. But she described three men to me. There's one of them right there!" Jason pointed at the tall man with the tan hat.

The patrons of the place whispered among themselves as they listened to the conversation. Joe remained silent and made a pretense of wiping an already gleaming bar. Elaine's heart pounded as she anxiously watched the scene, wondering how the big man would react to Jason's accusation.

The man glared at Jason, then spoke nonchalantly to the officer. "You know better than that, Deputy. I've been around here for years. I don't make trouble for nobody."

"Deputy!" Jason cried out for the man's attention but the uniformed man held up his hand, signaling that he wanted no more outbursts.

"Boy, you got no business comin' in here, accusing folks of such a thing as murder. If your sister witnessed a crime, then tell her to come out of hiding so I can talk to her."

"I don't know where she is!"

"If your sister is lost, then let's get the facts straight so we can do a proper search for her…"

"She's not lost!" Jason shouted. "She's hiding! She's scared! And what about the man that was murdered? Aren't you even going to look for a body?"

"Yeah, yeah. Calm down. I'll go out back and look around. It's probably a wild goose chase, but I'll check it out," the officer said as he turned toward the door.

Joe signaled one of the patrons to exit out the back door. As the man slipped around the bar, Joe handed him a flashlight. Most of the other patrons followed the deputy outside as if the possibility of a real murder on the sparsely-traveled stretch of road was an event not to be missed.

Elaine Henderson watched quietly through the dark window glass as the deputy headed to his car to drive to the service area at the back of the buildings. A troupe of onlookers marched toward the vacant, shuttered motel. Several patrons scurried to their vehicles to retrieve flashlights before joining the crowd.

Elaine was left in the tavern with only her son, the bartender, and one lone customer seated at a window table. She wondered briefly if she should follow the group. Given the deputy's reluctance at looking for a murder victim, she couldn't help but question how thorough his search would be.

"Boy!" the man at the table shouted to Jason once the room had cleared. "You may as well save your breath accusing any of Trent Dominic's men of murder. The sheriff and his fine deputy here are in Dominic's pocket and those guys are not about to get locked up."

"Chase, don't be tellin' these folks such stuff!" the big man behind the bar reprimanded. His thick, dark brows knit together in a scowl as he warned his patron.

"Well, it's the truth," Chase slurred. "We ain't gettin' no justice 'round here since Higgins got elected sheriff. And Dominic's money put that skunk into office."

"You want a beer, young man?" the bartender asked in an attempt to distract his out-of-the-area customers from heeding Chase's advice.

"No, I don't want a beer," Jason replied emphatically.

Joe turned to Mrs. Henderson and offered her a lemon-lime soda, which she declined. "What does your daughter look like, ma'am?"

Elaine brightened a bit at the thought that someone was making an effort to help. "She's five feet nine inches tall, slender, has long, blonde hair and green eyes."

"I'll bet she's a pretty girl," Joe ventured.

Elaine's eyes filled with tears. She smiled up at the bartender and admitted, "Yes, she is."

"Shoot!" the man named Chase rejoined the conversation. "I know where she is!"

All eyes turned to the man seated by the window.

"She's with Brady Hollister! They pulled out of the parkin' lot a long time ago! Brady wasn't in here with no girl, but he walked out the door and just a few minutes later came up with a tall, blonde one. Walked all lovey-dovey like over to his truck and they took off together."

Elaine and Jason began questioning the man further, but Joe interrupted. "Now, you're not gonna go tellin' that to the deputy are you, Chase?"

"Shoot, no! I ain't tellin' him nothin'! That would get her killed faster than anything, sending Higgins' outfit after her along with Dominic's men."

"What should we do?" Jason demanded of Joe. "Who's this Brady guy who's got my sister?"

"Brady will take good care of her. Don't worry about him," Joe assured Cassidy's anxious family. "He'll do his level best to keep her away from Dominic's thugs. But he's gotta get out of the county and get help from the law somewhere else. In the meantime, just sit tight and act like you're cooperating with the law. Do you have a picture of this gal?"

"I've got one in the motor home in my purse," Elaine stated.

"Well, if the deputy asks for one, you might want to delay finding it. Let the trail get as cold as possible. Give Brady a good head start."

Elaine looked up at her son. She wondered whom they should trust. The deputy who wouldn't believe Jason or the bartender who encouraged them to let a strange man flee the county with her daughter.

Jason looked down at his mother and echoed her thoughts. "Mom, who are we supposed to believe?" he asked.

Elaine breathed a silent prayer for wisdom and took a deep breath before she talked about her inclinations. "I've always trusted the law to be honest, but I don't like that deputy," she replied emphatically. "I can't believe when you tell him there was a murder that he would discredit the witness as the first step in his investigation. And he didn't even attempt to question the big man you said was one of the murderers."

Elaine's fears and confusion were turning to anger. "What does Brady Hollister's truck look like?" she questioned Chase.

"White Ford with black trim, extended cab with a short box," Chase replied. "He went that way." The man indicated the direction with his thumb.

"Let's go," Elaine told her son as she headed for the door. "The motor home is fueled up. Maybe we'll find them along the highway…"

"Ma'am," Joe interjected. "I think you'll do better sittin' tight. If you take off, they'll think you know where your daughter is or where she's going and these guys will come after you like flies after cow dung. You'd be putting yourself and your son in danger. You'd best stay here awhile and see what comes of this search out back."

"But I don't feel safe here!" Elaine insisted. "Cassie wouldn't lie about what she saw and if she described the killers and they're still here…"

A creaky hinge at the back door alerted Joe to the return of the customer who had slipped out the back. The wiry, leather-faced man addressed Joe with a grin.

"Well, the deputy didn't expect to find a body and didn't seem to be tryin' too hard to do it, neither. He was lookin' around with his flashlight a hundred feet from where they dumped it when one of the gals leaned against the guard rail and got her hand full of fresh blood. You probably heard her scream all the way down here. Anyway, the deputy couldn't deny any more that something hadn't happened. And wouldn't you know the body didn't crash all the way to the bottom of the gulch. It got hung up on a rock outcrop. So now they've got a body and blood and a witness. The sheriff's been called in. Looks like poor ol' Higgins has got to work for a livin' tonight!"

"He doesn't have his witness. She's long gone!" Chase spoke quietly to himself and laughed. Elaine heard the man's comment, but scarcely had time to ponder it when her attention was returned to the bar.

"And while that was goin' on I checked around the alley out back. I found this," the wiry man said as he unfolded the red jacket that was tightly clenched in his fist, "and this." The man produced a springy hair-clip that Elaine immediately recognized as the type Cassie often used. "The jacket was in the dumpster and the hair thing was in the dirt in the alley. I checked the dumpster, and there's nobody hiding in there."

"You recognize these things?" the bartender asked Elaine.

She nodded. "They're Cassidy's."

Joe took the jacket, wadded it up, and stuffed it under the bar. "We'll keep that out of sight for awhile," he explained. "Let Dominic's thugs keep thinking they're lookin' for a gal in a red coat."

The thunder of footsteps on the boardwalk alerted those inside the tavern that the crowd was returning. Elaine and Jason listened silently to the hubbub of talking as the saloon refilled.

"So, what's going on out there?" Joe asked.

"Looks like there's been a killin,' sure enough. A couple guys are going down with ropes to try to bring the dead person up," came an excited answer.

The stir continued for several minutes. As one couple headed toward the exit, they were met by a brawny uniformed officer.

"Hold it!" the lawman ordered as he strutted into the smoky room. The throng gave the stout, sandy-haired officer wide berth. "Everybody sit tight. Much to my surprise, we've got what appears to be a murder here in our quiet little community."

Elaine was certain that the man spoke mostly for her and Jason's benefit to assure the visitors that this was not an ordinary occurrence. Elaine bristled as she listened to the gravelly voice of the haughty officer that she knew instinctively was Sheriff Higgins.

"From what my deputy has told me, we have a body in the gulch and we've had a phone call from a young gal who said she witnessed a murder. Before anyone leaves, I want to know if you saw anything suspicious and if anyone has seen this young woman."

"What does she look like?" one of the patrons questioned Elaine and Jason.

"She's tall…" Elaine began.

"Almost six feet," Jason interjected.

"She has green eyes and long blonde hair…" Elaine continued quietly.

"She was wearing a red jacket," Jason informed the crowd. "And she had her hair pinned up on top of her head, so you can't really tell how long it is."

"That's right!" Elaine agreed, thankful for Jason's quick thinking. "She had her hair clipped up in a big fluffy pony tail."

"Well?" Higgins questioned. "Did anyone see anything? Has anyone left here in the last hour or so?"

Elaine breathed a silent prayer, hoping that no one but Chase had seen anything and that in his inebriated state he would have enough self-control to bridle his tongue.

"You should probably check the restaurant and gas station," Joe suggested. "The same crowd that's in here now has been here for quite awhile. I don't recall anyone leaving but to go out back to help search for the body."

"Brady Hollister was in here," one patron mentioned. "But he's been gone a long time. Long before the ruckus started."

"I didn't see him here in the saloon, but when we came, his truck was in the parking lot," another suggested.

"If he was outside, he might have seen or heard something," commented another. "And if he did, Brady's not the kind of guy to walk away and ignore it. He'd check it out."

The tall man with the tan hat joined the conversation. "Does this Hollister fella drive a white Ford truck? I just drove in when a young couple was leaving here," he lied. "They left in a white truck."

Elaine cringed at the man's bold question. *Here stands one of the murderers,* she thought, *acting as if he's trying to help the investigation while he's really trying to pinpoint Cassidy's location so he can hunt her down.*

"Brady drives a white truck, but he was in here alone," the first customer insisted. "I sat next to him and talked to him! He wasn't with anyone."

Sheriff Higgins interrupted and directed a question to the tall man. "What did the young lady look like that got into the white truck?"

"She was tall and skinny and had long, light-colored hair. She was wearing a white shirt and tight blue jeans."

"And what did the guy look like?"

"Who cares? I wasn't lookin' at him!" the tall man said with a chuckle. The crowd laughed with him. "I guess he was average height and build and he wore a black hat and coat."

"Yup," Higgins resolved after confirming that the description offered by the tall man matched that of the bar patrons. "I think we'd best be lookin' for Brady Hollister. Sounds like he mighta run off with the young woman…"

"Sheriff, you haven't even checked in the restaurant or gas station or motel. There's likely been people coming in and out of those places all night!" Joe insisted.

"I will. I will. As soon as my deputies get that body up here, we'll scout around some more," Higgins assured the bartender. "But I don't want to be lookin' for a murderer if this turns out to be an accident or something."

"Sheriff, are you done questioning us?" the tall man with the tan hat asked.

"Yeah, I guess. But you all leave your names and phone numbers in case I need to get hold of you for further questioning," the sheriff ordered. "Joe, you got a pen and paper?"

Joe produced a tablet and pen and laid it on the bar. Patrons signed their names. Elaine watched as the big hand of the murder suspect scribbled an almost indecipherable signature on the page. When he was finished, the man headed for the door. Joe motioned to the wiry informant who had found Cassidy's jacket in the dumpster. The man moved toward the window. Elaine nonchalantly followed suit and watched a couple minutes of heated discussion between the tall man in the tan hat and a lean man in a brown jacket. The pair climbed into the cab of a silver truck and sped away, after which a shorter, stouter man in a worn denim jacket silently strode to a Jeep and headed in the opposite direction.

When they were gone, Elaine returned to the bar, as did Joe's informant.

"They split up," the wiry man spoke quietly to the bartender. "Two of 'em headed south in the silver truck. The other went north in a Jeep."

"Thanks," Joe nodded and turned to Elaine and Jason who waited anxiously at the corner of the bar. He opened a couple cans of soda without asking them for their preference and spoke quietly as he poured the drinks into glasses of ice.

"The three that probably did the killin' just took off, heading in opposite directions. By now, Brady's got a good lead on 'em. I doubt they'll know where to start lookin' for him."

"Where do you think he'll go?" Elaine whispered, but Joe didn't answer for he seemed to sense that the sheriff was moving toward them.

"Ma'am?" Higgins asked politely, gazing at Elaine. "Do you have a picture of your daughter? I think we should get a search started right away for her and it would help a lot if you could supply us with a picture."

Elaine regarded the smug uniformed officer, a stocky, athletically built man who looked to be in his early to mid-forties. Though his words were meant to sound sincere and caring, his eyes belied the fact that protecting Cassidy was not his first priority.

“I…don’t understand why you want to search for her…” Elaine hesitated.

“Do you know where she is?” the officer asked as if speaking to a dunce.

“No,” Elaine admitted.

“Do you know this man that she’s supposedly with? Do you know whether she’s safe with him?”

“No, but…”

“I don’t think you grasp how much danger your daughter may be in. I’m trying to help her! If you have a picture of her, we’ll mount a formal search for her.”

Elaine slid down off the bar stool, pulling her coat tightly around her. “I think I have one in the motor home. I’ll go look,” she offered, grateful that she had an excuse to get away from the man. As she headed toward the door, she paused long enough to say to the bartender, “Thanks, Joe.”

Mother and son stepped out of the smoke-charged atmosphere of the bar into the crisp, dark Wyoming night. They walked in silence across the gravel lot together. As Jason unlocked the door of the motor home, Elaine searched through the blackness for the faint outline of ridges and mountains that surrounded them.

“Jason, she walked right across this parking lot just a little while ago,” Elaine said with a sigh. “She got into a truck with a man she didn’t know and now they’re gone. Are we doing the right thing by delaying the sheriff in his investigation? Are we trusting the right people?”

“I honestly don’t know, Mom,” Jason replied with a shake of his head.

The pair entered the motor home where an excited Pansy greeted them. Elaine laid the dog on the bed beside her as she searched for the small folder of family pictures that was stashed in her purse. With shaking hands, she sorted through the photos. The only good close-up of Cassidy was her high school graduation picture, which was six years old. She decided it was the only one suitable to take to the sheriff.

As she clutched the pictures and looked around the trailer, Elaine blinked back tears. Cassidy’s shoes lay in the corner. Cassidy’s travel bag rested on the top bunk along with her sketch pad and pencils. Cassidy's books were tucked into a pocket near the table.

"I'd like to make a phone call, Jason," Elaine resolved. "Can I use your phone?"

Jason drew the instrument from his pants pocket and handed it to his mother. She dialed a number and waited as the phone rang several times before someone answered.

"I'm sorry, Pastor. I probably woke you."

Elaine paused a moment as the pastor assured her it was okay to call anytime.

"This is Elaine Henderson. I have an urgent need for prayer on behalf of Cassidy. She…" Elaine sobbed and struggled to put into words the hurt that tore at her heart. "She witnessed a murder. The killers saw her and she ran away from them. A man gave her a ride away from the scene but at the moment we have no idea where she is or how much danger she's in. Jason and I have to go talk to the sheriff, but I wanted to ask you to put this on the prayer chain at church."

Elaine listened briefly as the pastor assured her that Cassidy would be kept in fervent prayer. She quietly told the man, "I'll keep you informed. Thank you."

Returning the phone to Jason, Elaine dried the tears that had erupted. With a deep breath, she straightened her shoulders and left the motor home to return to the tavern where the officer waited.

With the photo in hand, the sheriff inquired about Cassidy's full name, age, and identifying marks. *He doesn't expect to find my daughter alive,* Elaine thought during the grueling interview. *Does he even want to?*

When the interrogation finally ended, Elaine silently led the way to the motor home, anxious to shut herself away from the cruel world and enter a quiet place. She needed to pray in earnest for her daughter's safety. And she needed to cry.

THREE

Brady pulled the white Ford to a stop in a dark ranch yard, then bolted from the truck and loped to the front door of the house to rap on it. As Cassidy climbed out of the vehicle, she sensed that the buildings were nestled between high ridges, for the only stars visible were those high above her. Though she couldn't see the vegetation, she detected a hint of sage mingled with the dust that stirred around her.

"Hi, Toby!" Brady exclaimed as an old hound rose on stiff legs and plodded toward him in the darkness. "Long time, no see!" Brady reached down to scratch the dog behind the ears. Cassidy waited at the bottom of the steps. Faint light spilled from a window at the back of the house, leaving the front yard shadowed until the door creaked open, spewing a bright shaft of yellow light into the blackness.

"What kind of trouble you in now, Boy?" a raspy voice questioned as a weathered, vein-riddled hand reached out to push the screen door open for the young man.

"How did you know it was me?" Brady asked as he stepped into the light and held the door open until Cassidy moved inside.

"Hound didn't eat ya," the old man replied curtly. He eyed Cassidy and asked, "Who you got here?"

"Murder witness," Brady responded, imitating his uncle's habit of using as few words as possible. As he tossed his hat on the nearby rack he added, "The killers spotted her and are hot on our trail. Could I leave my truck here and use your black one? They're looking for us in a white truck."

"Traded it off three months ago," came the reply. "You'd have known that if you'd call on me now and then."

"Yeah, I know. But I've been out of town," Brady defended. "Well, if we can't swap trucks can I at least get a sandwich or two for the road?"

"Didn't say we couldn't swap trucks. You just ain't gettin' a black one. It's red and it's a Dodge," the old man announced as he moved to the kitchen.

"A Dodge!?" Brady said with a laugh. "I've never known you to drive anything but a Ford!"

"Yeah, well, variety…you know, s'posed to spice up your life or somethin'."

"You starting a second childhood, Jubel?" Brady teased.

"'Bout time, ain't it?" came the gruff reply.

Jubel handed Brady a half loaf of bread and a package of lunch meat from the refrigerator. "Got salad dressing in here somewhere," he mumbled as he searched the shelves.

"Jubel, just bread and meat is fine," Brady assured the man. "This will get us by until we get down the road a ways."

The old man straightened and questioned his nephew. "When did you get into witness protection?"

"'Bout an hour ago," Brady replied. "I was snooping around The Alibi when I recognized a couple of Trent Dominic's boys. They caught a guy who had been hiding in the abandoned motel at Lone Pine and drug him out back and knifed him. Cassidy was out walking her dog and saw the whole thing. I took off with her in my truck."

Jubel regarded Brady in silence for a moment as he sacked up a small jar of salad dressing and a chunk of cheese along with a couple of apples. Brady added the bread and meat to the bag.

"Dominic's boys, huh?" Jubel twisted his jaw as he pondered what his nephew had been telling him.

"Hey, they're not gonna come here lookin' for me. They don't know you, Jubel," Brady responded hopefully.

"Don't be so sure, Boy," the old man answered. "It's been a lot of years, but Dominic might remember me from the trial. You've been gone a while and things have changed around here. Folks suspect the new sheriff is Dominic's puppet. If he is, he'll use the county resources to get information to Dominic. If they make the connection between you and me, you can bet this is one of the first places they'll look for you."

"If the sheriff is in cahoots with Dominic, that answers some of my questions..." Brady stated. He ran his fingers through his thick hair and looked away from his uncle for several seconds. Cassidy noted the alarm in his eyes.

"You can't stay here alone, Jubel. You've got to come with us..."

"I ain't up to no wild chase across the country!" the old man interrupted. "I'd only slow you down. Just take my truck and take the girl and git down that road!"

Jubel grabbed the keys from atop the kitchen counter. Lifting Brady's hand, he slapped the keys hard into his nephew's fist. Brady opened his mouth to argue, but Jubel cut his words short. "It's in the shed. Git!" he ordered.

"But, Jubel, what will you do if they come here lookin' for me?"

"I reckon I won't be here. I haven't slept under the stars up on the ridge for many years. Think I'll try it. Just me and the old dawg." Jubel turned toward the cupboards once again and grabbed a couple cans of beans and a pan. When he found that Brady and Cassidy hadn't moved, he ordered once again, "Git!"

Brady opened the door for Cassidy, who pulled the blanket tight around herself to ward off the chilled night air. As he grabbed his hat off the rack, he paused long enough to ask his uncle if he could spare a coat for his passenger. Jubel silently went to the closet and lifted a clean brown chore jacket from a hook. He handed it to Cassidy, who grasped the garment, thanked the elderly man, and stepped out into the night.

Brady stopped at his own truck to gather the cooler, the box, and other belongings, which Cassidy helped carry to the shed. Nudging the unlocked door open with his foot, he deftly switched the light on with his elbow.

"Wow!" he exclaimed. "Jubel went all out! I don't think he's ever owned a truck with chrome on it in his life. Look at this, would ya!"

After setting the box on a nearby workbench, Brady took the cooler from Cassidy and filled it with the food Jubel had provided. Opening the door of the truck, he shoved the cooler inside and turned his attention to the cardboard box from which he extracted a small travel bag and a case of compact discs. Cassidy noticed that under the pile of file folders lay a laptop computer. She couldn't imagine this man, who dressed like a cowboy, to be proficient enough on a computer to own a laptop. From the pile of folders, Brady extracted an envelope and tossed it into the truck cab. The box was then stashed far under the dusty old workbench with a pile of tools set upon it. Brady kicked up some dirt from the floor to settle on the newly placed box, allowing it to blend in with its surroundings.

"We're ready," Brady stated as he opened the large shed door.

Jubel was outside loading his bed roll, rifle, and food items into Brady's truck and coaxing the lame hound up into the cab.

"Jubel, I really appreciate…"

"Git, Boy!" Jubel commanded as he followed the dog up onto the seat. Without looking back, he started the engine of Brady's truck and drove beyond the buildings, heading up a narrow trail toward the ridge above.

Brady backed Jubel's truck out of the shed as Cassidy swung the big door shut and latched it. He was turned sideways in his seat, organizing the litter of items he had tossed into the cab when Cassidy opened the passenger door. She stopped short of getting in when she saw a shoulder holster and pistol under his opened jacket.

Brady immediately noted the fear in her eyes. "Cassidy," he reassured her quietly. "I promise I am not going to hurt you. I told you before, I'm a private investigator. I pack heat because I get into sticky situations. I have a license to carry a gun. Now, let's hurry and get out of here." He spoke gently, as if trying to calm the fears of an untamed filly that was ready to bolt. "Those guys might be able to trace me to my uncle. If they do, they'll come here."

Cassidy weighed her options. She didn't like the prospect of hiding around the creaky old buildings all night or running away into the unknown hills. And this man appeared to be sincerely trying to help her. After all, he was a witness to the same crime she was, putting him in equal danger. Besides that, there was no one else to defend her.

"I guess since you've got my supper in there, I'll ride along with you for awhile," Cassidy decided as she climbed into the truck cab. Once again, the side of Brady's mouth twitched in the faintest of smiles.

Scarcely settled into her seat, Cassidy started digging in the cooler. With bread, lunch meat, and salad dressing, she made sandwiches. The pair ate in silence for several minutes as Brady concentrated on traversing the winding road at the highest speed he safely could while devouring food.

Once several sandwiches were put away, Cassidy ventured to ask, "How old is your uncle? He must be a lot older than your parents."

"He's in his early seventies, I guess. He's actually my great uncle. My father's uncle on his mother's side of the family," Brady explained, "so he doesn't have the same last name as me. His name is Jubel Post. That's why I didn't think I might be putting him in danger. Dominic's men couldn't put the connection together by themselves. But Jubel's right. Dominic himself might remember."

"I did the wrong thing by not running to the gas station for help," Cassidy suddenly lamented. "I've put you in danger. And now your uncle may be in danger, too."

"I made the decision for you, remember?" Brady reprimanded her. "I hauled you outta there without giving you any options."

Brady pulled the red truck onto the nearly deserted highway and sped up, heading east. He punched a button that turned on the radio and fiddled with the controls without finding a station that came in clearly. "Can you try to find something on the radio?" he finally asked Cassidy. "It's been a couple hours. They might have news about the murder by now."

Cassidy scanned through the available stations and found a country one. She listened in silence to the familiar tune with the volume turned low enough that the pair could still speak to one another over the music.

"How long have you been a private investigator?" she wondered aloud.

"Several years. When I was in college, I majored in police science," Brady answered, "though if you asked Jubel, he'd tell you I was wasting good money payin' a school to let me be on the rodeo team. And my dad feared I was spending all my time studying female anatomy."

Cassidy laughed aloud, the sound of it filling the enclosed space.

"I didn't finish college back then," Brady continued. "I went full time on the rodeo circuit instead. There were times I wasn't raking in much prize money so I started doing private investigation to keep from starving. I've been able to make a decent living at it."

"You still do rodeo, too?"

"Not since late last year," Brady responded. "I ripped my arm up pretty bad so I had to put rodeo aside for awhile. I was hired to do an investigation that landed me in Reno, and while I was there I uncovered some dirt on Trent Dominic. Since then, I've been doing a lot of snooping into his affairs. That's why I happened to be at The Alibi this evening. The bartender had some information for me."

"What is this Dominic guy doing?" Cassidy asked.

"He was dealing drugs back when we were in college. He still has his fingers in that but he's also into some other crap with this outfit out of Reno. I think the man that died tonight was an illegal immigrant who escaped from Dominic's ranch."

"He was a prisoner there?"

"I kinda think so," Brady answered. "I think Dominic's got several people that are being paid very little, if at all, and aren't free to come and go as they please. He may be supplying people for certain businesses. There's always desperate people in desperate circumstances. Trent Dominic is one link in a long chain of scum who'll take advantage of them."

Cassidy found Brady's words disturbing and frowned as she contemplated them.

"Let's change the subject," he suggested as he noted his passenger's furrowed brow. "You don't need any more worry than you've already got. Tell me about your little dog that caused so much trouble. What kind is it?"

"It's my mother's Yorkshire Terrier," Cassidy replied with a smile.

"I've heard of 'em, but I've never seen one in action," Brady said with a wide grin. "Kind of a rowdy little thing, ain't it?"

Cassidy laughed. "Yes, it's rowdy," she agreed. Feeling more comfortable with her companion, she asked what event he was in when he was involved in rodeo.

"All of them." Brady smiled fully at the mention of his favorite subject. "I tried everything when I was younger and really wanted to be the best all-around. But I'm not quite big enough to pull down the steers in good time and I struggled with the calf roping. I've pretty much stuck with riding bulls the last few years."

Cassidy considered the lean, muscular frame of the man next to her and imagined the grueling sport in which he participated. "What did your parents think about you riding bulls? Weren't they concerned?"

"My dad encouraged it because I was so intense about it. I guess he figured spending my time around the arenas was going to help keep me out of trouble."

"Did it work? Keeping you out of trouble, I mean?"

"For the most part," Brady replied with a smile.

"What about your mother?" Cassidy questioned. "I'll bet she was scared half to death."

There was a long pause before Brady answered. "She wasn't around to comment one way or the other."

"I'm sorry," Cassidy muttered, remembering how she felt when he questioned her about her father. She hesitated to continue to speak further of Brady's mother, but ventured to do so anyway, thinking perhaps this man could understand how she felt about her own recent loss.

"Is she still living?" Cassidy asked quietly.

"I have no idea," came the reply. "She left me and Dad when I was six years old."

Cassidy was stunned. She could think of no appropriate words to offer her companion. Rather than risk offending or angering him, she said no more.

"I had a little brother that was born with heart problems," Brady offered, breaking a long silence. He kept his eyes on the road as he explained further. "He was always sickly and his only hope of surviving was major surgery. He didn't live long after the operation. He was only three years old. My mom, she couldn't cope with it. She went to the pastor for counseling for a long time and seemed to be getting better. And then one day, she up and left town…with the pastor."

"Oh, no!" Cassidy exclaimed. "What did you and your dad do?"

"We changed churches," came Brady's smirk reply. Several quiet seconds passed again before he added, "My dad raised me with the help of Jubel and the neighbors. I thought I was in heaven down at the neighbor's place. They had kids about my age and their dad competed in rodeos. When my dad was working, they hauled me along with 'em and that suited me just fine. And Mrs. Knowlton's cookin' was a lot better than Dad's, too!"

Cassidy listened to the soft music playing on the radio as she pondered Brady's childhood. He drove on, seemingly deep in thought until Cassidy ventured to speak.

"You must have spent quite a bit of time with your Uncle Jubel," she observed. "I certainly noticed similarities."

"What kind of similarities?" Brady wondered aloud.

"Mostly, your decisiveness. You guys seem to make up your minds about something and then plunge ahead."

Brady laughed aloud. "You're right about that. We don't leave too many things up for discussion. Just bully ahead."

"Is your father like that, too?" Cassie inquired.

"Oh, yeah," Brady assured her. "There must be some unwritten code among us. 'You believe in God. You love your country. You help your neighbors when they're in need. You make up your mind and stick to it.'"

Cassidy considered the country mentality that had been part of her childhood, which was so scarce among the city people with whom she now lived.

"Why are you scowling?" Brady asked as he glanced over at her.

"I was just thinking that I sure miss being around country people," Cassidy sighed. "I think that's what bothers me most about living in the city. The attitude is so different compared to what I was raised in. I don't even know my neighbors. I only know the people I work with or go to church with. And even then, the businesses are so big and the churches are so big, you only get to know a handful of people."

"So you weren't raised in Minneapolis?"

"No. I took a job and an apartment in a suburb after college. I was raised on a dairy farm in northwestern Wisconsin."

"So…you probably didn't appreciate my comment about you being a big city girl."

"Not especially," Cassidy admitted.

"You don't like living in the city," Brady observed.

"No."

"So, why do you stay?"

"I've got a great job as a graphic artist at an ad agency. I love my work, but there's not much demand for it in the country."

"Maybe some day you can freelance and live wherever you want," Brady encouraged.

"I sure hope so!" Cassidy responded with a sigh.

FOUR

Brady concentrated on the road as he peered through the darkness for the entrance to the freeway, which would take him and Cassidy to Sheridan County. Jubel had made it clear he didn't trust the Johnson County sheriff, so Brady intended to appeal for help from the police in Sheridan. Easing the truck onto the freeway, he accelerated to match the pace of the northbound semi trucks.

When at length he glanced over at his companion, he found that she had her eyes closed. The gentle rise and fall of her shoulders as she breathed told him that Cassidy was in deep, peaceful slumber.

Brady considered the young woman who rested beside him. He'd never had a case quite like this. He would have to count this as one of his more daring adventures, and having a young woman as pretty as this to look out for certainly was a bonus. He smiled to himself as he recalled the girl's nice curves that he had eyed earlier. He studied Cassidy in the dim light–her dark lashes, creamy smooth skin, shapely lips…and smooth hands that sported no wedding or engagement ring…

A blaring horn alerted Brady that he was intruding into a big rig's territory. Righting the path of his truck, he reprimanded himself for his carelessness. *Keep your focus, Brady,* he warned himself. *It's a good thing you don't work with women like this every day. You'd go to daydreaming and get yourself killed.*

Brady suddenly realized that the songs on the radio had ended and a news flash was being aired.

"Police are searching tonight for twenty-four year old Cassidy Henderson of Apple Valley, Minnesota. She was abducted from outside her family's motor home where it was parked at a gas station in Lone Pine, Wyoming. Cassidy is five feet eleven inches tall and has long, blonde hair and green eyes. She was last seen wearing a red jacket, white blouse, and blue jeans. Her abductor is described as a man in his early thirties, six feet one inch tall with dark hair and a short beard and mustache. He is wearing a black Stetson and black leather jacket and was last seen driving a white Ford F-150 extended cab truck. Anyone with information on the whereabouts of either of these people is urged to call the Johnson county sheriff's office at…"

Brady hit the button angrily and the radio silenced. Cassidy stirred only slightly when he punched the dash in his fury.

"That was done deliberately," Brady spoke quietly through clenched teeth. He kept his eyes intensely on the road as he pondered the untruthful report. News of a murder witness who had fled the scene of the crime would not raise the attention of law officers in surrounding counties as quickly as the news of the abduction of a young woman. With an urgent radio broadcast like this, the sheriff now had the law and private citizens across the entire state on the lookout for him.

Brady had a feeling that the sheriff was not the brains behind this desperate search, nor were Dominic's hit men. These lies were being perpetrated by Trent Dominic himself. *Dominic and his men have come to the conclusion that Cassidy wasn't the only witness to their crime,* Brady thought. *They know I was there, too, because there's no other way I could have gotten the girl out of there so fast. Cassidy was too far away and the light was too dim to ensure that she could identify the murderers to the police. But they don't know where I was or whether I can finger them.*

Dominic knows that I know this country. I could hole up for a long time in Wyoming and stay out of his grasp, Brady considered. *But if I get out of Wyoming with the girl, this farce of a kidnapping becomes a federal matter. They're trying to flush me out by daring me to try to cross the border into one of the neighboring states. That means they're putting cops in place on every road leading out of Wyoming….*

Brady smiled to himself as a plan began forming in his mind. Trent Dominic was chasing him. He anticipated a wonderful game of cat and mouse with his most hated enemy, especially when he held bait such as he had in an innocent, trusting young woman named Cassidy Henderson.

Brady glanced at the slumbering young woman who rested peacefully beside him and wished immediately that he hadn't looked her way. While the devious plan still unfolded in his mind, in his heart he knew he would scrap it. He recalled the promise he had made to her an hour ago–that he would not hurt her. How, then, could he risk her life by leading Trent into a confrontation that would surely end in a gun battle? Cassidy's safety must be his priority, Brady decided. He would deal with Trent Dominic once she was out of danger. But where should he take her? He considered remote mountain cabins and ranchers who would aid him. But Cassidy was already apprehensive about him. If he forced her to go with him and they were found, Brady didn't trust the law to correctly sort out the situation.

I have to do exactly what they don't want me to do, Brady told himself in the silence of the truck cab. *Getting the two of us across the state line is the only way to clear up this mess. Once we're out of Wyoming, this so-called kidnapping will become a federal case for the U.S. Marshal and these local cops won't be able to pin anything on me.*

Brady glanced again at the dozing Cassidy. *What kind of person is she?* he wondered. *Can she be trusted to tell the honest truth if we're caught? Or will she say whatever she needs to in order to save herself and leave me to suffer the consequences?*

The gas gauge showed little more than enough fuel to get across the border into Montana, which was a very risky level if they were pursued. Brady decided to stop before news of the so-called kidnapping could spread any further.

The bright lights of the island of pumps at a truck stop glared through the window. Cassidy awoke as Brady pulled the truck to a halt.

"Where are we?" she asked as she stretched and yawned.

"The outskirts of Sheridan."

"I have some cash in my pocket. I'll help pay for gas," she offered.

"Hang on to it. There's a store inside. If there's anything you need, now's your chance to get it."

Discarding the blanket in which she was wrapped, Cassidy reached behind the seat for Jubel's coat and slipped it on.

"You might be able to reach your brother's cell phone from here," Brady suggested as he opened the truck door and pulled the keys from the ignition.

"I'll try it," Cassidy said with a smile and opened the door.

"Cassidy?" Brady instructed as she exited the vehicle, "when you're talking on the phone, be careful not to mention my name or yours. You never know who might overhear you and tell the wrong people we were here."

Cassidy nodded that she understood the need for caution and trotted across the pavement toward the building.

Brady zipped up his coat and climbed out from behind the steering wheel. As fuel pumped into the truck's tank, he studied the details of his surroundings, noting the few tractor-trailer rigs and the little building that would be his only hope of refuge if he were discovered here.

Alarm welled up inside the man. He hated being so vulnerable. Did Cassidy realize he could be put behind bars for a long, long time? He wondered again if he could trust her and contemplated taking off without his passenger–leaving her here to fend for herself. No one would blame him, for he had inherited far more trouble than he anticipated when he gave that pretty gal a ride in his truck.

A vision of the three murderers came to mind. Grabbing up the stack of pictures that he had tossed into the truck cab, Brady quickly sorted them as he mentally reviewed the evidence he had against Trent Dominic's organization. He knew too much about these ruthless men to leave Cassidy without a means of escape and promised himself he would not walk away until he knew she had help.

Brady wondered briefly if he should have told Cassidy what the news reports were saying. No, he decided. They would be far less likely to attract attention if they seemed unconcerned and unwary. By letting Cassidy go into the store alone, no one would consider that she was the object of a statewide search for a kidnap victim.

The pump handle snapped, stopping the flow of fuel. Brady returned the hose to its resting place. With a deep sigh, he steeled himself and headed across the pavement, wondering what might transpire once he entered the building.

Cassidy located the pay phones, dug through her jeans pocket for change, and inserted coins into the slot.

"Jason?" she cried as her brother answered his cell phone.

"Cassidy, where are you?" he demanded.

"We're at a truck stop outside Sheridan. I just wanted to call to let Mom know I'm doing okay."

"Cassie?" Elaine's voice came over the phone.

"Mom, I'm fine. Everything is going to be all right."

"Oh, Cassie, just tell me we did the right thing. We tried to delay the sheriff's investigation for a while to let you get far away," Elaine cried. "That bartender told us not to trust the sheriff. And now with these lies that have been put on the news…"

"What are you talking about?" Cassidy interrupted. "What lies?"

"About you being kidnapped by Brady Hollister."

"You can't be serious!" Cassidy exclaimed in shock. "That isn't true!" She started to elaborate, but stopped short when a customer passed within easy earshot of the phones.

"Thank God! We've been praying that it wasn't," Elaine assured her daughter. "I'm glad now that the only close-up I had of you was your high school graduation picture. They've started showing it on the news."

Brady walked past the phones on his way to the restroom and stopped near Cassidy to whisper, "How's your family holding up?" Cassidy gave him a thumbs-up signal and nodded, indicating that they were fine under the circumstances.

She watched him move confidently across the room. *If this is a kidnapping, this was the slickest job of it ever,* Cassidy considered. *Make a young woman think she is being rescued from murderers when she's actually being whisked away without a struggle and without any help from the law…*

A sudden feeling of terror welled up in the pit of Cassidy's stomach. *What was Brady's comment about supplying people to certain businesses? What if it's not Trent Dominic but Brady Hollister who should be feared?* Cassidy could well imagine what kind of business Brady had been referring to. *And he is armed,* she reminded herself.

"We described you to the sheriff as a blonde, but your hair is actually light brown with blonde streaks in it," Elaine's voice broke into Cassidy's thoughts. "Maybe that will help confuse things."

"I think it will, Mom," Cassidy replied weakly, so distracted by her confusing thoughts about Brady she could scarcely pay attention to what her mother was saying. "Mom, thanks for all you're doing for me. We'll get through this. I'm not sure what Br…" Cassidy hesitated. "I'm not sure what the plan is or where we're heading. I'll call again as soon as I can. I love you! Tell Jason I love him, too!"

Cassidy listened to the phone for a few more seconds as her mother told her they were praying for her safety. Tears stung her eyes at the reminder of her mother's unfailing trust in the Lord. "Thanks, Mom. Bye," she whispered and hung up the phone.

Brady was scanning a clothes rack full of T-shirts when Cassidy emerged from the ladies' room. She watched him quietly. *I told Mom that I didn't know what our plans are,* she thought. *The truth is, Brady and I never discussed plans. I've meekly gone along with him and never asked where he intends to take me. I've let him take the lead. Am I like a sheep being led to slaughter?*

"How are you doin'?" Brady asked when he discovered her presence, though she knew the strain on her face was probably evident.

"Okay, I guess."

"This has got to be hard on your whole family," he sympathized as he picked up a shirt and held it in front of Cassidy. She shook her head.

"I guess I'm not in the shopping mood," she said quietly.

"You've gotta be kidding! You hear so much about women and shopping, I didn't know they had to be in a certain mood to buy something," he said with a laugh.

Cassidy smiled back. She wanted so much to believe in him. To trust him. She needed to trust someone.

"How about some snacks?" Brady asked as he headed toward an aisle laden with chips and candy.

"We have some cheese and apples left in the cooler," Cassidy reminded him.

"Do you like peanuts?" Brady asked. "They're nutritious, aren't they?"

"I suppose."

Brady stopped short in his fervent search through the food aisle. "What's wrong?" he challenged.

Cassidy looked away and whispered, "Mom told me they're charging you with kidnapping. That's serious…"

Brady sobered quickly. "Yeah. I heard it on the radio. I probably should have told you," he said with a sigh as he studied Cassidy's worried face.

Fishing the keys out of his jacket pocket, he held them out to Cassidy.

"Take the truck and go. They probably haven't figured out yet that we're driving Jubel's truck. You can be in Montana in less than an hour. Head for Billings. I'll call the U.S. Marshal and tell him where you're going. He'll catch up to you.

Cassidy fingered the keys that Brady offered her and told herself, *He did it to me again. About the time I decide not to like him or trust him, he does something totally unexpected.*

"What about you?" she asked.

"They're out to kill me, Cassidy. You'll get hurt if you stay with me."

Cassidy's eyes filled with unshed tears. She had been the cause of so much trouble for Brady that he now feared for his life. She didn't like the idea of going alone, but could understand his desire to be rid of her.

Cassidy heard her name spoken across the room. She moved toward the sound of it and found a small TV in the dining area that was airing the latest news broadcast regarding her kidnapping. She watched the screen intently as her picture and that of Brady were displayed and descriptions given for both of them.

"Brady Hollister is thirty-two years old. He is six foot, one inch tall and has blue eyes and dark brown hair. He was last seen wearing a black leather coat, black Stetson, and blue denim jeans. If anyone sees this man," the reporter urged, "please contact the Johnson County sheriff's office at the number on the screen. Do not approach the suspect. He is armed and dangerous."

"What a bunch of crap!" Cassidy shouted angrily. "I haven't been kidnapped!"

She looked around at the few people who were in the room. A pair of elderly ladies sat in a booth with coffee cups in front of them, whispering to one another. A lone trucker with a half-eaten sweet roll occupied another booth. The teller at the cash register was the only other person in the store besides Cassidy and Brady. Everyone remained still with their eyes intently on Cassidy.

"I don't know where all these lies are coming from," Cassidy spoke emphatically to the people around her, "but they are lies! I was not kidnapped by Brady Hollister! I went with him willingly!"

She turned to Brady and sobbed, "I'm sorry I got you into this mess…"

"You didn't get me into this mess!" he answered sharply. "I dealt my own hand!" Brady tossed a few items on the counter and pulled money out of his wallet to pay for them as the teller silently rang up the total.

"Take the truck and go, Cassidy!" he ordered. "You've got to get out of here!"

Cassidy bit her trembling lip. Tears filled her eyes and spilled silently down her rosy cheeks.

"Excuse me?" one of the elderly ladies rose from her seat to place a comforting hand on Cassidy's arm. "If these news reports are lies and you went willingly with this man, my sister and I guessed that you two are probably running away to get married. Is that right?"

The concept of such a thing took Cassidy by complete surprise. She brushed at her tears and looked over the short woman's head at Brady. He grinned and nodded his head slightly. Cassidy blushed at the thought of running away to marry a man she didn't even know. But with everyone in the truck stop staring at her, awaiting her response, she smiled weakly at the woman and breathed a soft, "Yes."

"We knew it, didn't we Alethea?" the elderly woman asked excitedly.

"Who's trying to stop you, Honey?" the woman named Alethea asked as she, too, came to stand near the young woman.

Cassidy felt committed to perpetuate the story, though lying was uncharacteristic of her. "My…brothers," she ventured. "My stepbrothers, that is."

"How awful," both of the women concluded, shaking their silver-gray heads.

"Why would anyone do such a thing?" wondered Alethea. "You are such a nice looking couple!"

"Thank you," Cassidy whispered with an uneasy smile.

"What are your plans?" the first woman asked.

"To get out of Wyoming," Brady said as he joined the conversation. "We have friends in Red Lodge, Montana that will help us. But Cassidy's brothers are some very influential people. They've convinced the police that Cassidy was kidnapped in order to stop us from getting there."

"Alice, they can go with us!" the woman named Alethea cried.

"Yes, we'll take you to Red Lodge!" agreed Alice with a wide grin.

"That's a long drive from here," Brady protested. "We can't ask you to do that."

"We can do it! This is our 'Wild Weekend'!" declared Alice.

"Yes! Alice and I are on our 'Wild Weekend'!" Alethea confirmed with a giggle. "Our husbands are gone fishing. We ditched our kids and grandkids and hired a babysitter for the dogs."

"We were heading to Deadwood to gamble," Alice whispered conspiratorially. The pair giggled again. Brady and Cassidy, along with the truck driver and teller, couldn't help but laugh at the mischievous pair.

"Ladies, we don't want to ruin your weekend…" Brady started.

"No! This will be cheaper, won't it Alethea?" Alice pointed out. "We can go gambling some other time! But how many times do we get to help a young couple elope?"

"We can still get a motel and–what is there to do in Red Lodge, Montana?" Alethea wondered. "I don't think I've ever been there."

"There's a rodeo going on this weekend," Brady told them. "That's where our friends are."

"Oh, a rodeo!" Alice exclaimed. "We can go to the rodeo!"

"Come on!" Alethea urged. "Let's go!" She grabbed Cassidy by the arm and headed toward the door.

"Hurry!" Alice ordered Brady. "We've got to hurry before her wicked stepbrothers catch us!"

"You take Cassidy with you. I'll meet you in Red Lodge. It's too dangerous for us to ride together," Brady stated firmly. "I don't want to see anyone get hurt."

Brady looked squarely at Cassidy, silently conveying the message that his mind was made up. They would travel separately.

"We'll pretend Cassidy is my granddaughter," Alethea spoke up. "You are my granddaughter who is going with us to the rodeo." She pulled on Cassidy's arm, urging her toward the door.

"Alethea!" Alice scolded her sister. "You have to give them time for a good-bye kiss!"

"Oh!" Alethea exclaimed. "Oh, of course!"

The woman dropped Cassidy's arm and pushed her toward Brady as the two sisters giggled. Cassidy blushed as Brady took her hand to pull her several steps away from the group in the small dining area. He removed his hat and spoke quietly, aware that all eyes were on them and ears were straining to hear what was said.

"When you get to Red Lodge, look up Skeeter, the rodeo clown. I'll give him a call and let him know you're coming. He'll be performing at Saturday's show and probably preaching a Sunday morning church service, and then he'll be at Sunday afternoon's show. You'll have to catch him between obligations, but he'll be easy to find."

"Okay," Cassidy agreed. "And you?"

"Don't worry about me. I'll get out of Wyoming," Brady assured her, then added, "Cassidy, if you ask Jason and your ma to come help you, they'll be followed. I'll call the U.S. Marshall and tell him where you're heading. Once he catches up with you, you'll be in safe hands."

Cassidy was about to say good-bye to the man who had probably saved her life. Though he had angered her and confused her, she suddenly felt lost without his firm guidance. There was so much she wanted to tell him, but she couldn't say any of it without rousing suspicion.

Brady placed his right hand softly under Cassidy's chin, lifting it until her eyes met his, and ran his thumb gently across her lips. Resting his other hand lightly on her shoulder, he held his hat in a position to partially shield them from the stares of those who watched the scene as he whispered, "Do you mind?"

Cassidy slipped her arms around him. "No," she whispered. She allowed him to kiss her–an unexpectedly passionate, lingering kiss that left her breathless. When Brady released her from his strong grasp, she felt the hot flush of embarrassment spread over her face. She hardly dared look up at the man. Never had she made such a public display of affection, and especially not in a performance such as this. Still reeling, she turned quickly toward the exit door.

"Cassidy, take this with you," Brady instructed as he extended his hat toward her. "Skeeter will recognize my hat. Guard it with your life, okay? And by the way, the news reports have it all wrong. It's not a Stetson, it's a Rodeo King."

Cassidy accepted the black felt from his hands. Well-worn and shaped to suit its owner's ruggedly handsome style, she detected the scent of Brady's cologne mingled with sweat and leather. Clutching it tightly, she followed the pair of chattering women toward the door.

"Don't you ladies go corrupting my sweetheart, you hear?" Brady admonished as they filed out.

Alethea turned back with a laugh. "We won't corrupt her, kid, but we might educate her. I'll bet there's a lot she doesn't know about married life."

Brady watched through the window as the trio of women took their places in Alice's car. He noted the make and model and license plate number as the vehicle pulled out of the parking lot and didn't turn away from the scene until the car was far down the road.

"Mister, you forgot your bag!" the lady at the cash register called as Brady moved toward the exit.

He retrieved it and smiled at her. "Thanks," he said, then asked, "You didn't call the cops on me did you? Or press a silent alarm?"

"No, I didn't," the middle-aged woman replied as she rested her meaty hands on the counter. "I thought about it, but she didn't act like she was kidnapped. I figured something was fishy. And when you gave her the keys to the truck and told her to go without you…"

"The keys to the truck!" Brady exclaimed. "I didn't get them back! I can't believe it! She couldn't have walked off with them!"

Brady searched his pockets and looked around the counter, though he knew full well they weren't there. He had handed them to Cassidy. She had her hands in the pocket of Jubel's coat…

"How could she leave with the keys?!" Brady threw up his hands and folded them behind his head as he walked around the store in panic. "I can't believe I can't even keep track of the truck keys!"

"You told her to take them," the teller pointed out. "I figured you must have a spare or some other idea about getting out of here."

"No, I didn't! I just knew we couldn't safely travel together any more," Brady lamented.

The lone trucker had been watching the scene in silence. He pushed his generously padded frame from his place at the table and came to stand near Brady at the cash register. He looked up at the younger man and addressed him with a sheepish grin.

"You know, when I first fell in love, my mother set a plate of pancakes in front of me and I poured coffee on 'em instead of syrup. Anybody can make a mistake like that when they're daydreaming, but…dadburnit, I ate 'em that way!"

The teller slapped the counter and laughed aloud. Brady couldn't help but grin, too, even in the midst of his distress.

"I'm headin' in the opposite direction of Red Lodge, Montana, but I'll be back up that way in a couple days after I unload. You're welcome to tag along with me if you'd like," the trucker offered.

"I appreciate that, Mister," Brady replied. "I really do. But you're wearing a wedding ring. That tells me you're a family man. With guys like Trent Dominic after me, I'd be putting you in danger."

"Dominic, you say? Is he any relation to Dave Dominic?"

"Dave's son."

"Well, if the kid's anywhere near being the crook that his old man was, I'd be more than happy to stick my neck out for someone who's standing up to him. And besides that, you're low on options at the moment."

"I am low on options," Brady admitted and made his decision. "I'll take you up on your offer."

Brady extended his hand to the trucker, who shook it with a firm grasp.

"I'd like to make one quick phone call, then I'll be ready to go," Brady stated as he indicated the pay phones along the wall.

"Sounds good. I'll settle up my bill and then go update my log book. I'll be in the blue Kenworth pullin' a cattle trailer."

With his battery charger locked in Jubel's truck, Brady knew he didn't have the option of using his cell phone indiscriminately. He extracted a slip of paper from his wallet and studied the number written there as he inserted coins in a pay phone's slot and punched the numbers.

"Marshal?" he asked after letting the phone ring several times. "Cassidy Henderson is crossing the border into Montana with a couple of little old ladies. They're taking her to the rodeo in Red Lodge."

Brady paused to listen to the voice at the other end of the line. "Well, I don't know exactly how safe she is," he answered. "These ladies are in their late seventies, maybe even eighty-something. They're driving an old Lincoln with a lot of thunder under the hood and this is their 'Wild Weekend'."

Obviously the cashier could hear Brady's half of the conversation, for he heard her laugh aloud at the verbal picture he painted of Alice and Alethea speeding down the freeway with Cassidy in tow.

"I'm headin' in the opposite direction," Brady answered the voice at the other end of the line. "No. I'm hitchin' a ride with a trucker. I gave Cassidy the keys to Jubel's truck and then we made arrangements for these ladies to take her and I never got the keys back. That's one reason I'm calling you. There are a couple of computer discs and a digital camera locked in the truck that you need to get your hands on fast. There's evidence there that can be used in court, but it will never make it there if the boys from Johnson County get hold of it first."

Brady listened once again to the voice of the marshal.

"Yeah, yeah, I know. You're short staffed and short tempered and you don't like gettin' called out of bed at two o'clock in the morning. Watch for Cassidy at the rodeo. Look for the Rodeo King."

Brady hung up the phone and headed for the exit. He stopped to speak to the cashier. "If the store manager complains about the truck sittin' out there in front of the pump, tell him the U.S. Marshal is coming to pick it up. No one else is to move it, open it, or search the contents. Okay?"

"Got it," the woman behind the counter assured. "Good luck to ya."

"Thanks. Thanks for everything," Brady said and headed out the door.

FIVE

The bright lights of Billings, Montana stretched before the trio in the dark blue Lincoln. Cassidy turned from looking out the window in time to catch Alice yawning. Alethea had long ago laid her seat back and was dozing.

"Are you going to be able to stay awake until we find a motel, Alice?" Cassidy questioned. "Do you want me to drive?"

"I'll stop at this motel just ahead," Alice assured her. "We'll be lucky to get seven hours of sleep before we have to check out, but that should be enough for what we've got planned for this afternoon, right? We'll go to the mall and find you a change of clothes, then we'll show you the bridal shop. I want to see you try on a wedding dress. With your height and figure, you're going to make a beautiful bride!"

Cassidy decided that modeling a wedding dress or two was a small price to pay for the ladies' generosity. They were so thrilled for her, she couldn't bear to disappoint them by telling the truth about her and Brady. She was determined to play this charade until she reached the rodeo arena and a trip to the bridal shop fit nicely into the script.

Alice pulled up to the entrance of a motel. "You don't mind sharing a room with us do you, dear?" Alice asked Cassidy. "I'll get one with two big beds if that's okay."

"I would really appreciate it. That will save me a lot of money. But I can help pay…"

"No. No. I get a senior citizen's discount," Alice insisted. "I can get the room cheaper than you can and we were planning to pay for a room anyway."

Alice exited the car and walked to the entrance of the motel. Cassidy laid back in the car seat and stuck her hands in the pockets of Jubel's jacket, drawing it close around her. Sudden dread washed over her. *The truck keys!* She had dropped them into the coat pocket and forgotten to give them back to Brady!

"Oh, no!" she cried.

Alethea roused from her nap. "What's wrong, dear?" she questioned.

"I have the truck keys in my pocket! What is Brady going to do?"

Cassidy envisioned a gun battle with Trent Dominic's men as they caught up with Brady at the Sheridan truck stop. Or Brady walking for miles under cover of darkness to elude his pursuers. Would he hitch a ride? Or take a bus?

"Alethea, do you know the name of the truck stop in Sheridan? I have to call them to find out if Brady's still there!"

"Oh, my…Let me see…" the woman pondered. "I was the one who gassed up the car…"

"Did you pay for the gas?" Cassidy asked.

"Of course I paid for it!"

"With a credit card or a check?"

"Oh! With my credit card! I would have a receipt, wouldn't I? Alethea flipped on the overhead light and dug in her purse. Coming up with a yellow slip of paper, she searched for a date on it.

"This is the one!" she exclaimed, handing the paper to Cassidy. The young woman bolted from the car and nearly collided with Alice in her haste to look for a pay phone in the motel lobby.

"What's wrong, dear?" Alice asked with concern.

"Oh, Alice, I left the truck keys in my pocket! I forgot to give them back to Br…" Cassidy didn't finish the sentence in case the front desk clerk would hear the name 'Brady' and be alerted. "I've got to try to call the gas station."

"Here's a key to the room," Alice said as she placed it in Cassidy's hand. Room 145. Down that hall. Go make the call."

Cassidy hurried in the direction of the room, then turned back and caught up with Alice.

"I'm sorry," she apologized. "I'm sure you have luggage that needs to be carried in."

"We just have small overnight bags. We'll manage just fine," Alice assured her. "You hurry and make that call."

By the time Alice and Alethea arrived at the room, Cassidy had found out from the truck stop clerk that Brady had gotten a ride with the driver of the cattle truck. She also learned of the truck's destination.

"Well, he got a ride," Cassidy told her companions with a weak smile. "The clerk thinks they were heading to South Dakota."

"Was he angry with you, dear?" Alethea asked.

"The woman said he was upset with himself."

"So much better than my first husband," Alethea exclaimed. "Everything that went wrong was always my fault!"

"Well," Alice added cheerfully, "it sounds like your man is taking the long route to Red Lodge. That means we can shop all afternoon. We'll get to Red Lodge in plenty of time to get some sleep and go to the rodeo tomorrow."

Once the lights were out and the women were settled under the covers, Cassidy removed her shoes and slipped out of her jeans and shirt. She pulled the cool sheets tightly around her.

Only five or six hours ago, Cassidy calculated, she had been on a pleasant ride with Mom and Jason on a mountainous Wyoming highway. How could life change so rapidly? She had been feeling safe and comfortable one minute and was being hunted by killers the next. She wondered once again what she could have done differently. She replayed the scene in her mind with different scenarios and always came up with the possibility that innocent people might have gotten hurt. *Don't waste any more time worrying about it,* she scolded herself in the dark silence. *What's done is done. If you could be more like Brady, you wouldn't always second-guess yourself. He makes up his mind about what to do and then deals with his decision no matter what comes along.*

As she listened to the soft snoring of the women in the other bed, Cassidy contemplated her situation. She felt that she was out of immediate danger from her pursuers, yet gnawing fear still knotted her stomach. It was not fear for herself, but fear for her rescuer. Brady had promised he would send help for her–help he trusted in. But who would help him?

Trent Dominic's men are out to kill Brady. Why? Cassidy wondered as she lay quietly in the darkness. *They must suspect that he witnessed their crime. Do they also know he's been investigating them? Maybe,* she considered, *but there seems to be something deeper than that. You can tell when Brady speaks of Dominic that he loathes the man. What happened to make them bitter enemies? Jubel did mention a trial…*

As the morning sun cast a pink glow through a sliver of a crack in the draped window, Cassidy finally drifted to sleep, knowing she may never see her rescuer again. Someday this nightmare would be behind her. The memory of her trauma would fade and the unsettling fears would dull with time. But Cassidy knew she would never forget the man named Brady Hollister.

Jubel stood on the rim of the high cliff, watching the oncoming truck kick up a rolling cloud of dust as it came nearer the ranch house. The vehicle was within a hundred yards of the buildings before he could make out with the help of his binoculars that it belonged to the local police department. A deputy stepped out and strode up to the front door of the house. Finding no one there, the man searched for tracks in the yard. After several minutes of studying the dirt, he returned to his truck and followed the same trail that Jubel had driven the previous evening.

Jubel turned from his lookout spot and made his way to the campsite. As the tires of the lawman's truck rumbled over the cattle guard at the base of the hill, the old man stepped to the meager campfire and poured himself a steaming cup of thick, black coffee. By the time the vehicle topped the rise, he was leaning on the front of Brady's white truck with coffee cup in hand and his rifle lying casually across the hood.

Toby rose from his bed to investigate the stranger who had come all the way up the hill to disrupt the old dog's early morning nap. Jubel breathed a sigh of relief when he found that the man who emerged from the vehicle was a friend who attended church with him.

"John," Jubel acknowledged the deputy who stooped for a moment to pat Toby on the head.

"Mornin', Jubel," John said. "I see you've got Brady's truck here."

"I reckon."

"He's got yours?"

"I reckon."

"Jubel, you know I've got to ask you where he went. How are we going to get this mess cleared up if we can't find him and the girl?"

"What's to clear up?" Jubel demanded.

"The kidnapping charges against Brady…"

"Kidnapping charges!?!" Jubel glared at the deputy and spat on the ground. The old man began a furious, raging protest against the sheriff for his unethical practices.

"Jubel, I only know what I was told when I came in to work this morning!" John spouted when he could get a word in. "If you know somethin' different, tell me!"

Jubel flung his coffee grounds onto the nearby vegetation. He took a deep breath before he relayed to the deputy what he had been told by Brady.

"The girl was here with him?"

"Yes."

"Did she appear to be captive in any way?"

Jubel shook his head. "She was no more kidnapped than I am! John, she followed him to the house and helped him carry stuff from his truck to the shed. She might have been upset about what went on in Lone Pine, but she didn't seem to have a bit of a problem taggin' along with Brady."

"Where were they heading, Jubel?"

"I wasn't dumb enough to ask," the old man insisted. "If Trent Dominic's men got hold of me, they weren't gonna beat outta me what I didn't know. They pulled in here in the middle of the night, searched the tracks and figured out Brady switched trucks with me. But they knew I was around and watchin' 'em. They left without comin' up here lookin' for me."

"Dominic's men?" the deputy wondered aloud. "What do they have to do with all this?"

"They're the ones the girl saw knifing that guy last night."

John shook his head in disgust. "I was told that a body had been found at Lone Pine," he explained, "but I thought this missing girl was a separate incident."

"It ain't," Jubel told the man bluntly.

The deputy sighed. "Jubel, do you have any idea where Brady might be hiding? You know I'll help him as much as I possibly can…"

"I don't have the faintest notion," came the terse answer. "He met cowboys from all over the world in his rodeo days and some of 'em are from the most remote ranches you can imagine. And there's plenty of 'em that would stick their neck out for him when he's in trouble. All I know is, if anybody's gonna find Brady Hollister, they'd best be lookin' outside of Johnson County.

Alice pulled on Cassidy's toes to arouse her. The young woman opened her eyes slowly until she was told that it was past noon. Bolting out of bed, Cassidy grabbed her clothes on the way to the bathroom as Alethea stood in the doorway and peaked into the hall, standing guard in case the housekeeper caught the trio overstaying their welcome. Within minutes, Cassidy had plunged through the shower and reentered the motel room fully clothed with hair dripping wet. She grabbed Brady's hat and Jubel's coat and her shoes. On a signal from Alethea, the trio of women tip-toed down the quiet hall and rushed from the building. As they crossed the parking lot, Cassidy learned that the key had been turned in two hours before and the luggage was already stowed in the trunk of the car.

"I can't believe I was sleeping so soundly. I didn't hear a thing!" Cassidy said as she took her usual place in the car. She donned her shoes as Alice eased the vehicle out of the motel parking lot and onto a side street.

"We stalled as long as we could," Alethea assured her. "Poor dear. You probably didn't sleep right away, did you? I'll bet you're worried about your man."

"Yes, I am," Cassidy admitted shyly. A twinge of color rose in her checks at the mention of Brady being 'her man.' *This lie is getting easier,* she warned herself.

"Don't you worry about him!" Alethea urged. "I can tell. He's a man who can take care of himself. You two will be back together before you know it!"

Alice pushed the gas pedal and the Lincoln plunged from the relatively quiet side street into a barrage of heavy Saturday afternoon traffic. Cassidy's eyes fell to Brady's hat and she studied the unique angles and bends of the felt rather than watching Alice maneuver the big car through the fast-moving throng. In silence, she prayed that the flighty navigator would not make the driver nervous or upset, for after surviving last night's ordeal, it would be a shame to perish in a freeway accident.

"There's the road I want!" Alice suddenly shouted. She plunged toward the exit ramp at the last possible second, much to the dismay of a horn-honking truck whose bumper was far too close for comfort. She turned the car down a side street. Deciding she had taken the wrong exit, she maneuvered the Lincoln through some business parking lots and down a frontage road. Cassidy was so relieved when the trio located the intended mall, she bounded out of the vehicle.

"You know what?" she asked as Alice and Alethea inched their way out of the car. "I'm starving! Can I buy you ladies lunch?"

"Oh, that sounds good!" Alice agreed. "I'm famished!"

"I'm not," Alethea insisted. "I never eat breakfast. I'll just have a cup of coffee and a sweet roll."

"It's not time for breakfast," Alice reminded her. "It's past time for lunch!" The older woman turned to Cassidy. "Do you like Chinese food?"

"I love it!"

"Good! Let's go this way!"

Alice led the way toward a favorite restaurant with Alethea trailing behind, muttering that Chinese food was so spicy, she might have a stomach ache all afternoon. Cassidy wondered at Alethea's prickly attitude.

As the trio dined, Cassidy mentally tried to calculate what time they might arrive in Red Lodge. They wouldn't be finished with lunch until two o'clock in the afternoon and hadn't even started shopping. She felt an urgency to hurry the women along.

"Alice, do you think we'll be able to get a motel room tonight?" Cassidy ventured.

"It's all set up," the woman assured her. "It took a couple of phone calls, but there was a last-minute cancellation and we got a room right in town."

"Oh. Good," Cassidy replied. She had hoped that the need to search for a motel room might spur them on, but the pair seemed content to spend the afternoon in Billings. *Beggars can't be choosers,* she reminded herself. *I should feel more grateful for their help.*

Cassidy finished her lunch and asked for the meal ticket. Encouraging the sisters to stay at the table and relax, she located a pay phone and dialed Jason's number.

"Hello?" Jason's voice sounded on the other end of the line.

"Jason. It's me! Is Mom there?"

"She's sleeping. I'll go wake her up."

"Don't! Let her rest. I'll call back later."

"Are you doing okay, Sis?" Jason asked.

"Yes. How about you?"

"Better, now that we moved the motor home. This morning some people came and brought food and offered to let us move to the back of their church's parking lot where we wouldn't be so conspicuous. Mom finally got some rest after we did that."

"I suppose she hasn't gotten much sleep," Cassidy sympathized.

"No, she hasn't. After they found the body, the sheriff came and started asking questions. It was really late before mom got to sleep. Then, that stupid news report said you'd been kidnapped so reporters started showing up at the crack of dawn to get an interview. Mom told them there was a mistake, that you weren't missing and that she had talked to you on the phone. She refused to answer any more questions and slammed the door shut. They finally gave up and went away."

"I feel so bad for mom," Cassidy lamented. "She doesn't need any more grief."

"She'll be okay, Sis, as soon as she knows you're safe. Are you and Brady still in Sheridan?"

"No. I'm riding with a couple of elderly women. Right now, we're at a mall in Billings."

"Shopping?!" Jason asked.

"Well, Brady thought it was too dangerous for me to travel with him, so we went separate ways. These ladies took pity on me and offered me a ride," Cassidy explained.

"Do you want us to come pick you up?"

"No! You're probably being watched and you'll only lead them to me. Then we'll all be in danger. I'm going to meet one of Brady's friends at the rodeo in Red Lodge, Montana tomorrow. Brady was going to call the U.S. Marshal and tell him where I'll be."

"Are you going to be safe until the marshal finds you?" Jason wondered aloud.

"Safe, but maybe a little crazy..." Cassidy began to confide in her brother about her situation but realized Alice and Alethea were approaching. "Here come my escorts now. I'll call back later."

Alethea's mood improved tremendously as the day wore on, and Cassidy found the pair entertaining as they shopped. The sisters had a knack for sniffing out bargains for themselves and their young charge. Cassidy was pleased with her purchase of a simple shirt and flattering jeans that would pair nicely with Brady's black hat. After buying a few personal items, she made a mental note that there must be no more purchases, for the cash in her pocket had dwindled considerably. She still needed to eat a couple meals, get to the rodeo, and purchase a ticket to get inside.

"It's time!" Alethea announced as she motioned to the display of glistening bridal gowns in the window of a nearby store. Taking Cassidy by the hand, she led the young woman through the doors.

Cassidy was overwhelmed with the bustle of prospective brides, mothers, and bridesmaids among the wide array of gorgeous gowns. *This is nuts!* she told herself. *I shouldn't be doing this. But these dresses are gorgeous! It won't hurt to try on a couple....*

When a sales clerk appeared, Alethea did the talking, telling the woman that her granddaughter was in need of a wedding dress. With that, she picked out the first dress–a strapless one with sequined top and flowing skirt. Cassidy knew she would never wear such an ornamented and immodest gown, but humored the woman by taking it to a dressing room and putting it on. A saleswoman swept Cassidy's hair upward and pinned it, then slipped a veiled tiara over the crown of her head.

When Cassidy glided onto the show room floor, Alice stood from her chair and Alethea gasped aloud.

"Oh, Cassidy!" Alethea exclaimed. "You are such a beautiful bride! If your man could see you now!"

Cassidy felt the heat of a blush creep into her cheeks. To hide it, she quickly turned toward the bank of mirrors that flanked her and made a show of admiring the dress from different angles.

"It looks wonderful on her," Alice agreed, "but I don't think it's quite her style. Too gaudy and too revealing. I think she should try on something like this over here." Alethea protested her sister's choice, but in fairness Cassidy agreed to don the dress. Once it was modeled, the sisters agreed that it didn't show off their charge's lovely figure to its best advantage.

Cassidy returned to the dressing room with another dress, then another, and another. She humored the sisters to the best of her ability, but her patience wore thin. She finally decided she had to take control of the situation.

"You know what?" Cassidy pointed out to the sales clerk when another garment was selected for her, "This is my first day looking for a dress. I feel like I have to stop and think about what I want for awhile. I'm not ready to buy yet."

After thanking the saleswoman for her help, Cassidy was finally able to steer her guardians from the mall. Her heart sank as she glanced at a clock and found that it was after six. *We won't get to Red Lodge until midnight at the rate we're going,* she sighed.

Alice, too, looked at the clock. "Oh, my! Where has the day gone? We're going to have another late night if we don't hustle!"

Packages were stashed in the generous trunk of the car before the women took their customary places. The vehicle had hardly reached the main road when Alethea began wondering where they should stop for coffee. Cassidy cringed, but remained silent.

"We'll take a potty break in an hour or so," Alice remarked. "We'll stop and eat then."

"I think we should stop for coffee and a sweet roll right way," Alethea insisted. "When we get to Red Lodge, we can check into our motel room and then we'll go find a place to eat. I wonder if they have a supper club or a steak house. I'm hungry for a good steak, and I want to wash it down with some beer! Doesn't that sound good, Cassidy?"

"Well, the steak sounds great…" she admitted.

Alethea turned in her seat to study Cassidy, who sat behind Alice in the back seat. "You don't drink, do you?" she accused.

"No, I don't," the young woman answered.

"Imagine that!" Alethea sputtered. "I didn't think there was a teenager alive these days that doesn't use alcohol…"

"I'm not a teenager!" Cassidy interrupted. "I'm twenty-four! And there happen to be a lot of young people who don't abuse alcohol!"

Alethea ignored the protest and changed the subject. "Twenty-four! By the time I was your age, I'd had two husbands and three kids!"

"And she wasn't happy with any of them!" Alice interjected. "Her kids were brats and her second husband was worse than the first."

"No, he was not!" Alethea argued.

"He was mean!"

"Well, we did fight a lot," Alethea admitted, then added wistfully, "but we sure could kiss and make up!"

Cassidy leaned back in her seat and tried to tune out the discussion that intensified in the front seat of the car. The young woman found herself blushing more than once as the elderly sisters chattered about their love lives. She wondered if this kind of candid talk was normal for them or if they thought they were helping prepare their young passenger for marriage. Cassidy was uncomfortable with the discussion. Trying to turn her mind to other things, she closed her eyes against the late-afternoon sun streaking through the window and wondered if it would be totally disrespectful to plug her ears also.

How would I have survived in such a household as these women raised their families? Cassidy wondered. *There seems to be so many different con-*

cepts of love in the world. But I know I've seen the real thing. I'm so glad Dad and Mom showed genuine love for one another.

Suddenly aware that Alethea had turned in her seat and spoken to her, Cassidy snapped to attention. "I'm sorry," she apologized. "What did you say?"

"I was telling Alice that you seem to be sleeping, but I don't know how you can when we're talking so much!"

"I wasn't sleeping," Cassidy replied, then fibbed, "I just had my eyes closed...because I was trying to picture the dresses and which one I liked best..."

"The strapless one, Cassidy!" Alethea insisted. "The first one you tried on!"

"I have to admit," Alice agreed, "you looked splendid in that dress! But I especially liked the one that was about the same style but had fewer sequins and narrow straps that criss-crossed in back."

"Well, I know which one her man would want her to wear!" Alethea argued. "The strapless one! Believe me, Honey, if he saw you in a dress like that, you would drive him wild. And he wouldn't want to be messing with a hundred fancy buttons..."

"Alethea!" Alice scolded her sister. "You're going to scare the poor girl!"

Cassidy smiled shyly. *This is almost funny,* she thought. *I am not getting married, but I have to try on wedding dresses and listen to raw talk about sex from two little old ladies who probably have a combined total of a hundred years of marriage. All for a ride to Red Lodge, Montana.*

SIX

Brady slid from under the back wheels of the tractor and brushed streaks of amber dust from his clothes. Wiping his greasy hands on a shop cloth, he contemplated the situation as Wayne crawled from the shadows of his disabled rig.

"I'm sorry, Kid. This isn't good," the trucker apologized as he wiped his hands and dusted off his clothes as Brady had done. "I make this run all the time without a lick of trouble. Wouldn't you know when we really need to get back to Montana, we blow a seal. I can't keep goin' with the rig rattling like this or I'll put the whole rear end out of my truck!"

Brady pulled the bandana off the top of his head to wipe the sweat that beaded on his brow. "How far is the nearest shop that can fix it?" he asked the older man as he eyed the meager little station to which they had limped the tractor and trailer.

Wayne scratched his head. "They can fix it here. Whether or not they have parts on hand is another story. But my main concern right now is for these cattle. They can't stay on the trailer in this heat. They need water!"

"There were some holding pens several miles back," Brady recalled.

"There are plenty of them around. The first order of business is to find some empty ones with water. Then we'll have to find a tractor to pull the stock trailer for us."

Wayne led the way across the expanse of the gas station parking lot toward the entrance door. Once inside, the trucker began checking with patrons and clerks in order to locate a place to unload the cattle.

Brady headed for the restroom. He scrubbed for several minutes to remove the black grease from his hands before splashing water over his dirty face and hair. He paused to study his image in the mirror. The neatly trimmed beard had gone two days without attention and the near-black whiskers that were usually shaved away now shadowed the entire lower portion of his face. Dark circles underlined pale blue eyes dulled by fatigue.

The young man stood for several minutes, gripping the edge of the sink, letting the water drip off his face and hair until it further soaked his sweat-stained shirt. He considered once again if he should have done things differently. *You did what you always do,* Brady reprimanded himself. *You made your decisions. Now you live with them. It's better that you and Cassidy are traveling separately. It's safer. You did all you could for her. Now leave her in someone else's hands and forget about her.* Forget her? Brady knew he wouldn't soon do that. He wondered for the hundredth time how she was faring.

The restroom door opened and Wayne walked in. "You okay, Kid?" he asked.

Brady nodded his head to indicate that he was, but knew that the misery in his eyes probably told a different story.

"We've got a place to corral the cattle and a truck to hook up to the trailer and haul it. Are you up to helping?"

"Sure," Brady nodded and straightened to his full height. Squaring his shoulders, he wiped the remaining droplets of water from his face, then jerked the door open and entered the crowded little station. He nearly collided with a woman. As he moved to skirt around her, she looked up at him in shock.

"You're that man they're looking for!" she cried loud enough for everyone to hear.

In a room gone suddenly quiet, with several pairs of eyes focused on him, Brady steeled himself to remain calm. He was in no mood to be confronted, but sighed deeply and spoke as politely as he could, keeping the force of his rage bottled up inside him.

"Lady, I know I'm the right height. I'm the right age. I have the same color hair and the same color eyes as Brady Hollister. But Brady Hollister is running around with a cute blond and I'm stuck with a broken down truckload of stinky steers!" Brady pulled his bandana out of his pocket and tied it over his hair as he marched out of the building without looking back.

Wayne found the young man leaning on the shady side of the truck.

"Are they calling the cops on me?" Brady wondered aloud.

"I didn't see anybody runnin' for a phone. I think when I told 'em you were my hired man they believed me."

"Thanks for going to bat for me, Wayne, but you can be charged with harboring a fugitive. I don't want to make trouble for you. We'd probably better part ways."

"What are you going to do, Kid?" Wayne asked.

Brady paused. He had no plan and could only think of one place to go. "If you don't mind, I'd like to stay with the steers out at the corral."

"I'd appreciate it," Wayne assured him. "I really would. But this truck isn't going to be fixed for several hours."

"That's okay. I need to be alone for awhile."

"Well, if you're willing to camp out with the cattle, I'll get you some food," Wayne offered. As he strode across the parking lot toward the store, he called, "There's an extra blanket on the top bunk. Plan to take that with you."

As Wayne made his way back to the cattle trailer with Brady's supper, a tractor maneuvered through the lot. Locating Wayne, the driver backed up to the trailer he indicated. Once they were hooked up, Brady retrieved his belongings and the blanket and climbed into the cab of the rig that took him and Wayne several miles down a dusty road toward a big empty corral. Brady rode solemnly in the lower bunk while the truckers in the front seats conversed about cattle prices and weather.

As the western sun dipped below the horizon, the rig was backed up to a chute, the trailer was opened, and the anxious steers were released from their cramped quarters. Bounding from their confinement, the cattle quickly located the water tank and fought mercilessly for a place at the edge of it so they could quench their thirst.

As the trucker unhooked the trailer, Wayne approached Brady.

"The man who owns these corrals filled the water tank for us. He's roundin' up some hay and he'll be back with it in a while. When he comes, I'd appreciate it if you'd pay him," Wayne said. "If you take care of this end of the deal, I can get back to town and start work on the truck."

He pulled out his wallet and counted out some bills, then handed the cash to Brady.

"Wayne," Brady said as he looked at the man. "What makes you think I won't take this money and run off with it?"

"Where you gonna go?" the man retorted. "Look around you, Kid. There ain't nobody here and nobody comin' by." He smiled and slapped Brady on the shoulder as he added, "If I had a bad feelin' about you, I wouldn't back you and I wouldn't trust you. And you wouldn't be ridin' around in my truck."

"Thanks for everything, Wayne," Brady spoke sincerely. The trucker again offered the cash. Brady took it and secured it in the front pocket of his shirt as the other driver joined them near the corral fence.

"We all set?" he asked.

"Yeah, I'm ready to go," Wayne assured the man. "The kid's gonna stay with the cattle and feed hay when the load comes." Wayne climbed the truck steps and handed the bundled jacket, bedroll, and sack of supper down to Brady.

"Thanks, Kid," he called as he settled into the seat and closed the door.

The diesel engine rumbled far into the distance, the sound of it lingering long after the lights faded into a dark cloud of dust, and Brady stood alone under the silent stars.

Cassidy sat on a bed in the motel room and dialed the front desk. "Hi. Can you tell me if there is a shuttle or a cab that I can take to the rodeo tomorrow?" she asked.

"We have a complimentary shuttle running all day," came the response.

"Great! I understand there's a church service tomorrow morning?"

"It starts at ten o'clock."

"Thank you!" Cassidy exclaimed as she hung up the phone.

Good! she thought. *I won't have to spend money for a taxi or wake Alice up in the morning to get a ride.* The way the two women had been talking about drinking, they would probably be coming back to the motel room quite late and in a sorry state. Cassidy had begged them to go alone to the steak house and leave her behind, telling them she had to get up very early in the morning to meet Brady's friend.

A quick search through the information on the desk yielded the phone number of a restaurant that would deliver meals to the motel. After ordering supper, Cassidy placed a call.

"Jason?"

"Cass! We were beginning to wonder if you were going to call back. Here's Mom."

"Cassie! Jason tells me you were shopping today! What in the world is going on?" Elaine asked with a voice that sounded as if she were only half teasing.

"Well..." Cassidy explained, "I got a ride with these elderly ladies–they're sisters and they're seventy-nine and eight-two years old–and they said they would take me to Red Lodge, Montana. They had seen the news reports that said I had been kidnapped, but I...we...led them to believe Brady and I were trying to elope and they wanted to help us...."

"Honestly!" Elaine exclaimed. "Who came up with an idea like that?"

"They did, actually! And Brady and I just...went along with it," Cassidy replied sheepishly and was thankful no one was in the room to see her blush as she recalled their pretense at being lovers. "Anyway, I needed a change of clothes so these ladies brought me to a mall and begged me to try on some wedding dresses..."

"Oh, Cassidy! Why didn't you just tell them the truth?"

"No way! And I'm not going to either!" she defended. "First of all, I don't want them to panic. If they knew I was being hunted by murderers, I can't imagine what Alice's driving would be like. It's scary enough as it is. And they have totally changed their whole weekend plans to bring me here. They would be so disappointed if they found out this was a hoax. This way, they can still have a fun weekend! They got to go shopping all afternoon, tonight they're out on the town, and tomorrow they're going to the rodeo."

Elaine changed the subject by asking Cassidy where she was, if she had gotten much sleep, if she had been eating well, and if she had any money. Cassidy assured her mother she had been well taken care of and had plenty of cash to pay for her dinner and ticket to the rodeo if she ate continental breakfast at the motel and took advantage of the free shuttle to the rodeo grounds.

"Tell me about Brady Hollister," Elaine ventured. "What is he like?"

"He's a really nice guy, Mom," Cassidy said with a deep sigh. "I feel so bad for him! He's in so much trouble because he helped me!"

"I don't understand how anyone would suspect him of kidnapping unless he was already in trouble with the law," Elaine pointed out. "Do you think that might be part of the problem?"

"I don't think so," Cassidy answered with a slight quiver in her voice. "He told me he was a private investigator on the trail of a guy who's a drug dealer or gangster or something. His uncle even told us the sheriff is taking money from the guy. That's why Brady decided to take me to another county. But when we found out about the charges against him, he said we had to get out of Wyoming."

"So you don't think he's a dangerous man like the news reports say?"

Cassidy hesitated as she considered what to say to her mother about the dangers of Brady Hollister. She felt the hot rush of embarrassment rise in her cheeks. Should a man be considered dangerous who dared kiss her so provocatively within hours of meeting her? Whose embrace made her heart pound furiously and took her breath away? He was very dangerous in a way Cassidy's mother was not referring to.

"I wasn't sure at first," Cassidy admitted. "He got me to his truck and we took off and I was really scared. I was scared that those men would come after us, but I was kind of scared of Brady, too. I didn't know where he was taking me and he's too strong for me to fight him off if he had tried to do something to me. But he knew I was scared and he promised he wouldn't hurt me. He was really considerate and while he was driving, he tried to keep my mind off the murder by talking to me about a lot of different things."

A knock sounded on the door of Cassidy's motel room.

"It sounds like my supper has arrived," Cassidy told her mother.

"I'll let you go," Elaine said hastily. "Call again as soon as you can. And you know we're still praying for your safety. We'll pray for Brady, too."

"Thanks, Mom. I love you!" Cassidy cried and hastily hung up the phone.

Stars were out in full force and a silver moon was high enough in the sky to shed feeble light over the great expanse of plain. The herd of cattle had been fed and the rancher who provided the hay was gone back to his warm house. The only sound was the slow munching and rustling of the feed as the steers ate their fill.

Brady had reserved a small pile of hay outside the corral fence to make a fluffy bed for himself. He lay down on it and tossed the blanket over his legs. Pulling his cell phone from his jacket, he turned it on and read the time in the feeble light. It was past eleven. Skeeter would probably be in bed by now, but Brady felt an urgent need to talk to him.

"Hello?" came Skeeter's groggy voice at the other end of the line.

"Skeeter, it's me. Brady."

"Brady!" Skeeter seemed to come fully awake. "Where are you? Are you okay?" he questioned.

"I'm about as good as can be, under the circumstances. I'm layin' in a nice, soft pile of hay about as far as I can get from nowhere in the middle of Nebraska. Just a herd of steers to keep me company."

"Where's the girl you supposedly kidnapped?" Skeeter asked. "Did something happen to her?"

"She was fine last I saw her. She's the reason I'm calling you. She got a ride with a couple of ladies to Red Lodge. I told her to look you up. Obviously you haven't seen her yet."

"No, I haven't."

Brady voiced his concern to his friend. "I wonder what's taking them so long!? It doesn't take a whole day to get from Sheridan to Red Lodge! I shouldn't have sent her with those two! They're way up in their seventies. Maybe in their eighties. I don't even know if they can drive decently and of all things, they were planning to party all weekend. Skeeter, I'll never forgive myself if something happens to Cassidy."

"Brady, why are you afraid something might happen to her?"

"She and I witnessed a crime, Skeeter. A murder. Done by a couple of Trent Dominic's boys."

Skeeter let out his breath slowly. "Ohhhh, boy," he sympathized. "And they know you saw them?"

"They know Cassidy saw them. But they've put two and two together and figured out I was the one who got her out of there and I must have seen the murder, too. Dominic and the sheriff of Johnson County made up the kidnapping charges so there would be an all-out search for us."

"Did you tell Cassidy to look me up at any certain time? I'll still be here all day tomorrow, you know."

"I told her you would probably be preaching the Sunday morning cowboy church service and then you'd be in the show in the afternoon," Brady recalled.

"And when did she leave Sheridan?" Skeeter questioned.

"About two o'clock this morning."

"Brady," Skeeter reprimanded his friend. "Did you really expect these old ladies to drive all night? They probably went two blocks down the road and got a motel so they could get some sleep."

Skeeter asked Brady how he found such a pair who would give Cassidy a ride in the wee hours of the morning. He laughed aloud as his friend related the details of the early morning escapade with the truck stop patrons who thought he and Cassidy were eloping.

"Ahhhh, Brady," Skeeter said with a chuckle. "I've never seen the beat for a guy who could bluff his way out of tight situations. And ain't it just like you to get a kiss out of a pretty girl besides!"

The pair talked amiably for a few more minutes before Brady told Skeeter he had to make one more call before the battery went dead on his phone. As the men said their good-byes, Brady asked Skeeter to take good care of Cassidy.

"You know I will," Skeeter promised. "I'll be looking for her tomorrow."

In the dim glow of the cell phone screen, Brady searched through the list of recently called numbers in the device's memory. He found an unfamiliar one and pressed the call button.

"Hello?" a man's voice came on the line after a few rings.

"Jason?" Brady asked.

"Who is this?" the voice countered gruffly.

"Brady."

Jason paused for a long moment. "Brady!?"

"Jason, have you heard from Cassidy?" Brady asked hurriedly, fearing the young man would hang up.

"Yeah," Jason answered cautiously.

"What did she say?" Brady persisted. "Is she okay? When did she call?"

"Listen," Jason warned, "I'm not going to tell you what she said or where she is or anything else until I know for sure you're Brady Hollister. There's been so much crap going on, I'm not going to trust anybody!"

Brady spoke hurriedly. "Jason, I can tell you things about her that weren't on the news releases! The little dog is your mother's, and she's a Yorkshire terrier. Your father died just a short time ago. She's only about five foot nine, not five eleven like they said on the news…"

"Okay! Okay!" Jason responded. "Cassie called about two o'clock this afternoon from B…"

"Hold it!" Brady suddenly cried into the phone. "Jason, I've got to ask you something before you say the names of any towns where Cassidy might be. Are you inside the motor home right now?"

"Yeah," Jason answered.

"Did the sheriff or any of his deputies or anyone come into the motor home at any time?"

"Yeah. The sheriff and one deputy stopped this morning."

"And they came inside the door of the motor home?" Brady asked anxiously.

"The sheriff took a couple steps inside. The deputy stayed at the door."

Brady sighed. "Jason, please look around for a small listening device in case they planted one. It would be in the least conspicuous spot where they could have reached."

"Jason, what are you doing?" Brady heard a woman's voice question. Jason's answer was to quietly tell his mother, "Shhhhh."

"Got it!" the young man's voice came over the phone. Brady could hear the faint sound of a toilet being flushed before Jason spoke once again into the phone.

"Mom and I were wondering what in the world the sheriff came here for. He hasn't caught any of the murderers and didn't have a clue where Cassidy was. He didn't have anything to tell us and the only question he asked was whether we had heard from Cass again. We told him we had gotten another call that didn't come through very good and we didn't know where she was calling from. She actually called us from Sheridan, then Billings, and then from a motel in Red Lodge."

Brady was relieved to learn that Cassidy had spoken to her family just a short time before, yet he did not rest easy. A persistent question gnawed at him. He was sure he already knew the answer, but asked Jason anyway, "After you talked to Cassidy this afternoon or this evening, did you and your mother discuss where she was or where she was heading?"

"Yeah," Jason responded.

"While you were in the camper?"

"Oh, God! God help her!" Jason lamented as the significance of the well-planted listening device dawned on him. "We really screwed up!"

"No! You didn't screw up!" Brady assured him. "I did! I never told Cassidy not to tell you where she was. I only told her not to let you come help her because you would be followed. I should have thought ahead of time they might eavesdrop on you, but I didn't!"

"Jason, what is going on?" Elaine demanded. "Tell me!"

"They know where Cassidy is, Mom!" Jason explained. He turned his attention back to Brady. "Is there anything we can do?" he wondered.

"Get a pen and paper!" Brady ordered. "I'm going to give you the direct phone number of the U.S. Marshal out of Cheyenne. I called him once and told him where Cassidy was headed, but I want you to get in touch with him right away and tell him about this visit from the sheriff!"

Brady recited the number from memory and Jason repeated it back.

"My phone is going to go dead on me or I'd make the call. Can I call you back later?" Brady asked.

"Sure!" Jason agreed.

Brady shut the small cell phone off and was immediately enveloped in blackness. At what point he had thrown off the blanket and risen from his warm bed of hay he couldn't remember. He paced back and forth on the lonely, dusty road.

"God! How could this happen!?" Brady shouted furiously. Never had he felt such panic. "Everything is going wrong! I can't reach Cassidy! I can't help her! She's in more danger than she realizes! Where is the marshal?!"

Brady wanted to hit something. He wanted to throw something. He clutched the small cell phone in his strong hand, but came to his senses enough that he pocketed it instead of destroying his only possible link to Cassidy. He searched the distant horizon all around him for any hint of man-made light that would reveal civilization within walking distance, but each faint twinkling seemed as unattainable as the stars overhead.

"How in the world did I ever end up in Nebraska at a time like this?" Brady lamented aloud.

"You're right where I want you," he sensed the answer to his question and suddenly had the unshakable feeling that God had orchestrated everything that had happened in order to bring him to this solemn place in his life.

As he meandered back and forth on the road, he reluctantly turned his thoughts to spiritual things. Brady believed that Jesus Christ was the Son of God. He believed Christ died to redeem people from the penalty of their sin and that Christ was raised from the dead. But he had never surrendered himself to live in obedience to the Word of God. He had attended church throughout his childhood and knew many of the same songs and scriptures that his friends did. Yet his friends called Christ the Lord of their lives. They studied the Bible. They prayed. They trusted in God. And they lived very differently than Brady did.

Have I ever asked God for anything? he wondered. It didn't take much thought to answer his question. *Not since I asked Him to make my mother come back and she never did. I have never since that day trusted God to help me with anything. I always tried to blame God and blame the church, but it was just an excuse to go my own way. It wasn't either of them that caused my mother to leave. One man led her astray.…Maybe she led him astray. It doesn't really matter. I haven't been living any better in God's eyes than Don Rice or my mother.*

The young man pulled the bandana from his head and absent-mindedly knotted it around his fingers as he leaned on the rails of the corral. *Independence,* he told himself. *You wanted your independence.* He hung his head. *Stop lying to yourself, Brady. It's not independence. It's rebellion…disobedience…sin.*

"God, I don't even know how to talk to you!" Brady admitted in anguish, feeling utterly alone and discouraged. He wasn't sure God was listening, but talking seemed to bring a measure of peace. Not wanting to dwell on his own misery, Brady talked about his fears for Cassidy.

"God, I don't even want anything for myself," he lamented. "I don't care that I'm in trouble! I'll get out of it somehow! Just watch over Cassidy, Lord. Please! Please protect her…"

Brady stopped short in his plea. *That's not what You want, is it?* he considered. *I'm still not asking anything from You for my own sake….* He struggled with confusing thoughts and wondered if he had enough battery power in his cell phone to call Skeeter back. He could ask Skeeter what to say…

This is between you and God. Skeeter can't do this for you, Brady admonished himself.

The realization of his sinful disobedience felt like a crushing weight upon the young man, and he struggled for several minutes before he allowed his pent-up hurts free reign. With true brokenness, he prayed quietly, "God, forgive me! I know I haven't been living right. All I can do is promise that I'll try to change my life, and I'll start by asking You for help…I need help! Help me get through this! And help Cassidy, too, Lord! You know how much I l…"

Was I about to say that I love her? Brady was startled at the thought. He had never in his remembrance declared his love for anyone nor said such words about anyone. He wondered what was happening to him.

When he finally settled back down in the bed of hay, Brady pondered the events that had brought him and Cassidy together. He knew his friends had been praying for him for many years. What had they asked God for? Definitely, for his commitment to Christ. Perhaps, also for his happiness. Maybe that he would know love. He considered that his present troubles could actually be a part of God's answer to their prayers.

"Lord, what do you have in mind for me?" Brady asked aloud as if he were conversing with someone sitting right beside him. "And for Cassidy? Lord, I've never felt this way about any girl. I've never worried so much…or cared so much."

SEVEN

Cassidy awoke in plenty of time to get ready for the Sunday morning church service at the rodeo grounds. She felt well-rested despite being roused at two thirty in the morning by a very drunk Alethea who had trouble finding her own bed. Thankfully, Alice was able to guide her sister in the right direction, whereby Alethea collapsed onto the mattress with all her clothes on. Alice flung a blanket over the limp figure and turned out the lights, quickly leaving the room quiet except for steady snoring.

After a leisurely shower, Cassidy dressed in her new clothes and placed her soiled ones in the shopping bag along with Jubel's coat. She ate breakfast in the motel lobby and was ready to catch the shuttle as soon as she said good-bye to her companions.

"Alice?" Cassidy spoke softly and touched the woman's hand gently.

Alice's eyes fluttered open.

"I'm ready to go, Alice," she said quietly, kneeling at the edge of the bed. "The motel has a shuttle to the rodeo. I wanted to say good-bye and thank you so much for everything…"

"Oh, Honey, it was our pleasure!" Alice whispered hoarsely as she raised up on one elbow. "I'm so glad we could help you!"

"Alice, would you give me your address? I'll send you some money to pay for the motel rooms and gas…"

"Nonsense!" Alice interjected as she sat up in bed. "I won't take a penny! We were going to drive and get motel rooms anyway. Like we told you before, this is cheaper than going to Deadwood."

"Really, Alice, I should…"

"No, Young Lady! This is my treat! I'll only give you my address on one condition."

"What's that?"

"You send me a wedding picture."

Cassidy's heart sank. It would have been easier to send money. She couldn't bear to hurt these women's feelings and there was no time to explain the truth now even if she wanted to. She quickly agreed to Alice's terms and allowed the older woman to scribble the information on a note.

Folding the paper with Alice's address and stuffing it into the pocket of her jeans, Cassidy whispered good-bye and gave Alice a quick hug. Glancing Alethea's way, Cassidy wondered if she should risk waking her.

Alice shook her head.

"Let her sleep. I'll tell her you said good-bye. And we might see you at the rodeo this afternoon!"

"Is he alive?" a man's voice sounded as Brady was nudged with the toe of a boot.

Brady wasn't ready to open his eyes. He wanted to continue the dream, but voices kept intruding.

"Maybe not," Wayne's voice answered the question. "You'd think the sound of the trucks would have woke him up."

Someone grabbed one of Brady's hands as it rested on his chest and lifted it in the air. When the limp appendage fell, Brady stirred. He slowly raised himself up on an elbow, yawned, and rubbed his eyes until a pair of cowboy boots came into focus. He finally awoke enough to squint up into the sunlight where he saw Wayne and the rancher's hired man who had helped unload hay the previous evening. The young man then looked around and located Wayne's truck, already hooked up to the empty cattle trailer. The ranch hand's pick-up truck was parked nearby.

"You got her fixed!" Brady said hoarsely, speaking of Wayne's rig.

"Yup. And we can get goin' as soon as we get the steers loaded."

Brady stood up and stumbled slightly, still groggy from his deep sleep. He shook his head to clear it.

"If I didn't know better, I'd think you packed a bunch of booze in here last night," Wayne commented. He turned to the ranch hand. "Did you boys leave anything for him?"

"No, sir!" the hired man insisted. "We only brought hay. Besides, he wouldn't be shakin' his head like that if he'd been drinking. He'd be holdin' it."

Brady laughed aloud as he brushed hay off his clothes. He silently admitted to himself that waking up with thoughts of a pretty blond sure beat some of the wretched hangovers he had survived in recent years.

Wayne told Brady there was coffee and doughnuts in the truck. The young man gathered up the blanket and his belongings, climbed into the cab, and retrieved the food. He began gulping it down as he made his way back to the corral. Climbing easily over the fence with breakfast balanced in his hands, he began driving the steers toward the chute.

"You're almighty chipper this morning," Wayne observed as Brady chased several animals up the chute toward the trailer.

Brady responded with a wide grin as he retreated back around the herd to force more steers toward the chute.

"The kid's got himself a girlfriend," Wayne explained to the hired man as they worked at driving the animals into the trailer. "He's fixin' to get married when we get back to Montana."

"No wonder he's so smiley," the man replied. "He wasn't near so perky last night when your truck was broke down."

Brady continued to work the cattle toward the trailer without comment as the men discussed him and his "girlfriend." The habitual slight twitch of a smile curled the edge of Brady's mouth whenever he harbored unspoken thoughts. It rested on his lips now as he pondered whether Cassidy might have a boyfriend. She hadn't mentioned anyone special. *If she's got guys calling on her, they've got some new competition,* he reasoned. *I don't want to pretend anymore....*

The steers were loaded and the trailer hauled down the long, dusty road before mid-morning. Once they were under way, Brady tried to calculate the hours before he might arrive in Red Lodge. An hour to their destination to deliver the load, then the unloading, then back across parts of Nebraska and South Dakota, the corner of Wyoming and a good share of Montana. Seventeen or eighteen hours, he guessed, not including time for refueling, meals, and the hours Wayne would have to shut the truck down and get some rest.

I'm over a day away from seeing Cassidy again, Brady mused. *If I ever see her again. The rodeo will be done. Everyone will pack up and go home. The marshal will take Cassidy into custody and keep her safe until the murderers are caught. But where will he take her?*

"Thanks for feeding the stock and paying the rancher for me," Wayne said as the men made small talk while rolling across the Nebraska plains, "When I talked to him over the phone this morning, he said he'd gotten all of his money."

"It's the least I could do for all you've done to help me out. You really stuck your neck out for me," Brady stated sincerely.

"That's not a problem. I appreciate the help and I appreciate the company, even if you do get a little owly at times."

"Have I been hard to get along with?" Brady wondered aloud.

"Not too bad, but you were kinda touchy for awhile. Especially when that woman at the truck stop pointed you out. It's probably a good thing your gun was locked in the truck. You had to use your head and talk your way out of the situation."

"I usually do that anyway," Brady said with a laugh. "I've never shot at anybody, but I tend to get into some rough neighborhoods in my line of work, so I go in armed."

Conversation lulled for a time when each man left the other to his own thoughts. Brady reasoned that Cassidy was probably at the cowboy church service by now. If she hadn't met Skeeter or the marshal yet, she would soon. Once again, he breathed a silent prayer for her safety.

"You're sobering up again, Boy," Wayne teased his young companion. "Are you going to get ornery on me again today?"

Brady looked over at Wayne and retorted, "I'll be all smiles as soon as this rig starts heading in the right direction."

Cassidy climbed to a spot near the top of a section of bleachers and watched as a substantial Sunday morning crowd gathered. Song sheets were passed around as a pair of guitar players tuned their instruments. Cassidy glanced at the familiar songs that she could have sung by heart and turned her attention to the people around her.

The rodeo advertisement posted at the motel had announced that Pastor Jeremy "Skeeter" Varness would be conducting the cowboy church service. Cassidy watched as a man of shorter than average stature and slight build pinned a portable microphone to the front of his western-cut shirt. *Is that Brady's trusted friend?* she wondered.

The crowd followed the song leader, a petite blonde woman, through three hymns, after which the man hailed as "Skeeter" stepped forward with Bible in hand to confidently address the crowd.

"I'd like to talk to you today about slaying giants," the man announced. "Do any of you kids know of a giant slayer in the Bible?"

"David!" several youngsters shouted.

"You bet! David was a young man, a teenager, when he stood up to a bully of a giant named Goliath. Now, before David even knew there was going to be a giant to fight, we read in 1 Samuel, chapter 16, that he was secretly anointed to be the future king of Israel. When he was anointed, the Bible tells us the Spirit of the Lord came upon him in power.

"Some time after this anointing ceremony, we read in chapter 17 that the Philistines were challenging the Israelites to war. David volunteered to fight the giant named Goliath who was nine feet tall. That's about as tall as if this little guy sitting here in front of me were to stand up on top of the arena fence. His head would be way up there! And David was probably shorter than me!"

Cassidy watched the reaction of the crowd as Skeeter addressed them. The children were excited at being involved in the story and gave the preacher their undivided attention. The rest of the audience, too, seemed to sense the extraordinary energy of the man. As Skeeter moved about in front of them, a feeling of expectation pervaded the place.

"Now David made it clear," Skeeter continued, "that as a shepherd, he had rescued his sheep from a lion and a bear. He told King Saul, 'The Lord, who delivered me from the paw of the lion and from the paw of the bear, He will deliver me from the hand of this Philistine.' And we know David won that battle just as he said he would.

"But do you know we all face giants? Not only do adults face giants, but teenagers and little kids face giants, too! They don't often come in the form of a physical nine foot tall person, but we face broken relationships, hurts and disappointments, health problems, financial problems, depression, peer pressure, and a whole lot of other troubles. How many of us face these things the way David faced Goliath–with the confidence that we will have help from the Lord when we need it or knowing that we can get power from the Lord to fight those battles? Most of us try to fight our battles on our own and we get clobbered!"

Skeeter laid his Bible down on a nearby podium as he addressed the people in earnest.

"I'd like to tell you today about the biggest, meanest giant I ever faced in my whole life. When I was a young man about David's age, I was not confident like he was. I was self-conscious. I was small for my age and my father, who was a pastor, took a parish in Wyoming and relocated our family during my sophomore year of high school. To top it off, back home in Illinois, we lived in a city and there were all kinds of things to do. I was in a lot of gymnastics classes and competitions, and I had a pile of fancy ribbons that I'd won. I thought gymnastics was the only thing I was good at and I took it very seriously, but when we relocated to Wyoming, it didn't take me long to figure out that unless they're wrestlers, men in tights are not well respected in cowboy country."

Cassidy looked around at the crowd as they laughed in agreement at Skeeter's statement.

"There were few gymnastics classes or competitions within hundreds of miles of our town and when my parents asked the principal of my new school about it, he had this look on his face like, 'Gymnastics? What's that?!' and tells me they could really use a small guy like me on the wrestling team. So, I'm in a new school where I don't fit in. I'm teased because of my size with remarks like, 'Hey, Kid, the grade school is in the building down the road.' Stuff like that.

"I had a sense of humor and I oftentimes cut up in class to get attention. The kids found me hilarious, but the teachers didn't get the joke. One day in gym class, we're supposed to be playing flag football and some bigmouth made a wise crack about using me for the ball and I hollered at him that I could do things he never thought of doing. I then proceeded to take a running start and did a flip and another flip and a no-handed flip and a round-off and a couple of back flips and no-handed cartwheels and landed in the splits!"

The audience roared with laughter at Skeeter's gyrations as he painted a verbal picture of his acrobatic stunts before wowing them with a small sample of his athleticism.

"Did I get their attention!?" Skeeter hollered.

The crowd clapped and laughed and acknowledged that he did. Skeeter continued when the audience quieted.

"You know I should have let it go at that, but I didn't. As I'm walking back over to these guys that are standing there with their mouths open, I said, 'I bet none of you can even do a decent somersault!'

"One guy says, 'I do 'em all the time! Usually off the back of a bucking horse!'"

There was more laughter from the audience.

"You know, kids could have a lot of fun in class if the teacher would just butt out. These big cowboy dudes were finally talking to me a little. You know, we're starting to interact. And then I get sent to the principal's office for 'doing unsafe stunts in class without the aid of equipment or spotters'." Skeeter imitated the stern gym teacher as he quoted the man, to the further amusement of the crowd.

"Later that day, this cowboy that somersaults off horses caught me in the hall between classes. His name was Brady and he says to me, 'You know, you'd make a great rodeo clown! Pete and Aaron and I are planning on bucking a bull out at my uncle's ranch on Saturday. Wanna come along?'"

At the mention of the name 'Brady,' Cassidy gave Skeeter her undivided attention. She was anxious to learn more.

"I was so overwhelmed that these guys would invite me anywhere, I said, 'You bet!' I didn't bother asking for details like, 'You want me to *be* the rodeo clown, even though I've never in my life been within a hundred yards of a cow? What, your uncle's gone for the weekend and we're doing this without his knowledge or permission?' Minor details! Hey, these guys are high school rodeo studs! They're so good, everybody knows they're going to the state competition! And they invited *me* to go with them!

"The guys picked me up at my house on Saturday. My mom and dad were so thrilled to see me finally getting along at school that they gave me their blessing to go see a real ranch and watch the guys 'work cattle.' My parents thought this would be educational for me. Boy, they had that right!

"Now, I had only attended one rodeo in my life, and that was when we first arrived in the West. I sat and pouted the whole time to show my father my disgust at being moved to this forsaken wilderness, so I never really paid attention to what was going on. In other words, I'm clueless. I was sitting on the top rail of the fence while these guys are rigging up a makeshift chute out of some old gates and they turned this bull in there. While Pete and Aaron were trying to get a rope around him, Brady came over and stuffed great big hankies in my pockets so they dangled down all around me. He said, 'Do you know what you're supposed to do?'

"'I'm supposed to scare the bull so he bucks?' I guessed.

"'No.' Brady laughed at me. 'He'll buck just fine on his own. When I come off of him, you try to get his attention so he doesn't attack me. Keep him busy long enough for me to climb out of the corral and you get out, too.'

"'Okay,' I said and hopped down from the fence. I was standing there, waiting for the action to start, and I looked over at this bull. The shoulders on him were up to these guy's eyeballs, which meant this bull was way taller than me. And did I hear them say he probably weighed seventeen hundred pounds? I thought, 'I might as well be standing in front of a locomotive.'

"Brady climbed over the gate and sat on the bull. Pete and Aaron were holding up the gate and getting ready to turn the monster loose. I started sweating and shaking like a leaf.

"You know, that bull never did buck an ounce. When Brady grabbed up the rope, that bull just snorted and whirled. He hit the gate so hard, Pete and Aaron couldn't hold it. The bull buried them under it, stumbled over the top of it and wiped Brady off his back by smashing into a corral post. It all took about four or five seconds and he had three guys down on the ground. The bull shook his big head and lowered it. He bellowed this deep, deep thunderous roar and pawed the ground. He was looking right at Brady.

"'Brady, get up!' I hollered. Brady didn't move.

"'Brady, he's coming after you!' I screamed. Brady wasn't moving. But my screaming and jumping attracted the bull's attention. He swung his big head around and looked at me. Oops!

"He came at me with his head down and I put the pedal to the metal. When I dove under that corral fence, he was so close, I could feel his breath. When he snorted, he got bull snot all over the back of my pants!"

Skeeter made the comment about the bull snot with a whining tone, as if he didn't like getting his clothes dirty. He got laughs from the kids and grins from the adults, which lightened the serious intensity. Still, everyone sat in rapt attention as they awaited the outcome.

"As soon as I was out of the pen, the bull turned his attention back to the other guys. Pete was trying to crawl out from under the gate, but he was stuck about half way and he was like a sitting duck if that bull took a notion to come after him. Aaron still had this whole big gate on top of him and he wasn't escaping very fast either. Brady was laying in a pool of blood and his leg was in a position a human leg wasn't meant to be in. We're miles from nowhere. I'm their only source of help, and I don't know what I'm doing!

"Being the son of a preacher, I'd witnessed prayer in action. It was my father's habit to pray about everything. I saw him put his trust in the Lord over and over and over again. All of a sudden, I understood how David could by choice face a giant of a man. He had put his confidence in the Lord–the "Living God" as he called him. He knew that God would be there for him and I knew I had to get back into that pen. As I climbed through the fence, I asked God to be there for me, too. As I hollered and screamed to get the big boy's attention, I was also praying for God's protection and for wisdom in dealing with the giant in front of me.

"'I'm back!' I hollered at the bull. I stuck my thumbs in my ears and waved my fingers and stuck out my tongue and went 'Spppptttthh! Nah, nah, you can't catch me!'

"The bull came after me. I jumped to the top rail of the fence and teased him with my hankies, but as soon as I was out of reach, he'd go stalk the other guys. I'd keep jumping back in the pen and running around and hollering until he'd chase me out. This went on for what seemed like an eternity.

"I was getting exhausted and loosing my voice and this bull wasn't quitting and Pete was trying to pull Aaron out of the corral and Brady wasn't moving. I couldn't leave. I couldn't go call 9–1–1. I couldn't go help the guys. So I just ran and hollered and prayed.

"All of a sudden, a gate at the far end of the corral was opened. A gate I hadn't even noticed. I ran for it and dove under the fence as the bull flew past me and headed for the pasture. Brady's dad had come home from work and after asking around, he'd put two and two together and figured out where the boys were and what they were up to. I was never so happy to see anybody in my life!

"You know, that bull was only the first giant I battled that day. Another one came along–named 'Guilt.' I knew I had done wrong. I hadn't told my parents the whole truth about what we were doing at the ranch. And I knew I shouldn't have agreed to do something I wasn't ready to handle. Granted, if I hadn't been there, the bull might have killed all three of the guys or maybe they would have been more cautious and done things differently. All I know is that the devil was having a heyday with me. The Bible tells us he is out to kill, steal, and destroy. Instead of me feeling good that my friends are still alive, I'm convinced I'm stupid, no-good for nothing, can't do anything right…

"Has the devil ever tried those lies on you?" Skeeter asked and waited for the audience to respond to his question, then asked again, "Has he?" Several people shook their heads in the affirmative and Skeeter continued.

"I refused to go to church the next day or attend school for the first couple of days of the week. Hey, we lived in a small town. Everybody knew about what happened, and I just knew they were talking about me and blaming me for everything.

"Pete showed up at the door of our house on Wednesday morning and ordered me to get ready for school. I started to protest but he told me if he could go to school with two black eyes and his knee in a brace and his arm in a cast, I could show up, too!"

Skeeter laughed as he recalled the sight. "He did look a fright! And beat up as he was, I still wasn't about to mess with him 'cause this guy was six foot five and weighed about 250 at the time.

"Well, I went to school knowing everyone was thinking terrible things about me, and wouldn't you know everybody got called to the gym for a special meeting. The students were not only there, but so were half the people from the community, including my folks!

"The principal got up and told everybody that what us boys did was foolish and irresponsible. He explained to everyone the extent of Brady's injuries and that he wouldn't recover in time for the rodeo season and therefore wouldn't be able to participate in the High School Rodeo finals, for he wouldn't qualify. To top it off, Pete and Aaron's injuries were such that they would doubtfully be recovered in time to compete up to their full potential. This was a huge disappointment to a community whose boys and girls excelled in rodeo events year after year.

"Then came the kicker. The principal asked Pete and Aaron if they had anything to say. They got up front and offered their apologies to the community. I nearly died! I was thinking, 'Don't make me get up there! These people hate me! I know they blame me for everything that went wrong!' All of a sudden, Pete and Aaron were done talking and the principal looked over at me.

"'Skeeter?' he says. 'I want you to come up here.'

"I couldn't move from my seat. I was mortified. I was wondering, 'What do these savages want from me!?'" Skeeter shouted as the audience remained unmoving and silent in their seats. "Pete took me by the scruff of my neck with his one good arm and stood me up and hauled me up front. Once he had me planted squarely in front of all these people, the principal turned to me. I was so close to tears it wasn't funny. I knew there was no way I could talk if he asked me to. Thankfully, he did the talking. He said, 'Skeeter, we want to give you this.'

"He reached over to his podium and picked something up and held it in front of me. It was a shiny medal that hung on a ribbon. Now, I'd been awarded a lot of medals for gymnastics and I was proud of every one of them, but this one just made those horrible guilt feelings wash over me again. I took the medal from the principal's hand and instead of thanking him, I let anger well up in me. I said, 'I hope this is a medal for stupidity, because that's the only kind I deserve!' I threw that thing across the gym floor and headed for the exit!"

The crowd stirred, mortified at Skeeter's ungrateful actions. Cassidy gripped Brady's hat nervously as she waited for more of the story.

"Brady's dad stopped me in my tracks halfway to the door. He put his strong hands on my shoulders and I knew there was no getting away from that man. He bent down enough to look me square in the face and spoke to me loud enough that everyone in the place could hear him. He said, 'Skeeter, we're not giving you a medal for going into the corral the first time. The first time *was* stupid. But Skeeter, you went into that corral a second time. And when you did, you were making a conscious effort to try to save lives. That was a courageous thing to do and we want to show you our appreciation.' Then he gives me this big old bear hug and says, 'Let's go get that medal.'

"I had a good talk with the Lord that night, and I prayed until I made things right. That's the week I became a real live giant slayer, just like David. Even though I was still in a little body, I learned what I could overcome with God's help. I'd not only fought off a raging bull, but I also came to know that, as David himself said in Psalm 139, 'I am fearfully and wonderfully made.' God didn't make a mistake when he made me small and wiry and quick, and I had no business putting myself down all the time. I finally came to grips with who I am. I started to believe what the Bible said about me! And best of all, the community had forgiven me and God forgave me, too. By accepting that forgiveness, I finally conquered the guilt and shame that had been weighing on me.

"In Philippians, chapter 4, verse 13 we read the words of the Apostle Paul who declares, 'I can do all things through Christ who strengthens me.' I'm here to tell you, if you're facing a giant, don't try to tackle him by yourself! Draw strength from the Lord. Ask Him to fight your battles!

"I'm going to ask Crystal to lead a hymn in closing while I step over to these bleachers." Skeeter indicated a bank of empty seats a short distance from where the audience sat. "First of all, if there is anyone here who doesn't know the Lord Jesus Christ as your personal Savior, I would encourage you to start a relationship with Him today. Feel free to talk to me about how to do that. And for those of you who are wrestling with a giant of any kind, I would be more than happy to pray with you. God wants you to be released from the strongholds of the enemy. You don't have to face health problems or financial problems or broken relationships alone. Maybe you think God wouldn't help you with anything, because you haven't been living right. I'm here to tell you, the Bible says in Romans, chapter 5, verse 8 that 'while we were still sinners, Christ died for us.' He doesn't ask us to get our act together *before* we seek Him. He's ready to help *now.* I encourage you to take that first step toward Him today. I'll be happy to pray with you. Come, as Crystal sings."

Skeeter turned off his portable microphone as the petite blonde woman stepped in front of the crowd. As she led the sober congregation in a song, several people rose from their seats and moved toward the bleachers where Skeeter awaited them. *This is my chance to talk to him,* Cassidy thought. She lifted the bag and settled Brady's hat on her head before following a small group as they made their way down the steps.

Cassidy chose a seat well away from the others and watched in silence as the pastor spent several minutes with each person. He moved from one to another, speaking with young and old alike, praying for them and reading scriptures to them.

Brady had told Cassidy to seek help from Skeeter. She wanted someone to befriend her until the marshal found her, but Cassidy was suddenly overwhelmed with her need for help. Hot tears surfaced and flowed down her cheeks as she silently acknowledged that it had been a long time since she shared her troubles with the Lord. Even now, while running for her life, she had left the fervent praying for her mother and church family to handle.

Cassidy buried her face in her arms as she folded them over her knees. Shutting out the world around her, she let her tears flow and was unaware that Skeeter sat down beside her until he rested his hand on her shoulder and whispered, "Cassidy, are you okay?"

She lifted her head and wiped tears away with the back of her hand until she realized that the man was holding out a hankie to her. She took it and thanked him as she dabbed at her eyes.

"I don't know where Brady is," she spoke quietly. "I don't know if he's all right…"

"Brady is fine. But that's not the reason you're crying, is it?" Skeeter challenged. "Do you know Jesus Christ as your personal savior?"

Cassidy kept her eyes averted from the preacher. She was reluctant to speak openly with a stranger about her troubled heart. "I…" she hesitated before plunging forward. "I went forward when they had an altar call at church camp when I was fourteen. And I stayed really involved in church and youth group until college. Then I moved away from home and I haven't found a local church I'm comfortable with. I'm not really involved anymore. I guess I haven't made any good Christian friends where I live now…"

"So you've been drifting away from the Lord?"

"I guess. Especially since my dad died," Cassidy admitted.

"What happened to him?" Skeeter asked patiently, as if he had all the time in the world to sit and talk. Cassidy looked around and found that nearly everyone else was gone from the immediate area. Skeeter had left her until last among the people that he had counseled this morning.

"He had a brain aneurism," Cassidy spoke quietly as tears threatened to spill over once again. "He was only fifty-two."

"I'm sorry. How long ago did this happen?"

"This past April."

"He knew Jesus Christ as his Savior?"

"Yes."

Skeeter paused for a moment as if reflecting on Cassidy's situation before he chose his next words. "Grieving can take a long time, Cassidy. You only lost your father three months ago. And even though you know in your heart he's in a better place, maybe your mind wants to blame God for not intervening in his death. The Bible tells us our days are numbered even before we're born. Be thankful for the time you had with him. The important thing, Cassidy, is to learn to trust God in this, even though you can't see the reason for it."

Cassidy shared down at her feet, silently considering Skeeter's words.

"Am I making any sense to you?" he asked.

"Yes," she nodded tentatively, trying to put her feelings into perspective, and finally admitted, "You're right about me blaming God. I've been feeling totally…betrayed…like He doesn't really care."

A fresh trickle of tears coursed down Cassidy's cheeks, and she brushed them away. "I don't know how my mother can take it. She loved Dad with all her heart, but she doesn't cry about him all the time like I do," Cassidy said apologetically.

"I'm sure she still hurts," Skeeter said confidently. "But she has children to focus on and be strong for. And unlike you, maybe she's learned to rest in the Lord and believe His promises."

Cassidy smiled a weak smile, acknowledging with a nod that perhaps Skeeter was right.

"God is not out to hurt you, Cassidy," Skeeter assured her. "The Bible tells us He disciplines those whom He loves. It also says our tribulations produce perseverance and perseverance produces character. May I make a suggestion?"

Cassidy shrugged her shoulders and uttered a soft, "Sure."

Skeeter grinned as he offered Cassidy his advice. "Being that God is going to so much trouble with these character-building lessons, learn them the first time so you don't have to go through anything like you're going through again."

Cassidy couldn't help but smile at the cowboy preacher.

"Renew your commitment to the Lord, Cassidy, and put your trust in Him."

Crystal finished speaking with some people at the far end of the row of bleachers and climbed the steps to join Skeeter and Cassidy.

"Do you mind if Crystal and I pray with you?" Skeeter asked.

Cassidy nodded her head and closed her eyes. Crystal sat down next to her and placed a gentle hand on her shoulder while Skeeter prayed.

"Lord, first of all, we thank and praise you for bringing Cassidy safely to us. We thank you for protecting her and supplying her needs and we ask that you continue to watch over her. Now, Lord, we ask for peace for Cassidy. Send your Holy Spirit to comfort her, Lord. Reveal yourself to her as a God of love and of mercy. We ask these things in Jesus' name. Amen."

EIGHT

Crystal carried her meager lunch toward an empty table with Cassidy following close behind her. Skeeter was delayed several times as he was greeted by patrons of the lunch line. When he finally sat down next to Crystal with a generous plate of food, Cassidy mentioned that he must have known Brady a long time.

"Oh, yeah," Skeeter said with a smile. "That little incident must have been, let's see…seventeen years ago. Did Brady tell you much about his rodeo career?"

"He told me he didn't finish college and went on the rodeo circuit," Cassidy recalled. "He said he wanted to be the best all-around, but he eventually stuck with riding bulls. And the neighbors were the ones who got him interested in rodeo."

"Those neighbors were the Knowlton family. Pete Knowlton was the Pete that was with us on our little adventure," Skeeter explained between mouthfuls of food. "He was a year ahead of Brady and me in school. Brady stayed with the Knowltons whenever his dad was out of town."

"Brady mentioned that the neighbors and his uncle Jubel helped raise him after his mother left."

"Yeah, and his uncle Jubel's place was where we were foolin' around with that bull!" Skeeter admitted.

Cassidy noticed that Crystal only picked at her food. She studied the woman who sat across the table in silence. Dark circles under Crystal's light eyes contrasted sharply with her colorless complexion. Crystal looked up and caught Cassidy watching her.

"You look really tired," Cassidy stated.

"I am," the young woman admitted. "I'm always nauseous early in the day, but today I'm not getting over it and I feel totally exhausted."

Cassidy smiled as she realized what Crystal was hinting at. "You're going to have a baby?"

"Our first!" Skeeter beamed with pride as he placed a gentle arm around his wife's shoulders. "We just found out a couple weeks ago."

"Congratulations!" Cassidy said with a smile. A flush came to her cheeks as she addressed Skeeter, "I didn't even realize until now that the two of you are married. Brady didn't tell me anything about you."

"That figures," Skeeter retorted. "He's the lone holdout among his old buddies. The rest of us are all hitched!"

The dining area was filling up fast, and a couple approached the table where Crystal, Skeeter, and Cassidy sat. "These seats reserved?" a huge cowboy asked. Being over six and a half feet tall before donning a cowboy hat and heeled boots, the man towered over the surrounding shuffle of people.

"Sit down, Pete!" Skeeter invited and introduced the newcomers. "Cassidy, this is Pete and Jennifer Knowlton."

Pete sat at the end of the table across from Skeeter while his wife slid into the space between the big man and Cassidy. Cassidy studied the couple as she greeted them. Pete's ruddy, freckled face and reddish-brown hair contrasted with his wife's light olive complexion and dark hair and eyes. His athletic build indicated he was probably still very active in competition.

"We were just talking about you, Pete," Skeeter admitted. "I was telling Cassidy that Brady stayed with your family."

"So this is the Cassidy we've been hearing about on the news, huh? How in the world did Brady get himself into such a mess this time?" Pete addressed the young woman at the end of the table.

"What do you mean, 'this time'?" Cassidy countered. "Does he get into trouble often?"

"No!" Pete assured her. "Only once every few years or so."

Cassidy briefly related the circumstances that led to her rescue. "Brady and I got to the walk in front of the buildings just as one of the three men drove his truck around the corner and came toward us. He pretended we just stepped out of the tavern. He walked me over to his truck, and we got in and drove away."

"I can picture Brady pullin' somethin' like that off!" Pete exclaimed.

"Yup," Skeeter agreed with a smile. "Cool as a cucumber! He can usually outtalk or outsmart most anyone."

"Weren't you scared?" Jennifer wondered.

"I was scared spitless!" Cassidy acknowledged. "And I didn't have much trouble pretending I'd just walked out of a tavern. My legs felt so rubbery, Brady had to hold me up!"

The small group laughed.

"Who in the world came up with kidnapping charges?" Pete wondered aloud.

"Apparently the local sheriff is hooked up somehow with a man named Trent Dominic..." Cassidy began.

"Oh, no!" Jennifer exclaimed. "Not him again!"

"What do you mean?" Cassidy questioned the woman next to her.

All eyes were on Cassidy as Jennifer told her, "He's the one that got Brady into trouble in college. Didn't Brady mention Black Mesa?"

"No," Cassidy shook her head. "What's Black Mesa?"

Crystal fanned her face to ward off the intense heat filtering into the dining area. Jennifer suddenly became intent on greeting friends at a nearby table and didn't reply to Cassidy's question. The two men glanced at one another before Pete broke the uncomfortable silence.

"Black Mesa," he explained, "is just a dumb, steep hill with a flat top that sits behind my folks' place. It's not a real mesa at all and it's not on any map. We just named all the hills around our place so we'd know what part of the cattle range we were talkin' about."

Pete pondered his next words so long, Cassidy wondered if he was going to tell her more.

"Brady and Trent Dominic and I all went to the same college. One weekend when my folks weren't around, we had a party out in a ravine at the bottom of Black Mesa. A lot of drinkin'...and a few people doing some drugs, too," Pete admitted reluctantly. "A bunch of guys started playin' 'King of the Hill' with their four-wheel-drive vehicles to see who could get to the top first. Brady and Trent were in the lead along with a guy and his girlfriend in a Jeep. The Jeep got ahead, then hit a rock and rolled over. The driver was thrown out and he got run over and killed by one of the trucks behind him. His passenger lived, but she was paralyzed and never did fully recover.

"Dominic told everyone that Brady was the one who ran over the guy. Brady maintained that Dominic was the culprit. Somehow, Dominic's daddy's money seemed to come into play. A bunch of charges were filed against Brady–manslaughter included–but Trent Dominic was hardly even investigated."

"So Brady went to jail?" Cassidy asked.

"No," Pete assured her. "There were enough witnesses who testified that he was acquitted of the manslaughter charge. But Brady holds a grudge against Dominic to this day."

Skeeter rose from his seat. "I've got to get moving. Got a show to do," he announced. "You stick around, Cassidy. We'll get together later, okay?"

Crystal rose and apologized. "I'm sorry I'm such a party pooper."

"That's okay. Go get some rest. I hope you start feeling better!" Cassidy called as the couple walked away.

"Is Brady here?" Pete asked quietly as he polished off his lunch.

"No," Cassidy answered with a shake of her head. "Last I knew, he was in South Dakota."

"How did you get here?" Jennifer asked.

Cassidy briefly related their parting in the early morning hours of the preceding day, which eventually brought her to Red Lodge while Brady hitched a ride with a trucker.

"And ended up in South Dakota," Jennifer pointed out. "What now?"

"Brady said he was going to call the U.S. Marshal and tell him where to find me. I guess I just have to stick around here and wait for him to show up."

Cassidy caught a glance and brief smile that was exchanged between husband and wife. She wondered about it but didn't have a chance to ask before several people walked toward their table, seeking places to sit.

"We're finished here!" Pete assured the group and gathered up his plastic plate, cup, and utensils, tossing them in the nearby trash can. Jennifer and Cassidy followed Pete's lead and swiftly cleared the table as they rose from their seats. Retrieving her bag from the floor under her feet and settling Brady's hat on her head, Cassidy followed the couple out into the bright noonday light.

"Where do you think I should go so the marshal will find me?" Cassidy asked the pair.

"You just stick with me," Jennifer told her. "We'll sit together over here. He'll find you."

Cassidy shouldered the awkward bag as she moved toward the area of the stands that Jennifer indicated.

"Would you like to put that bag in our camper?" Jennifer asked.

"I would really appreciate it!" Cassidy replied. "It's mostly dirty clothes and a coat I won't need for several hours."

Pete left the women and headed in the direction of the corrals behind the arena as Jennifer led the way to a large parking area filled with campers and horse trailers of every size and description. Cassidy pulled Brady's hat off her head and fanned her face with it, detecting a hint of Brady's cologne wafting through the air as she did so. Clutching the black felt in her hand, she followed Jennifer through the crowd, letting the faint breeze cool her perspiring brow.

"We're parked near the end of this row," Jennifer indicated. "I have to stop in to check on the kids anyway. Our daughter and a friend were playing games and making pizza for lunch."

"How old is your daughter?" Cassidy asked as she followed Jennifer through the maize of vehicles.

"She just turned eleven. And we have a son who is thirteen."

The women arrived at the door of the Knowlton's camper. "Come on in," Jennifer offered.

"No thanks," Cassidy declined. She could see through the doorway that the space was very limited with both of Jennifer's children and a couple of their friends gathered around the tiny table. "If I could just set this inside the door, I'd appreciate it."

"I'll put it in here," Jennifer said and extended her hand for the bag. She took it from Cassidy and moved around the crowded table to a small closet. As Jennifer reminded the youngsters to clean up when they were finished, Cassidy stepped back away from the door to give the family a few moments of privacy.

Cassidy smoothed her hair and replaced Brady's hat, adjusting it on the crown of her head. As she did so, she caught movement out of the corner of her eye and turned toward it. A man stepped from between two trailers and walked quickly toward her.

Alarm welled up as Cassidy recalled the three men she had seen behind the motel. She turned and walked hastily away from the Knowlton's camper and stepped between two horse trailers. The man followed. She changed direction again and the man shadowed her. Cassidy broke into a run toward the edge of the camping area. With only a few trailers left to pass, she headed for the crowded vendor area. Another man stepped into her path–the tall man with the tan hat! He barred her exit along her chosen route.

Cassidy bolted between one trailer after another and passed several campers as she tried to elude her pursuers. She rounded the corner of a vehicle and grabbed a folded camp chair. As the shorter of the men stepped into view, she swung the lightweight chair with all her might and smashed it into his face. The man nearly warded off the blow, but one corner of the chair knocked his hat off and gashed his forehead above the left eye. With blood trickling down his face, the attacker moved toward Cassidy once again. She swung the chair once more and the man stepped back to avoid the blow. As he did so, the trailer hitch caught him behind the knees. Off balance, the man flung his arms upward to try to right himself. Cassidy seized the moment and swung her weapon once more, bending the steel frame over the man's head and shoulder. Enraged, Cassidy's attacker steadied himself against the camper with one hand and grabbed the dilapidated chair with the other. Just as he flung it aside and stood upright to come at Cassidy, Jennifer appeared behind the man with a stout stick of firewood with which she delivered a hardy blow to the back of the attacker's head. His knees buckled. He slipped slowly to the ground and fell face down at the women's feet.

Cassidy's heart beat wildly as she approached her fallen pursuer and rolled him over. Opening his vest, she found that he sported a gun in a shoulder holster similar to the one Brady wore. Slipping the pistol out of its leather sheath, she located the safety mechanism and slipped the lever into fire position. Jennifer stared wide-eyed at the younger woman who stood shaking before her.

"Jennifer, there's at least one more man after me," Cassidy explained with an unsteady voice that scarcely sounded like her own. "A tall guy with a tan hat."

"He's coming behind you!" Jennifer whispered.

"Split up!" Cassidy whispered back.

The women separated and Cassidy headed to another narrow passage between trailers. As she stepped out of view of the tall man, she glanced back toward Jennifer, making sure she was well out of harm's way. Cassidy ran past the trailer and stepped into the next lane just as the tall man did the same. He walked deliberately toward his victim, an intense stalker hoping that his prey would panic and make a mistake in her attempt to escape. As the man drew steadily closer, he drew a long, glistening blade from under his vest.

Cassidy took a deep breath and stood her ground. She slowly raised the pistol that she had kept from her enemy's sight until now. The man showed momentary alarm but continued forward. Cassidy held her breath and concentrated on the menace before her.

The man suddenly lunged forward. A gun shot exploded. Cassidy stood as if frozen as her pursuer dropped the knife from his clenched fist and clutched at his bleeding side.

In disbelief, Cassidy stood motionless as she watched the stalker fall. She knew she had not pulled the trigger of the weapon she held so tightly. She was scarcely aware of the gathering of people around her until someone approached and ordered, "Cassidy, don't shoot! It's over! Nobody's gonna hurt you now."

A stranger cautiously stepped in front of the young woman, holding one hand toward her as he holstered his own gun. Cassidy looked around to find that numerous people approached and were waiting for her to lower the pistol before rushing to the aid of the wounded man at her feet. She slowly dropped the gun to her side as the lone man produced a badge from the pocket of his western cut shirt, which he flashed before Cassidy's eyes. She read the insignia of the U.S. Marshals Service.

As the marshal grasped the weapon from Cassidy's clenched fist and flipped the lever to the safety position, Cassidy eyed him. "Where were you ten minutes ago?" she accused.

The marshal seemed taken aback by Cassidy's grilling question. He stared at her with unflinching, narrowed eyes from under the brim of his black hat for several seconds until Cassidy shifted her gaze away from him.

"I'm sorry," she apologized. "I just…." Cassidy didn't finish her sentence. In frustration, she turned away to lean against a nearby trailer as the trauma of the last few minutes engulfed her. Jennifer appeared beside her to enclose the shaking Cassidy in comforting arms.

The marshal spun on the heel of his boots and shouted, "Sykes, has an ambulance been called?"

"Yes, sir! It's on the way," came the reply from a tall, thin man dressed in blue jeans and a t-shirt.

"How did you guys lose track of her? I thought you'd spotted her," the marshal demanded, placing his hands on his hips as he awaited an answer.

The deputy named Sykes responded in a steady voice, "She was in a big crowd heading toward the grandstand bleachers, then she turned in another direction. We thought she'd gone to the restroom. Gladys went in there to check. By the time we figured out she wasn't there, we had to scatter all over to look for her again. That's when we radioed you."

"I took Brady's hat off!" Cassidy gasped as the realization struck her. She spoke to Jennifer. "When we decided to go to your camper, I took Brady's hat off! That's why they couldn't find me!"

The marshal shook his head and looked at Cassidy as he spoke to his deputies and the police officers nearby. "Thank God she's a fighter or we'd be dealing with a murder about now." The marshal then addressed Jennifer. "Remind me to wring Brady's neck next time I see him. What was he thinking, sending her here in the middle of a rodeo?"

"He knew his friends were here and that we would help her!" Jennifer defended.

"And she did, too," Cassidy said with a timid smile as she indicated a blood-covered handcuffed prisoner being escorted to the scene of the shooting by two deputies. "Jennifer is the one who knocked that guy out. She hit him over the head."

A local deputy laughed aloud. "We were wondering how this girl beat him up so bad. We didn't know he was double teamed."

Emergency medical personnel arrived on the scene. Pete Knowlton pushed his way through a crowd of onlookers, followed by Skeeter in full make-up and half dressed in his clown outfit. The men made their way to the trailer where Jennifer stood with a protective arm around Cassidy.

The marshal addressed the local lawmen arriving at the scene. "I need to have these men watched around the clock. One needs to be stitched up and the other will need a bullet dug out of him," he said, indicating each of the prisoners in turn as they were being hauled away. "I don't have enough deputies to guard both of these guys and Miss Henderson too, and we've still got another murder suspect to contend with. How many officers can your department spare in the next few hours?" the marshal asked.

"With the rodeo goin' on, we've got everybody doing extra duty now," one of the deputies replied.

"I'll borrow help from the next county if I have to!" the marshal grumbled.

As the prisoners were escorted away, the remaining deputies questioned the marshal.

"What about this other murder suspect that you mentioned?" one asked. "Do you think he's here?"

"I don't know. These are the best pictures that we have of him," the marshal responded as he retrieved a couple photos from one of his deputies. "Deputy Cole has been working most of the night trying to clear up these pictures of the murder in Lone Pine a couple of nights ago. This is the murder that Cassidy Henderson and Brady Hollister witnessed, and these pictures are from Brady's camera."

"The pictures are kinda dark, but good enough that I'd say you just caught a couple of murderers," a deputy stated as he studied the paper. "But that third guy is going to be hard to identify."

"Yes, he is," the marshal agreed. "All three of the suspects apparently work for a man by the name of Trent Dominic. Dominic and the rest of his men were not directly involved in the murder. They're strictly here to look for Brady."

"Dominic is here?" Pete questioned.

"He and some of his men," the marshal confirmed. "He must suspect that Brady has been investigating him and can connect these three hoodlums to his organization."

"Marshal, I'm confused," a local deputy admitted. "Is this the Cassidy Henderson that was kidnapped in Wyoming a couple of days ago?"

The marshal turned to Cassidy and asked, "Young Lady, were you kidnapped?"

"No," Cassidy stated clearly. "Brady helped me escape when the killers came after me."

"So, where is this Brady Hollister?" the deputy questioned.

"He was in Nebraska when I talked to him on the phone last night," Skeeter offered.

Cassidy's heart sank. *He's getting farther away all the time,* she silently reflected. *I never had a chance to thank him for all he did for me. And I may never see him again…*

"Trent Dominic and his men have a beef with Brady, and they've come to the wrong place looking for him," the marshal explained. "They found out Cassidy was coming here and assumed Brady was coming too."

The marshal turned to Cassidy. "We picked up Jubel's truck and have been looking through the pictures and notes Brady left in it, but nothing is making a lot of sense yet. Did Brady take anything out of the truck or give you anything to bring to me? Pictures? Papers? Anything?"

"He left a box full of stuff at his uncle's place," Cassidy said with a shrug. "The only thing he gave me was his hat."

The marshal smiled. "He told me to look for the Rodeo King! I thought he just sent it with you to help identify you."

As the small group looked on with anticipation, Cassidy handed the battered black felt to the marshal who quickly turned it over. He pulled at the liner inside the crown until he found a section of the silky material that had been loosened from the inside band. Slipping his fingers into the slit, the marshal pulled out a couple of pictures and a minute memory card that had been secured inside. Beaming, he glanced at the photos and passed the card to Deputy Cole.

"Gladys, put that in your computer and see what you can make of it," the marshal commanded as he carefully handed the miniature record to the stout, dark-haired woman who stood nearby.

The tall, lanky Deputy Sykes studied the photos the marshal handed him. After reading the notes on the back of the pictures, he asked his superior, "Marshal, if Brady's evidence is enough to arrest Dominic, are we gonna try to nab him here?"

"No, I want these guys out of here. They're dangerous."

"We wait until the rodeo is done and trail them?" Sykes asked.

"That'll be near impossible if they leave when the rest of the crowd does," the marshal said. He turned Brady's hat around in his hands as he contemplated the situation. "They're looking for Brady," he stated as if he were speaking his thoughts rather than addressing the small group around him. "They're waiting for Brady to make the first move. If they were led to believe Brady is here, but leaving the rodeo grounds, they'd go after him."

"How about Black Mesa, Marshal?" Skeeter suggested after a few moments of thought. "Maybe you could arrest them there, where no one else would get hurt."

"How in the world would we get 'em to go there?"

"I've got an idea," Skeeter assured the man with a sly grin. "Wait until the rodeo gets started, then give me some time."

As if on cue, the loudspeakers that had been blasting country music around the grounds came alive with a hearty welcome to the overflowing crowd. As the announcer introduced the town mayor, Skeeter hurried away to finish dressing for his role as clown.

The marshal thanked the local deputies for their help as the group dispersed. Steering Cassidy toward the bleachers, he addressed his own deputies. "Let's pick through that new evidence while we're waiting to see if Skeeter can come up with something."

A local deputy turned back for a moment to ask, "Marshal Hollister, is this Brady Hollister a relative of yours?"

The marshal looked squarely at the man and acknowledged quietly, "He's my son."

NINE

Cassidy stood rooted to her spot and let the rest of the group move away as she faced the marshal, noting that he had the same lean, muscular build as Brady, but seemed to be slightly taller. Both had near-black hair and similar mannerisms, but Marshal Hollister's eyes were dark, unlike Brady's light blue ones.

"Judging by the look on your face, Brady didn't tell you his dad is the marshal, did he?" the man asked after the others had gone.

"No."

"He didn't say anything about me?"

"The only thing he told me about his father was that he raised him alone with the help of Uncle Jubel and the neighbors. He said we had to get out of Wyoming so the kidnapping would become a federal case for the U.S. Marshal. He told me I would be safe once the marshal caught up with me."

The man smiled, curling only one side of his mouth as Brady often did.

"He hasn't called me 'Dad' for years," the man sighed as he gently grasped Cassidy's elbow and steered her through the maze of trailers. He surveyed the area carefully as he spoke above the clamor of fast-moving horses entering the arena for the rodeo's opening ceremonies.

"He started calling me 'Marshal' when he was about twelve or thirteen," the man explained. "I shouldn't have let him get away with it, but he used to be so proud of me! I'd come home from work and we'd sit for hours discussing trials and witnesses and fugitives…and rodeo. He always had to talk about rodeo."

"The two of you don't get along anymore?" Cassidy questioned.

"We get along okay," the marshal said with a shrug. "We just go our separate ways. I'm based out of Cheyenne and he's been working around northern Wyoming and as far away as Reno."

The marshal led the way to some seats in a small press box he had confiscated for a temporary command post. Cassidy settled into one of the seats and tried to observe the marshal at work while paying attention to the rodeo at the same time.

Through emails and computer sleuthing, Deputy Cole acquired Trent Dominic's cell phone number. With that information on hand, the trio of officers huddled around a laptop computer in which Brady's file had been inserted. Amidst the noise of the rodeo arena, Cassidy occasionally heard comments from them indicating that there was some excellent evidence to bring a case against several people. Apparently, there was some very disturbing information also, as indicated by a discussion of a fourteen-year-old runaway who was working in a strip joint. Obviously Brady had gone to great lengths to put together detailed files. Cassidy shuddered to think of the places he frequented and the people he came in contact with in order to gather such information.

As the rodeo progressed, Skeeter frequented the arena amidst the serious competitive events with various funny cars and motorcycles and trick props. He kept the audience well entertained with his fast-paced, energetic antics and a hilarious string of jokes.

A matched pair of white horses with trick riders astride exited the arena and the audience waited in anticipation for the steer wrestling to begin. Skeeter entered the arena with a wooden box and sat on it with his elbow on a knee and his chin resting in his hand, striking the pose of a famous statue. The rodeo announcer, astride a sorrel horse with a white star on its forehead, looked over at the clown and studied him in silence for awhile.

"Skeeter, what are you doing?" the announcer finally asked.

"I'm pondering," Skeeter replied.

"Pondering."

"Yes, pondering. You know–thinking! I do exercise my brain cells every now and then."

The announcer commented, "It looks to me like you're imitating the statue called, 'The Thinker.' Does it help to sit like that?"

"Well, not really," Skeeter admitted. "But come to think of it, that guy was in his birthday suit when he did his thinking. Do you think a man thinks better when he's in his birthday suit?"

"I doubt it," the announcer commented before introducing the first contestant. A steer plunged from a gate. A rider on horseback chased him down, slid from the saddle to grab the steer by the horns, and in a flurry of dust, toppled the animal to the ground in little more than eight seconds. The crowd clapped and cheered as the contestant dusted himself off and acknowledged their applause by waving his hat in the air.

Skeeter remained in his thinking position.

"Skeeter, if you're having trouble figuring something out, maybe we can help," the announcer offered. "I'll bet there are a lot of brilliant minds around here."

Another contestant had to be announced quickly as he chased a steer across the arena dirt. The man missed his grip on the steer as he slid from the saddle and the steer trotted proudly to the far end of the fence. The announcer led the audience in an "Aw, shucks!" that was frequently awarded to unfortunate contestants.

"Okay," Skeeter proclaimed to the crowd in a moment of quiet. "I'm pondering a poem."

"You're pondering a poem," the announcer repeated. "You mean you're thinking of a new poem for us? You haven't recited one of your poems for a long time."

"Well, this isn't one of *my* poems. This is someone else's poem. Every now and then, someone in the audience wants to get into the act. So what do they do, they put a poem on the windshield of my truck."

"Someone put a poem on your windshield. Is it a good poem?"

"Well, it rhymes real nice and has a good rhythm to it. But I can't for the life of me figure out what it means. I guess you'd call it one of them there riddles."

The announcer turned to his agenda for a moment and announced the next contestant, Pete Knowlton, who successfully wrestled the steer to the ground in less than seven seconds. As soon as the audience cheers died down, the announcer turned his attention back to Skeeter.

"Maybe you should read the riddle to us. I'll bet someone here can figure it out."

"Okay," Skeeter announced. "Here is a riddle for you all to ponder. It was stuck on my windshield."

Skeeter stood and ceremoniously pulled a sheet of paper out of his deep pants pocket and read:

> I used to be King of the Rodeo
>
> But I found something better still.
>
> Until I'm six feet under
>
> I'd rather be King of the Hill!

The announcer turned his attention once again to the steer wrestling at hand. Again, as soon as the contestant finished, Skeeter continued with his own agenda.

"Speechless! He is absolutely speechless with the gravity of this fine poem!" Skeeter proclaimed, teasing the announcer.

"No, I'm speechless 'cause we're so far gone from the script I don't know what to say!" the announcer admitted with a laugh. The attentive crowd laughed with him.

"You don't know who made up this poem?" the announcer asked.

"Nope. The paper was only signed with initials–BJH."

Skeeter repeated the poem in the short span of time between the next two contestants. In the press box where the marshal and his team sat, Cassidy was suddenly aware that the marshal had risen to his feet and was watching an area across the arena intently. The deputies eyed their leader.

The marshal dialed Trent Dominic's number and spoke on the phone as if he were his son Brady. "Dominic. The marshal's got the girl. Now it's just you and me and I've got a lot of dirt on you. If you want to buy your freedom, you know where to find me."

The marshal laid down the phone and silently raised a pair of binoculars, focusing on a certain few seats across the arena. "We've had all the rest we're gonna get, boys and girls. They're headin' out. Let's pack up."

"Marshal, where are we going? What are we doing?" Sykes asked his supervisor.

"We're heading for Black Mesa!" was the excited reply.

Marshall Hollister removed his hat and ran his fingers through his grey-flecked hair as he relaxed in the passenger seat of the van. He closed his eyes. Things had been happening so fast, he needed to spend a few minutes in quiet thought, rehearsing the orders he had given.

He had placed the captured suspects in the hands of local lawmen until marshals from the Great Falls, Montana office arrived to take custody of them. His staff had circulated pictures of the third murder suspect. Those pictures and a vast majority of Brady's evidence had been forwarded via email to other Marshals Services offices. Trent Dominic and three of his men were being tailed with two vehicles as they traveled on the road heading south. A helicopter had been arranged to fly him and deputies Cole and Sykes down to Jubel's ranch in Wyoming where he would retrieve Brady's truck and drive it to Black Mesa. Deputy Cole had made copies of several of the pictures and much of the evidence against Dominic, which would be carried in Brady's truck. He had Cassidy in his custody and Pete Knowlton along because of his knowledge of the Black Mesa country. If everything went according to plan, Trent Dominic and his accomplices would be confronted by the U.S. Marshals Service within a few short hours.

As Sykes pulled into the airport parking lot, the marshal opened his eyes and turned to Cassidy, who sat quietly in the rear seat.

"Have you ever had a helicopter ride before?" he asked her.

"No," was Cassidy's quiet reply.

"You're not afraid of flying, are you?"

"No."

"Good answer," the marshal said gruffly. "'Cause you're goin' whether you like it or not."

When the vehicle pulled to a stop, the marshal stepped out onto pavement that danced with heat waves. He helped his team gather their equipment, which included the laptop computer, surveillance equipment, and weapons. Cassidy grabbed her bag of clothes, which Jennifer had retrieved from the camper, and followed the marshal's lead as he ducked under the whirling blades and through the doorway of the chopper.

Once inside, the marshal arranged seating so Pete and Deputy Sykes were close enough to study a map of the Black Mesa area. As soon as the chopper lifted from the ground and leveled off, the trio studied the paper before them as they discussed the rugged terrain at length. The conversation quickly became heated.

"Marshal, I'm tellin' ya, you don't have enough people to cover you if you're sittin' up on top of the mesa," Pete insisted. "There's a big draw that circles part of the base of that hill and leads all the way to the top under cover of trees and brush. Plus, there's a couple of other ravines that have good cover. If Dominic's men scatter, Sykes and Cole can't cover all the hiding spots and you'll be sittin' up on top with no protection!"

"Pete," the marshal explained with growing impatience, "we have enough evidence from Brady right now to charge Dominic and his men with felonies. We've got to confront them and make an arrest where innocent people won't get hurt. And if we can do that today, we have a chance to stop them before the rest of the organization is alerted. We have two deputies in separate vehicles trailing behind Dominic. So there's four of them and there's going to be four of us. You and Deputy Cole will be staying at the ranch to guard Cassidy and your folks."

The marshal eyed the big man who sat so close before him that he could see the muscles in Pete's jaw tighten as he clenched his teeth. "Pete, don't you get any bright ideas about coming to my rescue," the marshal warned the man. "If things go sour for any of us up on that hill, you just remember, they might bring the fight down to the ranch buildings. If they do, Deputy Cole will need all the help she can get."

The marshal continued to study the man who was as close as a brother to his son. His manner softened. "If you want to help, arm yourself, get up in the loft of that barn, and watch for anyone coming near the place. The last thing in the world I want is to see either of your folks get hurt. And

I can't let anything happen to Cassidy. I'd feel a lot better if you'd help Deputy Cole keep an eye on 'em."

Pete let out a deep sigh and turned to search the innocent green eyes of Cassidy. After several moments of silent thought, he turned back to the marshal and nodded his head. He would do as the man asked. He would stand guard at the ranch.

TEN

The K Bar B Ranch was nestled at the base of a long slope that extended upward to high plateaus and ridges stretching for miles to the rugged mountains beyond. As soon as the helicopter set down in an area of flat open pasture a short distance from the buildings, Pete, Cassidy, and Deputy Cole exited with their gear. When they were well clear of the whirling blades, the copter took off again in a ferocious cloud of dust that momentarily darkened the rays of the late afternoon sun.

The trio headed wordlessly across the open space and passed through a gate where they were greeted by a pair of mixed breed dogs who protested their presence until Pete called them by name. Upon recognition, the dogs followed quietly behind him.

Stepping up to the front door of the spacious, well-kept ranch house, the group was greeted warmly by Pete's mother. Beth Knowlton had been warned that Pete and a couple of house guests were coming. Her first instinct, as always, was to prepare food in case they were hungry. Pete set a couple of cases on the porch and ushered the women through the door where they were met with the wonderful aromas of a hearty stew simmering on the stove and apple pies in the oven.

"Where's Pa?" were the first words Pete uttered as he instinctively ducked his head while stepping through the doorway. He pulled his hat off and tossed it onto the nearby rack.

"He's not back from town yet," Beth replied as she wiped flour-speckled hands on her apron. "But I got hold of him at the feed store and told him what was going on so he wouldn't drive onto the range when he got home."

Pete sighed with relief. If there was any light at the end of the day, his father often drove up to the high pasture to check on the cattle. He silently thanked God that his mother got the warning message to him.

"Ma, this is Deputy Cole from the U.S. Marshals Service," Pete said as he indicated the officer. "And this is Cassidy Henderson."

"I am pleased to meet you both. I had no idea when you would arrive, but I hope you brought an appetite with you. Although by the looks of the two of you, I've made more than enough food."

Pete smiled as his mother surveyed her house guests. The rancher's wife dwarfed the short and muscular Deputy Cole and the lanky, fine-boned Cassidy. Her six foot height and generous frame gave the woman an automatic aura of command even though her smile spoke of generosity and gentleness.

"Pete, take the ladies' things," Beth ordered and motioned toward the nearby living room. "And you ladies can set a spell while I finish supper."

"I appreciate the offer, but I've got a lot to do," Gladys Cole protested. "I really have to set up this equipment somewhere."

"Go ahead and use the living room if you want," Beth suggested.

"I need as much quiet as possible," Cole pointed out. "The deputies have radios and we're going to try to record any conversation they might have with Trent Dominic. If there was an upstairs room I could use, I wouldn't feel like I was putting you out in your own house."

"You can use Pete and Brady's old room," Beth suggested, clearly concerned that her cooking efforts were going to go to waste.

The deputy put Beth's mind to rest. "As soon as I'm set up and making contact with the other deputies, I'll find out how long it will take for Dominic and his men to get here. I sure hope I have time to eat before the action starts. That food smells so good, I'd hate to miss it!"

"Well, if need be, we'll bring it upstairs to you," Beth promised.

Pete ducked outside, shouldered the two heavy cases of equipment that sat on the porch and carried his burdens upstairs to his old bedroom. Deputy Cole followed with more bags and immediately began unpacking. Pete noted the scoped rifle that rested in a long rectangular padded case and recalled his promise that he would keep watch from the barn.

"If you don't need my help any more, Deputy, I reckon I'll go haul a chair up into the barn loft where I can watch the action," Pete told her.

"I'll let you know if I need anything," Cole replied as she cleared a small table on which she began to arrange her equipment. As Pete left the room, the officer looked up from her work long enough to tell him, "Thanks for your help."

Nudging the protesting door open with his toe, Pete stepped inside the old barn where light filtered through cracks between the vertical boards of the walls. Fine specks of dust danced in the shards of sun rays, animating the stark wooden posts of well-worn horse stalls. He paused to let his eyes become accustomed to the dim light before proceeding toward the steep ladder that led to the loft. With an old dining room chair in his meaty fist, Pete hoisted his big frame upward, testing each weary step before putting his full weight on it. *How many years has it been since I've climbed to the loft in this old barn?* he wondered.

After treading uneven floor boards and skirting around a small pile of baled hay, Pete arrived at the wide opening at the end of the barn. There, he stood gazing out across the familiar sage-covered hills that spread over the ranch that had been his boyhood home. He couldn't help but think back to the countless hours he and Brady had spent here in the barn. They had built hay forts. They had played cowboys and Indians. They had fought battles in a make-believe war and talked about girls. *When did it all end?* Pete wondered, then smiled to himself. *I remember meeting Brady in the barn loft only once since he broke his leg. That was the day I told him about Jennifer. We never came to the loft together again. I guess it was time for us to grow up and move on.*

The sound of Bud Knowlton's truck racing up the long drive shook Pete out of his reverie. He scurried across the loft and down the ladder to meet his father. *I've got to let dad know what's going on,* Pete told himself, *and I'm gonna grab a bite to eat while I've got the chance. Something tells me this is going to be a long night.*

The sound of a truck coming up the drive alerted the women in the house to the arrival of Bud Knowlton. Pete followed his father through the front door where the two big men expertly tossed their hats onto the rack as they entered the room. Pete made a quick introduction of his father to Cassidy, who was busy setting dishes on the table. Beth wordlessly loaded the center of the huge table with food, utilizing Cassidy's proffered help as if a sense of urgency were hurrying the woman along. With the food in place, the four of them sat down, leaving an empty space for Deputy Cole in case she joined them. The group bowed their heads in prayer while Bud asked for blessing on the food and protection for each and every one of them, including Marshal Hollister and his deputies.

Conversation during the meal steered away from the events of the day. The Knowltons seemed to prefer to get acquainted with their guest rather than press her to relive the circumstances that had brought her to their home. They asked Cassidy questions about her family, her home, and her job. Much to her delight, the trio of Knowltons then joined together in relating some of their experiences in raising Brady.

All too soon, the delicious meal was consumed and the easy conversation ended. Beth rose from the table to get coffee and pie, but Pete declined. "I'd better get out to the barn," he explained. "Pa, I promised the marshal I'd watch the place in case any of Dominic's men get ideas of coming down here around the buildings. You got a rifle I can take up to the loft with me? And I'll need a pair of binoculars, too."

"Sure!" Bud answered. "You know where they are. Take one of the big rifles. We'll keep that ol' lever action Winchester and the shotguns here in the house."

As Pete left the room to fetch the rifle, Beth prepared a plate full of food and arranged it on a tray for Deputy Cole. Cassidy offered to take the supper upstairs. When she arrived at the door of the room, she found the deputy standing rather than sitting in front of her equipment. With headsets on, she paced a couple of steps each way, then retraced the short route, clearly agitated. Cassidy set the tray on a nearby dresser within reach of the officer and waited a moment, hoping for news of some kind.

Deputy Cole pulled the headset down around her neck, keeping it close to one ear so she could continue to listen. "We've got trouble," she told Cassidy. "Dominic stopped at a gas station and while one of his men pumped gas, the rest went inside. The one that pumped the gas stole a vehicle and took off down the highway. One of our deputies pursued him and there was an accident. While the traffic was backed up, the guy ran to another vehicle, threw a woman and her baby out of it and took off. Our other deputy went to the aid of people hurt in the accident while Dominic and his other two men left. So at the moment we have nobody on their tail."

Deputy Cole returned her attention to her equipment for a moment, then looked at Cassidy. She bit her lip as she contemplated something and then made her decision. "In case I have to leave this room, maybe you could keep recording everything. The marshal ordered me to stay here, but I think we need a back-up plan."

Cassidy readily agreed and sat down next to the officer. After several minutes of instruction, the deputy put the headset on her pupil with orders to signal her if the deputies began talking. Cole then began the job of polishing off the plate full of food as she stared out the window at the vast landscape before her.

Scarcely had Cassidy grown familiar with the buttons and knobs before her when a cloud of dust rose at the base of the distant hill, signaling that a vehicle was making its way along the road. The deputy dropped her plate back on the tray and grabbed a pair of binoculars, then checked her watch. She came fully alert.

"That can't possibly be the marshal arriving yet!" she reasoned aloud. "And Dominic would have to drive a hundred miles an hour to get here so soon!"

The officer spun around and headed for the door. "Cassidy, stay here!" she ordered. "I've got to go talk to Pete to find out who's going up that hill!"

"He's out in the barn," Cassidy stated. "But his dad is still in the house. Maybe he knows who it is."

The officer bolted out the door. With the headset on, Cassidy could scarcely hear her retreating steps and her hasty conversation with Bud Knowlton. Within a few minutes, the deputy bounded back up the stairs and raced down the hall to the room where Cassidy manned the equipment.

"Any chatter going on?" she asked Cassidy.

"Yes. The marshal said he would be heading up the road to the mesa in about fifteen minutes."

Officer Cole grabbed the headset from Cassidy and donned it. She spoke excitedly to the marshals in Brady's truck as she raised the binoculars in the direction of the road to Black Mesa. "There's an SUV heading up the mesa road! It's a light tan one. One of the bigger models. Bud Knowlton doesn't know the vehicle."

"Where do you have the equipment set up?" the marshal questioned.

"Upstairs in the house."

"Where's Pete?"

"In the barn."

The marshal expelled a long draught of air before he demanded, "We've got to be able to communicate with Pete! Go set him up with some of your gear and tell him to keep us posted on what he's seeing."

"Are you guys going to stop for a few minutes to give me time to get up there?"

"No! We're not going to get caught out on the road with Dominic coming up behind us!"

Cole snatched the headset from her own head and shoved it at Cassidy before grabbing a nearby bag. Quickly double checking that she had everything she needed, the deputy called behind her as she raced out of the room, "She's all yours! I've got to go see Pete!"

Pete turned to see who was climbing the ladder behind him. As soon as he recognized Deputy Cole, he returned his gaze to the hills.

"What are you seeing, Pete?" the officer asked as she scrambled to the end of the barn in which the big man had set up his guard post.

"A sport utility heading to the top of the mesa. Two guys got out at the point where the hill starts getting steeper. One went north up into the brushy ravine. The other went south and he's holed up in a washout. They're both carrying rifles."

Pete lowered his binoculars and glanced at the officer. "I hope you're not going to tell me these aren't your guys."

"Okay, I won't tell you," the officer agreed. "Put these on and tell the marshals what you just told me."

Pete donned the proffered headset and relayed his message, then listened to the comments of each of the officers.

"Turn back, Marshal! It's an ambush!" one voice shouted. "We're too far behind to help you!"

"I'm not turning back! Sykes thinks he spotted Dominic on the road behind us! The only other place to go is to head for the ranch and I'm not taking the fight there!"

The marshal shouted, "Pete!"

"Yeah, Marshal," the man answered.

"Can you see either of the guys who got out of the vehicle?"

"I can't see the one who went north, but I've got the other one in sight."

"How long a shot?"

Pete knew instantly what the marshal had in mind. He swallowed hard and answered cautiously. "'Bout seven hundred yards or so."

"Cole?"

"I'm here, Marshal."

"You got your rifle with laser sights with you?"

"No, it's in the house."

"Pete, you got any rifles with you?"

"Yeah, but they're not gonna shoot that far…"

"They will if you have a spotter to tell you where the bullet is going," the marshal argued. "One of you be the spotter and the other the shooter. If you can't take the guy out, at least distract him. I'm going to take the old trail and head toward that guy after I drop Sykes off at the bottom of the ravine. That way I'll be out of the line of fire from the guy who went north."

"Cassidy! Can you hear me?" Deputy Cole spoke over the radio.

"Yes, I can."

"I don't have time to run back to the house and get my rifle before the marshal gets up the road. Can you bring the whole case to me? We'll make do with Pete's hunting rifle if we have to, but I'd just as soon have my own gun up here."

"Send Bud!" the marshal ordered over the radio. "Cassidy, you stay in the house! How did she get involved in this anyway?"

The echoes of gunshots resounded across the hills as Bud struggled up the ladder to the barn loft with the cumbersome rifle case. Pete was aware of his father's arrival, but ignored the man as he concentrated on the view he beheld through his binoculars.

"Higher!" Pete called as he watched the puff of dust that signaled that the bullet landed a few feet under the intended victim. The deputy raised the gun barrel a couple of inches and fired another round. The gun blast boomed through the old building.

"He's moving to the left! Swing it an inch and fire," Pete commanded.

A third blast resounded through the timbers and Pete slowly lowered the glasses.

"He's out of commission," the big man whispered quietly.

Two men waited atop the plateau near their SUV. Deputy Cole fired in their direction with the hunting rifle, kicking up dust and startling the men, but not causing them to evacuate their positions. Bud readied the deputy's rifle and handed it to her. The next shot from the deputy slammed into the vehicle on which the assailants leaned just as Brady's truck cleared the rim of the steep hill. Both men abandoned their posts while trying to fire at the marshal. One of the assailants lurched to the ground as a pistol shot split the air. The other attempted to leap sideways, but the white truck plunged forward, pinning the man between the front bumper and the side of the SUV. The grating of metal was heard even to the barn rafters.

"Marshal! Are you all right?" demanded Deputy Cole over the radio.

Several seconds passed with no answer.

"Marshal Hollister! Trent Dominic's truck is heading up the road! He's coming your way! Can you hear me!?"

A slight click on the radio sounded, giving hope that the marshal was unharmed. Another few anxious seconds passed before more sound came across the radio.

"Yeah. I hear you," the marshal's deep voice echoed. "I lost this dumb gizmo on the floor…"

Pete and Deputy Cole expelled their breath in sighs of relief.

"Is Dominic staying on the road?" the marshal questioned his deputy.

"Yes," Deputy Cole assured him, then quickly spoke again. "He stopped. He's getting out of his truck."

"Brady!" a distant voice was barely discernable across the otherwise still airwaves. "Brady! Are you still alive up there?"

The marshal answered by revving up the engine of his son's truck and backing it away from the vehicle he had hit, turning it, then driving forward to the rim of the hill. He stepped out of the truck, using the door as a meager shield, and faced the three men who stood halfway down the hill. Wearing Brady's hat, with the failing light at his back, and being nearly the same height and build as his son, Pete prayed that the men wouldn't recognize the marshal until the other officers could get into position to make an arrest.

"I found the package you left at the gate for me!" Dominic's voice called again. Even at such a distance, with the man's voice faintly echoing outside as well as coming from the radio, Pete detected the familiar arrogant, self-important nature of the man.

"Interesting stuff you've collected. I'm surprised by it. Had I known you had this much information on me, I would have had you killed long ago, before you made copies of everything and hid the originals."

Dominic paused in his rhetoric, but got no comment from the marshal.

"How much money will it take to keep this information to yourself?"

"What's your freedom worth?" were the marshal's only words.

Dominic answered smugly, "I imagine you've been barely scraping by, trying to collect reward money for a living. How does two hundred fifty thousand sound to you? That's all the cash I can come up with in the next few hours."

The marshal suddenly dove to the ground and rolled under the truck as two shots rang out. The body of a man rolled downhill from his hiding place in the brush at the edge of the deep ravine. A rifle clattered as it tumbled across the rock strewn ground. Dominic and the two men with him dove behind outcroppings of boulders.

"Brady, I didn't know he was there!" Dominic shouted. "I swear! You call your friend in the bushes off and we'll get this settled! Let's meet tomorrow. I'll bring three hundred grand for you and your friend. You hand over all the information and walk away."

The marshal remained silent, but reappeared at the side of the truck. Pete wondered how close Deputy Sykes was to Dominic and his men, for he never detected the officer's position during the last exchange of bullets.

"What do you say, Brady?" Dominic called after a couple minutes of quiet.

"I say it's high time you started callin' me Marshal!" came the answer. "This is U.S. Marshal Bret Hollister! You're under arrest Trent Dominic! You and the men with you! Throw down your weapons!"

Silence pervaded and no one moved from his position. Long shadows had spilled to the bottom of the east facing slope of Black Mesa and twilight slowly enveloped the valley. Chilly evening air wafted through the opening in the barn as Pete, Bud, and Deputy Cole watched the scene. The rosy glow of sunset light faded to pale lavender, then deep blue. Still, no one moved until Bud decided he'd better get back to the house in case one of the men slipped away from the marshals under cover of darkness.

Pete and Deputy Cole were startled when several shots were fired from the top of the hill, penetrating the metal of Dominic's vehicle.

"I tell you what, if they plan on gittin' outta here in the dark, they're walkin'!" the marshal mumbled over the radio.

The standoff continued until twilight prevailed. Silence continued over the air waves until Cassidy's voice cried out, "Cops are coming!" From their vantage point, Pete and the deputy could see several lights in the distance. Within seconds, the full sound of the wailing sirens was screaming through the air. Two of the cars turned up the road to the mesa while another proceeded toward the Knowlton ranch driveway. Another sound also–the whirling blades of an approaching helicopter–thumped overhead.

The airwaves came alive when a spotlight was turned on, flooding the rock-strewn slope where Trent Dominic and his men had last been seen. Two figures emerged from cover to stand silently in the stream of white light. They threw down their weapons and raised their hands above their heads in surrender. Pete watched intently as Deputy Sykes cautiously made his way toward the two men, keeping his pistol trained on them, and knew instinctively that the lone fugitive yet to be captured was Trent Dominic.

As soon as the state patrol evacuated their vehicles to take custody of Dominic's men, the helicopter moved with its bright spotlight as Sykes directed to points up and down the long slope. Sykes tried several times to reach the marshal by radio, but received no answer.

"What's going on?" Pete asked the officer beside him. "Why isn't the marshal answering?"

Cole assured him this was not unexpected. "Knowing him, he's turned his radio off so the noise won't give away his position."

"Why don't some of the other officers help hunt Dominic?" Pete wondered.

"They've got two prisoners that might be persuaded to testify against him," Deputy Cole explained quietly. "Dominic might try to kill his own men before they have a chance to talk. That's why they're taking the prisoners down the road. Dominic will have to get past Sykes and the spotlight and a lot of open ground to get near those patrol cars. But if he fires so much as one shot, he'll give away his position."

Pete remained in the barn loft long after Deputy Cole returned to the house, her ultimate responsibility being the guardian of Cassidy. He continued to study the terrain for any sign of Trent Dominic.

Now that he had witnessed Brady's father in action, Pete thought at length about the man. *He's done this job for over twenty-five years. Has he always been this foolhardy? Plowing headlong into ambushes. Challenging professional gunmen. He has a reputation for being tough as nails, but I wonder how he's lived so long. I know he's desperate to catch these men, but I also know Trent Dominic. He's not going to give up without a fight!*

As the spotlight from the helicopter flooded the brushy ravine nearest the buildings, a shadowy figure stepped onto the rim of the hilltop, outlined only by a backdrop of faintly twinkling stars. The marshal stood quietly on the rock-strewn plane and waited as Dominic approached.

"I don't suppose you came up here to give yourself up," the marshal commented wryly.

Dominic answered sarcastically with an evil laugh, "No. I'm playing 'King of the Hill,' remember? How I wish Brady was my challenger!"

"Why is that?"

"He's the one who dug up all the dirt on me, isn't he?"

"Yeah."

"That figures. The law didn't go to such lengths to put me out of business. But a bounty hunter with a grudge…doesn't that beat all?"

The rifle in Dominic's fists swung rapidly to point at the marshal. Dominic squeezed the trigger as he spun, sending a bright flame exploding from the barrel. The marshal sidestepped and dropped to a knee as he fired his pistol at the shadowy figure before him. As the echo of the two shots reverberated through the hills, the clatter of a rifle falling to the rocky ground and a hoarse gasp told the marshal that his bullet had found its mark.

The helicopter swiftly made its way to the top of the hill, highlighting the badly wounded Trent Dominic. With a wave from the marshal, the airborne machine settled down on the flat and lawmen spilled out. Marshal Hollister stood unmoving in the distant shadows until the chopper was loaded with the injured and fallen men.

Once the whirling blades lifted the machine back into the night sky, the marshal stumbled in the blackness to Brady's bullet-riddled, crunched, and dirtied truck. There, he sank down to the ground and leaned his back against a tire. He pulled Brady's hat down over his eyes and closed out the dark world around him as he expelled a long breath of air. The adrenaline rush that had kept him going for the last several hours was over. Fatigue stole over the man and the chill air penetrating his sweat-soaked shirt made him shiver.

Deputy Sykes appeared, short of breath from his climb over the treacherous hill, and sat down on the ground beside his supervisor.

"What do you think, Marshal?" the man asked.

The marshal didn't move nor remove Brady's hat from over his eyes. He was slow to answer. "I'm tired. I'm hungry. I'm cold. But I tell you what, we sure did a stroke of business today, didn't we?"

"Yes, we did," the deputy agreed and asked, "You suppose any of these rigs are drivable or do we have to walk all the way down the hill?"

"I'm thinkin' Brady's truck'll make it to the ranch house. Want to give it a whirl?"

"You bet!" Sykes said as he rose to his feet. He offered a hand and helped the older man up from the ground.

As the pair of officers climbed into the white truck, Marshal Hollister turned on his radio.

"Gladys, are you back in the house?" he addressed Deputy Cole.

"Yes, Marshal," came the officer's reply.

"Warn Beth Knowlton that I'm hungry as a bear. Ask her if she'd be so kind as to whip up something to eat. Sykes and I are comin' down!"

ELEVEN

Brady's cell phone rang shortly after sundown as Wayne climbed down from the cab to fill the truck with diesel fuel. A worried Elaine Henderson spoke as soon as Brady answered.

"I'm sorry to bother you, but I haven't heard from Cassidy all day. I've tried to call the marshal, and he's not returning my calls. Something is wrong and I don't know what to do! I've called the police in Red Lodge. They said the marshal left hours ago with her."

"I've tried to call him, too," Brady said, speaking calmly. "But Mrs. Henderson, just because he doesn't answer, that doesn't mean he's ignoring us or that something is wrong. I gave you his direct number, not the one to his office. When he doesn't answer that number, it usually means he's not available. He's coordinating things with his deputies or chasing criminals or something."

"And where's my daughter while this man is chasing criminals?" Elaine demanded. "I knew more of her whereabouts *before* she met the marshal. It would only take her two minutes to call and let me know she's okay. He could be a little considerate…"

Brady laughed out loud. Elaine stopped speaking abruptly.

"Ah, ma'am," he said as he continued to chuckle. "Before you start bashing the marshal, I think I should tell you–he's my father."

Elaine remained silent for several seconds. Apparently she decided to let a simple apology suffice, rather than try to justify her outburst. When she uttered a quiet "I'm sorry," Brady wondered if she was sorry for criticizing or sorry that he had a father like the marshal.

"Mrs. Henderson, I called my friend, Skeeter, after the rodeo was over and talked to him about Cassidy. She had an eventful day, but she's fine."

"What do you mean by eventful? What happened?" Elaine demanded, worry edging her voice.

Brady decided he'd better share the good news with Cassidy's mother and omit the details of the murderers' pursuit of her. The woman probably had heard all the bad news she needed for awhile.

"Well, the marshal and his deputies caught up with a couple of the murderers at the rodeo, and they have them locked up. But first thing this morning, Cassidy showed up at the rodeo grounds and attended the church service. Skeeter preached a sermon and offered to have special prayer with anyone who wanted it. Cassidy was one of the people who came to him and Skeeter had a good talk with her and prayed with her. Apparently, she admitted to him that her faith in God was wavering, especially since her father died. Skeeter encouraged her to keep trusting the Lord."

"I have been praying that she come to grips with her father's death. She's been taking it so hard," Elaine confided with a faint quiver in her voice as if she were on the verge of tears. "Thank you for sharing that with me, Mr. Hollister. You know, I wouldn't have worried so much about Cassidy's safety when she was with you if I'd known you were a Christian."

Brady paused for a time before he confessed in a quiet voice, "To tell you the truth, Ma'am, I haven't exactly been living right. This whole situation with running from the law and hiding…well, I think God was backing me into a corner. I finally took a good hard look at myself and decided I was tired of doing things my own way, so last night I made things right with Him. My friend, Skeeter, was really excited when I told him about it today. He's been preachin' at me and prayin' for me for years."

"Obviously, church must have been a part of your life," Elaine observed, "because you seem to understand disobedience and repentance and forgiveness."

"Yes, Ma'am. I was raised in church," Brady conceded.

Wayne climbed a nearby ladder and stretched his portly frame over the hood to wash the truck windows. Brady quickly begged Elaine to be patient in waiting for a call and told her he had to go.

"Wayne, let me do the washing," Brady offered as he scooted out of the cab.

"Don't mind if you do," the trucker said. "You get up and down a lot better than I do."

Brady wetted the squeegee and climbed up the steps to the side of the truck where he could easily lean over and scrub the windows clean.

"Was that your sweetheart on the phone?" Wayne asked. "You looked like you were in pretty serious conversation."

"No," Brady replied with his winning smile. "It was her mother. She's worried. She hasn't heard from Cassidy all day."

"Your future mother-in-law, huh? You'd better stay on the good side of that woman," Wayne advised with a laugh.

Brady's only reply was a wide grin. Inwardly, he sighed. Elaine was not his soon-to-be mother-in-law. She was simply a close link to Cassidy. Someone he could talk to about her. He silently wondered if he would ever see Cassidy again.

Brady suddenly realized that two men had exited a nearby car and were walking toward Wayne's truck. He paused in his washing as he eyed the pair. His gun lay on the seat just a few feet away inside the open window. But Wayne was standing between him and the approaching men, unaware of possible danger.

Brady breathed a sigh of relief when one of them pulled a familiar badge from his shirt.

"Brady Hollister?" the man asked. "U.S. Marshals Service. Would you mind coming with us?"

Marshal Hollister sent the late-arriving deputy marshals to transport the surviving gunmen to a secure location. Over the phone, he dispatched federal officers to Trent Dominic's ranch where, according to Brady's documents, they might find people who were being held against their will. Now, after wolfing down a hot meal, he took his business and his phone outside the confines of the house.

Cassidy assisted Beth Knowlton in pouring coffee and dishing up thick slices of apple pie as Bud and Pete relaxed in the living room with deputies Sykes and Cole. Conversation indoors was minimal as the muffled voice of an irate Marshal Hollister could be heard from the front yard. With everyone's attention on the marshal's distraught conversation, Cassidy ventured to ask Beth quietly if she could call her mother.

"Of course, dear!" Beth exclaimed. "We should have had you call her hours ago! She must be worried sick by now!"

"Probably," Cassidy agreed.

"Use the phone in my bedroom," Beth suggested. She led the way down a short hallway to the master bedroom and flipped on the light. Once the room was illuminated, Cassidy located the phone by the bed and dialed Jason's number. She had scarcely made the call and asked her brother to give the phone to their mother when the marshal burst through the front door and stomped into the living room.

"That stinkin' Higgins!" the marshal ranted. "He absolutely refuses to drop the charges against Brady! I told him I've got Cassidy in custody, and she denies that Brady kidnapped her! He insists that I'm trying to cover up for my son and I need to hand both of them over for questioning before he'll drop any charges! I told him to take a short walk off a long cliff."

Cassidy gave the bedroom door a push so that it swung nearly shut as Elaine questioned what was going on.

"It's the marshal," Cassidy explained. "He just got off the phone with Sheriff Higgins and he's not very happy. Higgins won't drop the kidnapping charges against Brady."

"So Brady has to stay in hiding?"

"I don't know. I hope the marshal can do something," Cassidy lamented.

"Where are you? Are you still in Red Lodge?" Elaine questioned.

"No, we're at a ranch near a place called Black Mesa. I think the nearest town is either Ten Sleep or Worland."

"Cassidy, you're not that far from us! Ask the marshal if we can come see you! Now that they've caught the murderers..."

"Only two of the three....How did you know that?" Cassidy wondered aloud.

"I talked to Brady a little while ago."

"You did?"

"Yes, I called him," Elaine explained. "I hadn't heard anything from you and the marshal wouldn't return my calls, so..."

"How did you get Brady's phone number? And the marshal's?"

"Brady gave them to us when he called us."

"But I never gave him Jason's number!" Cassidy puzzled. After a moment of consideration she admitted, "I forgot, recent calls can be saved on a cell phone..."

"Cassidy, I want to come see you!" Elaine exclaimed. "Tell me where you are and how to get there."

"I can't describe to you how to get here," Cassidy replied in frustration. "We came by helicopter!"

"Helicopter!"

The bedroom door pushed open slowly and Beth peaked her head inside.

"Cassidy, is something wrong?"

Cassidy blushed as it dawned on her that from the kitchen, Beth probably overheard some of her conversation, even above the loud talk going on in the living room. She replied to Beth's question without covering the mouthpiece on the phone so that her mother could hear every word.

"Mom wants to come see me, Beth. She's been camping out in a church parking lot for two days near Lone Pine. Do you know where that is?"

"Sure. It's not far from here," Beth answered. She held out her hand for the phone. "I'll give your mother directions."

"What if the marshal decides to leave before Mom gets here?" Cassidy asked. "He'll make me go with him!"

"I'll put my foot down!" the big woman spoke firmly. "Nobody is leaving until every one of you has gotten some rest! Just because he can go two days without sleep doesn't mean everyone else can."

Beth took the phone from Cassidy's hand and greeted Elaine warmly. She dictated directions to her home and promised to have coffee and pie waiting when Elaine and Jason arrived. Once the receiver was replaced near the bed, Beth reached out to Cassidy and gave her an encouraging hug before leading the way out of the bedroom.

"Pete Knowlton, don't you dare touch another piece of pie!" Beth scolded as her son headed toward the kitchen with his empty plate. "I'm saving the rest of it. We've got company coming."

"Tonight?" Pete questioned.

"Yes, tonight. Cassidy's mother and brother are on their way."

The marshal overheard the exchange. He stared at Cassidy as though he had totally forgotten about her. She glared back in defiance. After several long moments, the marshal spoke without dropping his eyes from the young woman.

"I'm surprised you didn't call your family a long time ago to come pick you up."

"Brady asked me not to," Cassidy replied firmly. "He said they'd be followed and they would lead those men to me. Then we would all be in danger."

"He was right."

"Will they be followed when they come here?"

"Not by any of Dominic's men. Higgins will have someone watching your folks in order to try to find you. But his jurisdiction ends at the Johnson County line. We're in Washake County. I'll let your folks come see you, but don't get any ideas about leaving with them, young lady. You're still under protective custody," the man instructed.

The marshal's words infuriated the normally mild-mannered young woman. "You'll *let* them come see me!?" she shouted without regard to the audience watching the scene in stunned silence. "What am I? A prisoner? I'm just supposed to sit down and shut up while you drag me around the country? And now I have to have permission from you to see my mother? You..."

The marshal rose slowly, menacingly, from the chair he had been sitting on. He stepped toward Cassidy, eyeing her. She stopped her tirade in mid-sentence and swallowed hard but didn't back away. Cassidy could see the muscles in his jaw tighten as he continued to stare at her with narrowed eyes.

"I owe you an apology," he conceded with a deep sigh. "You are not a prisoner. If you were, you probably would have been treated better than I've been treating you."

He reached down and took Cassidy by the hand, leading her into the living room and steering her to the couch. After only a moment of defiant hesitation, she sat in the place that the marshal indicated.

He's just like Brady, Cassidy thought. *About the time you get mad at him and decide you don't like him, he becomes considerate and you melt.*

The marshal sat down in the chair nearest Cassidy and gave her his full attention. "You should understand some things that are going on," he said and paused as he chose his words carefully. "Brady infiltrated a criminal organization and gathered a lot of valuable evidence that coincides with some of our own investigations. He had the stuff we needed to make some key arrests, but we had to put everything together fast to catch these people by surprise. That took all the manpower we could muster, so we didn't have extra people to guard you. Normally, we wouldn't take someone in protective custody by helicopter to a remote ranch. Especially where there was any chance of a major confrontation."

The marshal sat back in his chair and looked outside the large living room window in the general direction of the nearby hill that was long ago totally cloaked in darkness. "You know some men died up there tonight, don't you?" the man asked Cassidy without turning toward her.

"Yes, I know."

"I'm sorry you had to witness that," he apologized as he turned to face her. "And you witnessed a shooting at close range this afternoon. Do you need to talk about it?"

Cassidy shrugged her shoulders. With all of the other excitement of the day, she had actually dismissed the scene from her mind. "They killed that poor man behind the motel and they would have killed me too. I would have shot that big guy myself if you hadn't come along."

"I'm glad you didn't have to do that, Cassidy. It can be a hard thing to live with."

"I'm just glad there are people who are willing to deal with criminals like that," Cassidy assured the officer. She was feeling bolder and more at ease now that things were coming out in the open, so she continued. "Marshal, I have a question."

"What's that?" the man asked.

"If Brady's evidence is so valuable and he infiltrated this organization, then he can identify these people, right? So why isn't he in protective custody?"

The marshal grinned with approval. "He should be by now. We asked a couple of deputies from Nebraska to catch up to that cattle truck he's been riding around in. They'll pick Brady up and bring him here tomorrow. Beth has offered to put us up for a night or two so we can get some rest. Once we get some sleep, we'll pick through Brady's evidence more thoroughly."

"So you found the box of stuff at Jubel's ranch?" Cassidy questioned.

Dead silence prevailed. Deputy Sykes looked at the marshal, then at Deputy Cole. Cole glanced sheepishly at the marshal and rolled her eyes, then glanced at Sykes. The marshal lowered his head and ran his fingers through his course, grey-flecked hair. After several moments, he responded to Cassidy.

"You told me that before, didn't you? That Brady had taken some things out of his truck..." With a deep sigh, the marshal rose slowly from his seat. "I've got to get back up to Jubel's and find it. Bud, can I borrow your truck?"

"No!" Bud spoke emphatically. "You haven't had an ounce of sleep for God knows how long and you're dead on your feet! You've already wrecked enough vehicles for one day and you ain't drivin' my truck nowhere!" Bud pushed his bulky frame from his overstuffed chair and stood tall before the marshal. "I'll take you up there."

The marshal smiled at the reprimand and followed the broad-shouldered man meekly toward the front door as Bud turned to his wife and asked her to give Jubel a phone call to warn him that he would be getting some middle-of-the-night visitors. Pete volunteered to accompany the pair. As each of the men retrieved their hats from the nearby rack and headed for the door, Marshal Hollister stopped for a moment.

"Cassidy," he asked, "where is that box?"

"In the shed where Jubel parks his truck. There's a work bench off to the left and the box is under there with some tools sitting on top of it."

"Thanks, young lady," the weary marshal said with a polite nod. As he stepped out into the night he added, "Give my regards to your folks when they get here."

TWELVE

Cassidy awoke slowly, well after full daylight had dawned over the K Bar B ranch. A single bird chirped outside the window opened wide to allow the still-cool breeze to sweep through the upstairs bedroom. She rose up on one elbow, searching the unfamiliar room, and discovered that the other bed, which had been occupied by Deputy Gladys Cole, was now vacant.

Hearing only the faintest of sounds, Cassidy lay back down and closed her eyes, drifting back to sleep until the sound of a truck coming up the driveway penetrated her dream. *Maybe that's Brady coming!* she thought. She leaped out of bed and ran to the window where she discovered that Skeeter had driven alone into the ranch yard.

Rummaging through the luggage she'd retrieved from the motor home the previous evening, Cassidy selected a flattering blouse and slacks, scarcely considering that they may be more dressy than necessary for a day at the ranch. Brady was coming! She had so much to tell him about the past couple of days. And so much to ask him.

Still in her pajamas, Cassidy scurried to the bathroom down the hall. By the time she emerged, freshly showered and fully clothed, she could hear the voices of Skeeter, Bud, Pete, and the marshal drifting from downstairs. Returning to the bedroom, she straightened the bed covers and arranged her personal items in her suitcase, then sat down in front of the window to let the morning breeze dry her long hair.

The banging of the screen door and scraping of chairs indicated that some occupants of the house had moved to the porch below the bedroom window. Cassidy learned quickly that they were in the midst of a discussion about her and her family. The marshal questioned what time Cassidy's folks had pulled out of the yard and wondered why they hadn't stayed longer. Bud informed him they left about six o'clock because they were scheduled to be home in Wisconsin yesterday. They had livestock to tend to and the neighbor that had been doing their chores was not going to be available after today.

"She's a farm girl, huh?" the marshal questioned, speaking of Cassidy.

"Yeah. They don't have a lot of animals anymore, mostly crops," Bud added.

"So who came in the camper?" the marshal asked. "I've only heard mention of her mother and brother."

When Skeeter informed the group Cassidy's father had died a few months ago, Cassidy left the room, opting to stop eavesdropping rather than relive her heartache.

Beth was scrubbing pots and pans in a sink teaming with fluffy suds when Cassidy bounded downstairs. She smiled at the young lady and grabbed for a nearby towel to dry her hands. "I've got some breakfast for you," she offered. "Do you like biscuits and gravy?"

"That sounds great! I'm famished!" Cassidy answered. As she dished up a plate of food, she noted that deputies Sykes and Cole were seated at a small table in a quiet corner of the living room with the box of files from Jubel's shed at their feet. She briefly wondered if Brady would be angry with her for telling the marshals about it.

"I'm sorry I got up so late," Cassidy apologized, turning her attention back to her hostess. "Everyone else has eaten, haven't they?"

"They finished just a few minutes ago. Bud usually does some chores before he eats breakfast. He was outside this morning when your mother was getting ready to leave, so he visited with her for awhile. She and your brother have a long drive to make in a short time, don't they?"

Cassidy worked at polishing away the generous breakfast as she replied, "Yes, they do. And they sure haven't gotten much sleep lately."

As soon as the food was gone, Cassidy took over the dishwashing while Beth rounded up dirty laundry throughout the house. The conversation on the porch suddenly became animated. Skeeter's voice came through the open kitchen window where Cassidy stood at the sink.

"I kid you not!" he exclaimed. "Brady told me over the phone what happened! There were two little old ladies who thought he and Cassidy were trying to elope so they offered to give Cassidy a ride to Red Lodge. Then they stood right there watching until Brady gave her a good-bye kiss!"

Pete's laughter was especially loud amidst the revelry on the porch. Cassidy blushed deep crimson as she realized Beth had come around the corner and heard Skeeter's tale. As she wondered how she could ever look these people in the face again, Pete burst through the doorway, shouting as he charged into the room.

"Ma, is Cassidy outta bed yet?"

Realizing that the mortified girl stood at the sink near the open window within earshot of the men on the porch, he flashed a wide, sly grin at her.

"Cassidy, you left some details out of your story about getting a ride with the little old ladies!" he teased.

"Pete Knowlton!" Beth scolded her son. "You leave this poor girl alone! Don't you be picking on her!"

"But Ma, Brady kissed her!"

"Good grief! They're not twelve years old. They're both adults. They can kiss if they want to," Beth defended and waved her hands at the strapping young man to shoo him out of the house.

Pete turned on his heel and stepped back out onto the porch, laughing loudly. The chorus of jocularity from the men echoed across the front of the building and wafted through the open window where Cassidy stood as if rooted to the spot. Beth stomped around the kitchen counter and followed her son outside with her meaty hands straddling her wide hips. Cassidy could not hear a word being uttered. She imagined Beth glaring at the men, intimidating them to stifle their guffaws and end the silly conversation.

When Beth returned to her household chores, the marshal's voice was the first to break the imposed silence. "You know, I should get up in that barn loft of yours, Bud, and see what kind of shots Deputy Cole was making last night. I've got a load of reports to write, trying to explain everything that went on."

The moving of the chairs and stomping of boots on the steps indicated that the men all moved off the porch. As Cassidy returned to the dishwashing, she watched the retreating backs of the quartet. *I hope they forget about this by the time Brady gets here,* she thought, but knew that wasn't likely to happen.

A car pulled into the yard in a flurry of brown dust. Brady bounded from the back seat without waiting for the deputies to exit and skipped steps to leap onto the porch, bursting through the ranch house door without knocking.

He found Cassidy at the kitchen counter in the midst of peeling a mountain of potatoes. With a broad smile, he breathed a sigh of relief. "You okay?" he asked.

"Yes, I'm fine," she answered, feeling warm, rosy color creep into her cheeks as she looked up at him.

Beth turned from her corner of the kitchen where she was preparing chicken to bake in the oven. "I see I'm about as appealing as chopped liver anymore, now that Cassidy is in my house," she teased as the pair stared uncomfortably at one another.

"Hi, Ma. How are you doing?" Brady asked as he scurried around the end of the counter to plant a kiss on the woman's cheek. He put his arm around Beth's broad shoulders and added, "I see you're making my favorite meal. You must have known I was coming."

"All my meals are your favorites, young man, but you'd better cut the chit-chat and head out the back door," Beth warned as she indicated through the window the quartet who strode across the yard together. "The hecklers have come out of the barn and they're heading this way."

Brady ducked his head to look out the window and spotted the marshal, Bud, Pete, and Skeeter heading for the house.

"How did Skeeter get here? Did he come with Pete?" Brady wondered.

"Pete came with the marshal yesterday afternoon and Skeeter brought Pete's truck to him today. They were supposed to head home a long time ago, but they changed their plans when they found out you were coming…"

Brady needed no further prompting. As the group paused with Marshal Hollister to greet the deputies outside, Brady turned from the window and grabbed Cassidy by a hand. He led her past Sykes and Cole toward a sliding glass door leading from the house to a shaded deck. The deputies took in the scene without comment as the pair escaped the house.

Once outside, Brady silently led Cassidy to a split rail fence that marked the border between lawn and pasture, where he stopped and turned toward her. As he gazed into Cassidy's innocent, trusting eyes, he felt an overwhelming sense of remorse again well up inside him–the same feeling he had experienced while camping out at the corral. He had intended to pursue a serious relationship with her, but now, seeing the expectant look on her face, he asked himself, *What made you think she could have a decent life with someone like you?*

Brady looked away as he removed the bandana from his head and twisted the cloth nervously in his hands for several moments before he spoke.

"Skeeter told me over the phone what happened at the rodeo yesterday. It makes me sick, thinkin' about how close those guys got to you."

He glanced once again into Cassidy's eyes. "I'm so sorry…" he whispered.

"For what?" she asked with a confused look on her face.

Brady struggled to put into words what he wanted to say. "I just…I could have gotten you killed…" He paused and let out a deep sigh as he confessed, "Cassidy, I have to tell you…I wasn't helping you just to be a good guy. I hated Dominic so much that I was actually considering trying to keep you with me, hoping he'd chase after me."

Cassidy's brow furrowed. She started to speak, but Brady held up his hand and touched her lips to quiet her. As she raised her eyes to study his face, he gently caressed the outline of her jaw with the back of his fingers.

"I didn't change my mind until just before we got to that gas station," he continued. "That's when I decided I would protect you as much as I could…but it was too late. By then I was a danger to you. I had to let you go."

Brady stared at the toes of his boots for a while. When his gaze returned to Cassidy's, it harbored sadness.

"Will you forgive me?" he begged.

Cassidy searched the deeply tanned face and shrugged as if she were unaffected by his words. "Everything turned out okay in the end. You did all you could," she weakly assured him.

Leaning over the fence with his forearms resting on the top rail and setting one foot up on a lower rail, Brady silently stared out over the vast landscape.

"I could hardly wait to see you again," Cassidy spoke with a slight tremor in her voice that hinted at her unease. "I wanted to tell you about what happened to me and find out about you…I thought we'd have a lot to talk about…"

"We do…" Brady uttered and glanced at her where she stood gripping the top fence rail as if for support. "I had so many things I wanted to say to you but nothing's coming out right. I wanted to see you so bad…but…"

"You're going to tell me this is where the cowboy rides away, aren't you?" she whispered. "Don't expect anything more from him…"

Brady didn't deny it. His jaw clenched tightly. He sighed as he quietly studied her face. "You're gonna haunt me for the rest of my life, Cassidy Henderson. I could love you with all my heart."

"You have a wife and kids everyone forgot to mention?" she asked, her voice nearly failing her.

"No, Cassidy, there's never been a wife and there's no kids."

"There's someone else?" she guessed.

"There's no one," he insisted.

"What then?" she demanded. "More people to hate? Ghosts to chase? *What?*"

"It's just that…you don't deserve a man like me."

"Don't tell me what I deserve!" she argued. Tears trickled slowly down her cheeks. She took deep breaths as if to calm herself, but each gasp threatened to become a sob. Brady stepped close to gently brush the tears away with the back of his fingers.

"Cassidy, if I'd known an angel like you was going to come along, I swear things would have been different in my life," Brady lamented. "But I've done things that I am so ashamed of. When you're young and foolish you think about yourself, not the future. Cassidy, I've been drinkin' and partyin' and…"

She didn't have to be told that there had been women in his life, too, for he saw the hurt in her eyes and it wrenched at him. He hung his head. Cassidy stood mute as he struggled to find words to explain the remorse he was feeling.

"Skeeter told me he had a chance to talk to you," Brady whispered hoarsely, "so I know you can understand when I tell you I did one thing right since I met you. I finally made things right with God, Cassidy. A couple nights ago. I asked Him to forgive me."

"I'm happy for you," Cassidy said with a weak smile that briefly changed the course of the tears that glided down her cheeks.

"I need your forgiveness too," Brady pleaded.

Cassidy's brow furrowed. "I already told you, everything turned out okay…"

"Cassidy," Brady begged, "forgive me…"

"Okay! I forgive you for putting your hatred for Trent Dominic above my safety," Cassidy spoke quickly, as if trying to put the matter to rest.

"That's not what I meant! Forgive me for ruining everything we could have had together. For not waiting for you…"

Cassidy took a deep breath, choking on her words. "I don't like thinking about how you've been living, but if you've put it all behind you…I'll try to forgive you for it," she cried. "But I won't forgive you for breaking your promise!"

Brady's heart ached as he studied the tear-stained face before him, trying to comprehend her statement.

"You promised you wouldn't hurt me," she reminded him with a tremulous voice. "Well, broken hearts hurt, Brady Hollister!"

Cassidy turned to flee to the shelter of the house, the nearest place of refuge on the wide plain. Though his head told him to let her go, Brady's heart wouldn't cooperate. In a flash, he reached out and caught her, to draw her slowly into the circle of his arms. She tried to fight, but quickly gave in and let Brady rest his chin on the top of her head. Slowly, she leaned her forehead on his chest and slipped her arms around his waist. Like this, they cried together.

"Pete!" Marshal Hollister shouted in a disgusted voice that carried from the corner of the house to the fence where Brady and Cassidy stood. "If he walks away from a nice girl like that, you have my permission to pound him into the dirt!"

Brady slowly turned his head and found that a group of spectators had gathered outside the house. The young couple was probably out of hearing of the onlookers, but the obvious emotional turmoil between the two had spoken volumes. Bud had his arm around his wife as she anxiously twisted a kitchen towel into knots. The marshal stood ramrod straight with a deep scowl on his face and his arms folded across his chest. Skeeter chewed his fingernails and Pete slowly and deliberately rolled up the cuffs of his shirt, revealing the massive muscles in his forearms.

Brady sighed and released Cassidy from his embrace enough to slip his hand gently under her chin and lift it so she faced him.

"Then again, we only met three days ago. Let's not make any hasty decisions, huh?" he whispered as he smiled down at the woman he knew he was falling deeply in love with. "I've been through enough lately. I'd just as soon not get pounded into the dirt besides."

Cassidy smiled up at him and wiped at the tears on her face with the back of her hand. Brady kissed away a stray droplet.

"I've got a lot of changing to do in my life, Cassidy," he confessed quietly. "There's people in this world that I've hurt and I've got to make things right. I hope you can be patient with me, 'cause I already know I want you for all time."

Cassidy released her grip and stepped back to look up at Brady with a tentative smile. "I was hoping we could take some time to get to know one another a little…"

"I'm not asking for commitment yet," Brady assured her with a sly grin. "I'm just warning you that you'd better tell your other boyfriends to git."

He placed a strong arm around Cassidy's shoulders and confessed, "I don't have much to offer you right now. I bought part of Jubel's ranch with my rodeo winnings, but I haven't made much money lately and I'm nearly broke. I've got a bunch of evidence to give to the marshals. That will pretty much put me out of a job until I crack some new cases. All I've got is my truck," Brady lamented, then added with a sheepish grin. "And I've got this great bandana I can share with you." He smoothed out the red paisley-printed square of cloth and dabbed at the remaining tears on Cassidy's face. She smiled a shy smile. After wiping his own face dry, Brady reached down to grasp her hand and lead her slowly across the lawn.

"Brady?" Cassidy ventured as they drew within hearing of the group of spectators. "Did you mean what you said about turning over your evidence to the marshals?"

"Yeah. Why?"

"'Cause I already told them about that box in Jubel's shed and they have it. The deputies in the house have been looking through your files."

"Well, good," Brady replied cordially, though he would have liked to present it in a more professional manner. "I hope they make some arrests."

"They've already arrested a lot of people," Cassidy informed him. "And about your truck…"

Brady spotted it then, sitting alongside the shed. His mouth dropped open as he released Cassidy's hand and hurried toward the vehicle to inspect the damage. Bullet holes, broken windows, a dented front bumper and grill, and a smashed headlight were quickly noted. He peered through the broken windows to see if there was blood in the cab, but found none. Brady made a second circle around the truck, noting additional damage. A rear tire was flat and there were a series of dents and scratches low on the passenger side, indicating that the vehicle had lurched over rough terrain that included some good size boulders.

Straightening up to his full height after inspecting the underside of the vehicle, Brady brushed the palm of his hand across his beard-stubbled jaw. Anger rose up in him, but he took a deep breath and forced it aside. *It's only a truck,* he told himself. *It can be replaced.*

He turned toward the house to find that the group of onlookers had not moved from their places except to turn toward him. He approached them, contemplating what to say to make light of the situation.

"About that truck I told you I had," he said with an impish smile aimed at Cassidy, "well, it's kinda out of commission at the moment."

The young man had left the truck in Jubel's care. Now, it was here at the K Bar B and wrecked. He knew instinctively who to blame.

"Marshal, what did you do?" he demanded, searching the man's face expectantly.

"I borrowed your truck and your hat and led Trent Dominic to the top of Black Mesa," the marshal confessed.

Brady shook his head in disbelief. "That was a fool thing to do and you know it! Dominic was out to kill me!"

"I reckon."

"You could have died up there!"

"Could've, but I didn't," the marshal stated. He stared steadily into his son's face and added, "They would have killed you for sure if they caught up to you. But I'm not a lone ranger like you. I keep good help around to back me up."

Brady looked down at the ground as he considered what his father had done. *He knew what Dominic had in mind for me and took my place. He might have taken a bullet for me. And I've done nothing but cause him grief for years. It's time I made things right…*

"Dad?" Brady began, and sheepishly looked up at his father. "I, uh… I've been…"

"You've been doing a bang-up job on your investigations" the marshal interrupted and proudly slapped his son on the back. "We arrested ten people here in Wyoming in the last twenty-four hours, freed a half dozen that were incarcerated on Dominic's ranch, and we're closing in on his accomplices in Reno."

The marshal had spoken hurriedly, stalling a string of confessions and apologies that Brady intended to make.

"I think I left your hat in the back seat of your truck," the marshal suddenly recalled and strode away from the group.

As the marshal backed out of the vehicle after retrieving the hat, he found Brady beside him.

"Dad, we've got to talk."

"Yeah," the marshal said quietly. "Just you and me alone, for once."

Brady agreed. "Do you have time to get away right now?"

"I'll check with the boss," the marshal said with a grin. He shouted across the yard toward the group that lingered around the porch.

"Beth, how long before dinner is ready?"

"Dinner!" Beth exclaimed and threw up her hands. "I haven't been thinking about dinner! I don't have the chicken in the oven yet!"

The Hollister men strode toward the barn in silence. Brady turned suddenly, breaking the pace that matched that of his father. He looked back at Cassidy, who was watching their retreat from the front porch.

With a sheepish grin, the young man confessed quietly, "I'd never seen her in the daylight 'til today. She's kinda pretty, don't you think?"

THIRTEEN

The clanging of the iron triangle created an echo that reverberated around the ranch buildings. Beth didn't have to repeat the call. Bud and Pete and Skeeter filed through the door before Cassidy had finished setting out the dishes. Before they had washed the grime of machinery repair from their hands, the marshal and Brady drifted in. The four deputies that had sequestered themselves in the living room tossed files aside and rose from their seats.

As soon as everyone was washed and seated at the huge table, Bud offered a brief prayer asking the Lord's blessing on the food before platters of chicken, mashed potatoes and gravy, green vegetables, and rolls were passed around. There was little conversation other than compliments on the cooking until the marshal quietly announced he had been telling Brady about the previous night's shootout.

"Dominic wanted to play 'King of the Hill.'" he stated between mouthfuls. "He got his wish. I haven't even checked to see how he's doin'."

"He survived for a few hours, but died early this morning," Gladys Cole offered.

The marshal lowered his eyes to his plate. He remained still for some time before smiling up at the woman. "You're always a step ahead of me, aren't you, Gladys?" he commented.

"Not always, but once in a while," Deputy Cole answered as she buttered a roll. "By the way, when would you like to take Brady to Reno? Are you up to going tonight or should I make arrangements for tomorrow?"

The marshal cast a sidelong glance at the deputies who sat together at one end of the table, looked across the table at his son, then returned his gaze to his fellow marshals. "And why should I take Brady to Reno?"

"Because the box of evidence that you brought from your uncle's shed mostly concerns names, places, dates, and pictures from Reno," Deputy Sykes said with a grin. "Drug smuggling. Money laundering. All kinds of good stuff. We've been emailing it to the Nevada office and they've put several officers on it. They want to move in fast before anyone on that end finds out Dominic and his boys are out of commission here."

"When Marshal Connor from the Las Vegas office found out we had Brady in custody, he requested Brady be brought to Reno as soon as possible," Deputy Cole added, eyeing the marshal as she spoke. "He thinks they could use his insight on this case."

Marshal Hollister lightly tapped his fork on the edge of his plate as he considered the request from Marshal Connor. He breathed deeply and let out a long sigh. "Tim, you got vacation this week?"

"Starting Friday."

"Shoot! This is only Monday. We've got three days and four nights to work! You suppose we can shut down the whole operation in that time?" the marshal asked in a teasing manner. "How about you, Gladys? Can you handle a few more days? If we're going to take Brady and Cassidy to Reno, we can't be slack about guarding them."

The pair of deputies from Nebraska who had driven Brady to the ranch grinned in relief at their overworked Wyoming counterparts. The responsibility for guarding Brady was out of their hands, and they would be heading home as soon as they finished lunch.

Cassidy was startled at the mention of her name and wondered why she would be taken to Reno. Beth asked the question that was on her mind. "Marshal, do you have to drag Cassidy all over the country?" she challenged. "Why not leave her here?"

The marshal regarded the woman and said, "I can't do that, Beth. Number one, you're too close to Johnson County and that idiot sheriff over there. Number two, because we've only apprehended two of the three murder suspects and I have no idea where or who the third one is. I'm not taking any chances."

Brady had offered little to the conversation, being content to listen and learn. Now he asked which of the three was still at large–the big, tall guy, the skinny one, or the red-headed one.

“That guy that I wounded was a big guy. The one she and Jennifer beat over the head was a skinny, dark-haired guy,” the marshal informed his son with a smile in Cassidy’s direction. The others around the table grinned at the reminder of Cassidy’s triumphant fight with the criminal.

Brady sobered quickly. “That leaves the red-headed one. Kenny Chite,” he said with a sigh and sat back in his chair.

“What can you tell us about him?” the marshal asked.

Brady shrugged. “Very little. He travels alone between Dominic’s ranch and Reno. I suspect he’s a courier. He didn’t go to Lone Pine with those other two and I’m not sure how he got involved the night they killed that guy.”

When the meal was finished, no one lingered in conversation at the table. The deputies from Nebraska thanked Beth for her hospitality and headed for home. Gladys Cole started making flight arrangements. With Brady’s help, Tim Sykes continued to sift through his mess of files for pertinent information to send to Nevada. Marshal Hollister worked on reports, and the three other men returned to their repair work in the machine shop. Cassidy cleaned the kitchen while Beth laundered Brady’s one extra change of clothes.

Being silently engrossed in their duties, everyone was startled when Pete burst through the door with Bud and Skeeter close on his heels.

“You’re not going to believe this!” Pete shouted in agitation. “We had the radio on in the shop. They just said on the news that Sheriff Higgins is lookin’ for Brady as a suspect in the stabbing of that guy at Lone Pine!”

Everyone in the room paused in their activities. Brady sat in stunned silence.

The marshal moved first, rising deliberately from his chair and silently reaching for his phone. He dialed the number he had used the previous evening and identified himself in a well-controlled but sinister voice as he demanded to speak to Sheriff Higgins. As he waited for Higgins to come on the line, he stroked the sides of his jaw.

Higgins could be heard speaking first, apparently trying to defend his position before the marshal could begin questioning him. The marshal put a quick end to any discussion.

"You *shut up*, you sorry potlicker, and you listen to me good!" the marshal snarled menacingly. "We've already captured two of the three men involved in that murder and gotten confessions out of them," he lied. "And furthermore, your meal ticket is on a slab at the morgue! You just dug yourself one big, deep hole, and I'm gonna bury you in it!"

The marshal hit the off button on his phone and expelled a long breath of air. Silence pervaded. The others remained motionless while the marshal paced the floor from the living room, past the dining area, to the edge of the kitchen and back. He stopped suddenly and in frustration hit the large table with his open fist, making a thunderous clap that caused Cassidy to jump.

"I suppose you already told Connor we'd be coming to Reno," the marshal addressed Deputy Cole.

"Yes, sir," she answered.

"Marshal?" Deputy Sykes ventured in a deliberately calm voice. "Higgins is digging his own hole. And he's only one man. Let's just concentrate on getting the rest of this operation shut down. When we do, we're going to find evidence somewhere that will hang him."

The marshal resumed his pacing as he pondered the situation. "I know you're right, Tim," the man agreed through clenched teeth. "But oh! How I want to see that man go down!"

At length, the marshal eased himself into a chair in the living room, again stroking the sides of his jaw as he sat in quiet thought. The deputies made a pretense of turning their attention back to their work while Bud and Pete and Skeeter seated themselves at the table.

Cassidy stood in silence at the edge of the kitchen counter, saddened by the unfounded accusations being heaped upon Brady. He had given his all to put Trent Dominic out of business. He had nothing left. All of his hard work was dispersed to others to complete the mission he had started and he didn't even have the satisfaction of seeing Dominic behind bars. *Does that matter to him anymore?* Cassidy wondered. *Has he put revenge and hatred behind him? Will his new faith in Jesus Christ sustain him until this is over?*

Beth poured fresh coffee into large mugs, and Cassidy carried the steaming cups to set one in front of each person. Brady remained where he was, sitting in a dejected posture with his elbows resting on his knees and his hands folded in front of him until he became aware that Cassidy was standing nearby. She held a cup out to Brady, who bravely put on a smile when he looked up at her. She looked back at him with what she hoped was an encouraging grin, but the unshed tears that glistened in her eyes belied the worry within. Brady stood and took the hot mug from her hand. Setting it down next to the computer, he embraced her, holding her close and stroking her hair without uttering a word.

"I wish you two were doing what those little old ladies in Sheridan thought you were doing!" the marshal growled from his seat across the room as he eyed the pair.

Brady was taken aback. He released his hold on Cassidy and faced his father with a confused look on his face. "What?" he questioned. "Running away to get married?"

"Yes!" the marshal answered emphatically. "Nothing would discredit that fool sheriff faster than if the Feds found his kidnapper and kidnappee holed up in the honeymoon suite of a Reno hotel with a marriage license in hand! If you two are going to end up getting married anyway, now would be a good time to do it!"

Pete and Skeeter cast devious glances at one another and grinned.

"Brady, you look a little peeked," Pete ventured with a broad smile. "How are you feeling?"

"Like I've been sucker-punched!"

Pete rose from his chair and rushed to Brady's side. Ushering his friend to the nearby chair, he forced Brady to sit down, feigning concern. "Doesn't he look off color, Skeeter?"

"Bad. Real bad," Skeeter agreed. He came to fan Brady's face.

To the amusement of the nearby deputies, Pete placed his hand on Brady's forehead and announced, "It's fever! Bad fever!"

Cassidy would have found the scene amusing, had someone else been the target of Pete and Skeeter's ministrations, but their efforts upset her. She wanted to scream at them, but held her tongue. Thankfully, Beth took charge.

"You men are impossible!" the big woman shouted as she exited the kitchen. "How can you be acting like this when Brady is in serious trouble?"

Pete and Skeeter backed away, fearing they were about to incur the awful wrath of the normally gentle Beth.

"You know, Mrs. Knowlton," Deputy Sykes spoke cautiously, "if he and Cassidy were married, there's no way a kidnapping charge would stick. And if the media got hold of the story, Higgins would look like an absolute fool for launching a nationwide manhunt for a couple who eloped. That man would have a *lot* of explaining to do."

Pete slapped Brady on the back and laughed. "Brady, this is right up your alley! You usually jump into things with both feet!"

Beth stepped into the midst of the room, addressing her boisterous son as well as Skeeter and the marshal. "That's enough foolish talk for one day. You men don't have to be teasing Brady and Cassidy every spare minute."

"I wasn't teasing, Beth," the marshal retorted in a firm, even tone. The entire group sobered quickly as they realized the man was not laughing with them. He turned his attention to Cassidy, who stood in stunned silence. "But I'm sorry I mentioned it. I was only thinking of Brady…and myself," he said with a sheepish grin, "'cause I'd really like to have a daughter-in-law like you. But you've been through enough ordeals lately. You need time to heal from them before you start thinkin' about marriage."

Cassidy nodded in agreement. *He did it to me again,* she thought. *I get upset with him, then he shows understanding and compassion. And his son is so much like him. Would life with Brady be a continuous emotional roller coaster?*

FOURTEEN

Cassidy awakened slowly, brushing at her cheek to wipe away an irritating strand of hair that kept tickling her. When her long lashes finally fluttered open, she was startled to find Brady propped up on his side with one arm, twining her hair around the fingers of his free hand to brush the strands across her face.

"What are you doing?" Cassidy challenged her new husband in a raspy early morning voice as she pulled the sheet tightly up under her chin.

"Watching you sleep," Brady stated with a smile.

A flush of pink rose in Cassidy's cheeks as she looked up at him. "How long have you been watching me?" she yawned.

"Not long enough. This is my new favorite pastime. Watching you. Playing with your hair. Peeking under the covers…"

Cassidy flushed crimson at Brady's teasing.

"And wondering," Brady added.

"Wondering what?" she asked.

"How are you gonna tell your momma?"

Cassidy closed her eyes momentarily. When she opened them again, Brady was still watching her, his playful sideways grin etching his mouth.

"You should be the one to tell her," she resolved sternly. "You're the charming one."

Brady laughed aloud. "I'm the charming one, huh? Therefore I should tell your ma we got married? You're her daughter. I think you should tell her."

"You're the one who talked her into giving you permission to ask me to marry you."

"And she's gonna put all the blame on me, too," Brady argued. "I think you should tell her so you can explain that we decided this together."

Cassidy sat up in bed, pulling the sheet around her as she turned toward Brady. "My mother is not mean. She'll understand once we explain the circumstances."

"Once *you* explain the circumstances," Brady corrected. "I'm gonna tell my family and friends. You tell yours. That's only fair."

Cassidy tried to glare sternly at her husband, but a hint of a smile teased at her pouting lips. Brady laughed aloud at her.

"We've had our first fight," she pointed out.

"That's terrible. We've only been married half a day," Brady agreed soberly. He suddenly became teasing. "Now we can kiss and make up!"

Before Cassidy could dodge his grasp, her husband playfully wrestled her back to the mattress. The bulk of the blankets slid across the silky sheets to plunge over the side of the king-size bed as the newlyweds embraced.

Shouts outside the door caused Brady to pause in a lingering kiss. He raised his head and listened carefully. Someone was unlocking the door to their room! He scarcely retrieved the covers and tossed them over Cassidy before the door was kicked open, ripping the safety chain from the wall. Policemen burst into the room with guns aimed at his chest.

"Freeze, Hollister!" an officer shouted.

Brady slowly raised his hands above his head. Cassidy clutched the blankets tightly around her. Neither spoke nor moved as the policemen closed in on the young couple.

"Get away from the girl, Hollister," the officer ordered menacingly. "Move over here nice and easy."

"No!" Cassidy screamed. *"Don't hurt my husband!"* She threw her arms around Brady's torso, preventing him from leaving her side while shielding him with her own body. The officer who had shouted at Brady looked completely bewildered.

"Husband!?" he wondered aloud.

"Ahhh, Tom?" a fellow officer indicated a fancy white dress which was draped over a nearby chair.

“I tried to stop ’em, Brady! I swear I tried to stop ’em!” Deputy Gladys Cole announced as she barged into the room, pushing uniformed officers aside as she did so. “They wouldn’t listen! They shoved me to the end of the hall to keep me out of the way and wouldn’t even look at my badge!”

Deputy Cole marched to a nearby dresser where she snatched up a piece of paper, which she held up for the stunned policemen to see. “May I present to you the marriage license!” she said scornfully in case the officers had not yet grasped the fact they had interrupted a couple on their honeymoon.

Blinding camera flashes from the doorway gained the attention of the room’s occupants. “It’s true, isn’t it?” a reporter asked. “Brady Hollister and Cassidy Henderson are married! He didn’t kidnap her at all! They eloped!”

“Yes, they are married!” Deputy Cole said knowingly as she stepped toward the pair of reporters. “And there is a sheriff in Wyoming who is going to have a lot of questions to answer for bringing false charges against this young man!”

“But this guy is wanted as a murder suspect along with having kidnapping charges against him!” an officer insisted.

“Yes!” Deputy Cole agreed. “Despite the fact that the U.S. Marshals Service apprehended two murder suspects six days ago that match the eye witness descriptions and pictures that were taken of the crime. We have been keeping this couple under surveillance until the Sheriff of Johnson County, Wyoming withdraws the charges.”

As one reporter snapped pictures, the other hurriedly recorded the detailed information concerning the incompetent sheriff. Cassidy clenched the covers with white-knuckled fists, scarcely moving or breathing during the entire exchange. Brady slowly lowered his hands from above his head as the police officers sheepishly returned their guns to their holsters. The leader apologized for the entire group, explaining that a hotel employee had given them a tip that Brady Hollister was here with the girl he had kidnapped. He assured the young couple that all officers in the area would be immediately informed of the situation.

As the policemen and reporters filed out of the room, Brady called after the one who had done the majority of the talking. "Could you do me a favor?" he asked.

The officer shrugged and asked what Brady would like.

"Now that I don't have a safety latch on my door and the hotel staff hands keys out left and right, do you think you could provide an extra deputy to stand guard?"

"What do you think I was doing?" Gladys Cole protested. "I was guarding your room!"

"Yeah, well! About ten people just walked in on us!"

"I was outnumbered!" Gladys cried. "And they wouldn't take 'no' for an answer!"

"I want more guards!" Brady insisted.

"Fine!" Gladys shouted. She marched toward the door and was about to leave when she turned back to the young couple.

"By the way," she spoke in an even tone, "those ace reporters intend to air their story as fast as they can. They're hoping to get it on the nine o'clock news. It is now eight-thirty." The deputy smiled a broad smile at the unnerved couple and left the room, closing the door firmly behind her.

Brady flopped backward onto the bed as he breathed a huge sigh of relief. Cassidy remained sitting as she was until he caressed her arm and shoulder and gently pulled her toward him. As she lay down beside him, she didn't try to stem her tears.

"Don't cry, Honey," Brady tried to console her. "It's over. No one got hurt."

"I was so scared," she sobbed.

"I know. So was I."

Brady wrapped his arms around his wife, embracing her in such a way that she felt safe and secure. "I promise, Cass, someday we're going to have a nice, quiet, normal life," he consoled her. "We'll have kids. And a dog–a big dog–and a ranch of our own. As soon as we get back to Wyoming, I want to take you on a tour of Jubel's place so you can see it in the daylight."

"I'd like that," Cassidy whispered, loving the soothing sound of Brady's calm voice, which eased her tension.

"Jubel didn't like the idea of me buyin' the place at first. He told me if I'd just be patient and wait 'til he croaked, I'd inherit a bunch of it anyway. I told him I'd rather see him have some money to enjoy life, so we came to an agreement. I buy more parcels as I can. He'll live in the house and run the place as he sees fit until he decides its time to quit. I help with round-ups and any other time I can get there. But I have to confess, I haven't been a whole lot of help to Jubel for quite some time now."

"Since you started investigating Trent Dominic?"

Brady didn't audibly answer her. He didn't have to, for Cassidy knew she had guessed correctly.

The young couple rested in silence, each leaving the other to his own thoughts for a time. Brady finally broke the silence.

"Cassidy?"

"Hmmmm?" she responded, keeping her eyes closed while acknowledging that she heard him.

"How are you gonna tell your momma?"

Cassidy didn't utter a word as she rose from the bed and donned a robe. With a sigh, she picked up the phone. "I guess I'd better take Mom's advice," she said as she dialed her mother's number. "That which you must do, do quickly."

"Is that from the Bible?" Brady asked as he tossed the covers off. Cassidy narrowed her eyes as she watched her husband's retreat to the bathroom, trying to convey the message that he was a traitor to leave the room while she broke the news. He smiled broadly as he turned on the shower and closed the door behind him.

"Yes, Mom. Everything is fine," Cassidy assured her mother after a couple minutes of exchanging small talk. "The reason that I called is… well…are you sitting down?"

"No, I'm not sitting down," Elaine replied. "Why?"

"Well…Brady and I got married last night…" Cassidy blurted.

Elaine laughed at her daughter. "You mean you got engaged, Cassidy. Brady called and asked me for permission to propose to you. I can hardly wait to meet him in person. He seems so nice…"

"Mom, I said we got married," Cassidy interrupted. "We didn't get engaged, we got married. Last night."

A long pause ensued before Elaine muttered, "I'm going to go sit down."

The silence on the other end of the line caused Cassidy to wonder if her mother had fainted.

"Mom?"

"I'm here," Elaine assured her daughter. "Tell me again what you just told me."

Cassidy sighed. "Mom, you heard me right the first time! Brady and I love each other so much. We knew within a few days of meeting each other that we wanted to be together forever."

"Cassidy?" Elaine finally spoke after another lengthy silence. "Just tell me you're happy."

"I am, Mom," Cassidy assured her mother. "I'm very happy."

"You don't sound happy," Elaine pointed out.

Silent tears trickled down Cassidy's cheeks. Though she tried to quench the tide of emotion, she couldn't. Brady came to stand by her side as she poured out her frustrations. "The police just left here, Mom," she cried. "They broke into our room and tried to arrest Brady. They had guns pointed at him and everything!"

Brady slipped an arm around his wife's shoulders and took the phone from her hand, holding it so both of them could converse with Elaine. "Mrs. Henderson, Cassidy is really shaken up by what happened," he tried to explain. "We didn't plan to call you and make you worry. Neither one of us got hurt and now we have extra guards posted at the door to our room. We would have liked to call you after things calmed down, but a tip was leaked to the press and a couple reporters tracked us down about the time the cops raided our room. They got pictures and a big fat story and it's going to be on the news this morning. We thought you'd better hear it from us first."

"So…" Elaine wondered aloud in a strained voice that sounded as if she were forcing herself to be cordial, "you two have to spend your honeymoon locked in a room with guards outside your door…"

"Well, it's a big, fancy room," Brady quipped. "A honeymoon suite." In a more sober tone, he continued. "It's nearly over, now. The Feds have gotten all the help from me that I can give them. And they're confident the third man who was an accomplice to the murder in Lone Pine isn't going to come after us. His criminal buddies are in jail and he's wise to lay low and not do anything stupid. And now that this story is breaking, Sheriff Higgins will have to back off and withdraw the charges against me. We'll probably be heading back to Wyoming today or tomorrow. We'll come visit you as soon as we're sure I'm not going to be arrested every time I turn around."

"I'd like that. Let me know when you can come. We'll have a wedding reception for you," Elaine offered quietly.

"That sounds good," Brady agreed. "We'll get there as soon as we can."

An uncomfortable silence lingered. Cassidy sensed that her mother was on the verge of tears. Brady must have also detected the woman's anguish and attempted to make amends.

"Mrs. Henderson, I'm sorry if you're not okay with this..." he apologized.

"You take good care of her, Brady Hollister," Elaine commanded with a quivering voice.

"Yes, Ma'am," Brady answered as the phone went dead on the other end of the line.

FIFTEEN

The church fellowship hall was filled nearly to capacity. Guests lingered around the decorated tables and near the doorway, anxiously awaiting the arrival of the bride and groom. Elaine nervously bustled about the kitchen, checking once again that all the food was prepared. Her sisters assured her everything was ready and there was plenty of help in the kitchen. They urged her to relax and enjoy the occasion.

How can I possibly relax? Elaine wondered. *I haven't had a decent night's sleep for weeks. I met my new son-in-law in person for the first time yesterday. This morning, I briefly met his father and the more I learn about that man, the more I despise him. How could he allow a marriage like this?*

Elaine hung her head in shame as she silently admitted the resentment that was threatening to overwhelm her and reduce her to tears in front of the entire crowd of well-wishers. *No! No tears!* she resolved. *This is the first time since Keith's funeral that all of our friends and family have gotten together. This has to be a joyous occasion!*

Elaine steeled herself to step out of the kitchen and join the merriment. She moved quietly among the tables, going through the motions of checking to see that everything was in place. Inwardly, she was praying. *Lord, they seem so deeply in love with one another. But I have no peace about this marriage. You know how compassionate and caring Cassidy is. Has she sacrificed the marriage You had in mind for her in order to help Brady out of his troubles? Please, Father, help me be loving and supportive.*

Putting a smile on her face, Elaine began mingling with those who had gathered. She had greeted only a fraction of her guests when the entry door opened and a huge cowboy strode in. Dressed in black jeans and a flamboyant western shirt, he doffed his wide-brimmed hat, revealing reddish brown hair and tanned, freckled complexion. His size alone drew immediate attention from the chattering crowd. Conversation waned as the man raised a hand, signaling for silence in the room.

"Ladies and gentlemen," Pete Knowlton announced to the crowd. "May I present to you…Mr. and Mrs. Brady Hollister!"

Brady led a blushing Cassidy into the room to a round of applause, cheers and whistles. In black jeans and a crisp, white shirt adorned with tiny pleats, the mix of formal and casual dress flattered the man's ruggedly handsome features. He donned his most winning smile as he tipped his hat to the boisterous crowd.

Elaine had to admit that her daughter never looked lovelier. Her fitted white dress was elegantly simple with a minimum of embroidered adornment. The smooth lines, devoid of flounces and sequins, accented Cassidy's figure perfectly. With her hair swept up in a loose coil at the top of her head, no one could help but notice the new bride's radiant smile and bright eyes.

Brady held tight to Cassidy's hand as a group of young ladies rushed to her side, hugging and kissing and congratulating her. Pete stepped in front of the couple before too many over-zealous well-wishers could swarm closer and asked that everyone find a seat. The crowd noisily complied, quieting as Pete accepted a microphone from Jason, who had been busily setting up audio equipment.

"May I have your attention?" Pete spoke over the rustling of chairs as everyone adjusted their seating and turned toward him. "My name is Pete Knowlton. I've been a friend of Brady's since he was six years old. I got elected to make the introductions and head up a little program 'cause I wanted to and nobody fought me for the job."

The audience regarded the large, muscle-bound physique on the man who stood over six and a half feet tall with his cowboy boots on. They cheerfully agreed that Pete could take the floor if he wanted to.

"I'd like to begin by thanking Cassidy's mother for arranging wonderful accommodations for those of us who traveled from out of state," Pete announced. Elaine stood shyly at the far edge of the room, praying that this man would not ask her to say anything to the crowd. Thankfully, he simply acknowledged her preparations before turning his attention to introducing Brady's father and his own wife Jennifer.

"Brady and Cassidy are planning to go from table to table to visit with you while you're eating, so you'll each get a chance to get acquainted with Brady," Pete explained. "But first, Cassidy's brother, Jason, has put together some pictures from the bride and groom's growing up years. This video will be a fun review of Cassidy's life for those of you who know her and a great way to begin introducing you to Brady."

Each of the round tables in the fellowship hall accommodated six to ten people. The newlyweds sat at a table reserved especially for them. Jennifer joined them, as did Marshal Hollister. That left a chair for Pete and an empty one next to the marshal. Elaine glanced around the room and knew there were no other tables more appropriate for her to sit at. As the hostess of this affair, she felt obligated to give special attention to her out-of-state guests. She moved to the table where Cassidy and Brady sat and greeted Jennifer, then gracefully extended her hand to the marshal in a firm, welcoming handshake. He arranged the chair next to his so that it faced the video screen and politely helped Elaine into the seat.

As soon as the crowd was situated, lights in the room were dimmed. A huge white screen lit up with the name "Cassidy Jane Henderson." As country music played in the background, the audience was treated to an array of baby pictures, school photos, and scenes from Cassidy's home. She was shown with family and friends, with county fair projects and art awards. There were photos of Cassidy playing softball and volleyball, swimming in a river, hunting deer with her father, climbing an apple tree, milking a cow, and driving a tractor through a lush, green field.

The video then switched to photos of "Brady John Hollister." Unlike Cassidy's wide array of pictures, there were few photos from Brady's infant and preschool years. None showed him with his mother, only with his father, grandparents, or friends. There were a few touching scenes when Brady was hugging or kissing his frail little brother. The blue tint of the lips of the little toddler compared to Brady's healthy complexion spoke volumes to the silent audience. Brady's school years included numerous scenes on a ranch. One person present in a number of those photos was a youthful Pete Knowlton. The pictures included views of normal ranch life–fixing fence, herding cattle, making hay, and eating watermelon with a half dozen other children on a wide front porch. And there were lots of pictures of rodeo. Brady riding bucking horses and bulls, roping calves, and wrestling steers. Taking spills and rejoicing in successes. Laughing with a group of contestants and smiling amicably as a line of cowgirls young and old vied for his autograph.

"Brady and Cassidy" was the title for the third set of pictures, of which there were few. A short series of photos taken at the little chapel where they were married followed by pictures of their current ranch life together. The video ended with a stunning portrait of the newlyweds walking hand in hand beside a wooden corral fence while streaks of morning sunrays highlighted their images against a backdrop of distant rugged mountain peaks.

As the video ended and the lights turned on, the guests showed their appreciation with a round of applause. Pete again picked up the microphone and stood in front of the crowd.

"I know there's loads of questions about how Cassidy could go off on vacation to visit her brother in Idaho and come back a few weeks later with a husband from Wyoming. Rather than have the newlyweds answer the same questions over and over as they visit with you, we have one more guest with us today who's gonna give you the low down. Ladies and gentlemen, I would like to introduce to you...Skeeter Varness!"

"Oh, oh," Marshal Hollister said in a barely audible tone as Skeeter appeared from a side door where he had been in hiding. Elaine glanced at the man beside her with a questioning look. The marshal merely smiled, offering no explanation for his comment.

Elaine had not been informed that there were more guests from Wyoming. Pete had simply asked to make introductions and tell about the newlyweds–a job which she had gladly relinquished. As she looked toward Cassidy and Brady, she realized they, too, were surprised by this man's presence. They also seemed apprehensive.

Skeeter strode to the front of the room and took the microphone from the man who stood a foot taller than him. Turning it off and setting it aside, he turned on the portable microphone that was clipped to his shirt. Pete walked toward the table, slapping Brady good-naturedly on the back as he took the seat next to his friend.

"I am delighted to be here today to roast…I mean introduce to you a very dear friend of mine and to tell you a little of the events of the past few weeks," the man began. "My name is Jeremy Varness, better known as Skeeter. I am a rodeo clown and bull fighter by trade and I am also an ordained minister, which means I have a license to talk."

Skeeter obviously felt at home in front of a crowd and the group before him was already smiling in anticipation of what this energetic man was going to say. He began his adventurous tale with a brief description of Cassidy's escape from the murderers, then led the rapt audience through a maze of emotional turmoil experienced by Cassidy, Elaine, Jason, and Brady.

As Elaine listened to Skeeter's story, some of her own suspicions were confirmed. *"Brady said…Brady did…Brady decided…Brady led…" Cassidy often had trouble making up her mind,* Elaine considered. *Naturally, she would be attracted to a confident, decisive man to replace her father, who was the first one she turned to for advice.*

As Skeeter's story took the audience to the truck stop in Sheridan, the marshal turned his head toward the young couple and his mouth twitched in a slight grin. Pete and Jennifer were smiling broadly. Elaine quickly found out what kind of fun the three of them were anticipating from the rodeo clown.

"We've got to hurry, Alethea! We can't let those wicked stepbrothers catch up to us!" Skeeter said as he impersonated one of the elderly ladies in a high-pitched, squeaky voice. The audience laughed uproariously as he played the part of the other sister. "But Alice, we have to wait for him to give her a good-bye kiss!"

Skeeter changed back to his normal voice and laughed as he continued. "Let me tell you, Brady Hollister was not about to pass up an opportunity like that! With everyone in the building watching, he gave Cassidy a good, long two-minute smacker!"

Brady shook his head and protested loudly over the howls and whistles reverberating through the room. Cassidy's complexion became increasingly red as the revelry continued. Elaine sensed that Skeeter was embellishing his tale to wild proportions, but knew by her daughter's embarrassment there must be some truth to the story.

"Well, okay, maybe it was only one minute!" Skeeter conceded after the noise died down.

Brady again protested the accusation.

"Well, fine!" Skeeter announced. "You'd better just set the record straight and show us!"

With the crowd encouraging them, Brady stood and offered a hand to Cassidy, who rose from her chair. He moved slowly toward his wife and brushed the thumb of his right hand across her smooth lips as he had done the first time he kissed her. The couple moved into each other's arms and reenacted the tender yet passionate embrace they had first shared.

The gathering of friends and family whistled and clapped in delight until the newlyweds returned to their seats. Elaine's eyes misted as she silently prayed, *Oh, Father, may they always be so tender with one another…*

"I declare!" Skeeter exclaimed.

When the crowd quieted, he addressed them once again and reenacted scenes of misplaced truck keys, Alice's driving, Cassidy's fight at the rodeo, and the marshal's argument with the ruthless sheriff.

Elaine realized she was relaxing and actually enjoying Skeeter's tale. And even though she knew much of the story, Skeeter's version shed new light on the drama. She recalled the evening Cassidy had called her from Knowlton's ranch. The marshal had been speaking in a loud and angry voice in the next room. *I thought he was mean-tempered and irrational and selfish,* Elaine thought. *In reality, he was fighting for Cassidy and Brady. He was trying to keep them safe and serve justice, too.*

Skeeter's rendition of the marshal's deep-voiced comment, "I wish you two were doing what those little old ladies thought you were doing!" drew the attention of the crowd to Brady's father. The marshal remained stoic, neither trying to apologize or argue the statement as Skeeter imitated Brady's shocked, stammering reaction.

Skeeter briefly explained the need for Brady and Cassidy and the marshals to go to Reno. "When it was time for them to head out, Pete started ribbing Brady about getting married while he was in town. Brady argued that he was not going to do that and Pete asked, 'Why not?' Brady shouted at him, 'Can you imagine what Cassidy's mother would do to me? She'd probably kill me!'

"Pete and the marshal and I laughed at him. Then Brady said, 'You can laugh all you want, but you never had mother-in-law who could shoot you dead at three hundred yards!'"

A shocked audience turned all at once to see Elaine's reaction. She did her best to erase the mortified look from her face and slowly turned to her son-in-law. Brady smiled guiltily, shrugged, and whispered an apology, claiming that he didn't mean it in a bad way.

"Well, you all know how intimidating Elaine Henderson is, don't you?" Skeeter challenged the audience. The crowd continued watching Elaine as the quiet, mild-tempered woman blushed profusely. "And you all know about the trophy deer she shot a few years back when she was hunting with her husband? And you know what she's like when she blows a fuse and gets good and mad, don't you?" Skeeter prodded the crowd. They laughed and denied that Elaine had ever been intimidating and few had ever seen her get good and mad.

"Well, I tell you, Elaine Henderson has such a reputation in the West, the very thought of her gunning for Brady had a bull rider, a steer wrestler, and a U.S. Marshal shaking in their boots!" Skeeter proclaimed emphatically.

Pete, Brady, and the marshal laughingly protested as Elaine shielded her face with her hands in embarrassment.

Pete shouted across the room, "What about the clown? He was scared, too!"

"No, sir!" Skeeter denied the accusation.

"Oh, yes, he was!" Pete persisted.

"The clown was not shaking in his boots!" Skeeter insisted above the taunts from Pete and Brady. "The clown was not shaking in his boots. No, sir!" He suddenly changed his voice to a quivering, high squeaky one, and with knees knocking and his body trembling furiously, he admitted, "He was wearing tennis shoes!"

Elaine couldn't help but burst into laughter. The audience roared along with her.

When the noise finally died down, Skeeter stepped cautiously closer to Elaine as if he couldn't resist taunting the demure woman for a few moments longer.

"I'm not afraid of you," he stated with mock confidence. "I'll bet I can outrun you."

Elaine laughingly agreed that Skeeter could outrun her. She glanced around the room and saw that her parents were laughing so hard they had to wipe tears from their eyes. The thought occurred to her that she hadn't laughed so much since long before Keith died.

"I can outrun her," Skeeter stated confidently as he made his way back to the front of the room. "I learned way back when I was a toddler, if you're going to be mouthy, you'd better be fast, too."

Giving the crowd a few moments to settle down, Skeeter picked up the love story where he had left off.

"Brady and Cassidy were taken to Reno, where Brady shared with the feds the information he had gleaned about some criminals. Can you imagine trying to conduct a romance while you're under constant guard by law enforcement officers? They had to pass notes back and forth like they were school kids!

"One night, Brady was alone in a hotel room. He picked up the phone and called Elaine. He told her, 'I want to ask Cassidy to marry me. I'd like your permission.'

"Like any good, concerned mother, Elaine pointed out that perhaps it was a little early to think about becoming engaged. Brady explained to her that sometimes you just know when the right one comes along and could he please ask Cassidy. He turned on that cowboy charm of his and Elaine finally, reluctantly gave in. After all, the guy had risked his own life to save her daughter's."

Skeeter grinned broadly. The crowd anticipated what was coming next. "Well, Brady asked Cassidy on Friday morning if she would marry him and she said 'yes!' He asked if she needed a big wedding or if a chapel in Reno would do. She told him a small, simple wedding would be just fine. He said, 'How about tonight?' She said, 'Okay.' So while Brady was digging through police files, the marshal and one of his deputies were taking Cassidy shopping for a dress and a change of clothes for Brady and arranging a wedding. And the couple became Mr. and Mrs. Hollister one week after Brady ran away with Cassidy in his truck!

"And by the way, didn't the marshal pick out a beautiful dress for Cassidy?"

The crowd applauded and cheered while the marshal sat as stone-faced as he could with the attention turned toward him. The man shook his head and denied to Elaine any part of picking out the dress. Skeeter let the audience ridicule the somber man for some time before issuing his final remarks.

"Pete Knowlton and Brady Hollister and I have been friends for many years. And I know Pete agrees with me when I tell you Brady is one of the nicest guys you would ever want to meet. He's friendly, generous, and fun-loving. He was intense in his rodeo career and relentless as a private investigator. He rode hard and played hard. But he never ever put his heart and soul into loving anyone until Cassidy Henderson came along."

The crowd sat quietly, in a solemn, thoughtful mood. Elaine's eyes misted again at Skeeter's touching final words.

"None of us ever realizes how we influence other people. Cassidy's family and friends probably have no idea what you have done to help her grow into the wonderful young lady that she is today. And we probably won't see for many years to come what an impact a run-in in a dark alley is going to make on the lives of Brady and Cassidy and the people around them. But I believe God had His hand on both of them and He has wonderful plans for their future together.

"I would like to close by telling Brady and Cassidy, I am so happy for you. You know that I wish you all the best. May God richly bless you as you walk with Him. And Brady, you take good care of your new best friend."

SIXTEEN

The Sunday morning congregation filtered out of the church into a stifling hot August day. The marshal and Jason followed Elaine outside. While waiting for Cassidy and Brady, who were being greeted by several well-wishers, Elaine was complimented several times by passing parishioners on the previous day's beautiful reception.

Cassidy finally emerged from the building, bounding down the steps and skipping toward her mother. "Mom! Mark and Heather and everyone are going to the Country Café to eat. They asked if we'd like to go, too! I haven't spent time with them for ages! I'd really like to go!"

"What does Brady say about it?" Elaine challenged as a way of reminding her daughter to consult her husband. "He met hundreds of people yesterday and tomorrow he's helping you move out of your apartment. He might like to relax and take it easy."

"I'm fine with it," Brady assured Elaine with a smile. "It will be easier for you if we go out and eat."

"I do have a beef roast in the oven," Elaine explained. "I'll have to go home and turn the stove off, then I could meet you at the restaurant."

Jason invited Cassidy and Brady to ride with him. As Elaine hurried toward her car, she was hailed by one of the women of the church who reminded her she left a number of her dishes in the kitchen and a bowl of salad in the refrigerator. The marshal opted to follow Elaine and helped retrieve the items. By the time they emerged from the building, Jason's truck was nowhere in sight. Not knowing the way to the restaurant, the marshal followed Elaine to her home in his vehicle, helping her unload her car and carrying the dishes to the house.

Pansy greeted Elaine with excited jumps when she entered the farmhouse, and barked ferociously at the stranger who followed her master through the door. Elaine ignored the little dog as much as possible as she rearranged her refrigerator to make room for the salad.

With the food taken care of, Elaine moved past the kitchen window to turn off the oven. She stepped back to the window, sensing that something was not right. Then she saw it. Her garden! The cattle were loose in her garden!

"Oh, no!" she cried. She threw off her sandals and ran to the mud room where she stuffed her bare feet into tall rubber chore boots. Running toward the back door, Elaine commanded Pansy to stay in the house. The little dog instead escaped between its master's legs and raced across the lawn, its short little legs pumping furiously as it plunged headlong into the midst of the scattering heifers.

Elaine grabbed up a garden rake that was leaning against the side of the house and screamed to no avail at the dog. The marshal was left alone on the door step to watch as the animals evacuated the demolished produce patch.

The cattle fled in all directions, some loping off toward the distant soybean field while others raced across the lawn. Elaine tossed the garden rake aside and trotted toward the barn. Wading through a mud puddle, she opened wide the gate that had been tipped over, then ran to the shed.

Within a few seconds, the woman emerged from the building on an all-terrain vehicle. She had her skirt tucked up and her knees showed above the tall boots. She expertly maneuvered the four-wheeler toward the field, gunning the engine, spinning the tires and throwing mud several yards behind her as she raced after part of the wayward herd.

Once Elaine had overcome the fleeing Holstein heifers, they turned and trotted toward the buildings where the marshal stood ready with his arms spread, heading the animals toward the open gate while Elaine approached behind them. The animals suddenly bolted past the opening, lunging instead toward their comrades who dined on the grassy lawn. The marshal tried to stop them as they changed course. His boot slid on a patch of greasy mud. Off balance and with arms flailing, a fleeing calf brushed against him hard enough to topple him backward into the huge mud puddle. Before the marshal could crawl out of the muck, a dozen calves ran on either side of him. The marshal attempted to sit up and just as he did so, Pansy appeared, hot on the trail of the cattle. Rather than go around the puddle, the dog took advantage of the bridge in the middle. It leaped onto the marshal's chest and scurried across the front of his once immaculate white shirt, then hastened after the herd, barking with a high-pitched yip.

Elaine pulled up to the edge of the puddle and leaped from the four-wheeler. Wading into the muck, she asked the marshal if he was hurt.

"Only my pride," he admitted as he sat up, leaving mud and water to course down his sodden shirt into the puddle in which he sat.

"Mr. Hollister, I am so sorry," Elaine apologized as she extended a hand to help the man to his feet. The marshal accepted the offered assistance. Once he was standing upright, he reached down to retrieve his hat, which lay at the edge of the murky water and silently shook large gobs of mud off of it.

"Mr. Hollister…" Elaine began, shaking her head as she tried to find words to describe her anguish at the mess her livestock had made of her guest.

The marshal interrupted her. "You know, Mrs. Henderson," he spoke curtly as he studied the woman, "it sure seems redundant to me to be so formal when we're sharin' the same mud hole." With a broad smile, he added, "Would you please call me Bret or Marshal like other people do?"

Elaine breathed a sigh of relief. The man seemed not to be too angry for these unexpected circumstances. She returned the smile and nodded her assent.

Turning her attention back to the herd of cattle, Elaine found that they were trotting down the long driveway toward the road. She asked the marshal if he would mind driving the four-wheeler while she headed the animals toward their pasture. This time, the cattle were more cooperative. They retreated through the gate and ran toward the rolling green pasture hills behind the barn.

With the animals corralled and the fence secured, the marshal and Elaine regarded one another. The man was soiled from head to foot. His damp shirt, dark brown in back and white in front with a smattering of small footprints and dark splotches, clung to his muscular torso. Mud encrusted his jeans, his belt, and his boots. Elaine hadn't fared much better. Her blue blouse was sweat-stained and mud-spattered. Tendrils of dark hair were plastered to her flushed face by streams of perspiration. The hem of her ankle-length, flower-printed skirt dripped with mud and her hands and face were streaked dark brown.

The pair contemplated their situation in awkward silence. Elaine's thoughts were in turmoil. She couldn't send the marshal to his motel room to clean up. It was several miles away on one of the busiest streets in town. How embarrassing for him if anyone saw him like this! Yet, if he stayed here, what would he wear while his clothes were in the wash? Should she offer to go to his motel room and get clean clothes for him? Brady would be eating by now and he was miles away. She could hardly make the marshal wait in sodden clothes for him to come to his father's aid. Yet how could she invite a near stranger into her house to shower while she was alone?

Pansy scampered across the lawn and jumped excitedly around Elaine's legs. The once fluffy tan and black and silver-gray mop of hair was plastered to the skinny little pup's body with a mat of brown slime sprinkled with green stems and seeds. It leaped atop the step and scratched to get into the house through the back door.

"Nothing doing, you dirty dog!" Elaine scolded. "You are not setting foot in that house!" She seized the wiggly little creature and carried it to an outdoor faucet to which a hose was attached, then turned on the spigot. The pup fought wildly to get away from the flood of chilly water, but Elaine showed no sympathy as she rinsed the mud from the furry coat. Releasing the dog to run away across the lawn, Elaine turned the water off and stood to face the marshal.

"You gonna hose me down, too?" he wondered aloud.

Elaine shook her head. "There's a bathroom with a shower just beyond the laundry room. You can put your clothes in the sink. While you're showering, I'll go upstairs and look for something for you to wear."

Elaine kicked off the muddy chore boots near the back step and went through the back door, motioning for the marshal to follow. He hesitated.

"How about you go clean up first so you're not traipsing all over the house dripping mud?" he suggested.

Elaine agreed that would be easier for her. She hastened into the bathroom and showered quickly, throwing her filthy garments into the laundry tub. Wrapped in a large towel, she cracked the back door open and called outside to let the marshal know he could come into the house. She then sped upstairs to dress before the marshal entered.

Jason's jeans were too long and slender for the more muscular marshal and Elaine had already donated most of her deceased husband's clothes to charity. Rummaging through closets and drawers, she found a pair of cotton, elastic-waist lounge pants and an oversized t-shirt that Jason often wore around the house. Returning downstairs, she offered these to the marshal through a crack in the door.

Running cool water over the filthy pile of clothes that lay in the deep sink, Elaine worked at squeezing mud out of the garments. While she was busy at her task, the phone rang.

"Mom! Where have you been?" Cassidy asked. "And where's Bret? Brady and I have been trying to call you. Didn't you understand which restaurant we were going to?"

"I've been chasing cattle," Elaine stated flatly. "And Brady's father has been helping me chase cattle."

"Oh," Cassidy murmured. She must have sensed her mother's irritation, for she asked rather cautiously if the animals were back in their pasture.

"Yes, we got them in."

"Are you coming to the restaurant, then?"

"No, we're not coming."

"But, Mom…"

"Cassidy, we've been chasing heifers in ninety-five degree humid weather! And we just had three days of rain and storms. By the time we got those stupid things into the pasture we were hot and sweaty and filthy dirty from head to foot! Your father-in-law is just now getting cleaned up, and I've got laundry to do."

"What would the pastor say if he knew you two were alone in the house together?" Cassidy wondered aloud in a teasing manner.

"I know exactly what the pastor would say about me having a man here while I'm alone in the house. I never thought of it, but I probably should have thrown your father-in-law in the back of the truck and hauled him to the pastor's house to get cleaned up. Wouldn't he love that on the very weekend that his persnickety mother is visiting him!"

Elaine regretted the words as soon as they were out of her mouth. *What is happening to me?* she wondered. *I am so critical, so impatient, so… frustrated. I had no business saying what I did about the pastor's mother.*

She turned to find the marshal standing behind her with a wide grin on his face, which he quickly tried to conceal. She wondered what he found amusing and missed what Cassidy said to her.

"I'm sorry, Cassidy," Elaine quickly apologized. "I didn't mean to take my frustrations out on you. Just have a good time with your cousins. Tell everybody 'hi' for me. I'll see you later. Bye."

Elaine quickly hung up the phone before Cassidy could argue further. Rather than rinse any more mud off the garments, she threw the whole pile into the washing machine to rinse them in cold water, knowing they would all need to be run through the washer again.

Pansy scratched and whimpered outside. Elaine inched the door open to let the dog in, scooping it up with a towel before there was any chance the still-damp dog could run around the house. As she briskly rubbed the pet dry, the woman suddenly felt hot tears sting her eyes. *Everything that I love has become such a frustration for me,* she thought. *My family, the farm, the animals. Even Pansy angers me.* Elaine glanced up to see the marshal staring at her.

"Elaine," he spoke softly, "if you've gotta cry, just let 'er rip. I lost someone, too, you know. I know about the heartache and uncertainty and the loneliness…"

I have no intention of breaking down in front of this man, she promised herself. *No matter how mad I am at the world! And how dare he think we have anything in common!*

Elaine bit her trembling lip, fighting for control. The battle was nearly won until the marshal laid his hand softly on her shoulder in an attempt to comfort her. The unexpected touch unleashed a flood of pent-up emotion that Elaine could no longer stop. She hastily dropped Pansy to the floor and stepped past the marshal, intending to flee upstairs to be alone. His strong arm encircled her and steered her instead into the living room, where she plopped wearily into her favorite chair. As she reached for a nearby box of tissue, he left her there to weep.

Bret returned to the living room several minutes later to find Pansy laying quietly, curled up on Elaine's lap. The woman's arms were folded around a framed picture, which she clutched tightly. Tears trickled down her cheeks. She ignored the man at first until she realized he was standing with a plate of food and a tall glass of icy lemonade clearly meant for her.

"I tell you what," the marshal stated. "You sure know how to cook. That is great beef roast."

Elaine took note of the lunch he had prepared for her. A hot roast beef sandwich with a generous scoop of pasta salad on the side. She smiled weakly up at the man and thanked him as he laid the glass on the nearby table. He handed Elaine the plate while removing the picture from her grasp.

As Elaine savored her meal, Bret studied the portrait that she had been clutching tightly. It was a picture of Elaine, her husband, and three children in an informal outdoor setting.

"Cassidy and Jason sure took after their dad didn't they?" the marshal asked as he noted the Scandinavian features and fair complexion of the younger children. The oldest, with his darker hair and hazel eyes, more closely resembled Elaine.

Pansy hopped down from Elaine's lap and sniffed at the marshal's bare feet as he set the picture down on the coffee table that was strewn with photos. He moved toward a large recliner. As he sat down, the little dog unleashed a vicious growl and attacked the stranger's pants leg, gripping the cotton material and pulling with all her might.

"Pansy! Stop that!" Elaine scolded. She made a move to get up from her chair and retrieve the dog, but the marshal motioned for her to remain seated.

"I tell you what," the marshal said with a laugh as he watched the terrier wrestle with the pants, "it's a good thing you've got yourself a little dog. If you had a big one with an attitude like that, I'd be in a heap of trouble 'bout now."

The marshal got up from the chair and moved to the couch in an effort to appease the ornery pup. "Apparently that was your husband's chair," he noted.

Elaine nodded.

The marshal picked up the little dog and held the wiggly animal in front of him. "And you're probably not happy with me for wearing Jason's pants either, are you?" he asked the pup. It stared at him with beady black eyes. The little pink tongue hung out over miniature white canine teeth surrounded by long brown strands of hair.

"So this is a Yorkshire Terrier, huh?" the marshal asked as he studied the animal.

"That's what I'm told. They should have called this one a terror instead. She's so naughty."

The marshal set the dog down on the floor and after a few sharp warning barks aimed at the stranger in the house, Pansy trotted off to play with a toy.

Elaine asked the man if he'd gotten enough to eat, and he replied that he did and thanked her. He paused a moment before confronting her with a question.

"Elaine, why are you unhappy that Cassidy married Brady?"

She stared at the man in stunned silence for a moment, then looked away. "Unhappy?" she asked. "I'm not unhappy with it. I…"

"I think you put on a good show," the marshal challenged. "You threw a great party for them. You smiled for your family and friends and you've treated me and Brady's friends real nice. But you cry about it when you're alone, don't you?"

Elaine stood from her chair. Gathering the plate and glass, she walked out of the living room and into the kitchen without answering the man. *How dare he come into my house and talk to me like this?* she seethed in anger. *What more can I do to support Brady and Cassidy than what I've already done?*

The marshal followed the woman into the kitchen and stood behind her as she piled dishes in the sink.

"If you've got to be mad at someone, be mad at me! I gave them money and helped make the arrangements," the marshal goaded. "But I want to know what it is you don't like about it. You don't like Brady? You didn't want Cassidy to move away? You didn't get to plan a big, fancy wedding for your only daughter? What!?"

At the sound of the loud voice, Pansy raced into the kitchen, warning the stranger with growls the dog intended to protect its master. Elaine spun around to face the marshal, who stood with his hands on his hips, ignoring the noisy little creature at his feet. He stared at Elaine with dark eyes narrowed.

Elaine refused to let the tall man intimidate her. "I like Brady," she stated honestly. "I like him very much. I only want Cassidy to be happy! How can two people possibly be ready for such a commitment in a week? It takes a lot longer than that to get to know someone. I think you and that clown of a preacher take marriage far too lightly when you encourage something like this!"

"Skeeter did *not* encourage this!" the marshal vehemently defended. "He's a big tease and he's been picking on Brady for years about getting married, but he was as shocked as anybody when he heard about it. He's not to blame for any part of this and he takes marriage very seriously. Furthermore, so do I!"

"Then why did you let them do such a thing? They're not ready for it!"

"How long does it take to get ready, Elaine?" the man questioned. "Sarah and I dated for two years before I went to Viet Nam and for two more after I got back! We should have been as ready as anybody! But the first bump in the road that came along, we were history!"

Elaine studied the marshal. "A bump in the road!?" she challenged. "I was told your wife left you after Brady's little brother died. You call that a 'bump in the road'?"

The marshal regarded the woman in silence. He turned his eyes away from her to look up at the ceiling and spoke through clenched teeth as he admitted, "No. It was more like smashing into a brick wall. It still hurts."

Elaine scooped up the still-growling Pansy and quieted her, then turned her attention to the laundry. The sooner she got the marshal's clothes washed and dried, the sooner he could be out of her house. Plopping the dog down by her dish, she pulled all of the sodden clothes from the washing machine, tossing the dark ones back into the unit to be rewashed while the lighter clothes dripped in the sink.

When she retraced her steps through the kitchen to the living room, she found the marshal seated on the couch, looking through the folder of Brady's pictures that had been used for the video. Elaine sat down in her chair and watched the man as he fingered the photo of the six-year-old Brady reaching over the edge of the hospital bed to give his little brother, Brendan, a kiss.

He hurts, too, Elaine realized. *He's not the unfeeling ogre I thought he was.*

Elaine softened and asked quietly. "How did he die?"

The marshal remained silent for so long, she wondered if he heard her. He eventually cleared his throat and spoke.

"He, uh...was born with a hole in his heart and only half his heart worked right. You might say the plumbing was all screwed up. Arteries that were supposed to go to the lungs went back to the heart instead so he could never get enough oxygen. They did surgery a couple times before he was a year old, but those were only temporary fixes. We knew Brendan's chances of survival were slim. When it came time for major surgery, his heart just wouldn't go on its own. They wheeled him out of the operating room with life support on him."

The marshal tossed the picture onto the table, then stood and walked to a nearby window. He stared outside for awhile before he continued.

"I ordered the doctors to take the machines off of him. He didn't have a chance at ever leading a normal life. Sarah fought me. She insisted they leave the machines on–that everyone had been praying for Brendan and God was going to heal him."

The marshal turned to fully face the woman who sat upright in the chair across the room from him.

"So help me, Elaine, I believed with everything in me that God could and would heal people. But He'd had three years and two months to do it. And I wasn't going to watch my little boy suffer one more day..."

Elaine noted the clenching of the marshal's jaw as he spoke of the gut-wrenching experience of making such a decision.

"Sarah...she wouldn't leave his side. She fought every doctor and nurse that came near him so they couldn't unplug the machines and let him go. One of the doctors got too close and she turned on him, hitting and pushing him away from Brendan. So I physically restrained her. I told her to say good-bye and hauled her kicking and fighting out of the room. She screamed that I was a murderer. That we were all murderers. We sedated her, and I took her home.

"We kept her sedated until after the funeral. Then I took her to our pastor so we could get counseling. It took several weeks, but she finally settled down. She became less vicious anyway. She was more patient with Brady and seemed more loving toward me than she'd been in months.

"I came home from work about midnight one night and there were lights on in the house. I was hoping she was waiting up for me with romance on her mind, but when I walked through the door, there she was–dressed to go. Her bags were packed, sitting by the door.

"The first thing I did was look around for Brady. She told me he was sleeping in his room and I went to check. She hadn't moved him or dressed him to go anywhere. A car pulled into the driveway and she put on her coat. She asked if she should be the one to tell Brady she was leaving. I told her, 'No. I'll do it.' She said she was going to go kiss him good-bye. I told her, 'Don't bother.' She didn't say another word. Just flung the door open, picked up her bags and left. She never looked back."

Elaine was saddened by the marshal's story. "And it was the pastor who took her away?" she asked.

"Yeah," the marshal said with a nod. "He left his wife and three kids."

Elaine considered not prompting the marshal for more information, yet she felt compelled to learn more of her new son-in-law's past. She asked further questions and the marshal answered them honestly, though at times reluctantly.

Bret made the decision to move away from Buffalo, Wyoming when he learned that Pastor Dan's wife intended to stay in town. One of Dan Rice's children was in Brady's class at school. Even though they were only in the first grade, their classmates said things that prompted Brady to fight. Bret got too many calls from the school to allow the situation to continue.

He finally realized the pent-up frustration within his son when he awoke one day to the smell of smoke. Brady had taken clothing from his mother's dresser and had torn her image from every picture in the photo album. He was burning them in the back yard, watching the flames intently as each item turned to ash. Too late, Bret found out what his son had done. Fearful that he would explode with anger at the boy, he went back to the house. When Brady came in some time later, he found his father sitting on the couch, sobbing. The boy put his arm around his father and said, "Cowboy up, Dad."

Bret took Brady to visit his Uncle Jubel. It was at the Sunday morning service in the church Jubel attended that Bret met the Knowltons, who extended an invitation for the little family to come to their home for dinner. Once the Knowltons learned of Bret's plight–his need for a new job, new home, and someone to care for Brady while he was at work–they took the little family under their wing. They suggested Bret look at a little place nearby that was for sale and offered to take care of his son during work hours. Brady was ecstatic about the arrangement. Not only were there six Knowlton children to play with, Beth didn't make food that tasted like paste or charcoal as his father tended to do.

Looking for work in close proximity to the Knowlton ranch was no easy task for a police officer. Bret continued to drive the long treacherous route over the mountain pass to work in Buffalo until he got a letter from the U.S. Marshals Service. He had applied for a position with them a few weeks after Brendan died and with the more recent turn of events had nearly forgotten about it. Now, he was a single parent who was struggling to secure a good, loving home for his son. Was he to uproot him again to go to work in Cheyenne?

He sat down at the kitchen table to draft a return letter explaining that he was thrilled to be considered but his circumstances had changed.

A curious young Brady asked what his father was doing. After Bret explained, Brady took it upon himself to call the Knowltons to tell them his dad wanted to be a U.S. Marshal and asked if he could stay with them while his dad was at work. He promised he would do his homework as he was told and would go to bed on time every night. He would help with chores, even if it meant he had to help the girls wash dishes.

The Knowltons agreed to take care of Brady as long as necessary if Bret was serious about such a pursuit. Bret told them he would think about it. "I was near thirty years old," the man explained, "with an opportunity to do something I had dreamed of for a long time. I looked at the Knowlton kids. They were a happy bunch. I wanted so much for Brady, and I knew I couldn't give it to him alone. I could keep a roof over our heads and clothes on our backs, but I knew I'd fall short in other areas. So I went to work for the Marshals Service and left Brady with the Knowltons. Until he went off to college, Brady stayed with them whenever I was away."

By the time the white shirt was done washing and the dark clothes were dry, Elaine had also learned of the changes in Brady's life during his second year of college. "Kicking over the traces" was how Bret described Brady's revolt as he and Elaine sat outside under a shade tree, brushing dried mud off Bret's hat and belt and boots.

Brady started running with a rambunctious crowd and his grades suffered. When he got into trouble for an accident on Black Mesa, Bret hired a good lawyer and left the judicial system to determine his son's guilt. In the end, justice was served and Brady was acquitted. Yet Brady accused his father of never believing in his innocence. In one heated argument, Brady accused the marshal of abandoning him.

For the next several years, the two men drifted apart. They kept in touch, but lived very separate lives. That all changed when Cassidy appeared on the scene. Brady asked for his father's help for the first time in years–not for himself, but for Cassidy. And Brady's entire attitude toward his father had recently changed. It seemed the good relationship they had enjoyed when Brady was young was slowly being restored.

During the course of the afternoon, Elaine shared some of her own problems when the marshal prompted her. She confessed that she knew as soon as Keith died she would not continue to farm the land. Jason insisted he wanted to run the place, but Elaine doubted his long-term commitment to such a venture. Had most of the crops not been planted before Keith died, she would have tried to rent the fields out. As it was, no one was prepared to commit financially to operating hundreds of acres of additional cropland at a moment's notice. She looked forward to the day all of the harvesting and marketing was done and the remaining cattle were sold. She was determined to keep things as normal as possible until she felt confident about moving on, but felt as if she were in a sinking boat being buffeted by increasingly huge waves.

"With God's help, I know I'll get through this, but I have never in my life felt so despondent and so confused," she admitted.

Elaine washed the few dishes that were dirtied at lunch and tidied the kitchen while her guest changed into his freshly laundered clothes. She eyed the man as he entered the room, checking for any stains that might have lingered on his white shirt. He assured the woman everything looked good as new.

The marshal picked up his hat from where it rested on the table and moved toward the front door.

"I thought maybe our kids would be back by now," he stated. "Bein' they're not, I'll get out of your way so you can get a good old-fashioned Sunday afternoon nap. You probably need that more than anything."

Elaine smiled a weak smile, acknowledging that she was indeed fatigued.

"Thanks for everything," the marshal said as he donned his hat. Without another word, he stepped out into the sultry afternoon air and strode to his vehicle.

As she watched the man leave, Elaine realized her outlook had changed drastically in the past couple of hours. Learning that Brady had been raised by a loving and moral Christian family had brought great relief to her. And hearing of his change of attitude toward his father gave Elaine hope that Brady's recent commitment to the Lord was truly sincere. She felt more hopeful than she had in the past several weeks that everything would work out for the best–for her and for Cassidy.

Lord, Elaine prayed in the silence of the old farmhouse, *thank you for the encouragement I received today. Isn't it just like You to use the most unexpected people and circumstances to answer our prayers? What started out as a horrible afternoon has finally begun to give me peace about Cassidy's marriage–the peace I asked You for. So now, Lord, instead of complaining, I'd like to rejoice with Cassidy for the loving husband she has found. I thank You for Brady. I thank You for their marriage. I thank You for the love they have found in one another…and in You.*

SEVENTEEN

Brady settled into an old routine to which he had become accustomed as a child. Little had changed since his days with the Knowltons, except the modernizing and upgrading of machinery to compensate for the lack of help when all the children grew up and moved away. The seasonal responsibilities remained the same. With winter fast approaching, Brady's weekdays were filled with moving, sorting, and shipping cattle–tasks that were aided by Pete and his son while Bud recuperated from foot surgery.

The job at the K Bar B was only temporary. Bud would soon be able to handle the ranching on his own again, relying on Pete's family for help in the busiest seasons. Still, Brady was grateful he had income and a roof over his head this late in the year. Best of all, he and Cassidy could work on the chores together while looking forward to the day they would run a ranch of their own.

Brady had worked alone most of the morning, for Cassidy was preparing to accompany Beth to a baby shower for the youngest of the Knowlton girls. With the urgent chores finished, he strode to the house, hoping to get a bite to eat before the women left. As usual, Beth was prepared for him and dished up his meal. Brady carried his plate to the table and ate alone as Beth bustled around the house, finishing last-minute tasks before her departure.

Cassidy bounded down the stairs, looking lovely in a light-weight pink sweater and a colorful skirt. Brady smiled at her personal style–make-up done perfectly, an outfit from a big city department store, and hair done in a casual, unhampered fashion.

Cassidy leaned over and kissed her husband before silently handing him an envelope. The insignia of the U.S. Marshals Service was immediately familiar. Brady checked the typing to make sure the letter was addressed to him and not to his father. With furrowed brow, he ripped the end of the envelope and extracted the papers inside.

Cassidy watched in silence as she awaited Brady's comments about the correspondence. He handed the papers to her to read for herself and resumed the consumption of his lunch, keeping his eyes on his plate as he did so.

"They're thanking you for the help you gave them," Cassidy observed, "and commending you on your thorough investigation…and they want you to work for them…."

Beth stepped from her bedroom door with wrapped gifts in hand and indicated it was time to go. Cassidy gathered up her gift and paused near her husband as Beth exited the house.

"Have a good time at the party, Honey," Brady said as he grabbed her hand and pulled her close for a kiss.

"Brady, what about the letter?" she whispered.

"Hon, don't even give that stupid letter another thought," he commanded. "You go have fun!" He kissed her and shooed her out the door.

The folded papers lay in a heap on the table. Brady tried to ignore them as he finished his lunch. He reached for the sheets once with the intention of throwing them away, but hesitated.

U.S. Marshal–a childhood dream he held until his run-in with the law. *Why would I want to be a marshal now?* he wondered. *Cassidy enjoys ranching and she's making friends here. How can I ask her to start over somewhere else?*

Brady cleared his dirty dishes from the table. Bringing them to the sink, he took the time to wash them and set them in the drain as he had been taught as a youngster. Being preoccupied with the contents of the letter, he hardly noticed when Bud drove into the yard until the alternate thumping of crutches and boots on the steps brought him to attention. He snatched up the correspondence, folded it, and stuffed it in the back pocket of his jeans before opening the door.

The limping man hobbled indoors and headed straight for his easy chair, where he propped up his throbbing foot on an ottoman. When asked if he'd had anything to eat, Bud assured Brady he had lunch before he drove to town. Brady questioned whether the drive had been more than Bud had bargained for and the older man admitted he was painfully paying the price for doing more than he should. After a few minutes of discussion about the cattle, Brady was about to go back to work when Bud stopped him.

"What's this I hear about you getting a letter from the Marshals Service?"

Brady wondered how Bud could have gotten wind of such a thing so quickly.

"I met the girls down the road," Bud admitted. "Cassidy told me."

"I told her not to worry about it…"

"Brady…"

"Bud, I'm not going to do it!" the young man insisted. "The letter came from the office in Las Vegas. I'm not even going to ask Cassidy to move there! Being a U.S. Marshal was just a stupid dream I had when I was a kid."

"It's a dream you had *since* you were a kid," Bud corrected him. "You folded it up and shoved it in your back pocket like you did with that letter. But it's still there and it's still attainable."

Brady shook his head. "I never told Cassidy I was planning on being a marshal…"

"Whatever you do, Brady, tell her now," Bud advised. "Don't just turn down the job, assuming it won't work out. Weigh things out and discuss them together before you decide whether to try it or drop it."

Brady sat down on the couch and considered the options. Bud began asking questions, which was his way of helping each of his children put things in perspective.

"Did you like being a private investigator?" he asked.

"You know I did."

"Why?"

Brady thought about the question and finally told Bud, "I liked the hunt. Looking for clues, following the trail, and in the end, finding that missing person or that crucial piece of evidence…"

Brady's voice trailed off. He stood and paced the room before he continued.

"Bud, I can't do it anymore! I swore I was going to change. You know full well where I was going for information. I've been in some of the worst hell-holes and rubbed elbows with some of the vilest people you could ever imagine. I have to put all that behind me."

Brady ran his fingers through his short cropped hair and stopped his pacing. He stared unseeingly out of the big picture window.

"I felt dirty at first, going into those places, but I told myself it was part of the job. After a while you get hardened to it. Sometimes I thought it was kinda like dancing just outside the gates of hell. I wondered if there would come a day when I'd misstep with my two-step and fall on in."

Bud eyed the young man in silence, as was his manner to contemplate serious matters before speaking.

"Son, I can see the change in you since you gave your life to Christ. I can't thank God enough for what he is doing in you. The scripture comes to mind that God wants to give us the desires of our hearts. I know this was once a desire of yours and when you finished the rest of your police training a couple years ago, I thought maybe you were finally going to do it. Can I give you some advice?" Bud asked.

Brady smiled and nodded; sound advice was what he needed.

"If the job threatens your relationship with Jesus Christ or with Cassidy, then you've got no business taking it. But if you feel like you've got a mission to serve justice with the Marshals Service, then you should do it. I suggest you call this man who wrote you the letter and have a talk with him about his expectations. Get a clear idea of what he has in mind. It may be a job that isn't going to pose a problem for you. Since the terrorist attacks on nine eleven, they need marshals for all kinds of jobs and some of them wouldn't threaten your convictions. If this is God's plan for you, you'll know it if everything works out."

The newlyweds entered the little country church that they had been attending since they got married. In his youth, Brady had been well acquainted with several of the members. Cassidy was getting to know those in the congregation besides the Knowlton family and Uncle Jubel. The young couple greeted several people as they moved to an empty pew and sat down.

The service began with an opening prayer, followed by an old, familiar hymn to which the congregation sang all four verses. When a second hymn was begun, Cassidy caught Brady checking the clock. They both knew it was not like Jubel to be late for church. The faintest of bird calls could be heard outside a slightly opened window, but no vehicles disturbed the still Sunday morning air.

As another verse was begun, Brady pulled his cell phone from his pocket and motioned to Cassidy that he was going outside. Instead of remaining where she was, she slipped out of the pew and followed her husband. She watched in silence as Brady dialed Jubel's number and let the phone ring numerous times.

"Cassidy, the Knowltons will give you a ride home. I'm going out to Jubel's…"

"I'm going with you," she told him firmly.

Brady placed his strong hands on his wife's shoulders. "Honey, I'm so scared of what I'm gonna find out there…" he argued.

"Then let me come with you," she pleaded.

Brady sighed. He took his wife's hands in his own and looked into her eyes. "This might be another rough ride for us."

"I know."

As they scurried toward their truck, Bud Knowlton and two other men emerged from the church. Bud hobbled as fast as he could, only half using his crutches as he approached the young couple.

"John and I will follow you out to Jubel's," Bud informed them. "Gary will get a couple guys together and have the ambulance ready, just in case."

The morning sun was high in the clear autumn sky as the pair of trucks approached Jubel's ranch house. In a flurry of dust, Brady screeched to a halt and emerged from the vehicle on a run toward the corral. He had already located his uncle, lying on his side under the fence with the old dog resting quietly beside him.

Brady talked softly to the dog as he crawled under the rail toward his uncle. "It's me, Toby," he assured the animal. "Come here, Boy." The big hound whimpered, but did not move from his position next to his master.

While Brady laid a hand on his uncle to check for a pulse, Toby remained silent and unmoving.

"He's alive!" Brady called to the others waiting anxiously nearby. Brady pulled his cell phone from his pocket and called for the ambulance while Cassidy ran to the house for blankets. From his position along the corral fence, Bud offered prayer for the injured man, thanking God that Jubel's life had been spared and asking for quick and complete recovery for the man.

The horse that was trapped in the enclosure stamped restlessly and pawed the ground at the sight of the newcomers. Brady fetched a rope from the barn and expertly dropped a loop over the head of the skittish animal. He secured one end of the rope around a post, leaving the nervous filly with little room to move but ensuring the safety of the men in the corral. Brady returned to Jubel's side where John had kneeled to examine him.

"What do you think, John?"

"I think if that dog wouldn't have stayed by him, he'd be suffering from hypothermia by now. It was downright chilly this morning and he's been layin' here awhile. It's a good thing he had his coat on. Besides the blow to the head, it seems to me his hip is busted up. I don't know about his back, so we'd best not move him."

Cassidy ran back to the house and returned to the corral a few minutes later toting a couple of small garbage bags tied tightly and filled with hot water. "Maybe these will help warm Jubel up," she ventured.

John eagerly grabbed the bags she offered and slipped them under the blankets next to the wounded man. The old hound must have felt confident that his master was in good hands. He rose stiffly, plodding behind Cassidy as she ran back to the house to produce more of the make-shift hot-water bottles.

By the time the emergency team arrived, Jubel's eyes had fluttered open and he was attempting to talk. Brady calmly assured him that everything would be all right as he knelt in the dust and held his uncle's hand. When the old man had been loaded carefully into the waiting ambulance, Brady glanced at Cassidy. The EMTs were about to close the back door.

"Go ahead and ride with him," she urged. "I'll close up the house and meet you at the hospital."

"Feed Toby!" Brady called as he leaped inside the waiting vehicle. The doors were shut behind him and the ambulance sped away.

Assuring Bud and John she knew where the hospital was, Cassidy watched John's truck retreat until a movement at the far side of the corral caught her eye. She sighed. Everyone had forgotten about the horse that was tethered to the post. Hiking her skirt up high above her knees, Cassidy climbed over the rails of the corral and leaped to the soft dirt inside the enclosure. She spoke quietly to the captured animal and moved slowly, inching her way toward the head of the nervous filly–a beautiful sorrel with golden red mane and tail, a wide white blaze on its face, and four white stockings.

After several patient minutes of petting the animal's neck, Cassidy ventured to remove the saddle, the bridle, and then the rope. Once it was freed, the horse cautiously backed away from her and trotted around the corral.

Cassidy hauled the gear out of the enclosure to place them in the barn. She fed the horse and drained the water-filled garbage bags into a tank from which the horse drank thirstily until it had its fill.

With the horse taken care of, Cassidy turned her attention to Toby, who had been meekly pacing outside the corral. She spent several minutes with the hound, scratching him behind the ears and telling him what a good dog he was. As she did this, she studied the vast and beautiful landscape around her. The striped ridges amazed her. Their colorful layers were marked with centuries of erosion from wind and rain that scarred the surface of the rock but left protective pockets where meager vegetation grasped for a foothold. *What a fantastic place,* she thought. *How it must break Jubel's heart to leave in such pain.*

Cassidy checked the home, making mental notes of what needed to be tended to in Jubel's absence–the food in the refrigerator that would spoil and the leaky sink in the bathroom that dripped water into a bucket. With the immediate chores done, she said good-bye to Toby and climbed into Brady's truck. Driving down the long length of the dusty road, she paused beyond the imposing gate to look back at the scene once more.

Tall poles held a weathered sign that arched across the gravel drive–a sign depicting shadowed horses and horsemen on either side of the ranch's brand, a stylized JP with horizontal wavy lines on either side. Framed behind the arch, the noonday sun brightened high, steep ridges that were like fortress walls of protection, dwarfing the ranch buildings and ancient, gnarled trees at their base.

I know why Brady loves this place, Cassidy told herself. *And now, just when his job at the Knowlton's is soon to come to an end, God is providing another responsibility for us. We may have to stay here for a long time. Maybe that's Brady's answer about the job offer in Nevada.*

Cassidy headed for town, excited about the possibilities in store for her and her husband.

By the time his wife arrived at the hospital, Brady was pacing the floor, wondering as much about what was keeping her so long at the ranch as he was about the extent of Jubel's injuries. He breathed a sigh of relief at the sight of Cassidy and reprimanded her for worrying him. She quietly reminded him he had left a horse unattended, still saddled and bridled, with no access to food or water. She had fed Toby as she had been asked, then emptied an overflowing bucket of water from under a leaky sink and mopped up the bathroom floor. Showing amazement at her capabilities, Cassidy pointed out, "Brady, I'm a farm girl. I can figure out what to do."

Brady smiled and hugged his wife close, teasing her that he could smell the odors of horse and hay on her dress. She returned the favor by pointing out the patches of dust on the knees of his best jeans and shirt. Light-hearted banter continued until a nurse stepped from the emergency room and drew their attention, offering to let the couple visit Jubel for a few minutes.

The old man had been given pain medication. He appeared groggy, but was conscious. The doctor explained that Jubel's hip was broken and would have to be pinned back together. No broken bones were found in his back or legs, but they were severely bruised. The injury to his head was superficial, requiring a few stitches, but no skull fracture was found.

The medical personnel left the young couple alone with Jubel, who showed his cantankerous side as soon as they were alone together.

"Did you shoot that fool horse for me?" he growled at Brady.

"No, I didn't shoot your horse. I left her snubbed to a post. But my wife took pity on her and turned her loose in the corral. She even fed and watered her," Brady answered with a grin.

"What's her name?" Cassidy asked.

"Stupid!" barked the old man. "S'posed to be from good stock. I'd like to know what kind of stallion jumped the fence to create an idiot beast like that! To think I've been callin' her 'Fancy.' 'Flighty' is more like it. She did good the last few days, so I figured to put her through her paces again this morning. What does she do? Bolts and kicks at a jackrabbit that cuts through the corral!"

Brady and Cassidy exchanged glances as they laughed discreetly at the old man's tirade.

"You know what?" Brady asked Cassidy. "I think Uncle Jubel's pride is hurt as bad as his hip. He's been training horses his whole life, and he doesn't usually run into one he can't handle."

"I can handle her just fine!" Jubel argued. "As soon as the doc gets me bolted back together, that little filly is gonna learn some manners!"

The hospital staff waited until Marshal Hollister arrived from Cheyenne before they called the small family together to discuss their patient's prognosis. As Jubel's closest living relative, the marshal needed to be informed that his uncle would require therapy for many weeks to come. It was recommended he be put in the nearby nursing home so he could be given the care he needed.

The marshal shook his head. "I guarantee Jubel will fight tooth and nail if you so much as mention the words 'nursing home' to him. He'll go back to that ranch if he has to crawl there on his hands and knees."

"He needs care, Bret," the doctor insisted. "He cannot take care of himself, no matter how independent he wants to be…"

"I can take care of him," Cassidy blurted. All eyes turned to the young woman who had been listening in silence. "I worked in a nursing home for a while after high school. I know I could learn to help with his therapy…"

Cassidy hesitated. She looked over at Brady and confessed, "I wasn't thinking about your job…" *I was thinking about myself,* she silently admitted. *I want to stay on the ranch.*

"Don't worry about the job offer, Cassidy. This is more important at the moment. Do you really think you want to tackle something like this?"

Cassidy assured Brady and his father that she would like to try. If it didn't work out, other arrangements could be considered later. In the least, the prospect of Jubel being able to go home would certainly encourage him.

Discussion turned to what needed to be done to ready the ranch house for an invalid. By the end of the meeting, the hospital staff was confident they could release Jubel to Cassidy's care once his home was made ready. Brady and Cassidy left the hospital with a long list of tasks, the first of which was to find a carpenter to help them with their remodeling needs. Within minutes, Brady had gotten a recommendation from Bud Knowlton and was on the line with a local semi-retired handyman who promised to be at Jubel's place early the next morning. Brady ended the call and smiled at Cassidy.

"Looks like you got yourself a job, Cass," he said. "Tomorrow morning you get to tell the carpenter what needs to be done to the house. As soon as he gets the supplies together, the two of you can start the work."

"You're not going to help us?" she asked.

"I've gotta help Bud! We've still got cattle to round up and move down from the mountains to winter pasture. It's gonna be several days before I can get to Jubel's to help you with anything."

Cassidy was disappointed. She would be missing the huge round-up on the Knowlton ranch that always included mountains of food for the hungry crew and traditional campfire entertainment in the evenings. She suddenly realized that Jubel's cattle would have to be brought down from the mountains also.

"Who helps with the round-up at Jubel's?" she questioned.

"I reckon you and I are stuck with it," Brady said with a grin. "Don't worry. Jubel doesn't keep more'n a couple hundred head around the place anymore. We can handle it."

The marshal drove into the yard with an elated Jubel, who flung the passenger side door open and called for Toby as soon as the vehicle rolled to a stop. The old dog trotted toward the marshal's SUV, placing its front paws on the newly installed step. Resting its gray muzzle gently on its master's lap, the hound stood quietly as Jubel petted it until the wheelchair was unloaded and brought to him.

Cassidy helped to swing Jubel's legs over the side of the seat and ease his feet to the ground. From there, he had plenty of strength in his arms to lower himself into the wheelchair as the marshal steadied it from behind. With Toby plodding alongside, Jubel was wheeled across the gravelly drive and up the newly-built wooden ramp. Cassidy waited anxiously as she held the door open, wondering what Jubel's reaction would be when he saw what she had done to his home.

The old man's eyes scanned the place from one room to another as Bret gave him a tour. Not only was the house cleaned more thoroughly than it had been in recent years, much of the furniture had been moved or taken out to allow easy access through the rooms. Scatter rugs had been removed to ensure unhampered movement. Brighter lights had been installed. The short hallway that led to the two bedrooms at the back of the house now sported a hand rail, as did the bathroom. The marshal paused in the doorway of the bathroom as Jubel studied the taller toilet and the roomy shower that had replaced the deep old-fashioned claw-foot bathtub.

"What do you think, Jubel?" the marshal asked. "Are you and Cassidy going to be able to manage?"

Jubel's answer was as touching as it was unexpected. He reached for his young nursemaid's hand. Grasping it in his own rough one, he patted it gently as a couple of silent tears trickled down his cheeks.

EIGHTEEN

Ominous gray skies hovered over the snow-crusted mountain tops and a bone-chilling wind swirled around the ranch buildings as Cassidy fed Fancy inside the barn. Once the wily old horse-trainer learned of Cassidy's interest in the perky sorrel filly, it quickly became routine for Jubel to venture to the corral each day with his walker. Sitting on a chair outside the fence, he would coach Cassidy as she trained the horse. Eventually, she felt confident enough to take Fancy out of the corral, where horse and rider paraded in front of the gnarled trainer for workout instructions. Today, however, the biting wind and intermittent snow was postponing the show.

Brady will be here tomorrow, Cassidy thought as she gave the horse a final pat on the head. *We've got to get those cattle down from the hills before they're snowed in. I wonder if Fancy will help with the job.*

Cassidy spent most of the morning baking bread and preparing a dessert while a hearty stew simmered on the stove. As she worked in the kitchen, she noticed several times that Jubel shuffled with his walker to the window that faced the pasture, straining to see if the cattle were drifting down from the hills above.

Cassidy gathered her heavy winter clothes from the closet. "Jubel, how do you feed hay to the cattle?" she asked.

"The tractor in the shed," he answered, still staring out the window. "But the gate isn't open to let them down into the lower pasture. I wish Brady would hurry up and get here."

"How far away is the gate?" Cassidy asked.

Jubel turned to her then, suddenly realizing what she intended to do. He studied her in silence as if determining whether he should allow her to venture out into the gale or leave the cattle to fend for themselves until his nephew arrived.

"Jubel, can I drive there in the truck or do I have to go by horseback to open the gate?" Cassidy inquired.

"The trail past the barn," Jubel answered. "There's a truck track that follows the fence on the right. The gate's about a half mile from the big corner post."

Cassidy gave Jubel strict instructions not to venture outdoors while she was gone, then donned her heavy coat, gloves, boots, scarf, and stocking cap. Through the biting late-October wind, she trudged toward the shed and fought to tie the creaky door open so the truck could be backed out. Increasingly heavier snow drifted past the windshield as the young woman put the truck in four-wheel-drive and followed the faint outline of a track that led to the pasture gate.

By the time Cassidy had worked the gate open and returned to the ranch buildings, the snow was accumulating so quickly she could hardly see the tracks she had made a short time before. Instead of rushing back to the house after returning the truck to the shed, she climbed onto Jubel's tractor. It took a few minutes in the dim light of the building to figure out how to start the engine, shift the tractor, and maneuver the bale fork that would carry the hay. She knew Jubel might be concerned as she backed the tractor from the shed, but she didn't relent. She was going to try to haul some hay.

Slowly, cautiously, Cassidy lifted a thousand-pound hay bale from the huge stack with the bale fork, backed the tractor from the pile, and hauled the bale to the lower pasture. After two more trips, she returned the tractor to the shed. As she pushed the huge door shut, she heard the faint bellowing of cattle. Even above the whistling of the wind, the animals must have recognized the sound of the tractor and come running, hopeful that food was being served. She peered through the falling snow at the dark figures of the beef cattle that emerged from the brushy hills and wondered if Brady would be surprised at what she had done.

By the time the rosy-cheeked, snow-covered young woman made her way to the house, Jubel had been busy in the kitchen for some time. Anticipating that she would be ready for a good, hot meal when she returned, he had dishes placed on the table, bread sliced and stacked on a plate on the counter, and a fresh pot of hot coffee waiting to be poured.

The surprise on Cassidy's face must have showed. Jubel grinned sheepishly and apologized for not putting the food on the table. "Hard enough gettin' the plates over there with two hands on my walker," he explained. "Could only carry one at a time."

Cassidy grinned at her elderly patient and set the food on the table. When everything was ready, she took her seat and bowed her head, waiting for Jubel to say a prayer, as was their custom. Today, Jubel didn't merely ask for blessings on the food as he usually did. He thanked God for keeping Cassidy safe as she drove over the uneven terrain of the pasture and he thanked God for sending her to help him.

When Jubel finished the prayer with an "Amen," they looked at one another through eyes glistening with unshed tears. Cassidy realized that she enjoyed living here on the ranch with Jubel. Though he projected an outwardly gruff manner, he was uncomplaining and grateful, a patient teacher, a good listener, and an encourager. She felt she would be totally content here as soon as Brady came to join them.

Waking before sunrise, Cassidy tiptoed quietly to the kitchen to start breakfast and found Jubel at the living room window, straining to see the herd of cattle in the dim predawn light.

"Is something wrong?" she asked without offering the usual "Good morning."

"Just tryin' to count heads," Jubel answered. He turned away from the large window without further comment.

Breakfast was scarcely finished before he headed back toward the window. With his binoculars, he studied the high slopes, blanketed in several inches of fresh, glistening snow. He checked again the herd in the lower pasture, whose few inches of fluffy snow were already beginning to dissipate into white patches under bright rays of sunlight.

"How many cattle are missing, Jubel?" Cassidy asked.

He lowered the binoculars and turned to his nurse with a smile. "Thirty or forty," he admitted. "Kinda hard to tell from here. Brady should be here soon. That will be a good job for him, rounding up strays."

Cassidy washed the breakfast dishes and cleaned the kitchen before donning her winter clothes to do the outside chores. She was surprised when she stepped from the house at the warmer temperature the day offered. The air was still chilly and the wind raw, but it was a sharp contrast to the frigid temperatures of the previous day. She was immediately tempted to saddle Fancy and ride to the upper slopes to check for more cattle. Instead, she determined to ride through the herd in the lower pasture to count heads.

The ground beneath Fancy's feet was slippery as Cassidy walked the horse around the perimeter of the herd of cattle that munched contentedly on the hay she had provided for them. Leaving the herd behind, she rode to the house to report to Jubel the number of cattle in the pasture. It was as he suspected–around thirty were missing. And Brady had called to tell them the mountain pass was not yet plowed out. It might be some time before he would get to the ranch. After assuring Jubel she would be careful and that she wouldn't get lost, Cassidy remounted Fancy. Heading through the gate, she urged the horse up the long slope.

The going was fairly easy at first. Fancy stepped energetically through the carpet of snow, undeterred by the steady uphill climb. After nearly a half hour, however, the horse was plunging through drifts that were several inches deep. Cassidy reined in the filly to let her rest as she studied the terrain above. With numerous ravines crisscrossing the slopes, Cassidy had no idea where to start looking for the stray animals. She frequently checked the sky overhead to be sure no clouds were moving in that might bring more snow, trapping her in the hills. Seeing nothing but blue sky above, Cassidy continued forward, letting the horse choose the path.

Fancy seemed to sense the mission. The horse stopped frequently, raised its head, and tipped its ears forward as if listening and watching for a sign of life. Cassidy knew the cattle were found when Fancy stopped halfway through a snowdrift to whinny. A couple of cows answered back, affirming their location near a cut in a sharply rising cliff.

A snowdrift that reached nearly up to Fancy's belly had boxed the cattle into a corner. Reluctant to plunge through the pile, they huddled in a tight pack at the base of steep canyon walls. The filly pawed at the deep pack of snow while Cassidy considered her options. Before she could decide whether she should dismount or not, Fancy opted to lunge forward. Cassidy held on tight as the horse plunged into the drift, leaping over mounds of snow until it emerged on the other side within a few feet of the pent-up cattle.

The cows needed no urging. They skirted around the horse and plunged single-file down the newly cut trail that had fenced them in. One by one, cows and calves fought through the deep snow to follow the horse's track down the slope.

Cassidy kept a tight rein on Fancy, who was impatient to hurry the cattle toward home. Unexpectedly, a wayward calf balked at taking the well-trodden trail. It turned to run back to the shelter of the brush from which it had come. Without warning, Fancy lurched after the calf. Cassidy had casually rested her hand on the saddle horn. Grasping it was the only thing that kept the horse from running out from under her. She held on with both hands as Fancy faced the calf, forbidding it to return to the brush. When the calf tried to dodge to its right, Fancy was there. The calf bolted in the opposite direction to find Fancy once again in its path. Unconvinced, the calf tried to skirt around the horse one more time, to no avail. It finally turned down the beaten path and ran to catch up to the herd.

Cassidy breathed a sigh of relief as she watched the cattle retreat. She was shaken yet exhilarated and her heart pounded. *I've never had such a wild ride in my life!* she thought. *I wonder if this is how Brady feels when he's riding bulls.* As Cassidy urged Fancy along the trail, she said to herself, "I can hardly believe I stayed on this horse. Jubel must be praying for me."

Brady pulled into the yard with his mud-spattered truck and watched the long string of cattle make its way down the slope with Cassidy and Fancy trailing behind them. As the skies darkened and light snow began drifting on the wind, he stepped out of the vehicle and waited inside the doorway of the barn as Cassidy slipped from the saddle and slid to the ground. Leaving Fancy to stand in the corral, she ran to greet her husband, planting a cold, wet kiss on his face. Brady hugged her close for a moment before pushing her away at arm's length.

"You worry me so bad, Girl," he said with a shake of his head. "You shouldn't be out in this weather tending cattle."

"Brady, I'm from Wisconsin," Cassidy pointed out with a laugh. "I'm not afraid of snow."

"Cass, it's not just the snow!" Brady argued. "You're riding a horse that threw Jubel just a few weeks ago! You're up in the foothills where you have no idea what kind of weather is going to come at you from over the mountain. You could be in a blizzard within minutes! How would you find your way back to the ranch if you couldn't see where you were going?"

"Ride downhill?" she ventured.

Brady showed the exasperation that he felt. "You're not taking me one bit serious!" he reprimanded. "You could get yourself killed!"

"But I didn't," Cassidy defended. "And now you're home, so everything is okay."

She stepped toward her husband and hugged him close, resting her head on the front of his heavy coat. With a deep sigh, he wrapped his arms around her, returning her embrace in a fiercely tight hug.

After holding one another for a minute, Cassidy lifted her head and looked up into her husband's eyes. "I'm sorry I worried you," she apologized. "I was just doing what I thought needed to be done, like every other rancher does."

"I know," Brady confessed. "But one of the things that makes me most proud of you also scares me the most. You see something that needs to be done, you seem to find a way to do it."

"So, why does that scare you?" Cassidy wondered aloud.

"Because you don't need me," Brady whispered.

Cassidy pouted. "That's not true! I didn't want to take care of everything by myself! I wanted you here with me!"

Brady kissed Cassidy's rosy cheeks, then drew her close and kissed her passionately. She returned the affection, clinging to Brady as tightly as her thick winter coat would allow.

Releasing one another, Brady traced the outline of Cassidy's jaw with his gloved hand. "It's okay that you don't need me," he teased, displaying the hint of a smile that lifted one corner of his mouth. "It's enough that you want me."

With another quick kiss planted on Cassidy's forehead, Brady retrieved the horse his wife had been riding. Leading Fancy into the barn, he stripped the saddle and blanket from her back while Cassidy fetched a generous scoop of grain and an armful of hay. Brady rubbed down the horse's damp coat while Cassidy strewed fresh bedding on the floor. Once Fancy was secured in the stall, the barn doors were latched tightly shut against the rising wind and the young couple walked hand in hand toward the house.

"Why do you always do that to me?" Cassidy challenged Brady in a voice loud enough to carry above the cry of the wind.

"Do what?" he asked.

"You get me mad or upset, then you turn around and kiss me or say something nice or do something nice and you don't let me stay mad at you."

Brady laughed at her as they stepped up the ramp onto the porch. "So…you have a problem with that?" he teased.

He reached to draw his wife close for one more lingering kiss before they stepped inside the house. As the pair embraced, the front door creaked open and Jubel stood in the bright light, leaning on his walker with one hand as he held the door with the other.

"You got a bedroom at the back of the house. You don't have to stand out in a blizzard to do that," he reprimanded the young couple.

Without another word, the old man shuffled to the living room and sat down in his favorite chair. Grabbing the remote control from the end table, he turned the sound of the television to near deafening volume while Brady led his wife down the hall.

Cassidy's eyes fluttered open and she turned her face in time to catch Brady watching her. Closing her eyes again, she snuggled closer under his arm, then suddenly pushed herself up from the bed to look at the clock.

"Look what time it is!" she exclaimed. "I've got to start supper! I can't believe I fell asleep in the middle of the day!"

She started to rise, but Brady held her in his strong arms.

"Cass?" he whispered. "We've got to talk."

She sensed he had something serious on his mind. Something he was struggling with.

"Do you remember Tim Sykes, the deputy who was working with Dad? He transferred to Nevada. Tim recommended me to his boss and that's where the job offer came from. Tim found references and a picture in my notes about a guy they think has killed several people. He thinks if I found him before, maybe I can find him again."

Cassidy eyed her husband. "You're going to do it, aren't you?" she asked with a growing sense of dread.

Brady sighed deeply. "Cass, I just can't shake it. I've thought about it. I've prayed about it. I've asked God how He could let something like this happen. If I had an opportunity like this before you came along, I'd a snapped up this challenge in a heartbeat!"

Cassidy remained stubbornly silent, offering no comment, for it seemed Brady was blaming her for keeping him tied down on a ranch in Wyoming when there were more exciting places for him to be.

"Cass, I know you love the ranch, but…" Brady faltered as he tried to explain himself.

"How soon do we leave?" she interrupted.

"Cass, the marshal's training takes weeks. You're needed here and there's nothing for you to do in Georgia…"

Cassidy pushed her husband away and rose from the bed. *He's not even asking me to go with him!* she raged inwardly. Her hands shook as she quickly dressed in silence. She avoided Brady's eyes until she was gone from the room. *How can he do this to us?* she accused under her breath as she marched toward the kitchen. *He acts like he's so in love with me, yet he's leaving! I've given up everything to be with him! I've done everything I know how and he's not content to stay with me!* She choked back a sob so Jubel wouldn't detect her distress.

As Cassidy worked at preparing a meal, Brady joined his uncle in the living room.

"What does the doctor say about you, Jubel?" he asked as he sat down.

"My nurse is takin' good care of me," Jubel said with a broad grin. "I'm comin' along better than they expected."

"But it will be awhile before you're up and around on your own?" Brady prodded.

"I reckon. What you got in mind?" the old man asked suspiciously. "You hankerin' to run away with my nursemaid?"

"No," Brady answered with a shake of his head. "I'm hoping she can stay here while I'm taking the Marshals Service training. I'll be gone for several weeks."

Jubel's brow furrowed as he digested the news. He eyed Cassidy as she busied herself at the stove. She listened intently to the conversation in the next room and glared occasionally at the duo as they discussed her future.

"Cassidy okay with it?"

"Not exactly."

"Then why you doin' it?" the old man bluntly demanded.

"Gut feeling that I can help track down a fugitive that's slipped by everyone else," Brady stated. "And besides that, Jubel, it's a job. I need to make a living. Bud doesn't need my help any more, and I'll never get this place paid for just by ranching. You and I both know that."

"What about your bull riding?" Jubel posed the question.

Brady shook his head. "The best part about riding bulls anymore is the massages I get from my wife after I'm done. I'll always love doin' it, but I'm thirty-two years old, Jubel! I may never get into the big prize money again."

Jubel sat in silence for a time, rubbing his beard-stubbled jaw as he studied his nephew. "A man's gotta do what a man's gotta do," was the old man's decision. "Don't you worry about Cassidy. She's got a place to stay as long as she wants. She can stay forever if she can stand it. Between me and the cows and the horses, I reckon we can keep her outta mischief until you get back. And I've got enough doctor appointments, we'll have her back in civilization every week or two, whether she needs it or not."

Brady smiled at the old man. He patted Jubel on the back as he rose from his chair and strode toward the kitchen where he asked Cassidy if she would like help with anything. She merely shrugged.

"You know I don't want to make you unhappy, Cass," he said with a deep sigh. "If you tell me to stay, I will. I'll forget the whole thing."

"You'll stay if I beg you to stay, but you'll never forget about it. You might as well just plan on going and getting it out of your system."

"Not until you're okay with it."

Cassidy kept her eyes averted from her husband as she moved from cupboard to table with a stack of dishes. Brady leaned against a nearby counter and watched her work.

"You want me, but you don't need me," he reminded her with his sly sideways grin.

"And you don't seem to need me!" Cassidy blurted. Tears stung her eyes as she blindly moved about the kitchen.

"What can I do to convince you otherwise, Cass?"

"I feel like…I must be boring to you or something! Like you have to get back to your big city street life…or maybe there's a woman you've got to see…"

Cassidy knew as soon as the words were out of her mouth that she had hurt her husband deeply. The shock and sadness on his face were unmistakable. She bit her trembling lip, but refused to apologize.

Brady took several steps around the small room and breathed deeply before replying to her accusation.

"Cassidy, I can't believe you'd accuse me of such a thing!" he defended. "I love you! You're the only woman I love!"

"Son!" Jubel interrupted as he shuffled toward the young couple with his walker. "I'm not one to stick my nose in any man's business, but Cassidy has questions that need answering. Don't leave things to her imagination. If you haven't told her what this job is going to require, then you'd best level with her."

Brady studied Cassidy's face as he spoke quietly. "You know what kind of crap I was into before we met, Cass," he reminded her. "I told you everything before we got married. Everything!"

Cassidy remained silent.

"I'm not the same man I was before I met you, Cassidy! I swear there's nothing that can make me go back to that old life! But I like being a detective and I have a chance to be one for the Marshals Service!"

Cassidy stopped stirring the food and faced her husband. More than anything in the world, she wanted to believe him. Searching his face, she detected sadness rather than absolute resolve to do what he wanted. *This is tearing him up inside,* she admitted to herself. *But Lord, I'm so afraid to let him go....*

"Supper's burning!" Jubel cried as boiling water spilled over the sides of the pot and sizzled on the stove. Cassidy spun around and turned her attention back to the meal. She scarcely had things under control when the phone rang. Brady answered it.

"Cass, it's your mother!" he announced.

Instead of asking Elaine to call back after they finished supper, Brady conversed about the terrible weather they were having and told her about the job he had been offered. By the time Cassidy had finished preparing the meal and setting it on the table, Brady had divulged most of the couple's latest news, including Cassidy's misgivings about him going to work for the Marshals Service.

Why not just tell her we've been fighting, Cassidy fumed in silence. *Just tell her we've got a huge marital problem right now.* She motioned for the men to sit down and eat as she took the portable phone from Brady's hand. As Jubel led in prayer over the meal, Cassidy picked up the conversation where her husband left off, walking down the hallway toward the bedroom so she could speak to her mother in private.

"The way Brady talks, you're not too happy with him taking this job," Elaine observed. "Is it a dangerous one?"

"Yes! They want him to track down a murderer. There are all kinds of people working for the Marshals Service. I don't see why they need Brady..."

"Cassidy," Elaine interrupted, "what was he doing for a living when you met him?"

Cassidy didn't answer so Elaine posed another question. "What did you expect him to do for a living once you were married? Were you so infatuated with one another that you didn't discuss the future?"

"He said he wanted to settle down on the ranch someday," Cassidy defended.

"Someday. Apparently, 'someday' hasn't come yet. It probably won't come until he's busted up from his bull riding or sick and tired of chasing crooks. You should be happy that he'll have other people to work with instead of hunting criminals on his own like he used to."

"I never thought of that," Cassidy admitted quietly.

"Cassie, if he likes that kind of work and he's good at it, then don't try to convince him to do something he's not going to be happy with. You'll both end up miserable."

"But, Mom! Is it right for him to be going into casinos and bars and strip joints and every other kind of sleezy place to hunt criminals down? Why does he think he can do that and still call himself a Christian?" Cassidy argued.

"Don't use Christianity as an excuse to try to manipulate your husband into doing things your way, Cassidy!" Elaine warned sternly, then softened her manner. "Did you ever consider that he is doing this *because* he is a Christian? For the same reason that some people go to war. They know in their hearts they can make a difference to someone, somewhere. They may not like the circumstances, but they know there is a job to be done, so they go.

"Cassidy, he's competitive, he's a thrill-seeker and a risk-taker. You can't change that in him and it's not your job to change him. If he has truly given his heart to the Lord, the Holy Spirit will change what needs to be changed from the inside."

As tears stung her eyes, Cassidy asked her mother if she could call back later. Before she hung up the phone, Elaine gave the young woman one more piece of advice.

"You were the beautiful princess who married the daring knight in shining armor who rescued you, Cassidy. Now the end of this fairy tale is up to you. If you try to keep him locked up in your castle, he'll find a way out. Let him go...and give him good reason to want to come back home."

Sitting at the bedroom window, Cassidy stared into the darkness as she considered her life with Brady in the past few months since their marriage. Brady's temporary ranch job gave them income and a home until Jubel got hurt. Now, with Jubel's need for a helper, Cassidy had a place to stay and work to keep her busy while Brady was away. She suddenly recalled the day at the rodeo in Red Lodge when she was sitting next to the marshals as they scanned Brady's notes and discussed a fourteen-year-old runaway girl he had encountered. Cassidy learned later that the girl had been reunited with her family because Brady had alerted authorities.

'They know in their hearts they can make a difference to someone, somewhere,' Cassidy recalled her mother's words. *Is that what he's feeling, Lord? Is it a prompting from You? If so, Lord, what are you doing to us? I really believe You brought us together. Why are You separating us again?*

Cassidy prayed an earnest prayer. As she talked to God, a scripture from Proverbs that she had memorized years earlier came to mind. "Trust in the Lord with all your heart, and lean not on your own understanding; in all your ways acknowledge Him, and He shall direct your paths."

Trust. I don't trust him, Lord, Cassidy confessed in the silence of the dark room. *I'm not as worried about the job as I am about Brady's ability to resist the temptations that lured him in the past. And when I don't trust him...that means I don't really trust You to keep him under Your guidance....*

After several minutes of soul searching, Cassidy came to a hard realization. *The real decision is not whether Brady should go or stay,* she decided. *It's whether I'm going to put to work my faith in Jesus Christ or keep giving it lip service. If my faith is to be real, then I've got to show it. Brady is shouldering the responsibility for our financial welfare and the Scripture tells me to be his helpmate. Lord, help me make things right with him....*

Cassidy rose from her seat and dried her eyes. With new resolve, she walked toward the kitchen where Brady was just about to clean his dirty dishes from the table.

"There's pie in the refrigerator!" she blurted, then added in a softer tone, "I hope you saved room for it."

Brady flashed his easy, crooked smile and said, "I reckon I can choke down a piece of pie."

He opened the refrigerator, telling Cassidy he would dish up the dessert while she ate her supper, and served a thick slice of lemon meringue pie to each of them before returning to his seat at the table.

After sampling a few bites, Brady turned to Jubel and asked, "You eat good food like this every day?"

"Why d'ya think I've gained fifteen pounds?"

Cassidy looked up and caught Brady staring at her.

"I didn't even know you could cook," he admitted sheepishly.

"Brady!" she reprimanded him. "I helped Beth with lots of meals while we were at Knowlton's!"

"Well, it was so good, I thought Beth made it all!" he defended.

Cassidy laughed at her husband with a throaty giggle that eased her tension. She looked at Brady hopefully as he returned her gaze from across the table.

"You just got a mighty fine compliment," Jubel pointed out to Cassidy. "There ain't nobody in the country can cook better'n Beth Knowlton."

Jubel finished the last of his pie and pushed back his chair, savoring the final sips of his coffee. Turning to Brady he said, "I don't understand how you could up and marry a girl without even finding out first if she can cook."

Brady kept his eyes on Cassidy as he addressed his uncle. "To tell you the truth, she surprises me every day. I never know what she's gonna do next, but I'm finding out she can do most everything she sets her mind to. In fact, I was just teasing her a while ago that she doesn't need me, she just wants me."

Jubel rose from the table and reached for his walker. "Nothin' wrong with that," he said with a smile as he headed for the living room.

NINETEEN

Brady paused in front of the lifeless building. Neon lights no longer flashed overhead, beckoning passersby into the club that had featured exotic dancers and scantily clad waitresses. Trent Dominic's allies were no longer using the place to dispense shipments of illegal drugs or launder money, peddle stolen merchandise, or trade in human lives.

Brady remembered the first time he had stepped through the doors of the establishment. Never before had he ventured into a world of such blatant pornography, but he had been hired by a woman to find out where her husband was spending his time. He spotted the man, noting the key that was slipped to him and the way he sauntered through a side door. Brady had all the information he needed. As he turned to go, he nearly collided with Trent Dominic who didn't even notice his old college buddy, so intent was he on parading around the room greeting dancers and waitresses by name. Brady quickly slipped into a seat near the end of the bar, keeping several customers between him and Dominic, being as inconspicuous as possible while observing his enemy. He watched as Dominic was greeted warmly by a very shapely, rather elegant woman who stepped out from the back room. She quickly led him away through the door in which she had come.

A man next to Brady wondered aloud how much money Dominic spent in the place to get royal treatment from Lola herself. Another informed those around him the man was in cahoots with the owners of the place. Brady acted as if he was scarcely interested in the discussion, but his mind processed every scrap of information. Gradually joining the conversation, he asked if Lola was a waitress or dancer. One of the men answered sarcastically, "No, she's a school marm!" The others laughed at the remark and the man added, "She teaches all the young ladies their tricks."

Though Brady found his companions' language vulgar and their leering stares disgusting, he bought a round of drinks for them. Plying them with questions, he learned a great deal about the club, its owners, the clientele, and rumored illegal activities. Thus began his pursuit of Trent Dominic.

He had returned to the place several times–sometimes going inside, sometimes snooping outside at different hours of the day. Noting who came and went. Amassing computer discs full of notes and photos, he raised a lot of questions he had no answers for.

The whole picture started coming together when he followed Kenny Chite from Reno to Wyoming–first to Dominic's ranch, then to Lone Pine. There, he met Cassidy and everything changed. Within a week, the club was shut down and boarded up–its patrons scattered, its owners arrested, and its contents seized by the government.

The thought of Cassidy made Brady's heart ache. He had given her the option of relocating to Nevada with him and hiring someone else to stay with Jubel or staying on the ranch. Her decision was quick. She would stay on the ranch where she was needed rather than sit in a lonely house in Reno wondering each night when her husband would come home. There was no denying that Cassidy enjoyed the ranch. He could hear the excitement in her voice every time she told him over the phone about Jubel's progress and how well the livestock were fairing.

Brady found it ironic that he had been the one to accept the job challenge despite Cassidy's misgivings, yet she was the one remaining cheerful while he grew more discouraged each day. *I miss her,* he lamented. *But I needed work and I wanted this job. Now I'm on the cold, cold trail of a cold-blooded killer. Will more people die before I catch this guy?*

As Brady strolled down the street, he recalled the last night he and Cassidy spent together before he began his training for the Marshals Service. The young couple had been airing their concerns and wondering how they would cope with being separated for several weeks when Jubel went to his room and came back with a small green New Testament that had been given to him during the Korean War. In a touching moment, he presented the book to Brady and counseled both of the young people to use their time apart to become more diligent in studying the Word of God. It was a piece of advice Brady took to heart and he had been setting aside time each day to read a portion of the little Bible.

Brady reflected on the prayer time that followed. Having lived alone for many years, Jubel was rather shy about voicing his words with the Lord in front of anyone, but he spoke with God as if he were conversing with a well-thought-of neighbor and simply asked God to watch over Brady and to be with Cassidy so she wouldn't get lonely and discouraged.

I'm the one getting lonely and discouraged, Lord, Brady confessed silently. A sudden realization dawned on him. *You did it to me again, Lord. You've corralled me. Backed me into a corner. I'm beginning to figure out that's when You're trying to tell me I'm not doing something the way You want me to. And that usually means I'm trying to do things on my own without talking to You about it. So Lord, I'm asking for help. I need help in solving this case. I need wisdom. And I need your strength to carry me through these long weeks away from Cassidy.*

With a sigh, Brady mentally reviewed the notes he had made about the man he was looking for. The guy was big–about six foot four or five and around two hundred thirty pounds. His light brown hair was long, extending in a ponytail several inches down the middle of his back. Though he wore a shirt with a company logo on it, the black boots, tattoos, and accessory chains suggested he was a biker.

Tim Sykes had already searched for the company whose name was advertised on the delivery truck the fugitive unloaded, only to discover the business no longer existed. The truck itself was the subject of a search of every dealership that handled large vans and every business for miles around that might have purchased such a vehicle in the past few months.

Are we even chasing the right man? Brady wondered. *I took pictures of a man making deliveries to a legal-looking business that was a front for illegal activities. That man matches the sketchy descriptions we have of one who forced an elderly couple to drive off the road, beat up the old man because he didn't like the way he was driving, and left the pair to fend for themselves up in the mountains. A man of the same description was seen with a prostitute who was found beaten to death. A man of the same size and build was involved in an armed robbery in which a customer was slugged and knocked unconscious. The list is long–crimes with someone hit or beaten by a tall man with medium build. But the locations span an area from Reno to Sacramento and from Carson City to Salt Lake City. Eight victims died from blows inflicted upon them. Young, old, lawmen, street bums. No ties from one victim to the next. No pattern. No motive.*

A long alley ran behind the buildings along the street where delivery trucks serviced several businesses. Brady wandered down the narrow path, knowing others had long ago combed the area for evidence.

Slight movement under a stairwell caught the detective's eye and he stepped back into the shadows where he could watch as a dingy, haggard-looking man crept from under a pile of cardboard boxes. Though it was early afternoon, the man was just now rousing from sleep. As he stumbled from his hiding place, Brady detected the odors of stale cigarette smoke and booze.

The wiry man was startled when he discovered that someone was standing close by, but didn't hesitate to approach the clean-cut young man to ask him for money. Brady quickly insisted he would buy the man a hot meal, but would not give him money.

The man followed Brady to a nearby fast-food restaurant where he stuttered as he awkwardly placed an order. With the deputy's help, the man ended up with a sandwich, fries, hot coffee, and a pastry. Once several mouthfuls of food were put away, Brady asked his companion if he had a name.

"L-L-L-Lyle," came the answer.

"I'm pleased to meet you, Lyle," Brady spoke politely. "Tell me, Lyle, do you always stay in that alley?"

"N-N-Not always. I-I-I-It used to be J-J-J-J-Jerry's place," Lyle told him.

"Did Jerry move away?" Brady wondered aloud as he ate his sandwich.

"H-H-He's dead," Lyle stated with a shake of his gray-haired head.

Brady stared at Lyle. His heart beat faster.

"Lyle, did Jerry die in that alley where I met you?"

"Y-Y-Yup."

"When, Lyle? When did he die?"

The man hesitated. He pondered the question for some time before he answered, "L-l-l -last s-s-s-summer."

Brady feared he might frighten Lyle away with all of his questions, but he had to keep going. "How did he die, Lyle?"

Lyle shook his head and refused to answer. He turned his attention back to his meal.

"Lyle, can I show you a picture of someone who used to drive a truck into the alley? I need to know if you've ever seen this man."

Lyle eyed the younger man with suspicion as Brady pulled the photo from his shirt pocket and slid it toward his companion. Lyle picked it up and held it closer to the light as he studied it through narrowed eyes. Brady saw the recognition in Lyle's eyes as the man dropped the picture onto the table.

With shaking hands, Lyle gathered up his coffee and remaining food and headed out the door. Brady followed, pleading with him, but Lyle hurried down the sidewalk, refusing to utter another word until Brady physically stopped him by grasping his arm firmly.

"Please, Lyle!" Brady begged. "You don't understand how important this is! We have to find this man so we can stop him from killing people. Can you tell me his name? Can you tell me anything about him?"

Lyle looked around as if for a hiding place. The fear in his eyes was unmistakable. He avoided looking at Brady's face, but finally spoke in a whisper.

"D-D-Dragonman. D-D-Dragonman will k-k-k-kill me."

"Dragonman?"

Lyle nodded.

"Did the dragonman kill your friend Jerry?" Brady asked excitedly.

Lyle nodded again.

"Did he hit him?"

Once again, Lyle nodded.

"Lyle, why do you call him 'Dragonman'?" Brady questioned.

Lyle finally looked Brady full in the face. "B-B-Big d-d-dragon. O-o-on his arm." Lyle indicated his left forearm.

In the only decent photos that Brady had of the suspect, the man was wearing leather protectors on his forearms that reached from his wrist nearly to his elbow. Perhaps these were not to protect his arms as he loaded and unloaded trucks as much as to cover a unique, recognizable tattoo. Brady had studied the photo numerous times, unable to distinguish what the markings were. As he peered at it again, he envisioned the dragon's head on the back of the suspect's hand and the tail wrapped around the man's upper arm.

Brady looked up to find that Lyle had slipped away, joining a group of people who were crossing the street. He let the man go.

"Thanks, Lyle," Brady said quietly and ran up the street to retrieve his truck.

"I'm sorry to have to bother you," Brady apologized to the elderly woman who sat before him. Her daughter stood behind her with her hand resting on her mother's shoulder as if to offer strength. The younger woman eyed Brady suspiciously as the older woman's eyes misted with tears.

"I know there have been all kinds of lawmen who have asked way too many questions already," he sympathized. "I've read all their reports, but there are a couple of things I need to clarify. I don't want this to be painful, but I need to ask you about the man who attacked your late husband."

The older woman gave a slight nod of her head and lifted a hand to rest it on that of her daughter's. Brady rose from his chair to stand directly in front of the pair.

"After the man pulled your husband from the car, your husband was standing and the man was hollering at him. The man hit your husband with his fist. Did he stand like this and swing his arm like this?" Brady demonstrated the moves of a boxer, keeping his arms tight to his body and throwing punches with the force of his shoulder behind them.

"No," the old woman answered softly.

"He swung his arm like this?" Brady asked as he swung his fist in a wide arc.

"Yes," came the tentative answer. "More like that."

"Okay. The reports state he was wearing a black leather jacket. When he reached into the car to pull your husband out, did he grab your husband with his left hand?"

The woman closed her eyes momentarily. Brady wondered if she was trying to envision the details of the assault or block them from her memory.

"He…reached in with his left hand…and grabbed my husband by the front of his jacket," the woman replied with heart-wrenching sadness in her voice.

"Did he have a tattoo on that hand?"

The old woman nodded quickly. "It was an awful looking thing. I have nightmares about it. A big snake with teeth and a long tongue…"

"How about a dragon with flames coming out of his mouth," Brady suggested.

The woman looked up at him with a startled expression. "Why, yes! I think you're right! I saw the whole head. I believe it was a dragon instead of a snake!"

Brady picked up his hat from the chair where he had laid it and turned to go.

"Thank you very much for seeing me," he said with a smile.

"We didn't help much, did we?" the mother asked.

"You've helped a lot," Brady assured her, then added with a conviction he didn't really feel, "We're gonna get this guy."

Brady climbed into his vehicle and cruised back toward Reno. *Great!* he thought. *The guy isn't a fighter trained in boxing or martial arts. He's a street fighter. We won't find him around any sports centers. We have a good idea what the large tattoo on his left arm looks like, but there are countless tattoo parlors. The chance of us locating the one he used to obtain the dragon tattoo is slim. He dresses like a biker. Our only hope may be to find out if he has an affiliation with a motorcycle club or gang.*

As his mind churned with his new-found but perhaps irrelevant information, the thought suddenly occurred to Brady, *Where would motorcycle gangs be hanging out this time of year? Avid bikers would go south. Arizona. New Mexico. Texas. But that doesn't seem to fit him. He was alone when he attacked the elderly couple. He's a working man, not a full time biker. He's strong. He unloads trucks or works on shipping docks. The crimes were committed in northern California, Nevada, and Utah. That means he's traveling around or moving around or making deliveries in those areas. He drove a large delivery truck that requires a special license....*

"Tim, I've got to look through those files again," Brady said to himself as he gunned the engine, entering onto the main highway through Reno. He felt excitement rising within him. Though the clues were minute, he was slowly putting together a picture of the killer. Though he'd read through the files a dozen times, he finally was getting a vision of what he really needed to look for.

Lord, with your help, we're gonna stop this guy, Brady promised with new determination.

Wyoming's long winter evenings offered quiet time for Cassidy to gather her art supplies and work on the paintings she envisioned. Much to Jubel's delight, the only area large enough to spread canvas and paint was on a table set up in a corner of the living room. As the young artist applied color to canvas, Jubel explained the fine details of the gear used in a rodeo, which added realism and accuracy to the pictures.

Cassidy chose to create a portrait of Brady fighting with all his strength to stay astride a mottled red and white tornado of a bull called Shake Rattle 'n' Roll. The background gates and chutes were obscured by clouds of dust churning under the pounding hooves and rising off the animal's back as he kicked his hind feet high in the air. Also obscured were the handlers and pick-up men. Only a lone bull fighter stood ready for action near the rider and animal. This, Cassidy decided when she finished, was to be Brady's birthday present.

With Jubel as a co-conspirator, Cassidy would pack up her art supplies and canvases and store them in the old bunkhouse out of sight each time she learned that Brady was coming home. The evidence remained out of sight until he returned to work, and Brady never learned of his wife's creations.

The fine spring air that wafted through the valley brought the warmest temperatures northern Wyoming had seen for months. Jubel enjoyed the heat of the sun as he waited on the bench for Cassidy to finish her errands.

"Jubel!" a man named Charley exclaimed as he approached. "Ain't seen you for months! How you doin'? I heard you fell off a horse and got busted up real bad. Did they put you in a nursing home?"

Jubel didn't particularly like Charley's habit of minding other people's business, but decided to be civil in front of the neighbors who had stopped to chat with him. As he was about to answer Charley's questions, Cassidy drove to a spot in front of the building and parked the truck.

"They wanted to, but I got me someone to help at home instead," was Jubel's only reply as he indicated the truck in front of them.

The eyes of the men followed Jubel's gaze as he watched the lovely young woman climb out of the vehicle and approach the group.

"I've got all the errands done, Jubel," Cassidy spoke self-consciously as the men stared at her. "I'm ready to go whenever you are."

She headed back to the truck and waited there, not offering Jubel unneeded or unwanted help.

Jubel smiled an uncharacteristically devilish grin as he rose to his feet and steadied himself with his cane. He bade good-bye to his acquaintances, adding softly, "Eat your hearts out, boys."

As Jubel shuffled toward the vehicle where Cassidy waited, Charley said, "I'd fall off a horse, too, if I could get a nursemaid like that."

"Don't try it, Charley," one of the other men warned him. "With your luck, you'd end up with one that weighed 450 pounds and smoked stogies."

Jubel made his way to the truck with little help from his cane and pulled himself up into the seat with more energy than he ever had since his accident. As Cassidy backed the truck from the parking spot, he asked if she had remembered to pick up the photos for which she had dropped off a film on their last trip to town. Replying that she had, she quickly produced the packet from her purse. Jubel clutched the unopened envelope and without explanation, directed the young woman to an office building a few blocks away. He emerged from the building a half hour after he entered it, still clutching the packet of pictures as he made his way to the truck. Looking soberly straight ahead, he remained thoughtful as he climbed up into the cab.

"One last stop," he instructed his chauffeur. He pointed Cassidy in the direction of a well-known steak house. She looked at him quizzically after parking the truck there.

"Now, we're going to celebrate with the biggest, fanciest steak in town!" Jubel announced with a wide grin.

"Jubel, what are we celebrating?" Cassidy wondered aloud.

He handed her the opened packet of photos. She extracted them from the envelope and studied them–snapshot after snapshot of her rodeo paintings. Jubel apologized for giving the best photos to his friend and keeping only the poorest for himself. Cassidy asked him why he would show anyone her pictures.

"Well," Jubel explained, "the man is part owner of a print shop. I thought maybe he'd be interested in your artwork."

"What did he say?" Cassidy asked excitedly.

"He said he wants to come out to the ranch tomorrow and take a look at your paintings first hand. If they're as good as he thinks they are, he's got a use for 'em."

Jubel let himself out of the passenger door and slid carefully to the ground. As he made his way to the door of the steakhouse, he added, "By the way, this guy is on the committee for promotions for the professional rodeo association."

TWENTY

"Cassidy! Come quick!" Jubel hollered out the back door of the house. Cassidy heard the shout clearly through the open window of the old bunkhouse, which she confiscated for a studio when the weather warmed. She tossed her paint brushes into a container of thinner and raced out the door, where the cool evening breeze tossed her hair about her face.

Bounding up the steps to the back door, she entered the house and found Jubel waiting for her in the living room. He pointed to the television screen. "Bad storms in northwest Wisconsin. Some areas got hit pretty hard..."

As the weather report turned to other areas of the country, Cassidy grabbed the phone and dialed her mother's number. A recorded message said the phone was not in service. Cassidy envisioned the lush, green landscape of familiar fertile fields and hilly woodlands becoming a tangled mess of stripped and felled timbers, flattened buildings, and debris-strewn farmland. She called Jason's cell phone number and got no answer, but left a message asking him to call as soon as he could. Though the news had turned to other affairs, she plopped down on the couch in front of the television. Jubel sat down next to her and put his arm around her shoulders as he tried to comfort her. There was nothing to do but pray that Cassidy's mother and brother were all right, and they did.

It was late in the evening when the phone rang. Cassidy was startled from a fitful sleep and grabbed the phone with a hand that shook.

"Hello?" she cried anxiously.

Brady was on the other end of the line.

"I just watched the late news. Have you heard from your mother?"

"No. I tried to call her hours ago. I've left messages and she hasn't called back. I called Grandpa and Grandma and Aunt Joyce and they haven't heard anything either. All I know is that police have some roads blocked off. Only emergency vehicles can get through."

"Cassidy, if we need to go to Wisconsin, just let me know. I'll get home as fast as I can."

Brady didn't keep her on the line in case she got the call she had been anticipating. Within minutes, the phone rang again.

"Mom!" Cassidy cried with relief when she heard her mother's voice. "Are you okay? What about Jason?"

Elaine assured her daughter they were both fine, but had no way of calling until they got to Aunt Joyce's house. Local phone service was badly damaged. Jason had left his cell phone in his truck, which was overturned and smashed. To make matters worse, the pair had been unable to get out of the driveway because of the downed power lines that stretched across the road.

Cassidy voiced her concern about the extent of the damage. Elaine admitted every building had come to harm, though some was minor.

"Mom, what are you going to do?" Cassidy wondered.

"Get some sleep and deal with it tomorrow," was her mother's practical answer.

"Do you want me and Brady to come? He can get off work if he needs to…"

"Don't plan to come yet. I'll meet with the insurance man tomorrow and determine how bad things really are. I'll call you after we look things over in the daylight."

During supper the next evening, Cassidy got a call–not from her mother, but from an upset Jason.

"Cass, can you please try to talk some sense into Mom?" he urged. "She says she's going to bulldoze everything and sell the place and move away!"

Cassidy was stunned. She remained silent for some time before answering her brother, trying to speak as calmly as she could. "She's just stressed, Jason. And probably overwhelmed at the thought of all the work of cleaning up the place besides trying to put crops in…"

"Cass, we're not farming anything this year!" Jason cried. "She rented out every bit of land to the neighbors!"

Leaving the farm had been in the back of her mother's mind for some time, Cassidy realized. She voiced her thoughts to Jason, reminding him how their mother had insisted he enroll in classes at the technical school. Their mother had no intention of letting him stay home to farm the land. Renting out the fields was another step toward creating a new life somewhere else.

Cassidy suggested she call their older brother and discuss the situation with him in case Tom was enticing their mother to move to Idaho. The phone call to Tom was even more disheartening than Cassidy expected. He firmly told his little sister to mind her own business. Their mother had no reason to stay on the farm if she didn't want to and could sell the place for all he cared. And she was more than welcome to come to Idaho and stay with him.

As her supper went untouched, Cassidy called Jason back to let him know they were not going to get any support from their older brother. Her suggestion was to let their mother calm down for a few days and rethink things before bringing up the subject again.

By the time Cassidy finished with her telephone conversations and returned to the table, Jubel had cleaned his plate. When he finished the last of his coffee, he rose from his chair and carried his dirty dishes the short distance to the sink without the aid of his cane. Cassidy glanced up in time to catch the man eyeing her. He rubbed his beard-stubbled jaw as he mulled over what he wanted to say.

"Life's been dealin' your ma some awful blows. God help her, she'll get through it," he said. He hesitated before voicing the thought that was really on his mind. "Don't make things harder for her, Cassidy."

"I'm trying to help!" she shouted.

"Then quit lookin' at the way things used to be!" Jubel reprimanded. "Your daddy's gone! The rules have changed and all bets are off!" Jubel's tone softened as tears trickled down Cassidy's cheeks. He sat down at his place at the table and faced the young woman.

"Cassidy, if I would have left this world before my wife did, nobody would have expected her to stay here. This ranch was *my* dream, not hers. She made a home here because I asked her to. Did you ever think that maybe the good Lord's got something better in mind for your ma than slavin' away on that farm? You let your ma and Him work things out."

Cassidy didn't argue. Jubel had spoken the blunt truth, though it hurt like a punch in the stomach. She sat quietly and lowered her eyes.

Jubel is right, Lord. It's not up to me to fix everything. Mom will work it out with Your help. I'm the one hanging on while Mom is ready to let go and I haven't been thinking about her happiness. Lord, help me accept the changes. Whatever Mom chooses to do, Lord, please be there for her.

Another phone call later in the evening gave Cassidy a bit of hope that her mother might not make any rash decisions she would later regret. Brady's father called to inquire about her family. Cassidy poured out the details of the storm devastation and her mother's decision to move away.

"I know I don't live there anymore and I shouldn't feel so bad about it," Cassidy admitted to her father-in-law. "But I worry about what she's going to do!"

"Cassidy, do you want me to talk to her?" the marshal suggested. "It might be easier for your mother to get things in perspective by talking with someone who's not emotionally attached to the place. I started over once. I may know a little about how she feels."

As Elaine was summoned to the phone by her sister, the marshal thought back to the afternoon at the Henderson farm in which he and Elaine discussed her frustration with the responsibilities she was trying to shoulder alone. As soon as she came on the line, he simply said, "Stick to your guns, Elaine. You've thought about it long enough and hard enough. You know by now whether or not leavin' is what you need to do."

There was slight hesitation as if she was taken aback by the message, but Elaine must have recognized Bret's voice. "I want to go," she admitted quietly, then confessed, "but I haven't decided where. Or what I should do. I guess I've got a lot of options."

"That insurance money is your ticket out of there. Sell the place later if you need to, once you're settled somewhere else," Bret advised. He hesitated only a moment before plunging ahead with an idea that had been in the back of his mind for some time.

"If you care to come to Wyoming, I've got a job for you," he said. "I still own the little house Brady and I used to live in. We call it our cabin. It hasn't been fixed up or painted for way too long. You can stay there as long as you like, if you don't mind sprucing the place up a bit. It'll take work, but I know you could do it. You had your old farm house fixed up real nice."

Elaine didn't immediately respond as she considered the idea. The marshal urged her further.

"It's only about a half hour drive from where Cassidy is living right now. With Brady gone so much, she might appreciate that you're nearby. And you'd be a whole lot closer to that grandbaby in Idaho."

"I can't come right away," Elaine replied haltingly. "It's going to take most of the summer to get everything sorted out here."

"A few more months aren't going to matter to that old place," Bret stated. "Just let me know if you're interested."

Bright and colorful neon lights illuminated the crowded plaza as Brady made his way from one casino to another. The stifling August heat that enveloped Reno clung to the cement structures, emanating warmth that cool evening air whisking down from the mountains had not yet overcome. Brady pulled his hat off and wiped at beads of sweat forming on his brow.

It'll be a miracle if I run into any of my informants on a night like tonight, he thought. *Too much going on downtown. At least it's a change of pace after spending months in tattoo parlors, loading docks, and motorcycle shops. A couple more days of this and I can go home to Cassidy for awhile.*

Brady still marveled at the birthday present his wife presented to him when he was home in May. She had spent many long winter nights working on the painting. It was surprising to him that among all the bulls he had ridden since they married, Cassidy would choose to portray his ride on Shake Rattle 'n' Roll–the most cantankerous of the bunch. He never anticipated how heart-wrenching the experience might be for his new bride as the beast tried to crush its rider's leg against the chute gate and refused to stand with his weight on all fours as if he were trying to undermine the challenger's concentration. But giving up never crossed Brady's mind. When the animal was finally turned loose, his strength and will were tested to the utmost. Eight seconds had probably never passed so slowly for the agonized Cassidy as they did that day, which was probably why the image was so imprinted on her mind that she could create a portrait of it. The ride had not been Brady's best, nor had it won a prize. But it was his come-back ride–a signal that he wasn't giving up on a dream. With that ride, he proved to himself he still loved a challenge and he still enjoyed the thrill of riding bulls.

Brady steeled himself to concentrate on his work the same way he did while competing in rodeo. *Hold on 'til the end,* he cautioned. *Some rides are easy. Some are so hard. Some take eight seconds. Some take eight months. How many cases have we put behind us in that time? How many fugitives have we apprehended? Yet Dragonman still eludes us…*

Shrugging his shoulders to ease the tension he was feeling, Brady paused to study a line-up of fifties and sixties muscle cars that had been refurbished. He wandered around the vehicles, admiring the dedication and workmanship that had gone into restoring the popular antiques.

Pausing to listen to a conversation about the value of one of the cars, Brady glanced at a man who stood beside him in the crowd. As he looked at the man once again, their eyes met. The angular, jutting jaw and flat nose of Kenny Chite were unmistakable. Brady had never been this close to the man before, yet recognized him at the same instant Chite recognized Brady. The corner of Brady's mouth twitched in customary fashion as he studied the one before him. The other man's eyes narrowed as he glared at Brady.

"I ain't huntin' you," Brady spoke tentatively. "Are you huntin' me?"

Kenny Chite sneered as he studied the younger man. "Don't flatter yourself, Hollister. What would I want with a two-bit bounty hunter like you?"

Brady made a show of turning off and removing the minute communication device that kept him in contact with the other marshals as he spoke, "Well…maybe you had the mistaken notion that I could pin a crime on you or something."

Chite stepped out of the way of a group of passing pedestrians. Brady followed a few steps nearer the wall of a building, giving the two men a bit more privacy to talk.

"If you saw what happened, then you know I wasn't the one who knifed that guy. In fact, it was so dark, you can't even prove I was there," Chite pointed out.

"You're absolutely right," Brady said with a grin.

Chite lit a cigarette and made his way through the door of a nearby casino. Brady tagged along uninvited.

"Tell me something, would you?" he asked. "Off the record, I swear. No one will know anything about this conversation."

Chite stopped near a slot machine, eyeing the taller man suspiciously as he dropped coins into the slot.

"You were there at the rodeo in Red Lodge weren't you? And you were the one who bailed out of the truck at the gas station, right? How did you know enough not to go to Black Mesa with Trent?"

Chite stuffed several more coins into the slot and considered Brady in silence for some time before answering. "Trent wanted to get his hands on you so bad, he would have taken on the Marines. He was so sure all the cops were still at the rodeo, he just couldn't get it through his thick head the whole thing might be a set-up. I argued with him until we stopped for fuel, then I bailed out."

"Too bad he wouldn't listen to reason," Brady said with a shake of his head. "Trent must have figured that the marshal was there at the rodeo. He was the one who fired the shot. He should have known if the marshal wasn't behind that poem of Skeeter's, there was more than a good chance he could figure it out."

"That message didn't come from you?" Chite inquired.

"Shoot, no! I was in Nebraska. I had no idea what was going on."

A slot machine opened up next to Chite and Brady sat down, slipping coins slowly into the slot, concentrating on his conversation with Chite while watching the lighted screen and buttons before him.

"That marshal that shot Trent–he's your old man?" Chite asked.

"Yup," Brady acknowledged and turned to study the man's face to see what kind of reaction he would have. Chite stared straight ahead, a hint of a smile playing on his thin lips.

"You find that funny?" Brady challenged.

Chite nodded his head and smiled a broader grin than before. "I don't care who your old man is. All I know is he did me a big, big favor."

Brady waited expectantly for further information, but Chite offered none. "C'mon! What are you talkin' about?" he prodded.

The man turned fully toward Brady, eyeing him suspiciously. "Maybe I'll tell you–if you tell me something." Brady nodded in agreement, so Chite asked, "How did you get rid of Sheriff Higgins and dodge them kidnapping charges so fast? Your old man has a lot of influence somewhere?"

Brady laughed aloud and replied quickly to the question. "The girl had a lot more influence than my dad did. I brought her here to Reno and married her."

"What!?" Chite exclaimed. As if he didn't hear correctly, he asked again, "What did you say?"

"I married her," Brady repeated. "They couldn't charge me with kidnapping my own wife. All it took was for a couple of reporters to find out and spread it all over the news. Higgins looked so foolish he resigned from his sheriff job."

Chite shook his head in disbelief. "Married her! Don't that beat all?" He scratched his head as he considered the situation and asked, "You didn't know her before that night, did you?"

"No."

"You still married to her?"

"Yup," Brady grinned proudly.

"So, the whole thing worked out good for you too, huh?"

"It sure did," Brady agreed, then reminded Chite, "And you were going to tell me about my dad's big favor to you, right?"

Chite twisted his angular jaw, perhaps having second thoughts about telling Brady anything. He studied the younger man in silence for awhile before he talked.

"After I…borrowed that car out of the gas station and took off," Chite related, "I headed straight for Dominic's ranch. I carried a lot of money back and forth for him. He figured you'd gotten hold of way too much information and was going to offer you money to keep your mouth shut. Of course, he really intended to kill you if he had the chance. Anyway, I had a gut feeling the whole deal was gonna bust wide open. So I went to the ranch, gave the guards the password, and told 'em I needed three hundred fifty thousand out of the vault to bring to Trent."

"And you drove away with it," Brady guessed. He chuckled and slapped Chite on the shoulder. "Good for you! And the marshals nabbed everyone else so fast, none of 'em had a chance to come after you!"

The two men moved around the room, trying their luck at a couple of different games while talking amiably. After reviewing the stories they had heard about the shoot-out on Black Mesa, they began to discuss their present job situations. Brady let Chite know he was working at capturing a killer while Brady learned that Chite was driving a truck from California delivering food to Reno grocery stores. He had banked the stolen money in hopes that his ailing sister, a single mother, would accept some of it for her two sons' educations and for her medical bills.

Brady finally ventured to ask Chite if he ever ran into Dominic's girlfriend, Lola. Kenny was clearly reluctant to divulge any information about the woman, thinking the federal officers were still trying to round up the scattered few who had slipped through their fingers when they raided the club. Brady patiently explained that the marshals had put that case to rest, but they were looking for a dangerous man whom Brady had seen around the place.

Kenny listened to Brady's plight and wondered aloud how Lola could be of help. The deputy marshal told him the man had been making deliveries to the club and occasionally stopped at the casinos. Furthermore, he was known to have picked up prostitutes in the area. Brady showed a picture of Dragonman to Chite and asked him to watch for the man. After a lot of prodding, Kenny agreed to look Lola up and ask if she would cooperate with the search, but warned the deputy that chances of that were slim.

Brady thanked Chite for his help. He handed Chite a business card and glanced up from a black jack game to see Tim Sykes walk by. About that time, Chite tossed down his cards and picked up his chips, calling his gambling night quits.

"I've lost enough for one night," Chite announced. "How 'bout you buy me a beer?"

Brady picked up his few chips and stood, eyeing Sykes who stood a short distance away. "Maybe another night. I gotta get back to work."

Sykes and another undercover marshal approached the pair.

"How's it goin', Brady?" Sykes asked.

"Rotten luck tonight," Brady spoke swiftly. "Tim, I'd like you to meet Gary Swanson," Brady indicated Kenny Chite, who stood quietly next to him. "Gary's an old rodeo buddy."

Brady then introduced the two marshals to Kenny, using only their first names and calling them his co-workers.

Sykes eyed Chite suspiciously. "So, Gary, what did you ride in the rodeos?" he questioned.

Brady spoke up before Chite had a chance to try to make up an answer. "Him? He fell off of every critter he ever tried to ride." Brady slapped Chite on the back and grinned, then stuck out his hand toward the man. Chite shook the proffered hand without uttering a word. Brady quickly said, "Gary, I've got to get goin'. Been nice talkin' to ya. Hope to see you around."

As Brady turned to lead the officers away, he called back over his shoulder to Chite, "You take good care of them nephews of yours!"

The trio was hardly out of the man's hearing when Tim Sykes reprimanded Brady.

"What do you think you're doing?" he asked. "Wasn't that Kenny Chite you were talking to?"

"No, that's Gary Stephens."

"You're a rotten liar, Brady!" Sykes challenged. "You told me a minute ago his name was Swanson, now it's Stephens."

"No wonder he looked at me so funny," Brady casually remarked. "Gary Swanson was a calf roper from Utah."

Brady kept walking swiftly across the casino floor. Sykes finally called for him to halt. He steered the young man out of the pathway of customer traffic and faced him.

"I say that was Kenny Chite," Sykes challenged. "Why didn't you arrest him?"

Brady faced his supervisor and answered honestly, "Because he's worth a lot more on the street than he is in jail."

"What makes you think you should be making decisions like that!?" Sykes scolded. "The man is wanted for his part in a homicide in Wyoming! We're picking him up!"

Brady's eyes blazed. He had just worked for a couple of hours gaining enough of Chite's trust to possibly get a lead on their real prey. He would not destroy the informal pact he had with the man. Brady stood his ground before the tall, lanky man who was his boss and said, "Who's gonna testify against him, Tim?"

Sykes glared at his deputy. He well knew there were only two eye witnesses to the murder at Lone Pine–Brady Hollister and his wife. If Brady refused to testify against Chite, Cassidy would not do so either. And the pictures Brady had taken did not show the man clearly enough to convince any jury of his guilt. Without an eye witness account there was no way to make a case against the man.

Sykes changed the subject by asking if Brady had gotten any information.

"Nothing we can use yet. But I think he knows where to locate Trent Dominic's former girlfriend. She might be able to lead us in the right direction. He's going to see if we can set up a meeting."

"How soon will you know?" Sykes persisted.

"We didn't get that far in our conversation," Brady replied, turning to leave the casino. "I'll start over when I come back tomorrow."

Sykes' temper suddenly flared. "Maybe you shouldn't come back at all!" he hissed. "Maybe you're too used to working independently to be a member of a team of U.S. Marshals!"

"I'll think about it," Brady called over his shoulder as he headed for the door.

"Take a week to think about it!" Sykes shouted after him. "Your vacation starts tomorrow!"

"Fine!" Brady hollered, causing several patrons to look up from their games to see what was going on. With that, he stepped out into the night.

TWENTY-ONE

A hot, high-desert breeze wafted through the open windows of the little hillside house where Elaine busied herself removing the old and frail curtain rods from the living room windows. The battery-powered screw gun she used competed with the country music playing softly on the radio, creating noise in otherwise silent surroundings.

With the last of the windows laid bare, Elaine descended the ladder and retreated to the kitchen for a drink. As she sipped the cool water, she studied the room she had been demolishing. Mentally reviewing the list of things she wanted to do, she considered whether the next task should be patching the screw and nail holes in the walls in preparation for paint or turning her efforts to the unkempt yard.

The woman had spent the previous day cleaning the decades-old appliances in the kitchen, laundering bedding and rugs, and making a list of supplies that she would need to refurbish the disheveled but sturdy array of furniture in the living room and two small bedrooms. Now, with brilliant sunlight from the western sky filtering through dust-laden windows, Elaine decided her next task should be washing the panes of glass to eliminate the hazy appearance from the interior of the house.

Moving to the larger bedroom with a bucket of soapy water and a handful of towels, Elaine began the task of window washing. She heard Pansy's soft padding as the little dog jumped down from the living room couch. Seconds later, the pup started barking with high-pitched, ferocious growls and yelps. Elaine ignored the pet at first, for every new scent and sound was cause for a barking fit in the unfamiliar Wyoming surroundings. When the barking continued, she went to investigate.

"Pansy, what kind of varmint are you barking at now?" she called as she left her task behind.

Elaine headed toward the open front door in which she had secured a gate to keep Pansy penned inside the house. She was startled to see a man in the shadows of the porch.

"A big varmint," a deep voice answered her question from his position on the top step.

Elaine breathed a sigh of relief when she recognized the marshal. She backed away from the door to allow the man entrance.

"I didn't mean to scare you," he stated with a smile as he stepped over the pet barricade. "I would have called if I'd known you were here already. I was hoping to get here ahead of you. Maybe cut some brush in the yard or something."

Pansy suddenly launched a ferocious attack on the tall man's pant leg.

"I tell you what. It's a good thing I wear tall boots," the marshal commented as he lifted his foot, bringing the tugging and biting dog off the floor as it clung to his jeans. "They're good for fending off rattlers and Yorkies."

Pansy let go of the denim to drop to the wooden floor. She issued another series of sharp barks at the man, then sniffed and trotted away with her nose in the air.

"You must have gotten everything done in Wisconsin earlier than expected," the marshal noted as he surveyed the freshly scrubbed kitchen.

Elaine sighed. "I decided I was never going to get everything done, so I called it quits. I didn't think you'd mind."

"Your son still giving you trouble?" the marshal asked bluntly.

Elaine admitted that she and Jason weren't seeing eye-to-eye on the disposition of the farm. "We've compromised for now. I've had the house and the big shed repaired. Some of the other buildings have been demolished to make the place easier to sell if that's what I decide to do. In the meantime, Jason will stay there and fend for himself for awhile."

As the marshal studied the house, Elaine wondered what changes he would notice. Outside the door, some of the weeds and brush had been cut away, making a path to the clothesline, which had been sturdied to hold bedding and rugs. The kitchen had been stripped of adornment and thoroughly scrubbed. The living room furniture had been pushed to the center of the room and covered with sheets in preparation for painting the ceiling and walls. Every window was laid bare. Cans of paint, brushes, rollers, and a variety of tools were stacked in a corner. A glance into the nearest bedroom revealed a dismantled bed with mattress and box spring leaning against the wall and the single dresser moved from its customary location.

"How long have you been here?" Bret asked Elaine.

"I came four days ago," she answered. "But I didn't get much done the first day. By the time I decided what to do and went to town for supplies…" Elaine stopped in mid-sentence, detecting that the marshal was unhappy with her. "Is something wrong?" she asked.

"Yes, something's wrong!" the marshal stated emphatically. "I didn't ask you to come here to kill yourself with work! I was hoping you'd take several months to do this and relax a little! Go visit Cassidy…"

"I saw Cassidy when I first got here," Elaine defended. "But Brady got off work a few days earlier than expected, and they had a chance to go to a rodeo together. They go as often as they can because Cassidy's been selling prints of some of her paintings at the rodeos."

"What about visiting that grandbaby in Idaho?"

"Tom and his wife have vacation in two weeks. I'll go visit them then."

The marshal stared at the woman as he asked, "Have you been to the top of the hill to look over the country?"

Elaine admitted that she had seen the trail that led up the slope but hadn't taken time to explore it. Without another word, the marshal reached down and took her by the hand, pulling her along behind him. He politely helped her over the gate as they exited the house, leaving an irate Pansy behind.

The exhausting walk in the heat of the day became invigorating when, at the top of the rise, a cooler mountain breeze stirred the air. The scene around the hill was breathtaking. Elaine looked over the foothills to the surrounding mountains, noting the distant rugged peaks creating a backdrop for a multi-colored layered rock ridge that extended for miles.

"If you were to follow that ridge in that direction," the marshal explained, "you'd end up above Jubel's house, where Cassidy is living. And over in this direction is Knowlton's K Bar B ranch where you met up with Cassidy the night before you headed back to Wisconsin. Their house is on the other side of those hills. In fact, if you see any cattle up by this fence line, they're K Bar B cattle."

The marshal explained a bit about the surroundings as he pointed out the direction of the nearest towns. Elaine listened in silence as she studied the vast scenery until he ceased to speak. She quickly looked up at him, intending to thank him, and caught him studying her with his dark eyes slightly narrowed. Suddenly uncomfortable, she averted her gaze by glancing downward. When she did, she noted the man's habit of wearing a long-sleeve shirt. In heat like this, he rolled the sleeves up to just above the elbows and left open the front of the shirt halfway to his waist. She couldn't help but notice the rise and fall of his chest under the thin cotton material plastered tight to his muscular torso by sweat.

"Thank you…for showing me the country," Elaine muttered, the words nearly catching in her throat. Feeling uneasy, she backed away from the man and turned toward the trail. *Stay away from him, Elaine!* she cautioned herself as she made her way down the path. *He is physically attractive and you get lonely. Loneliness can be a dangerous thing and he is a dangerous man. He has a raging temper and he may be violent. His wife left him and never looked back….*

As the pair neared the house, the marshal asked Elaine if she was hungry and offered to take her to town for a meal. Though she was famished, Elaine was reluctant to agree to the offer. She finally decided it would be an opportunity to discuss her ideas for fixing up the house in a setting where there were other people around, thus keeping the man at a safe distance.

Turning toward his sport utility vehicle, the marshal extracted a piece of luggage from the cab. Elaine realized the man had intended to stay the night here in his own house, not knowing she had arrived earlier than expected.

"I'll drive my truck and meet you in town," she quickly suggested.

"Why?" he wondered.

"You obviously were planning on staying here tonight. I'll gather some of my things and get a motel room…"

The marshal smiled at her. "How 'bout if I drive you into town, bring you back here after dinner, and then I'll go sack out on Jubel's couch," he suggested.

Elaine considered the proposal in uneasy silence until the marshal ordered with a smile, "Go get cleaned up! I'll wait out here 'til you say I can come in."

Elaine stood in front of a faded mirror that rested on the dresser, combing her damp hair and tousling it into soft curls with her fingers. Sudden yelling outside the bedroom door drew her attention. It was obvious the marshal was irritated with Pansy, so Elaine stepped out into the hallway to reprimand the little dog. Pansy scooted around her legs, then turned and dashed back down the hall, streaking past the marshal. In its mouth, the dog carried a leather wallet as it growled playfully and ran in circles around the stash of living room furniture, daring anyone to catch it.

"Pansy, bring it back!" Elaine urged as she hurried toward her pet.

The dog made a full circle around the furniture. As the marshal approached, Pansy bolted away from him. Elaine sneaked in the opposite direction, hoping to corral the little dog. As it rounded the corner of the couch, Elaine dashed from her crouched position at the same time the marshal made a leap. The collision toppled Elaine onto the floor as the marshal tumbled over her and landed a few feet away. Her head hit the hard wooden surface. She lay there, stunned, as the room spun in surreal darkness with faint twinkling lights drifting in all directions.

Elaine waited a moment for her head to clear before trying to move. The marshal came to kneel beside her, slipping a strong arm under her shoulders. She grasped his arms to pull herself up into a sitting position. Too late, she realized the man took the move to be an embrace. The concerned look on his face turned suddenly to longing. Rather than assist her to sit up, he pulled her so tightly into his arms that Elaine could feel the beat of his rapidly pounding heart.

The marshal kissed her softly. Still reeling from her fall, Elaine hardly had strength to protest. She felt faint and dizzy. When she tried to push the man away, Bret seemed to mistake her weak struggle for anticipation of his affection, her faintness for relaxing in his arms, her soft moan of pain as that of pleasure.

Elaine was helpless until Bret moved his grasp around her arms to place a hand under her jaw, turning her face so he could kiss her more fervently. With one arm free, she weakly attempted to push him away. When the marshal clutched her in an iron grip to ply her with hard, reckless kisses, Elaine forced herself to struggle. She strained to pull away from him and pushed at his head to ward off any more advances.

Bret momentarily loosened his grip. He gazed down at her and softly whispered her name. She firmly raised a hand between them.

"Please!" she begged in a strained voice. "I hit my head..."

"Elaine?" Bret spoke her name again, this time as a question.

"I hit my head," she repeated in a hoarse whisper. "Please let me sit up."

The marshal helped her into a sitting position and cussed aloud. Elaine wasn't sure whether his disgust was at himself for being so careless or for a lost opportunity. He leaned back against the wall, sitting with his knees up and his arms resting on them while watching the woman in silence as she took deep breaths to quell the nausea that threatened to overtake her.

Pansy dropped the marshal's wallet on the floor near Elaine, apparently satisfied the chasing game had been won. The dog turned its attention to jumping onto Elaine's lap and stretching to lick her face. Bret watched the pair without comment as Elaine scooped up the folded leather wallet that the dog had relinquished. She handed it toward Bret. He took the smooth folded leather and clutched it in his fist.

"I'm sorry you got hurt, Elaine," he said with a sigh. "I don't know why I got so mad at that dog."

"She's a thief. You chase thieves for a living," Elaine pointed out.

"Yeah, well, they usually weigh a lot more'n five pounds. I had no call to get that riled that I'd end up hurting you."

"I'll be fine," Elaine assured the man, though slight nausea surfaced again.

The marshal rose from his place near the wall to stand over the injured woman. "Let's get you to the couch," he said, grasping Elaine's hands to lift her to a standing position. She allowed Bret to help her toward the stash of furniture. He quickly moved a couple chairs and plumped up pillows as Elaine lowered herself onto the well-worn sofa. Bret made a trip to the kitchen, returning with a bundle of ice cubes wrapped in a towel.

As Elaine positioned the cool cloth over the slightly raised bump on the side of her head, Bret said, "I'd better get you to the doctor. You act kinda drowsy. How does your stomach feel?"

"Not the best," Elaine admitted, "but if I rest awhile, I'll be fine. I'm tired because I've been working in this heat and my stomach probably doesn't feel good because I haven't eaten anything for several hours."

Bret studied the woman. "I tell you what, I'm gonna rustle up some food. But if you can't sit up to the table and keep it down, I'm haulin' you to the doctor!"

"Brady," the marshal's voice came over his son's cell phone.

"Dad? What's up?" Brady asked, sensing immediately that something was wrong, for his father seldom called him.

"Are you competing this weekend?"

"No. I was scheduled to work but I got off earlier than expected. Why?"

"I thought maybe you'd bring Cassidy home to stay with her ma tonight," Bret stated.

"Why? What's wrong?" Brady asked as he moved away from the noisily chattering friends that were relaxing together before the evening's rodeo performance.

"Elaine is hurt."

"What do you mean, hurt? How bad?" A gut-wrenching feeling of dread washed over the young man as he demanded, "Dad, did you hurt her?"

"Not on purpose. I knocked her over…" the marshal defended.

"Tell me what happened!" Brady screamed at the phone. Pete and Skeeter came to Brady's side as soon as they realized the phone call was a serious one. They overheard enough of Brady's side of the conversation to show alarm.

The marshal related that he was chasing the little dog that had stolen his wallet and accidentally knocked Elaine over when she sprung from behind the couch. She had hit her head on the floor.

"Is she conscious?" Brady demanded.

"Yes, she's conscious," Bret spoke evenly.

"Did she ever lose consciousness?"

"Not that I know of."

"Has she been sick to her stomach?"

"A little queasy but she's been eating a little."

"Where is she now?" Brady wanted to know.

"She's here. At the cabin."

"Can I talk to her?"

Elaine assured Brady she was okay except for a headache. She didn't need to go to the doctor and she didn't need everyone making a big fuss over her. Brady argued that someone needed to stay with her. He and Cassidy would be heading to the cabin immediately.

As Brady folded the cell phone with a snap, he closed his eyes and briefly covered them with his hand. He ran his fingers through his hair before he turned to his friends who wordlessly waited for an explanation for the call.

"Elaine told you she was all right," Skeeter counseled when he learned the story. "Your dad's worked up over the whole thing because he feels responsible. Don't worry!"

"I'm not half as worried about what they told me as I am about what they didn't tell me," Brady confided.

"What do you mean by that?" Pete asked.

"I wonder why my dad is at the cabin when Cassidy's ma is there alone."

"You think something is going on between 'em?" Pete questioned with a grin. "It's about time your dad started lookin' around for a woman friend instead of playin' marshal all the time."

Brady leaned over the hood of Skeeter's truck as he contemplated the situation.

"Your dad's been living alone for a long time," Skeeter reminded his friend. "Now that you're happily married, maybe he's decided he doesn't want to stay alone forever."

Brady sighed. "I never, ever really understood why she left."

Both of the men knew Brady was referring to his mother. It was a subject that seldom surfaced in all the years the three men had been friends. Pete and Skeeter glanced at one another in surprise as Brady quietly admitted to some of his fears.

"I've often wondered if Brendan's death was all there was to it. Maybe Dad hit her or threatened her to make her go away like she did. And I honestly don't know the answer." Brady considered the situation in silence for a few moments before he continued. "I'm wondering why he talked Elaine into coming to Wyoming. All of a sudden, I'm scared for her." Brady eyed his friends, who silently let him continue as he admitted to them, "What scares me most is how little I know my dad."

TWENTY-TWO

The pair spoke little as they sat at opposite sides of the table. Elaine was not angry with the marshal, but apprehensive. As she polished off a hamburger that was slightly charred and a scoop of beans that were barely lukewarm, she considered his apology to her. *"I'm sorry you got hurt…"* she recalled him saying. But there had been no apology for his advances. *Obviously, he has no regrets about that,* she considered as she wondered how soon Brady and Cassidy would arrive.

Elaine was determined to prove the lack of ill effects from her fall by eating a hearty meal. With the meat and beans gone, she looked up at the marshal to find him staring at her, as he often did.

"I have a way of losing my dignity when I'm around you, don't I?" he commented.

Elaine contemplated the statement. "I guess you do, at that," she admitted with a cautious smile, recalling the mud puddle incident and the ridicule the man endured from Skeeter at the wedding reception as well as the evening's dog chase that ended in unfortunate circumstances. "But it makes you more human," she said kindly. "Not so…," she paused, searching for the right word.

"Intimidating?" the marshal offered.

"I was thinking 'invincible.' You don't seem so invincible while you're losing your dignity."

Pansy made a dash for the front door, barking and growling, just as a truck topped the knoll in the driveway to come in full view of the house. The marshal rose to stand in the doorway until he recognized Bud Knowlton. He walked outside to meet the man as he climbed out of his truck.

“Evenin,’ Marshal,” Bud greeted the man. “I was passin’ by and thought I’d stop in to check on the place.”

The marshal regarded the portly man who had long ago offered to keep an eye on the Hollister house whenever Bret and Brady were away. He motioned for Bud to come inside. “Since when do you pass by here at supper time?” the marshal challenged. “Didn’t figure you for a man who’d risk missin’ any of Beth’s cookin’.”

Bud grinned as he patted his round stomach. “Well, I certainly don’t miss much of it.”

“You’re a good man, Bud, but you’re a rotten liar,” the marshal challenged. “The boys sent you.”

“Okay, the boys sent me,” Bud easily confessed as he mounted the steps.

As soon as he entered the house, Bud greeted Elaine, who was clearing dirty dishes from the table. Bret asked if she remembered meeting Bud the previous year. She acknowledged with a bright smile that she did remember the man and offered him a steaming cup of coffee.

Bud questioned Elaine about her trip from Wisconsin and the devastation that had taken place there. The discussion turned to Elaine’s ideas for fixing up the house. She moved from one room to another, describing the painting, reupholstering, and repairs she envisioned. When Bud realized Elaine would be spending several weeks in the area, he insisted she come to the ranch often to visit with Beth. Elaine promised that she looked forward to doing that, for she knew the first time she met Beth she would like to get to know her better.

The hillsides were enveloped in murky darkness when Bud said his good-byes. Within minutes of the man’s departure, Brady pulled his truck to a halt in the yard.

Brady walked in silence into the cabin. Cassidy followed, closing the door to the cool mountain wind. She was greeted by an excited Pansy and stooped to pick up the little dog as Elaine invited everyone to relax in the living room.

As the couch and chairs were being rearranged to positions comfortable for visiting with one another, Cassidy looked closely at her mother for the first time since she arrived. "Mom, what are those red marks on your face?" she asked.

Realization dawned and she spun around to face the marshal where he sat on a nearby chair. *"What did you do to her?"* she screamed at him.

"Cassidy, he tripped over me..." Elaine attempted to explain.

Cassidy glared at the marshal and repeated her question.

"I kissed her," the man confessed, maintaining composure in the face of his angry daughter-in-law. "I kissed her!" he repeated.

"Then what!?" Cassidy demanded.

"She pushed me away so I let her go," Bret answered in an even tone.

Cassidy searched her mother's face for any indication that the man was lying. Her mother denied no part of his story, but confirmed it.

"We crashed into each other and Bret's knee probably hit me in the jaw when he stumbled over the top of me. Then my head hit the floor. When he came to check on me he didn't know how badly I was shaken up. I grabbed his arms to pull myself up and...he thought I was trying to embrace him...and he kissed me. When I pushed him away, he let me go."

Silent tears rolled down Cassidy's cheeks. "I don't believe you!"

Elaine regarded her daughter. She had tried to make the incident sound like a minor thing, but as she recalled those moments in the marshal's iron grip, she had no doubt there might be bruises that indicated she had been handled roughly.

Brady rose from his seat to encircle an upset Cassidy in his arms. He held her tight as she leaned her forehead on his shoulder. Not wanting to give Cassidy another opportunity for an emotional outburst that might cause more hurt, Elaine tried to steer attention to the problem at hand. "So, now that everyone is so concerned about watching over me, are Brady and Cassidy staying here or not? We'll have to make up a bed for them..."

"Cassidy will stay here with you," Brady decided quickly. "Dad and I will spend the night at Jubel's."

"Brady! We hardly ever get to..." Cassidy started. She was interrupted by Brady's firm tone.

"Dad and I need to talk."

Cassidy quickly relented. Her husband's mind was made up. She would not argue or hamper the discussion with his father.

The recent long trip and hard work, coupled with an eventful evening, left Elaine feeling drained. She watched quietly, nearly dozing in her chair, as the marshal retrieved his belongings, some of which Pansy had relocated from the bathroom to a corner of the living room. Bending to pick up a pair of socks, he winced in pain.

"You ready to go, Dad?" Brady asked.

"In a minute," the marshal answered as he dug through his bag. "I'm gonna grab a couple pain pills before heading out."

As the marshal went to the kitchen for water, Brady explained that his father had been hit in the back by a ricocheting bullet years before. The injury still caused occasional problems.

Pansy suddenly scooted out of the kitchen, with Bret following. "I dropped a pill and the mutt's got it in her mouth!" he announced.

The dog darted past Cassidy toward a corner of the living room. Brady vaulted over the couch, cornered the pup and caught it. Pansy wiggled so furiously, he nearly dropped the dog, but Cassidy was there to rescue it from a fall. She pried the pup's mouth open to fish out the sodden pill before handing Pansy to her mother. The dog jumped excitedly on Elaine's lap and tried to lick her face.

"That thing is nothin' but trouble," the marshal mumbled as he headed for the door.

He turned to look at Elaine as he set his hat firmly on his head. His jaw was set. His eyes were unreadable. He offered a brief, wry smile before he wordlessly stepped out into the night.

Cassidy paced restlessly while her mother prepared to retire for the evening. Elaine emerged from the bathroom to find her daughter peering through the darkness of a living room window.

"Cassie, if you want to go home to be with Brady, then take his truck and go. I don't need anyone to stay with me."

"I don't want to go home with *him* there," Cassidy stated flatly.

"I thought you liked your father-in-law," Elaine reminded her.

"I did…"

"So, what's changed?"

"Mom! He can't go around throwing himself at women he hardly knows…" Cassidy stopped short in her tirade when she caught her mother smiling at her.

"The way I hear it, Brady kissed you within three hours of when you first met," Elaine commented.

"That's different. I wanted him to!" Cassidy confessed with a heated blush.

"I see," Elaine said with a grin. She sobered quickly when she caught her daughter studying her. "I did not want your father-in-law's advances, Cassidy," she spoke firmly. "And I did not intend to entice him."

"You were alone in the house together and his luggage was here," the young woman argued.

"He wasn't staying. He asked me to go to town with him for dinner and he came into the house with his luggage so he could clean up and change clothes. That's when Pansy got hold of his wallet."

The stubborn set of Cassidy's mouth remained. She would not drop the subject or accept her mother's easy explanations. "Mom, Bret can be really nice, but you're being too forgiving! I'm afraid you're going to get involved with him and end up being hurt! Please, Mom, go back home!"

"I've got a job to do!" Elaine argued. "I've been looking forward to a change of scenery for awhile, and I'm not crawling back to Wisconsin because things didn't go as expected here!"

Cassidy seemed to remain unconvinced that her mother knew what she was doing, so Elaine continued. "Furthermore, it's time for Jason to learn to live on his own. He thinks he wants to keep farming, but every one of his bright ideas involves spending money like we were growing it on the trees. I'm not ready to go back home and butt heads with him!"

"Mom, you might have traded one set of problems for another. Please promise me you'll be really careful around Bret. Take your time to think about things before…"

Elaine laughed at her daughter, indicating without saying it that Cassidy had no business instructing anyone in such fashion. Rather than remind her daughter she had married after one week of chaotic courtship, Elaine simply said, "I'll do that."

Cassidy eyed her mother with brows knit in a frowning expression.

"Mom, were you really worried when Brady and I got married?" she asked quietly.

"You can't imagine how scared I was for you!" Elaine confessed. "I think I would have gone crazy if I hadn't reminded myself over and over that Brady sounded like a really nice guy over the phone. He was always very polite and concerned for you. He had good friends like Bud and Beth Knowlton, and he told me he had given his heart to the Lord." Elaine smiled thoughtfully as she added, "And I prayed every day that he was nothing like his father, because I really thought that man was obnoxious and mean-tempered and selfish."

Cassidy laughed aloud and went to give her mother a big hug. "I'm sorry I worried you, Mom. I hope you don't worry about me any more."

"I don't. I think you have a wonderful husband. I hope you appreciate him," Elaine said as she returned her daughter's embrace. "And don't worry about me. I get lonely sometimes, but I have no intention of getting involved in a romance with your father-in-law or any other man. I'm not ready for that yet. What happened tonight was a simple misunderstanding. I promise I'll be more careful to keep him at a distance."

As Elaine turned out the bedroom light and slipped under the covers, she tried to put the evening's unfortunate incident out of her mind, for thinking about it would bring back memories of passionate times with Keith. That memory, she knew from experience, would bring a physical ache that would leave her crying until she fell asleep. Elaine forced her mind instead to turn to prayer. *I believe I was meant to come to Wyoming,* she told her Heavenly Father in the quiet room. *You said in your Word that in all things You work for the good of those who love You, who have been called according to Your purpose. Now that Brady has decided to obey Your Word, Lord, perhaps you are using me to help bring problems out into the open so restoration can take place in his family. Please give Brady wisdom when confronting his father. And Lord, give Cassidy peace about what happened tonight. If she harbors resentment and bitterness, she'll hinder the relationship between Brady and his father.*

While still talking to the Lord, Elaine drifted into an exhausted sleep.

Brady drove his father's SUV toward Jubel's ranch house, which had been home to him and Cassidy for nearly a year. The men rode in silence for several miles while Brady quietly pondered his relationship with his father. The marshal had provided for him financially, had found an excellent family for him to stay with, and spent every spare minute with Brady when he wasn't at work. Brady had never considered that the man may have sacrificed his own well-being to ensure his son's emotional stability.

"Dad," Brady finally ventured to speak. "I've been really selfish, haven't I?"

"What do you mean?" Bret wondered.

"I've never asked you how you were feeling. I never encouraged you to remarry. I never let you cry about Mom leaving....I remember the day you were sitting on the couch. You were really hurting. There were tears rolling down your cheeks. I walked up to you and told you to cowboy up..." Brady swallowed hard, trying to clear the lump in his throat. "I'm so sorry."

Brady stopped the truck on the side of the road as he tried to regain his composure. He rested his chin on his arms that were folded over the steering wheel. When he was ready to speak again, he asked a question that burned on his mind.

"Dad, why did you ask Elaine to come to Wyoming?"

Bret answered quickly and defiantly, "I didn't ask her here to take advantage of her, if that's what you're thinking!"

"You didn't intend to force yourself on her?" Brady questioned.

"No!"

"You had no intentions toward her when you asked her to come?"

The marshal paused before he confessed, "I wanted to get to know her better."

Brady knew he risked making his father very angry, yet he posed another question. "Why did my mother leave?"

Bret's jaw moved in customary fashion as he answered his son's question. "I never laid a vicious hand on her except for the day I restrained her when she attacked the doctor in the hospital," he spoke emphatically. "I did not abuse her!"

The marshal looked at a point in the distance and sighed deeply. "Your ma never had much of an upbringin'. She was raised mostly by her grandparents. They were good people, but never had any control over her. She came to church with 'em once in a while, but she generally ran pretty wild.

"I guess she was attracted to me because I was from a good solid family. I had discipline at home, in the army, in the police academy. I had goals and plans. Those were things she was lacking. In some crazy way, I was her hero. She thought I could do anything. But I couldn't keep Brendan alive...."

Another silence pervaded before the marshal talked again. "When you were a little guy, you were always into mischief. You tried your ma's patience to no end. When Brendan came along, she had a baby she could cuddle all day long. So much of her died when he did...."

Brady thoughtfully accepted his father's explanation and put the truck in gear. Miles of silence prevailed until Brady caught a hint of a smile on his father's lips.

"What are you thinkin' about?" he asked his dad.

"That stupid little dog. Never seen so much trouble wrapped up in a little fur ball like that."

Brady laughed aloud. He agreed with his father's assessment. "I told Cassidy before we got married she could have as many kids as she could handle, but don't be bringin' home no little ankle-biter dog like that."

It was Bret's turn to laugh. He then made a confession. "I tell you what, for a second I thought about not sayin' anything about that mutt taking the pill I dropped. But I figured I was already in more than enough hot water with Elaine, I didn't need to kill her dog besides. Trouble is, the little varmint probably wouldn't have overdosed, just been high as a kite for a week."

Brady shared with his father what he imagined the little dog would be like in such a state. It would maybe get on top of the refrigerator instead of jumping on the couch. Maybe run down a jackrabbit. Bret joined in the game and suggested that the mutt might stampede Knowlton's cattle or flush mule deer out of the hills.

As their imaginations ran wilder, the men laughed louder and louder. By the time they arrived at Jubel's ranch, father and son were rolling with laughter as they exited the SUV. Both were slow to notice the car in the driveway. When they did, Jubel had already stepped out onto the porch to investigate the commotion.

"You two been drinkin'!?" he demanded.

The pair laughed harder.

"I didn't think you were gonna be here tonight," Jubel pointed out to Brady as the young man stepped toward the door. Jubel blocked the entrance.

"What? Can't we come in?" Brady asked.

"Not if you're gonna act like hoodlums! I've got company."

The younger men sobered and took note of the sleek sedan parked in front of the house as well as their uncle's uncustomary new attire. Satisfied that his nephews were finally showing sufficiently somber demeanor, Jubel moved out of the way to allow them entrance.

The remains of a steak dinner for two rested on the table, graced by a single candlestick in which the fine taper had burned down to a short stub. The lights in the living and dining areas were turned down lower than usual and an old black and white western movie was showing on the television. Jubel wordlessly picked up the dirty dishes from the table to set them on the kitchen counter. He blew out the candle and set it out of sight in a cupboard. Bret and Brady stifled their grins as they watched the old man in silence.

The bathroom door opened and a petite gray-haired lady stepped out. She looked surprised to see that Jubel had visitors, but smiled warmly as she moved toward the men who stood just inside the front door.

"Edna, this is my nephew, Bret, and his son, Brady," Jubel said.

Edna stepped forward and offered her hand to each of the men in turn, giving them a warm and friendly handshake while she told them how pleased she was to meet them.

"So this is Cassidy's husband?" Edna asked as she grasped Brady's strong hand.

"Yes, ma'am," he answered. "I take it you've met Cassidy?"

"Oh, yes! I'm a volunteer at the hospital. I saw her nearly every week when she brought Jubel in for therapy. She did a wonderful job of taking care of him!"

"That's good to know," Brady commented, smiling pleasantly while wondering if Cassidy was aware of a romance going on under her nose.

Jubel asked where Cassidy was. Brady explained that she was staying the night with her mother at the cabin and he and his dad had expected to sleep at the ranch. Since Jubel had company, Brady suggested they go back to the cabin.

"Don't be silly!" Edna chided the young man. "I was going to leave as soon as we got the dishes cleaned up."

"Don't worry about the dishes, Edna!" Jubel said, then questioned, "Do you remember which road to turn on to get back to town?"

"Oh, I think so. There aren't that many of them," she answered with a giggle. Her dark eyes gleamed as she spoke.

"You might miss the turn-off in the dark. I'll lead you to the highway, just in case," Jubel told the woman as he grabbed his hat off the rack by the door.

Good-byes were said hastily as Jubel ushered Edna out into the twilight. Bret called after him that he might as well use the SUV, rather than getting his truck out of the shed. Jubel took the offer and climbed into Bret's vehicle to lead the way down the long dirt road.

When Bret reentered the house, he found Brady investigating the leftover food on the counter.

"Candlelight. Sirloin steaks. Baked potatoes. Green salad with who knows what in it. And some kind of fluffy stuff for dessert," Brady muttered as he tasted some of the concoction on the end of his finger. "This is serious business, Dad."

"Kinda looks that way," the marshal agreed. He fished a quarter out of his pocket. "Heads, you get the couch and I get your bed. How 'bout it?"

Brady agreed, having a feeling before his father flipped the coin that he would be spending the night in the living room.

"Are you gonna wait up and have a talk with Jubel when he gets home? Maybe get the scoop on what's goin' on between him and Edna?" Brady wondered as his father headed for the bedroom.

"Nope," the marshal replied wearily. "It'll keep."

TWENTY-THREE

Kenny Chite led Brady to the back of a dimly lit room. The woman who waited at the bar eyed the lean dark-haired stranger as he approached. Brady noted the low-cut blouse and short skirt of the shapely woman who watched him make his way across the casino floor and remembered her as the woman who had escorted Dominic to a back room at the club.

"Lola, this is the man I told you about," Kenny said by way of introduction. "This is Brady Hollister."

Lola's chin lifted and her eyes narrowed.

"You're not the Hollister who gunned down Trent Dominic?" she asked in a voice made deep and gravelly from years of heavy smoking.

"No, that was my father," Brady answered steadily. "I wasn't involved and that incident has nothing to do with the man I'm looking for now."

Lola studied Brady. "You're a cop?"

"Deputy U.S. Marshal," he acknowledged.

"A marshal. Like your old man," Lola stated.

Brady shrugged and didn't reply to the statement.

"Why should I help you?" she asked sarcastically.

"Because your girls may be in danger. This man has committed several murders and armed robberies. A store clerk was fatally wounded..." Brady started to explain.

"My girls aren't store clerks," Lola sneered.

A wry smile curled one side of Brady's mouth as he decided to speak bluntly to the woman. "He's been known to pick up prostitutes. Several months ago he picked up one in California. She was found beaten to death."

Lola glared at Brady. "That was in California," she pointed out.

"But he comes to Reno," Brady countered. "To this neighborhood. All I'm asking is that you be willing to circulate his picture among the girls so we can find out if any of them have been seeing him."

Brady saw that Lola clearly didn't trust him, but he sensed she was fiercely protective of "her girls." He pulled an envelope from the pocket of his western-cut shirt and extracted a number of copies of a single photo of the man he sought. He laid the stack of pictures on the bar as he apologized that he had no better ones to offer.

Lola picked up the top photo and squinted through a cloud of cigarette smoke to study it as Brady pointed out the dragon tattoo on the man's left arm.

"You may have seen this guy around the strip club. He delivered liquor there within a few weeks of closing. If you know anything about him, I'd sure appreciate it if you'd share it with me," Brady urged.

Lola made a slight shrug of her shoulders and shook her head, indicating she knew nothing of the man.

When the discussion ended, Brady wrote a cell phone number on the back of a couple of pictures and thanked Lola. After shaking hands with Chite and telling him he appreciated his help, Brady headed out the door.

The phone call came surprisingly fast. Brady had located Deputy Sykes and was informing him of his intention to call it a night and go back to his room to get some sleep. He interrupted his conversation to take the call from an unfamiliar number.

The message was short. Lola's voice simply informed Brady to return to the bar he had left just a few minutes ago.

"Gotta go," Brady informed his boss.

"We'll back you up," Sykes announced.

Brady hesitated. Did Lola despise him enough to lay a trap for him? Surely she would know every bouncer, thug, and hit man in the area. Yet Brady knew instinctively she was trusting him and him only with any information she had. He couldn't bring other marshals with him.

"I can't risk scaring off my informants, Tim," he concluded. "And I don't know if I can trust you not to try to arrest 'em."

Sykes considered the statement. He remained calm as he spoke. "Brady, I admit you have a real knack for gaining the trust of these people and you've produced good results because of it. But I have to ask, where do you draw the line between those who need to be apprehended and those who are more valuable left on the street?"

The younger man had no easy answer, but attempted an explanation. "I guess you have to take time to get to know 'em a little. You can find some good in a whole lot of so-called bad folks. But I know I'm taking awful chances with some of them. I wouldn't mind if you'd hang around the casino floor. Just don't follow me into the bar and scare her off."

Sykes nodded that he understood and called another officer for backup as he and Brady parted ways.

The slender young woman who waited at the end of the bar with Lola appeared to be in her mid-twenties, though Brady found it hard to determine with the heavy make-up and the dim lighting. She puffed on a cigarette and watched Brady approach through the haze of smoke around her.

Within a few minutes, Brady learned from the woman that she had accompanied a man who looked like the one in the photo to the edge of town where a number of motorcycles were parked. They partied for several hours together. Her date invited her to go with him to Sturgis. She declined and the man promised to look her up when he returned to town.

Brady was excited as he wrote down as much information as he could glean from the young prostitute. He handed a generous tip to the women. Before he left them, he let them know they would be seeing him around, watching for the tattooed man to return as he said he would.

Brady was well within sight of Sykes, who was pretending to watch a game of craps. Once the deputy left the casino floor, Sykes sauntered behind him to the exit. Another deputy soon followed. They met at the corner of a busy, brightly lit street.

"Well?" Sykes asked as soon as the three were together.

"First name Lance. Last name Janke or Janeke or something similar. He took a girl to the outskirts of town and they partied with some bikers three days ago. The whole bunch was on their way to Sturgis. Some were trailering their bikes over and then riding them back. They mentioned picking up a few bikes there. Our man with the tattoo was riding a chopped Harley Low-Rider with a one-of-a-kind purple dragon paint job on it. Like we thought, he's about six foot four or five, weighs around 220 to 240. He has blue-green eyes and a dragon tattoo that goes from his wrist to his upper arm. And he told the gal he's been using meth."

The officers discussed their next move. Bikers that were trailering their bikes one way and riding back indicated a possibility they intended to steal motorcycles. The stolen bikes would be concealed in the enclosed trailers while the thieves rode their own motorcycles back to Nevada. Brady provided his colleagues with the details of the trucks and trailers that the woman had given him. The marshals knew that locating one particular biker among the tens of thousands attending the annual rally in Sturgis would be a daunting task. The best option would be to try to locate the group as they returned west and hope Lance Janke was among them.

The man's use of methamphetamines was a concern. It explained the unpredictable, explosive, and violent behavior that had kept them from establishing a pattern of the fugitive's actions. *Where in the vicious cycle of meth use would they find their man?* Brady wondered. *During his high or his hallucinations? During a period of energetic sleeplessness or during a stage of paranoia?*

Brady wandered around a couple of casinos along Virginia Street where Lance Janke had stopped several days before. He thought the chances were slim that Janke would look up the woman as he said he would–but there was always a chance.

The information from the young woman had proved invaluable to the marshals as they studied Janke's background. While some did their homework on the fugitive, others followed a pair of trucks pulling enclosed trailers westward across Utah, keeping them under surveillance all the way to the chop shop where stolen motorcycles were being refurbished or parted out. The high desert location of the shop had now been watched for three days. A few hours ago, Sykes and Brady and the other officers on stakeout downtown were notified that a truckload of merchandise had left the shop. Yet there was no sign of Janke.

Did he party with the ring of thieves and then move on? Brady wondered. *Or does he work at the receiving end of this operation? If so, they'll pick him up with the rest of the bunch when they raid the place. That will be the end of it. I can go home to Cassidy.*

Tim Sykes had confided he wasn't comfortable with the few deputies working downtown Reno if Janke showed up. And he wasn't happy that his supervisor was so anxious to shut down the motorcycle theft operation and didn't want to wait a few more days. Brady sensed the same unease Sykes was feeling. A familiar tension gripped him. The same tension that knotted the pit of his stomach as he awaited his chance to ride a bull. Anticipation. An anxious wait. Familiar circumstances with unpredictable results.

Surveying the area to which he had been assigned, Brady watched for Lola's girl, who had left a casino with a short, balding man nearly an hour before. He wondered if she would reappear this evening. Rather than retrace his steps, the deputy wandered into the street to walk behind the establishments he was staking out. He skirted around a parking lot as he headed toward the flashing marquee lights of a casino entrance. In the shadows of the glaring signs, Brady nearly overlooked a trio of motorcycles parked at the back of the lot, for they were mostly obstructed from view by a large van. The neon glow that dominated downtown Reno cast an iridescent light on the bikes, making their true color undistinguishable. But the dragons painted on the fuel tank of one of the Harleys were not. "A one-of-a-kind paint job," the young woman had described it. She was right. Brady had never seen anything like it.

As he eyed the artwork, Brady sensed that people were approaching from behind him. He sauntered off as though he was a passing pedestrian who briefly stopped to admire the cycles. A shout behind him caused him to turn.

"What?" Brady asked the man who had hollered at him.

"Get away from my bike!" the big man screamed again as he hurried his stride.

Brady knew instinctively that a dragon tattoo lurked under the leather arm guards that covered the big man's forearms and that he was facing the man he had sought so long. He steeled himself to remain calm.

"Just admiring the artwork," he answered, raising his hands up toward the approaching group. "I didn't touch the bike. I promise."

The bikers continued forward as Brady backed away. With three men and a couple of women in the group, the deputy knew better than to confront them by himself. He calculated how far away Sykes and the other marshals were. The minute microphone hidden under his shirt was a worthless tool to help them locate him since he hadn't uttered a word when he turned aside to look at the bikes. The last they had heard from him was when he left the building down the block.

"Ah..." Brady spoke, feigning that he was a bit drunk. "I don't remember which parking lot I left my car in. Is this Center Street?"

One of the women laughed at him and directed him to a lot a couple of blocks away. The others laughed with her and teased Brady about his forgetfulness.

"Oh, yeah!" Brady exclaimed. "This is where I parked last night. This is the Sierra Street parking lot!" *Lord, I hope those guys got the message,* he prayed. *Help us get this killer off the streets.*

Brady thanked the woman and turned to leave. The laughter and jeers behind him suddenly halted. He knew before he turned to face the group that he was in trouble.

The men came after him and Brady bolted around a couple of parked cars to head toward the brightly lit street. One of the men had anticipated the move and ran toward the edge of the lot to head him off. As Brady opted for a different route, he tried to keep an eye on all three at once. He knew their locations, but didn't see until too late that Janke had thrown a short length of stout chain at him. It hit him square in the left side, wrapping around his stomach and back, punching his torso with searing pain and causing the air to explode from him. Brady hunched over the trunk of a car. As he attempted to recover from the blow, he reached under his vest and gripped the cold steel of his pistol.

Janke drew nearer and Brady looked up in time to see the raging evil in the man's face. "You touched my bike! I'm gonna kill you!" the man declared. He leaped upon the hood of the car where Brady was leaning. Brady felt the bounce of the vehicle as Janke jumped onto the top, ready to pounce on his victim.

Brady pulled the gun from inside his vest and aimed it squarely at the chest of Lance Janke. "Stop where you are!" he warned menacingly.

Janke paid no attention. He leaped into the air to come crashing down on Brady. Brady sidestepped as he fired the gun, the report piercing the din of the busy downtown. Janke landed on his feet on the trunk of the car in the very spot Brady had just vacated. The growing red stain in the middle of Janke's shirt told Brady that his aim was true, yet the man leaped off the car to continue his pursuit, oblivious to the bullet that had pierced his chest.

Brady ran a couple of car lengths away and used the few seconds that he could to locate the other two bikers. Both backed off when they saw the pistol. Knowing their companion had been hit by a bullet, they opted to discontinue their part in the fight.

"Halt!" Brady shouted as Janke approached him. "You're under arrest for murder!"

Janke only growled and leaped once again at Brady. The deputy's second shot hit the man square in the chest again. Janke was so close Brady could see the hole where the bullet penetrated the blood-soaked shirt. He could see a festering boil that marked Janke's cheek just below his right eye. The man plunged closer still, raging like a madman.

Brady spun around to get away from the huge groping hands extended claw-like toward him, but was closer to the wall than he realized. His only option was to clamor over the hood of a van whose bumper left no room to go around. As Brady scrambled over the hood, Janke caught the heel of his boot and tried to pull the smaller man toward him. Brady kicked furiously and loosed Janke's grip only to slide head first off the vehicle and land hard on the pavement. Rough gravel made torturous stabs into his back and shoulders as Brady gasped for breath.

The narrow passage between the parked cars left little room for Brady to roll over and get his feet under him so he could escape. He scooted backwards a couple of feet when Janke appeared on the hood of the van. Brady never warned the man again. As Janke rose above the deputy, ready to pounce, Brady fired a third shot and a fourth. The fatally wounded Janke toppled off the vehicle, landing on top of the deputy in a contorted heap.

The deputy shoved with all the power he had left to move the huge dead man in case the others continued their attack. His energy was spent and the crushing weight left little room to breath. Brady's back and side hurt horribly as he tried in vain to draw a deep breath, as much to calm himself as to gain strength to escape his imprisonment.

Footsteps approached. In desperation, Brady groped around the pavement for his gun. He found it in time to pull it out from under Janke's body and wiggled to move so he could see who was coming. He had the gun drawn over his head when Tim Sykes appeared at the back of the vehicles.

"Brady, it's me!" Sykes shouted.

Brady's pistol clattered to the pavement as Sykes holstered his own weapon and maneuvered between the cars to roll the body over. With the weight off of him, Brady rose stiffly.

Tim was startled at the sight of his deputy who assured his superior that the blood that soaked his shirt was not his but Janke's.

As a stunned Brady hobbled across the parking lot, he noted that deputy marshals and local lawmen had surrounded the other two bikers and the women with them. Sykes was on the phone, whether calling for the coroner or calling his supervisor to let him know Janke's fate, Brady didn't care. He walked down the street through the gathering crowd, who gave the blood-soaked young man wide berth.

In a sparsely populated area down one of the side streets, Brady leaned over a garbage can where he heaved uncontrollably, clutching his side in agony as he did so. A hand on his shoulder surprised him, but he was even more surprised as he recognized the voice of the man who stood beside him.

"You get shot?" Kenny Chite asked.

Brady steadied himself on the wall and turned to look at the man. Chite reeled at the sight of the deputy. Brady's shirt was plastered to his chest and stomach with oozing red blood. The young man's complexion was ashen and he clutched at his side.

"Have you been shot?" Chite repeated, more loudly.

Brady shook his head and turned back to the garbage can for another agonizing bout of retching. His knees felt weak and he longed for nothing more than to sit down for a few minutes to regain his strength. He turned to lean his back on the building.

Chite yanked the snaps apart on Brady's shirt, baring his torso. "Go home to your wife, Hollister," he advised as he studied Brady's chest and stomach for wounds. "You don't belong on the back streets of Reno."

Brady smiled the weakest of smiles. "I told my boss weeks ago I was getting out as soon as we caught this guy."

There were other voices around him. Brady detected Lola's raspy voice and that of another woman as firm hands grasped his arms and guided him to a chair that had been brought to the sidewalk. Lola helped Chite remove Brady's vest, unstrap the empty leather shoulder holster, and remove the microphone. The pair worked together to peel the deputy's shirt off of him. Another woman came with some warm, wet towels. She and Lola cleaned blood from Brady's neck and chest. When someone touched Brady's side and he grimaced in pain, Chite turned the young man around to find a huge welt across his side and back. The swollen area was darkened with severe bruising and there were scrapes and cuts on his back.

"What did you get hit with?" Chite asked the deputy.

"A chain," Brady mumbled.

"It wasn't an ordinary chain. The guy must have had something sharp fastened on it to cut you up like that."

Brady closed his eyes.

"Are you in a lot of pain?" a woman's voice asked.

"Only if I breathe," Brady retorted, wincing as he drew air into his lungs.

As the women continued to tend to Brady, Chite asked, "So, Hollister, was it Janke you shot?"

Brady nodded. "He accused me of touching his motorcycle. He tried to kill me for it."

Tim Sykes found Brady in the midst of the little group on the street. He approached quietly and studied the scene. Chite pulled gently on

Brady's shoulder to move him forward as Lola dabbed at the cuts on the deputy's back. They paused in their ministrations when they realized they were being watched. Sykes moved closer, frowning as he studied the extent of Brady's wounds.

"I thought you said you weren't hurt," Sykes reprimanded.

"I told you I wasn't shot," Brady retorted. "Janke belted me with a chain and then landed on top of me from ten feet up in the air."

"He can't breathe very good," Chite explained. "He's probably got broken ribs pushing on his lungs."

"I'll call an ambulance for him," Sykes told the group. "Would you mind waiting here with him until it arrives?"

"I can take him to the hospital," Chite volunteered. Lola offered to ride along.

"Are you sure?" Sykes asked the pair with obvious surprise in his voice.

"He did us a favor, getting rid of that woman killer," Lola stated. "I didn't think much of him, knowing who he was. But he's not like his old man. I'll bet his old man never got sick to his stomach when he gunned down Trent Dominic."

Brady stood up from the chair and pulled a blanket around him that one of the women offered. "Lola," he said, "if you want to know what happened on Black Mesa, this is the man you should ask. He was there. He worked for my father at the time."

Lola stared at the tall, thin lawman before her. Her eyes narrowed. After several seconds of silence, she shrugged, "I might ask him…someday."

Tim Sykes nodded at the woman and gave her a wry smile. "I might tell you about it. Someday."

Sykes thanked the group for their help and trotted down the street toward the parking lot that had become a crime scene.

As the medical personnel ushered Brady into the emergency room, Chite and Lola turned to leave. "Hey, Kenny!" Brady called after them. "You should maybe have Lola go with you and take those nephews of yours shopping for school clothes or something. Your sister would let you do that, wouldn't she?"

Chite seemed to consider it. Lola readily consented. As they walked out the door together, Lola was insisting that if they went clothes shopping, she was going to see to it that Kenny's threadbare duds were replaced, too.

Brady smiled despite his pain as he imagined Kenny Chite and Lola shopping together with two school boys. He could almost envision the four of them becoming a family together someday. *Why not?* he mused. *Circumstances change. Hearts change. What held true in someone's life a year ago doesn't necessarily pertain to today. I thought I wanted nothing more than to become a U.S. Marshal. I was excited about taking on a tough job in Reno, but I'm over it now. I'm coming home, Cassidy. I'm coming home.*

TWENTY-FOUR

The cool autumn breeze that drifted down from the mountaintops battled with a sun still intent on warming the surrounding landscape, making the temperature pleasantly warm one minute and cool the next, but Elaine found the day agreeable for laying a paving-stone pathway. Picking up the rake to level another patch of ground, she heard the faint sound of a vehicle coming up the road. Pansy perked up her ears and leaped to her feet on her sunny spot on the porch to bark at the vehicle that topped the rise in a cloud of amber dust.

Elaine knew she had never seen the car before. Seldom did any automobile venture up this road, for four-wheel-drive vehicles were the normal mode of transportation in this rugged country. As the sporty little red car pulled to a stop near the front of the house, Elaine noted the Ohio license plate. A young woman stepped out of the vehicle and cautiously approached.

"Hello!" Elaine offered a hearty greeting as she scooped Pansy up from the ground to quiet her barking.

The young woman seemed intent on studying the scenery around her. "Hi," was the timid greeting. "Ummm…I'm wondering if you could help me…"

Elaine focused on her visitor, who was clearly uncomfortable and would only glance furtively at Elaine before turning her eyes elsewhere.

"Are you lost?" the older woman asked kindly.

"I…don't think so. Is this the…Hollister residence?"

"It belongs to the Hollisters. But they don't live here," Elaine explained kindly.

"Oh."

Was that a sigh of disappointment or relief? Elaine wondered. She asked, "Is there something I can help you with?"

"Well, I'm trying to locate a distant relative," the nervous young woman spluttered.

Distant relative? Elaine thought. *The family resemblance is unmistakable. Didn't Cassidy tell me Brady had never sought out his mother or any of his half-brothers and sisters?*

"I've only been in the area for a couple of months, so I don't know many people here yet," Elaine told her guest. "But I'll call my son-in-law. He's lived here nearly all of his life. I know he can put you on the right track."

Elaine bounded into the house without waiting for a reply, leaving her guest to wait outside. Her hand shook slightly as she dialed the phone number for Jubel's house. Cassidy answered and when questioned about Brady's whereabouts, told her mother he was doing some repair work in the barn. Elaine explained that she had a visitor who needed the assistance of a detective and had mistakenly been directed to the cabin. Cassidy promised she and Brady would come as soon as possible.

Lord, I hope I'm doing the right thing, Elaine whispered a prayer. *If I told Brady I suspect a relative of his is here, what would he do? And if I tell this young lady Brady is coming, will she panic and leave?*

Deception was not normal for Elaine. She took a deep breath and steeled herself to remain calm as she went outdoors.

"I got hold of my daughter," she announced to her visitor with a bright smile. "She and her husband will be here in about half an hour."

A half hour seemed an achingly long time for Elaine to try to entertain someone so obviously discomforted. She asked the young woman's name and what part of Ohio she was from. The answers were rather curt, but Elaine learned that the young woman's name was Hannah and she lived in south central Ohio. Never having traveled through that part of the country, Elaine prodded her to talk about the area, then asked if she would like to climb to the top of the hill behind the house to look at the view. Hannah shrugged, giving neither a "yes" or "no" answer, but willingly followed Elaine up the steep trail.

At the top of the hill, Elaine explained a bit about the country as Bret had done for her. When she mentioned that the Hollisters moved to this place from Buffalo, Hannah finally ventured to ask a question.

"Do you know the names of the Hollisters who moved here?"

"Bret and his son, Brady," Elaine answered as casually as she could, pretending she didn't notice the sudden threat of tears in Hannah's eyes. Elaine turned her face toward the distant mountains as she explained briefly that the very same neighbors who found this house for them were the ones who took care of Brady while Bret was at work.

"So..." Hannah asked, "Brady was quite young when they moved here?"

"I believe he was six years old," Elaine answered with a curious glance at the young woman.

A dust cloud at the end of the road signaled that a vehicle was approaching the house. Elaine pointed it out to Hannah and started down the hill. They arrived in the yard only moments before Brady's truck rolled to a stop in the gravelly drive.

Elaine led Hannah to the driver's side of the truck and announced as soon as Brady had emerged from the cab, "This is Hannah."

Brady seemed momentarily taken aback at Elaine's failure to give the young woman his and Cassidy's names. He quickly took the initiative. With his winning smile, he introduced himself. "I'm Brady Hollister and this is my wife, Cassidy."

The shock on Hannah's face was unmistakable. Tears sprang to her eyes, clouding them as she hastened to her car. Brady followed. As she pulled the door open, his strong hand held it tightly enough that she couldn't get inside.

"You didn't come all the way here from Ohio to turn tail and run did you?" he challenged the young woman.

"I shouldn't have come!" Hannah wailed as tears streamed unabated down her cheeks.

"Well, you did," Brady stated flatly, as though he were impatient with the young woman for calling him away from his work only to find he may not have a case to solve after all. He let out a sigh and tried a different tack.

"There's obviously something going on that's very disturbing to you," he sympathized. "Let's go in the house and talk about it, okay?"

Hannah was still reluctant, but Brady encircled the young woman with a strong arm and moved her in the direction of the house. Elaine and Cassidy followed. Cassidy pointed Hannah to a chair, then seated herself next to Brady while Elaine fetched a box of tissue that she discreetly laid on the table at Hannah's elbow.

Surrounded as she was in a remote area of Wyoming with no friend to turn to and no one else to confide in, Hannah seemed finally resigned to tell the painful tale that brought her to this place.

"My mother died a couple weeks ago," she started, choking back a fresh flood of tears. "When she was really sick, I was sitting by her bed. She knew she didn't have much time left....I asked her if she had a lot of regrets about how she'd lived her life and if there was anything she would have done differently..."

Hannah averted her eyes from everyone as she continued. "She told me her biggest regret...was that she never asked Brady to forgive her..." Hannah sobbed and covered her face. Brady sat motionless, staring at the young woman before him.

"I said, 'Mama, who's Brady?' and she said, 'He's my son'....I thought the morphine was making her delirious. I argued with her...I said, 'No, Mama. Your son's name was Brendan. Brendan died when he was three years old.' She looked at me...so sad, and said, 'Brendan was the one who died...Brady was the one I left behind.'"

Brady was speechless. He sat as if riveted in his chair and hardly reacted as Cassidy's cool hands clutched his, but his eyes narrowed as he watched the young woman pour out her agonizing tale.

"I swear I didn't know I had another brother before then. And Mama was so weak I could hardly get her to say anything more. But before she got too sick to do anything, she packed up a box of pictures and mementos and gifts for each of us kids. I opened my box a couple days after her funeral...and found her diary at the bottom. She talked about leaving...and her regrets...and she swore she would never break up a family again as long as she lived, so she followed Dad wherever he wanted to go and kept us together as a family…and cried herself to sleep way too many nights."

With everything finally coming out in the open, Hannah breathed a huge sigh of relief. She spoke again, this time looking directly at Brady.

"It was like I couldn't get any rest until I came…."

Brady slid his chair back and rose from the table, turning away from her. Hannah hastily jumped from her seat. She stood behind her new-found brother and begged him, "Please tell me you've forgiven her. Tell me you had a good life…that you had good parents to raise you…"

Brady didn't answer. He walked out of the kitchen to pace around the living room in silence. When he finally returned to the kitchen, he found that Hannah had returned to her chair. Elaine was sitting next to her with an arm around her and Cassidy was holding her hand as she spoke softly to her.

"It's funny," Brady said in a raspy voice. "I've tracked down fugitives and runaways and missing persons, but never once did I try to find my mother. I wrote her off when I was a little kid. Told myself I didn't need her."

The young man slumped into his chair next to Cassidy and faced Hannah. He studied her features–the dark, naturally curly hair, the heart-shape of her face, her gestures.

"You look like her, don't you?"

"Quite a bit," Hannah confessed.

"Dad tried to tell me more than once I had some half-sisters and brothers. I wouldn't listen. Didn't want to hear it, I guess. But I couldn't help thinking about it every now and then. And I thought about my mother. It seems like her birthday was this time of year."

"She would have been fifty-six next week," Hannah remarked.

An awkward silence ensued. There were so many unanswered questions that no one seemed to know where to begin. While offering steaming cups of coffee to her guests, Elaine ventured to ask Hannah how many brothers and sisters she had. After learning that Hannah was the oldest of a family that totaled three girls and two boys, Cassidy took her mother's cue by asking more questions. Hannah answered them and ventured to ask a few of her own.

With conversation gradually becoming easier, Brady wondered aloud if Hannah was married. His question brought instant hurt to her eyes. She tearfully admitted she had broken off an engagement. In fact, the wedding rehearsal had been scheduled for that very evening. She had tried to tell her fiancé about a brother she never knew and secrets her mother had kept for decades, but he was unsympathetic. He insisted she needed no one in her life except him. Until that time, Hannah had not realized how controlling he was–and how uncompromising. She had taken the week off from work to make final preparations for her wedding. Instead of going to the bridal shop on Monday morning as planned, she packed belongings in her car and left a note and her engagement ring on the kitchen table of her apartment. She cleaned out her bank account and headed west with an old diary that raised numerous questions and offered only a few sketchy answers. Scared half to death of what she might find in Wyoming, Hannah wondered at times during her journey if she had gone crazy, yet she found a strange sort of peace in running away.

"You kinda like having a little sister, don't you?" Cassidy teased as she and Brady walked to the truck, having said good-night to Hannah. Elaine had kindly offered a bed to Hannah in the extra room of the cabin, for the young woman desperately needed rest.

"Well, after I got over the shock of it, I guess I decided it was okay," he muttered.

"Okay! You two talked steady for almost five hours!" Cassidy said with a laugh as she climbed into the vehicle. She folded up the console and slid to the middle of the seat as Brady climbed in behind the wheel.

After he turned the truck around and headed for home, Brady hugged his wife close. She snuggled under his arm, content to ride in silence, giving him quiet time for thinking.

"Cass," Brady asked after a long silence, "was it wrong for me to ignore my mother all these years?"

"It seems like she wanted it that way," Cassidy answered. "She never tried to contact you, and you would have been easy to find. You didn't move very far from Buffalo and anyone who knew anything about rodeos would have recognized your name."

"But she's gone now. I always figured she was self-centered and uncaring. But she stuck it out with Don and raised her family....I'm the one who was selfish and uncaring, for never having anything to do with her. Maybe I thought she'd reject me all over again. I don't know what it is in me that kept that big wall between us..."

Cassidy studied her husband in the dim light of the truck cab. "Things are pretty much black and white with you," she commented. "You make quick judgment calls–either you like something or you don't. It takes a lot of coercing to get you to try something different or to see things from a different point of view."

"Like trying to get me to eat broccoli?"

"Yes! Right or wrong, when you get an idea in your head, you stick to it."

Brady returned to his thoughtful mood for several miles. Cassidy was nearly dozing when he suddenly pulled her closer and spoke softly.

"I don't make up my mind about things as fast as you think I do. Why, it probably took me the better part of fifteen minutes to start thinking about this pretty blond that was ridin' around in my truck–how good it felt to have my arm around her, about her soft hair, her nice curves....Of course, I was distracted by murderers and all. That might explain the delay."

Cassidy laughed softly at her husband and asked, "In normal circumstances, how long do you think it would have taken you to notice me?"

"First glance, I'd a noticed you, second glance, I'd a started thinkin' things."

Brady suddenly pulled the truck to the side of the road.

"What's wrong?" Cassidy asked, sitting upright beside him.

"Nothing. I just made my mind up to do something."

"Like what?"

Pulling his wife into his arms, Brady plied her with tender kisses as he whispered, "Have I told you lately how much I love you?"

TWENTY-FIVE

The aroma of fresh-baked bread and homemade soup wafted through the cabin as Elaine unfolded lengths of drapery material. As arranged the previous evening, Brady and Cassidy had come to visit Hannah and take her for a drive around the countryside. Elaine elected not to tag along. She opted instead to fix lunch for the wanderers and work on decorating the yet unadorned windows in the living room.

With new drapery rods installed above the large front window, Elaine carefully folded fabric in soft pleats. Carrying the cloth up the ladder, she draped it over the rods. She tried to adjust the material, but it slid out of place. When she tried to drape the fabric in a different way, she disliked the arrangement.

Growing more frustrated by the minute, Elaine scarcely noticed when a vehicle topped the rise in the road and moved in a cloud of dust toward the house. Not until Pansy alerted her with alarmed barking did she pay attention to the SUV as it pulled to a stop. Though she had resolved to be more cautious around the marshal than she had been in the past, when he knocked on the door, Elaine called for him to come in. She nearly had the cloth in place and didn't want to release it to go to the door. Reaching to adjust an outside corner, the entire drapery rod tumbled down as Bret entered the room.

"Not havin' a good day?" the marshal asked with a grin while Elaine stood on the ladder with yards of cloth around her.

"I hate this material. I can't get it to cooperate," she pouted as she returned the rod to its holder and began gathering the mess.

The marshal stepped nearer and picked up a corner of the drape to hold it up to the light. "I don't like it either," he commented with a scowl. "Looks too much like dress goods."

"Dress goods!" Elaine repeated with a laugh. "Oh, I don't think so."

She climbed down from the ladder and reached for the material. The marshal still held one end of the fabric, clumsily attempting to help her fold it into a neat pile. As their fingertips brushed against one another, Elaine had the unsettled feeling the marshal was staring at her. She glanced up at him, wondering what was on his mind and whether he would put it into words or keep his thoughts to himself as he so often did.

Pansy again barked a warning. Elaine peered through the window in time to see Brady pull his truck to a stop in the yard. Without knocking, he bounded into the house.

"Dad!" he greeted as he came toward his father with a rather sheepish grin. "It's good to see you. We weren't expecting you."

"I reckon I'm outta the habit of announcing to anyone where I'm goin' or what I'm doin'," the marshal retorted, "but I've gotta come up here every now and then to replenish the bank account for all the fixin' your mother-in-law is findin' to do around here."

Cassidy and Hannah entered the house as Brady was remarking to his father that he must have just gotten there. The dust hadn't yet settled in the driveway. Bret acknowledged he had just arrived as he noted the guest who tagged along behind Cassidy. His eyes narrowed as he studied the young woman who stood next to his daughter-in-law.

"Dad, you tried to tell me a long time ago…," Brady stammered. "Well…this is my half-sister. Her name is…"

"Hannah," the marshal finished the sentence, much to everyone's surprise. "Hannah Rice."

"Yeah," Brady agreed as he stepped over to the shy young woman. Grasping one of her hands, he pulled her closer to his father. "This is Hannah."

The marshal was visibly shaken by the sight of her. His jaw clenched firmly as his dark eyes bored into Hannah's. He suddenly turned away to face the far wall of the living room. The rise and fall of his broad shoulders revealed that he was taking deep breaths. The clenching and unclenching of his fists showed how distraught he really was.

"I thought I forgave that woman everything. Everything!" he wailed. "How could she do this to me!?"

"Dad, it's okay…" Brady tried to console the man, resting his hand on his father's shoulder. The marshal spun around and flung it away.

"It's not okay!" the marshal raged. "Look at her, Brady! *Look at her!*"

Brady turned to look at the terrified Hannah as the marshal had ordered him to do.

"There's no way she's Don Rice's daughter!" the marshal sobbed. "She's mine!"

Slow tears slipped from Hannah's eyes as she stood riveted to her spot on the living room floor. The marshal plopped down on the couch and covered his face with his hands in a gesture that spoke of utter frustration and defeat. Brady folded his hands behind his head and paced in circles before going to Hannah to give her a hug of reassurance.

"You don't look like your brothers and sisters, do you, Girl?" Bret challenged the startled young woman. She slowly shook her head, not looking Bret or Brady in the eye as she did so.

"Do they have round faces like their dad? Green eyes? Light colored hair?"

Hannah didn't answer, but stood in silence as tears clouded her dark eyes.

"Where's your mother!?" Bret demanded as he stood and stepped close to the frightened girl. "I'm gonna have words with that woman…"

"She's gone, Dad," Brady broke the news. "She died of cancer a couple weeks ago."

The rage in Bret's dark eyes turned suddenly to sadness. What was done could not be undone. That which had been unforgiven could no longer be mended. The marshal closed his eyes as if to shut out the image of his wife that he saw in Hannah. After several moments of silence, he asked Hannah if her mother had suffered a lot. She nodded.

"I'm sorry," the marshal sincerely apologized in a quiet voice. "I'm sorry to hear it."

The man studied Hannah in silence for a time. "You're so much like your mother," he remarked quietly, then stepped past the young woman and out the front door.

Hannah's teary demeanor broke into sobs once Bret was gone. Brady helped his sister to the couch and sat down next to her.

"It's the truth, isn't it?" he asked. "Your eyes are like Dad's..."

"I didn't know until I saw him!" Hannah cried. "I don't expect him to love me...but I didn't think he would walk away!"

"He didn't go far," Elaine consoled. "He didn't take his hat with him."

"Dad has no right to be upset with Hannah!" Brady lamented. "She didn't do anything wrong!"

"He's not upset with Hannah," Elaine assured her son-in-law. "He probably needs to grieve." Tears welled up in her eyes as Elaine recalled the moment she had come to the realization of her own husband's death. "He used to love your mother, Brady. It was a shock for him to hear that she's gone. Not only did she pass away without the two of them making amends, she took a serious deception to the grave with her."

While Brady and Hannah remained seated on the couch, Elaine went to the kitchen to put the finishing touches on the noonday meal. Cassidy wandered silently from the living room to the kitchen and caught her mother checking outside the window for a sign of Bret.

"I'll bet he went up on the hill," Elaine remarked with a sigh. "He's going to freeze. He didn't take his coat or hat." She added a couple of ingredients to the soup kettle and asked Cassidy to set the table.

As Elaine reached for her jacket and Bret's coat, the phone rang. Cassidy answered and found that Beth Knowlton was on the line. After a brief greeting, she handed the phone to her mother. While Elaine discussed plans for Sunday dinner, Cassidy slipped into her jacket and grabbed Bret's coat and hat off the rack behind the door before stepping outside into the chill air.

Cassidy found her father-in-law sitting on a patch of near-barren ground at the top of the hill with his arms folded tightly across his knees. His face was downcast, his chin resting on his forearms while he stared at wispy blades of grass at his feet. He remained unmoving except for the chill wind that racked his body with shivers.

She had witnessed the harsh sides of the man–his anger, intimidation, impatience. She had also seen his sense of responsibility and streaks of kindness and gentleness. But never had she known the marshal to crumble under such a load of hurt.

Cassidy didn't relish the thought of coming to her father-in-law's aid, for she was still angry about his actions toward her mother, but a measure of sympathy surfaced when she realized the shock and hurt Hannah's visit had caused him. Her intention was to bring the hat and coat to the man and leave him alone with his thoughts, but seeing him like this compelled her to be more civil. She walked quietly toward him and placed the heavy coat over his shoulders, adjusting it tightly around him. He didn't stir nor look up.

"I don't know why I drug your hat up here," she remarked after a time. "It's not going to stay on your head in this wind."

Bret glanced up at his daughter-in-law as he slipped his arms into the sleeves of the coat and pulled the collar up around his neck to fend off the chilly gale.

"Watch me," he said with an uneasy grin as he held out his hand for his hat. When Cassidy gave it to him, he pulled it so tightly down around his head that his eyes were nearly hidden and his ears protruded. The wind buffeted the felt, but was unable to dislodge it from his head. When he looked up at her, Cassidy couldn't help but laugh aloud at the sight of the normally somber marshal looking so silly. He winced as he pulled the hat up, setting it on right and keeping a hand on the brim as a safety measure.

"I'm surprised you're the one who came to my rescue," the man commented as he stood and buttoned his coat. "It's a long, cold hike up here on a day like today."

"Mom was going to come, but she got a phone call from Beth," Cassidy explained.

"Well, you've gotta make sure your ma and I aren't left alone anyway, don't you? We can't have another incident like we had a few months ago..."

"She never mentions it," Cassidy quickly assured the man, hoping the sore subject would be dropped. "No one does. Everyone has forgotten about it."

"Everyone but me," the marshal stated in an even tone while keeping his eyes on Cassidy, "and you."

Stunned at the truthful accusation, she quickly looked away.

"I see the resentment in your eyes every time you look at me," the marshal accused.

"I just don't know how you could take advantage of her the way you did!" Cassidy lashed out.

"It was easy!" the marshal countered. "I swear, Cassidy, I didn't know she was hurt! But you don't know what it's like for a man to quench desire week after week! When she held me the way she did…"

Bret ceased to speak to the young woman who stubbornly kept her eyes averted. He wouldn't waste any more words trying to explain himself.

Cassidy knew how desperate Brady was for her affection whenever he came home after an extended absence. The marshal swore he had done nothing to intentionally hurt her mother and her mother obviously didn't think the incident warranted concern, for she remained cordial to the man.

"Brady told me you asked Mom to come here so you could get to know her better," Cassidy stated cautiously as she kicked at a clump of sparse grass. "Do you think about my mother a lot?"

"Yeah," the marshal quietly admitted.

"Does she know that?"

"She'll never know."

Cassidy raised her eyes to study the man. The reason for his statement dawned slowly. "It's because of me, isn't it?" she wondered aloud. "The reason you won't tell Mom how you feel about her…."

Bret didn't answer directly. He didn't have to, for Cassidy knew it was the truth.

"I'm not going to do anything that causes trouble between you and Brady after all you've done for him. He's really happy for the first time in his life. And Jubel is more outgoing and energetic than he's been in years.

I tell you what, before you came along, we threatened to be three ornery, unhappy bachelors in this family. You turned two of the three around. I reckon we'll just leave well enough alone."

Rather than directly challenge Bret about his intentions toward her mother and risk making them both angry again, Cassidy ventured to bring up the subject of affection in a different manner.

"Did you love Sarah?" she ventured.

The marshal seemed surprised at the question. His jaw clenched briefly, as if he were steeling himself against physical pain. "Enough to let her go," he said quietly. "And I'd a taken her back…"

"When did you give up hoping?" the young woman persisted.

The marshal sighed–a deep, long exhalation of air. "I guess after she had three or four of her kids and moved a half dozen times, I finally figured out she was gonna follow Don Rice wherever he went."

"I'm sorry," Cassidy muttered. She turned her attention to butting a nearby sage with the toe of her shoe, sending the fragrance of the plant wafting on the wind.

The twitch of a smile curled one side of Bret's mouth as he suddenly became thoughtful. He changed the subject. "You know, I saw the strangest thing a few weeks ago when I rode up to Black Mesa with Bud Knowlton," the man began, stroking the sides of his jaw as he so often did.

Cassidy searched the terrain for the little glimpse of the far-off hill that was visible from her vantage point.

"There's a tree trying to grow up on top of that hill. He's been there a long time. Right up on top, where the wind beats him up and the sun scorches him and the cattle step on him. If he'd a had any sense at all, he'd a rolled down the hill into the gulley with the others before he took root where he'd a gotten water and shelter and better soil. But there he is. Toughin' it out all alone up there. Actin' like he's on top of the world. Regrettin' it. But that's where he's put his roots down. I reckon that's where he'll stay."

Cassidy felt as though she had briefly breached the walls of a fortress, one of the marshal's own making, while the guard was laid low by grief and despair. But the ramparts had been raised again. The marshal had reverted back to his proud, self-reliant being and was shutting her out.

That tree is so much like you, she considered in silence. *So proud. So stubborn. So unmoving. You became the ideal U.S. Marshal that you dreamed of being–tough, relentless–and you've ignored everything in life that really matters. You've had the Bible at hand and good Christian friends to fellowship with, but you won't ask for help. You won't admit how lonely and miserable you really are.*

Cassidy cried out in silent prayer as her heart suddenly churned with remorse and compassion for the man. *Why would Bret want to be Christ-like? He sees people like me who call themselves Christians but are angry and resentful and unforgiving. I've been criticizing his hard exterior, but what does he see in me?*

"Bret?" the young woman asked in a quiet voice that quivered with emotion. "I'm sorry for the way I've been treating you. I know now you didn't have bad intentions toward Mom."

The marshal considered his daughter-in-law's words in stony silence.

"You need to tell Mom how you feel about her," Cassidy encouraged.

The man turned away, fixing his gaze once again on some point on the distant mountain. His jaw clenched and he remained silent.

"Can you forgive me?" Cassidy asked quietly while a couple of tears slid down her rosy cheeks.

The marshal met her pleading gaze with a steady one of his own. In a raspy voice he said, "You know I will."

Cassidy slowly raised her hand toward the marshal. He studied the long, slender fingers extended in his direction before reaching out tentatively to clasp them in his own. She stepped close and slipped her arm around him, hoping the touch would convey trust, forgiveness, and compassion.

Bret relented. He held his daughter-in-law tight in a brief one-armed hug around her shoulders and gently kissed the top of her head in a silent gesture of truce.

"Do you think they saved any food for us?" he asked.

Cassidy turned toward the trail and called, "Let's go find out!"

Chilly air cooled the room as Bret ushered Cassidy into the house. They found Brady, Hannah, and Elaine lingering at the table, though the trio had finished their meal. While the pair of wanderers hung their coats, Elaine ladled hot soup into their bowls and fetched a basket of fresh buns from the oven where she had been keeping them warm. Bret commented that he didn't realize he was so hungry until he walked through the door and smelled the food. He then focused his attention on Hannah and apologized for walking out like he did, citing the fact he was so overwhelmed with shock that he needed to be alone for awhile.

"Believe me, I always wanted a daughter," Bret said through mouthfuls of food. "But to find out I had one all grown up that didn't need me anymore…it really hurt."

"Hannah probably needs her father more than he thinks," Elaine said gently as she set a steaming cup of coffee on the table within easy reach of the marshal. "She was supposed to be married today."

Bret stopped eating and stared at the dark-haired young woman who sat across the table from him.

"I know what you're thinking!" Hannah defended. "That I'm just like my mother to leave the way I did! But I'm not! It's not the same!"

Bret shook his head. "Hannah, I wasn't thinking that at all," he said honestly. "But I would like to know what happened."

Hannah related the story to Bret that she had previously told the others–her fiancé simply refused to recognize her need to find out about her mother's past.

As Bret finished a second helping of soup and bread, he asked Hannah about her mother. The young woman confided that her mother never talked about her life prior to her marriage to Don Rice. Hannah was nearly seventeen years old when she came home from school one day and found her mother crying. When asked about it, her mother quietly confessed that day would have been her son Brendan's twenty-first birthday. Hannah had been stunned to learn of her mother's first marriage and of an older brother who had died of heart problems.

When Bret asked further questions, Hannah offered to let him read her mother's diary. She retrieved the volume from the bedroom and relinquished the tattered little leather-bound book into the hands of her natural father. Bret opened the book mid-way and studied the crumpled pages, focusing on the familiar handwriting rather than reading the words.

Hannah offered to read from the volume, but within the first couple of sentences, she was too distressed to continue, so she asked Elaine to do it. Scanning page after page, Elaine shared random passages that seemed to reveal the most about Sarah.

Hannah is a beautiful child. I love her dearly, but it is painful to hold her. She reminds me so much of Brady. She is lively like he was and she looks like him, too…

Moving again. Don't have much time to write, though we have little enough to pack. I am exhausted. The baby is due within a month. I think we have finally settled on names…

I am writing as I am rocking Adam. He is a colicky baby and keeps me up most nights. I'm always tired. And I'm scared. The bills are piling up. I would go find a job if I could, but I can't manage it. Don has got to find something better than the janitor work he is doing…

Don and I had a huge fight last night. I ask myself, what have I done? Why did I leave Bret for this? By now, he has a new wife and Brady has a new mother. And I have two kids in diapers and another one on the way…

Sometimes I wish Bret and I could sit down and talk the way we used to. It's funny, but he could be so rough on the outside, yet so gentle and understanding with me. I used to think Don was gentle and understanding, but he shouts at me and I feel just awful. I never felt that way with Bret…

I have made my bed and I must lie in it. This is my punishment for leaving Bret and Brady like I did. I'm sorry the kids witnessed our fight last night, but I never want my family to split apart again. I'll work things out with Don for the sake of the kids. If only he could find a job he enjoyed, he would feel better about things. I'll have to try harder to keep the kids quiet when he gets home so he can relax…

Grandpa Rice's funeral. This is the first time I have seen Don's first wife and older children since we left Wyoming. My, how they have grown! It makes me sad to look at the oldest girl, who is now a young lady. She is the same age as Brady…

I took the kids to church today. It's a different church than what we've been going to. Don was working, so he couldn't go along. The kids said they enjoyed the

Sunday School. We haven't been very faithful about attending church. I wonder why I bother at all, but it's important for the kids to know about Jesus. It's not His fault I didn't live like the Bible told me to. I have to do what's best for the kids and try to not think about the past. That's really hard to do sometimes...

Hannah caught me crying today. I couldn't help it. This would have been Brendan's twenty-first birthday. I still miss him so much. I just had to tell her about him. Now days, they could have fixed Brendan. Back then, they didn't know how. He was such a sweet baby. I would have taken care of him as long as I could. I prayed to God to heal him, but I know better than to count on God anymore. It's best to be like Bret–just take care of things yourself. Well, I guess that's what I've done. But that doesn't seem to be the best solution either...

Don told us today we would be moving to Atlanta. He has work waiting for him there. I told him to go ahead and go. I'm not moving anymore. The kids like their school and they have a lot of friends here. And they have relatives here–Grandma Rice and aunts and uncles and cousins. Ohio feels more at home to them than anywhere else. Don offered to leave Hannah with Grandma Rice so she could finish her senior year of high school. Then we would move with the other four kids. I hate the idea...

Atlanta is so hot, I can hardly stand it. And it's only April! I can't wait to go back to Ohio to see Hannah graduate. She has a job in a grocery store and is going to stay in Ohio and work for the whole summer. I miss her so much, but she's growing up and it's time to let her go out on her own. It will be easier for me to see her go than the others because she is a constant reminder of my past life. Someday, I'll tell her about it...

Elaine closed the journal–a book written intermittently over the course of twenty-five years. It seemed Sarah seldom found the time or energy to write, for there were gaps of several months between entries. She had never mentioned having close friends with which to share her feelings or discussing her deepest hurts and frustrations with Don. Perhaps her only outlet was to express herself on paper.

Somehow, it wasn't surprising that Sarah had passed away before the last of her children left home, for they had become the only love and focus of her life. As each one left the nest to lead an independent life of their own, a measure of her hope and joy had flown away with them.

TWENTY-SIX

Sunday dinner at the Knowlton house was an informal pot-luck affair, planned by Beth as soon as she found out Jubel and Edna intended to get married during the upcoming holiday season. The gathering would be an opportunity to acquaint friends and family with Jubel's fiancé. Pete and Jennifer and their children came, as did Skeeter and Crystal and their baby. Brady and Cassidy, Elaine, Hannah, and Bret rounded out the guest list. The dining room table was expanded as far as it would go with additional tables extending out into the living room so all sixteen people could be seated for the meal.

The talk was lively. Beth and Elaine sat nearest the kitchen where they had easy access to more food in case the laden table ran low. They discussed Elaine's problem window dressing while at the opposite end of the table, Skeeter teased Pete and Jennifer's kids, who clearly adored the man. Pete reprimanded Brady about keeping his little sister, Hannah, a secret so he couldn't pick on her while she was growing up. Crystal spent her time between visiting with Jennifer and Cassidy and Hannah and trying to catch food that her eight-month-old daughter threw from the high chair. Pete and Jennifer's daughter, Emily, had begged Elaine to bring Pansy for her to play with. The little dog quietly searched the floor, enjoying the spoils of the errant toddler high above her. Near the center of the ruckus, Bud and Bret sat across the table from Jubel and Edna.

"Bret tells me you decided to move to town, Jubel," Bud commented. "You've never lived in town in your life, have you?"

"Nope," Jubel replied. "But I reckon I'll give it a whirl. Edna likes her volunteer work at the hospital."

"My house is out at the edge of town," Edna added. "I have a big yard to take care of and my late husband had a woodworking shop out back. If that isn't enough to keep Jubel busy, he can always drive out to the ranch and find something to do."

"So Brady's gonna be a full time rancher now?" Bud guessed.

"No. Cassidy's still the rancher for now," Brady corrected as he joined the conversation. "I'm still on the Marshals Service payroll. My ribs are finally healed up so I can go back to work, but I'll be a lot closer to home and doing more guard duty than detective work for awhile. I'll stick with it unless Cassidy gets too busy with her art work to do the ranch chores."

"Speaking of ranching, are you gonna get the cattle out of the hills before snowfall this year or is Cassidy gonna have to do it by herself again?" Bud teased the young man.

Brady grinned sheepishly. "I think I'll manage to help her this year."

After a brief discussion of the pre-winter work yet to be done, the conversation steered back to Jubel and Edna.

"How long ago did you lose your husband?" Bret asked Edna.

"It's been nearly six years," she answered.

"It's been a long time since you lost your wife," Bud remarked to Jubel. "It must be near fifteen years that the only people in your family have been you and Bret and Brady."

Jubel nodded his head. "Rose died fourteen years ago. And Irene died just a couple months after," Jubel acknowledged, reminding Bud that his sister, Bret's mother, had been the last to go.

"Well, Bret's family is rebounding pretty good lately," Bud said with a laugh as he slapped the marshal good-naturedly on the back. "He got himself a daughter-in-law last summer and he found himself a daughter. Now he's gonna have a new aunt."

Bret looked across the table at Cassidy with a mischievous grin. "Cassidy, is there anything you want to add to that?"

She looked up from her plate, staring at the man with a blank look on her face. "What?" she asked, though she had heard the comment clearly.

"Would you care to add anything to that?" the marshal repeated.

"I don't know what you mean…," Cassidy stalled. Everyone around the table grew quiet as the young woman's face grew increasingly rosy.

"We've been talkin' about how my family is growing. Yesterday, you acted like you were hungry, but you picked at your lunch and then ate like a horse at supper time. Now you're pickin' at your lunch again. I tell you what, my gut feelin' says I'm gonna be a grandpa."

Cassidy's face flushed crimson. She hadn't even mentioned her unsettled stomach to Brady, but it was suddenly obvious by the way she had pushed her food around on her plate that something was not right. The thought she might be pregnant had been only a niggling suspicion resting in the back of her mind. "It's just the excitement...finding out about Hannah and all," Cassidy spluttered as she tried to divert the attention elsewhere.

Brady studied Cassidy's face. She glanced at her husband and shrugged. "Cassidy, do you feel pregnant?" he asked.

"I don't know," she answered quietly. "I've never been pregnant before."

Her remark delighted the crowd at the table and laughter abounded. Brady slid his chair back and pulled Cassidy onto his lap, embracing her and whispering in her ear while ignoring the jeers around them.

"I think we're going to have to rethink some of our plans," Brady commented. He turned his attention to his mother-in-law. "Elaine, are you just about done fixing up the cabin? Once Jubel moves to town, maybe you'd consider staying at the ranch with Cassidy. I think I'd better keep my job for the time being because that's where we're getting our health insurance."

"Brady, we don't even know yet..." Cassidy tried to interrupt, but Brady plunged ahead with his ideas for getting the ranch work done and making sure his wife was cared for.

Elaine and Beth rose from their places and began passing plates of dessert down the long table. As the dishes were handed down the line, Bud looked slyly around and remarked, "Yup, Bret, you've got a new daughter-in-law, a new daughter, a new aunt, and a new grandchild on the way. Now all you need is a wife."

The room suddenly stilled. Elaine did her best to ignore the statement as she continued passing out dessert. She nearly flipped a plate of the chocolate concoction onto the tablecloth and with a blush of embarrassment glanced up to find all eyes staring in her direction. Cassidy held her breath as she watched her mother's eyes slowly lift to meet those of the marshal.

"I committed a crime," the man confessed before a silent audience. "I imposed my own sentence by stayin' away from you, Elaine, but I'd like a reprieve. I'd like to talk to you about things other than fixin' up the house."

Elaine hesitated as she considered a reply. "Well…" she began, managing to keep a most sober look on her face while trying to answer the marshal's request in similar crime-fighter lingo. "I have done a thorough background check on you…and I don't find any horrible crimes on your record…"

Sly smiles surfaced on the faces of several adults at the table. Elaine kept her eyes on Bret as a mischievous grin spread across her lips. "But, I believe you need to be monitored, for I have yet to determine whether or not you're armed and dangerous."

Bret rubbed his fingers along his jaw as he eyed the woman across the table. A slow grin spread across his face. "Perhaps you'd like to step outside with me, Mrs. Henderson?"

"Outside?" Elaine asked sweetly. "Whatever for?"

"I tell you what," the marshal warned her. "I'm guaranteed armed and dangerous. And I'm thinkin' about breakin' parole. I don't care how many witnesses there are to see it."

Elaine blushed and held up her hands in a signal that she was unwilling to consent to a display of affection from the man in front of his friends and family. "We'll talk," she conceded. She didn't entice the man further, but moved toward the door. The marshal opened it and followed the woman outside.

Skeeter stuck his fingers in his mouth and let out a shrill whistle that pierced the air as the couple left. With everyone focused on the door, Pete stole a couple desserts off the table, hiding them on a shelf behind him.

"Dad!" Pete suddenly protested. "You just let an unmarried man and woman go outside together with nobody keepin' an eye on 'em!"

"Well, you go ahead and watch 'em," Bud advised his son while he savored the rich chocolate.

"Dad! You never let me and Brady go outside alone with a girl," Pete argued. "Last year when Brady was thirty-two years old he was never left alone with Cassidy!"

"My dessert is gone!" Skeeter complained. "I had one here! I didn't even get a bite of it yet!"

As conversation in the room returned to its normal, rowdy level, the young couple ignored the din around them. Brady continued to hold Cassidy close and quietly studied his wife's face as he whispered to her, "You aren't surprised by what's going on between my dad and your ma," he observed. "What happened up on the hill yesterday?"

"We had a good long talk…about Mom…about what happened. I told him I was sorry for treating him the way I have been and I know he didn't intend to hurt her. And I told him he should tell Mom how he feels about her. I think he really likes her."

"What if things get serious between 'em, Hon?" Brady questioned. "Will you be okay with that?"

Cassidy planted a light kiss on her husband's cheek as she whispered back, "I finally figured out I don't have to watch over Mom. She has her priorities straight and she'll take her advice from the Bible, not from me. She's not going to do anything hasty and it might be a long time before the marshal and Mom really see things eye to eye. We'll just have to wait and see."

TWENTY-SEVEN

An excited Cassidy hurried down the street with a precious bundle of paintings tucked under her arm. Focusing on her mission, she nearly collided with an unkempt, dour-faced man who came toward her on the sidewalk. She quickly maneuvered her large bundle out of the way to let the stranger pass and offered an apology for nearly bumping him. The man simply tapped the brim of his hat as he passed by, noting Cassidy's protruding stomach that overreached the boundaries of her jacket.

As Cassidy continued her trek down the sidewalk, the stranger paused in his journey, noting into which building she entered–the print shop. It was the very place he expected her to go, for he had seen her artwork displayed in a restaurant and learned that a local businessman was using it for promotional material.

The name "Cassidy" scrawled in the bottom corner of a painting had first caught the man's attention. After learning about the artist, it also gave him an idea for satisfying a hatred that had been festering for so long.

The stranger wandered down the street past a row of benches in front of a local café. There, several elderly men sat as they did nearly every morning when fine weather beckoned. The mention of Cassidy by the group brought the stranger to a halt. As he nonchalantly studied the auction bills and notices posted in a nearby window, the man intently digested every word of conversation.

"Cassidy's mother is stayin' 'til after the baby's born," a man called Jubel was telling the others. "She was a farmer back in Wisconsin and she's been doin' the ranchin' this winter while Brady's at work."

"Too bad she's not stickin' around here. I thought maybe the marshal would get around to askin' her to marry him," one of the men commented.

"He had that in mind," Jubel acknowledged, "but she told him she wasn't ready for another man. It's only been a couple years since she lost her husband."

"Is that the woman who comes to town with Brady's wife and Beth Knowlton every couple weeks?" another man asked.

"Yeah. They're all in town today. Cassidy's down at the print shop. They're getting a bunch of her artwork ready for sellin' this summer. Elaine and Beth are down at the grocery store," Jubel pointed out.

As the elderly men turned their conversation to other matters, the stranger sidled toward the hardware store, noting with a sidelong glance the women who were chatting with acquaintances outside the grocery store. He recognized the shorter, more fine-boned of the two as Cassidy's mother. If the trio came to town together every couple of weeks, they probably had a large quantity of groceries to purchase, the man reasoned. That would give him just enough time....

The stranger had thought long and hard about how to repay the marshal for ruining his career and he'd been drinking long and hard to build up the courage to do something he had never before attempted. The man had second thoughts about his plan when he saw Cassidy in her very pregnant condition. Now, his heart beat wildly as a better plot formed in his mind. With a final look at the women who entered the grocery, the stranger stepped resolutely into the hardware store before him.

With the back doors of Knowlton's Suburban flung open, Beth and Elaine busily arranged the numerous bags of groceries in the vehicle as they unloaded them from their carts. Pansy ran excitedly around Elaine's feet, happy that her master had returned to release her from the vehicle. As the women chatted amiably, neither noticed the blue truck that had pulled into a parking spot nearby, nor the unshaven, unkempt man who stepped out of it.

The strong arm that suddenly encircled Elaine's waist came as a complete shock to the woman. She was pulled backward, away from the Suburban, away from Beth. Stumbling backward with the force that held her, Elaine was several feet away from Beth before she could call out or mount a struggle to free herself. In shocked disbelief, Beth watched as an unknown assailant walked backward with her friend in tow while pointing a pistol in Beth's direction. The large woman stood helpless as the stranger shoved Elaine into the open door of his truck.

Pansy raced to the aid of her master, barking furiously and biting at the man's pant leg. With a swift and well-placed kick, the little dog flew through the air to land solidly several feet beyond where Beth stood.

Brandishing the weapon at Elaine in warning that she better not try to escape, the man snarled a message in Beth's direction before he leaped into the cab of the truck. "Tell the marshal Higgins was here."

Jubel's heart pounded as he gunned his truck in pursuit of the vehicle in front of him. On a quick turn that took the chase from the paved road to a dirt one, the old man feared losing control. Had not the early May sunshine been baking the surface, the greasy soil would have made passage doubly treacherous. As it was, there were still pockets of sodden gumbo soil that challenged the drivers' ability to keep their vehicles on the road. Jubel could do little but follow the truck ahead of him, noting in which direction it was going, hoping the driver would relent and release his hostage.

Without warning, the old man's truck spun sideways, swerving in one direction, then another. Turning the wheel as rapidly as he could, Jubel could not hold it on the slippery road. The red Dodge came to rest crossways over the tracks that the blue truck had made, its nose pointing into the ditch. As Jubel tried to back his truck out of its predicament, the blue truck slowed to a halt and the driver stepped out, brandishing the pistol.

"Old man!" the driver snarled. "You tell the marshal I've got his woman! If he wants to see her alive again, come find me! And he'd best be comin' alone!"

While Jubel watched helplessly, Higgins grabbed Elaine from the seat of the truck and pulled her from it. He slammed her against the side of the vehicle. Grabbing her hands together, he held them fast with his strong grip and wrapped Elaine's wrists with wide bands of duct tape. Shoving his victim back into the cab, he raced toward the distant mountains.

As Marshal Hollister stomped out of the courthouse, he silently cussed the judge who had let Larry Higgins post bail. After months of quiet investigation and a battery of charges finally ready to come to trial, Higgins had missed his appearance in court. Instead of putting closure on a case, the marshal now had another fugitive to hunt down.

Bret groaned as he opened the door of his SUV and checked his phone. The long list of messages could only mean one thing–more trouble. Settling into his seat, he played through the recordings, which included a frantic call from Beth Knowlton. The marshal backed hurriedly out of the parking lot. Speeding out of the city of Buffalo, he mentally counted the minutes it would take him to get to Worland as the haunting message reverberated in his mind. "Tell the marshal Higgins was here."

Elaine recalled her first meeting with the smug sheriff when Cassidy had disappeared. The man was hardly recognizable now. The arrogant, clean-shaven, and meticulously neat-uniformed officer had been transformed to a rough-looking, unkempt version of a bum that smelled of stale cigarettes and old booze. A few days of beard stubble and unruly hair testified to the recent neglect of his appearance, though these circumstances were probably not prolonged, for the man had not lost weight or his healthy complexion.

"Why are you doing this?" Elaine ventured quietly.

Higgins smiled and didn't answer immediately. When he did, his arrogance surfaced.

"I'm gonna watch U.S. Marshal Bret Hollister die," he grinned satisfactorily and turned his leering face toward Elaine.

"Why?" she demanded.

The man ignored her question. He drove in silence until he stopped the blue truck in front of a log building that advertised "J.J. Stearns, Outfitter."

"You set here real quiet and cooperate and you won't get hurt," Higgins instructed as he pulled a rifle from the rack in the back window of the truck cab. "But if you get out of the truck, I'll gun you down."

As Higgins strode up the plank steps to the office, Elaine studied the place. A variety of log and wood buildings rested in a secluded glen where tall stands of timber shrouded the surrounding foothills. Mammoth mountain peaks, spackled with patches of winter snow, stood tall behind the treetops.

Through the partially open truck window, Elaine heard the door of the house squeak as it opened. A lean, bow-legged cowboy stepped outside. "Larry! What can I do for you?" the man called as he seated his hat on his balding head and strode across the yard toward his store.

"J.J., I'd like to take a friend of mine on a horseback ride up into the hills."

The man referred to as J.J. glanced in Elaine's direction and smiled before returning his attention to his customer.

"It'll take me just a few minutes to get the horses saddled up. I have several in the corral. I've been working 'em, getting ready for trail rides we've got scheduled next week."

J.J. went around back of the barn and returned to the front of his store a short time later with a pair of sturdy mountain-bred horses, saddled and ready to go.

"How about a canteen of water and some grub?" Higgins asked. "You got some of that beef jerky layin' around?"

"Yeah, if the kids haven't snuck in here and ate it," J.J. said with a smile as he led the way into the building. "Help yourself to whatever you need."

Higgins gave a long warning look at Elaine as she sat rigidly in the truck before he followed the outfitter into his establishment. She calculated her chances of getting away from the man and decided it was too risky. Not only was Higgins watching her warily through the window, but an unsuspecting family man would be endangered if she tried anything foolish.

As Elaine watched helplessly, Higgins stepped out of the log cabin, propped his rifle against a post, and tossed a saddlebag over the back of a large bay horse. Adding a rolled sleeping bag, he secured the gear to the back of the saddle. A canteen was slung over the saddle horn.

J.J. stepped outside with a long leather sheath. Higgins slipped his rifle into it and nodded that it would fit fine. Elaine could scarcely hear the muffled voices of the men, but understood that Higgins was insisting on bringing a gun in case he ran into a bear. The leather case and rifle were secured on Higgins' mount and a second sleeping bag was tied on the saddle of a sorrel that stood quietly at the rail.

Satisfied that he was ready to go, Higgins strolled toward the truck, stepping to the driver's side. He opened the door and grabbed up the roll of duct tape that had been used to tie Elaine's wrists together. There was no doubt Higgins planned to do the same to the unsuspecting outfitter. As he strode back to the shop, he asked J.J. how much he owed him. The outfitter calculated the cost as he led the way back into the building. Higgins pulled a pistol from under his jacket and followed J.J. inside.

By the time the marshal reached Worland, townspeople had gathered along the streets. Several of them milled around the crime scene, waiting in anticipation, while keeping the streets clear for the vehicle that sped into town.

When the marshal's SUV screeched to a halt next to a marked police vehicle on the main street, a local deputy quickly handed him a paper with names, phone numbers, and a map drawn on it. Without words of greeting or introduction, the officer hurriedly explained that Larry Higgins' former staff of police officers had been contacted as well as his brothers. All concurred that Larry was probably taking his hostage to his favorite hunting spot in the Big Horn Mountains. Jubel had followed the man several miles in that direction, but had gotten stuck on a muddy road. Larry Higgins' family had provided the name and phone number of an outfitter who provided supplies for his hunting trips. There was no answer when they attempted to call the outfitter on the phone.

The marshal wordlessly digested all of the information the lawman gave him before he began asking questions of his own.

"Where's Jubel now?" the marshal asked, aware of the multitude of townspeople quietly taking in the scene.

"They got his truck pulled back onto the road. He and a deputy are heading toward the outfitter's place."

"Where's Cassidy?"

Someone in the crowd related the tale of the young woman's emergence from the print shop. When she learned her mother had been forced into a truck that was speeding out of town, Cassidy had run screaming down the street. A store owner caught up to her and stopped her, but she collapsed on the sidewalk and was clutching her stomach. People helped Beth Knowlton get her into the Suburban and they rushed to the hospital.

"Marshal, he watched Miss Cassidy go into the print shop," one man offered. "Then he came down here and stood in front of the café." The man hesitated and looked down at the sidewalk as he confessed, "Some of us were talkin' to Jubel about whether Mrs. Henderson was gonna move back to Wisconsin or stay here and marry you…"

Though inwardly raging, the marshal remained stone-faced as he studied the crowd. He hated the fact that people were using his private life as a topic for discussion. And if everyone in town knew he had approached Elaine with a serious relationship in mind, they probably also knew he had been put off. The revelation of the townsfolks' interest stabbed at his already wounded pride.

"He came into the hardware store, Marshal, and bought a length of rope and a roll of duct tape," a man in the crowd offered.

The marshal turned his full attention back to the matter at hand. "He never said anything to anyone?" he questioned the group.

Everyone indicated they had not spoken to the man except as they conducted business with him.

With a deep sigh, the marshal thanked the deputy and the people for their help and moved toward his vehicle. Extracting a card that contained his phone number, he handed it to the deputy. "Let me know if you hear anything more," the marshal instructed as he opened the door to his truck. He paused a moment as a call came through for the young lawman who held up his hand, indicating the marshal should wait for a message before he left.

When at length the call ended, the deputy was quick to relay it. "They found J.J. trussed up like a turkey, layin' in the doorway of his office. He'd been hit over the head, but he's conscious. Higgins is gone up into the hills on horseback with Mrs. Henderson. Along with horses, he got food, water, and sleeping bags. Besides carrying a pistol, Higgins is carrying a rifle–a 7mm with a scope.

The marshal wordlessly turned toward his truck once again.

"One more thing, Marshal," the deputy added soberly. "Higgins told J.J. if you want to see the woman alive, you go alone to meet him."

The marshal nodded that he understood. The directive was not unexpected. As the marshal put his vehicle in gear and fled town, he cussed himself for underestimating his enemies. Never did he dream a man like Higgins would do such a thing. A married man with kids. There was no doubt in the marshal's mind Higgins intended the confrontation to be a deadly one and if Higgins was capable of plotting to kill a U.S. Marshal, what were the chances he would keep Elaine alive?

Brady stopped in Gillette for fuel and a snack on his trek toward home. He had finished a stretch of several days work, most of the time transporting prisoners. The closer he got to home, the more his thoughts turned toward his wife. He wondered as he paid for his fuel if Cassidy's meeting at the print shop went well. She had been so excited when she called to tell him the spring rain had stopped and the dirt roads were finally dry enough to allow the women to safely make a trip to town.

As Brady eased his truck onto the highway, his thoughts drifted to Hannah. He wondered whether he should try to call her when he got home. She had stayed in Wyoming for a couple weeks before returning to Ohio where she had a good job, friends, and family. During their most recent conversation, Brady suspected she was still being influenced by her former fiancé. *Lord help her if she relents and gets back into a relationship with that guy,* he thought with disgust.

The cell phone hummed where it lay in the drink holder. Brady reached for it, expecting Cassidy would be calling. As he glanced at the small screen, he discovered the call was from a number he didn't recognize.

"Brady here," he answered.

"Brady, Cassidy's in the hospital," Beth's quivering voice began. "You've got to come home as fast as you can."

"What happened!?" he demanded.

Beth sobbed. "She panicked…and ran down the street…now she's bleeding…the baby may be coming early…"

"Why was she running down the street?" Brady wondered aloud as hysteria crept into his voice.

"Elaine…" Beth sobbed, "Elaine was taken hostage…by Higgins…"

Higgins! Too stunned to reply, Brady clenched the phone near his ear while his mind whirled.

"He grabbed her from behind when we came out of the grocery store," Beth continued. "He told me to 'tell the marshal Higgins was here'…then he drove out of town with Elaine in his truck."

"Are you at the hospital now?" Brady demanded.

"Yes."

"I'll meet you there!" he shouted as he stomped the gas pedal to the floor.

The silver and black SUV was so covered with mud and dirt that it matched the surrounding terrain when it wheeled into the yard and screeched to a halt next to Jubel's similarly mud-splattered red truck. Jubel waited quietly, leaning against a porch post under the J.J. Stearns sign until the marshal emerged from his vehicle. The marshal quickly noted the large buckskin gelding that stood ready, tied to the hitching rail in front of the store. Two more horses were tethered nearby with saddles and gear piled on the porch.

The marshal did not greet his uncle. "I'm going alone," he warned as he pulled his rifle, gear, and heavy coat from the truck cab.

"Yup," was Jubel's reply.

"Why are there other horses out of the corral?" the marshal asked as he approached the buckskin.

"Well, earlier today, J.J. took a couple horses on a trail that leads up through the trees to the right, in a different direction than Higgins took Elaine," Jubel patiently explained. "The way I figure it, if any help comes along and insists on following behind you, I'll lead 'em astray."

"Tell him to stay with his wife where he belongs," the marshal growled as he shoved his rifle into a case already secured on the saddle.

He and Jubel both knew Brady would show up unless Cassidy or the baby's health was truly endangered.

The marshal checked that the cinch was tight around the horse as Jubel calmly remarked, "That boy can find killers on paved city streets with the help of computers, but I'll wager he ain't much of a tracker in the mountains. I reckon I can delay him a good many hours."

The marshal paused in his preparations. "You up to it?" he questioned his uncle.

"I can still set a horse," Jubel retorted.

"Why don't you just tell him to stay out of the way?"

"I reckon he's gotta be doin' something. Keeps a man from feelin' so helpless," Jubel commented.

The marshal knew the statement held true for the old cowboy as well.

As the marshal secured his coat on the back of the saddle along with a bedroll, a young man bolted from the house with a sack clenched in his fist. "Here's some food, Marshal," he shouted breathlessly as he offered the bag. "Dad told me to give you the buckskin. He's one of Dad's favorites. A good mountain bred horse."

The marshal smiled down at the young man he figured to be about ten or eleven years old. "Did you saddle him and get all the gear together?" he asked as he deposited the lunch in one of the saddle bags.

"Mr. Jubel had already caught a couple of the horses before I got home from school," the lad excitedly explained. "But I went and got the buckskin for you."

"Well, you did a fine job. How is your dad doing?" the marshal questioned while checking that the clips for his rifle were full of ammunition.

"The deputy that was here took him to town a while ago to get his head stitched up. Mom just got home from work, and she's going back to town to be with Dad," the young man rattled on while the marshal checked his pistol and returned it to the holster.

After securing night-vision goggles and binoculars in the other saddle bag, the marshal untied the reins from the hitching rail and mounted the sturdy horse. Looking down at the lad, he tipped his hat to him.

"Thanks for all your help, young man. Tell your dad I'll settle up with him when I get back."

"Yes, sir!"

The marshal turned his attention to Jubel, who still leaned on the post. "Jubel, you're goin' to an awful lot of trouble for nothin'," the man commented.

"The way I figure it, Cassidy could lose her baby, her mother, and her father-in-law. No sense losin' her husband, too."

The marshal studied the weathered face of the old man whose somber words were an eerie reminder of the deadly potential of the situation.

"Higgins took a track to the left, heading for Buck Ridge, that open rock face above this stand of timber," Jubel informed his nephew. "You'll find the tracks of the two horses by the pasture corner post."

The marshal tipped his hat to his uncle and thanked him as he reined his horse toward the stand of timber. Jubel had garnered a wealth of trustworthy information, giving him a good start toward locating Larry Higgins and his hostage. The few hours' lead that Higgins had on him would make an immense difference in their location when nightfall crept over the mountain. The ex-sheriff knew the country well, while the marshal would have to carefully follow his enemy's tracks in order to locate him.

As the marshal loped the buckskin toward the trail, he glanced up at the graying sky and cussed his luck. The one thing that would make the trail hardest to follow and hardest to traverse was fast approaching–rain.

TWENTY-EIGHT

A pale Cassidy lay quietly on the stark white sheets of the hospital bed. Tears trickled down the sides of her face, wetting her hair and pillow. She kept her eyes tightly closed as if to shut out the world around her, ignoring the flowers that had been delivered to brighten her room as a reminder that several people about town were thinking of her plight.

The hospital staff tried to be cheerful as they monitored mother and baby. Beth Knowlton stayed at Cassidy's side, acting like a mother hen hovering over her chick. Yet there was no one who could console her. They finally departed from the room, leaving Cassidy alone in her misery to cry as she needed to.

A warm, firm grip on her hand and a kiss on her forehead signaled Brady's arrival. With a deep sob, Cassidy rose up in bed to enclose Brady in her arms as he sat at the edge of the mattress. Holding her tightly, Brady pressed his wife's face onto his chest. He didn't utter a word while offering the only comfort he could as the tears flowed.

When the flood of sorrow subsided, Brady released his hold on his wife and gently pressed her down onto the pillows. Leaning over her, he whispered, "Cassidy, the baby is okay."

She could only reply with a slight nod of the head. With the back of her hand, she wiped at her tears. Brady grabbed a handful of tissue from a nearby box and dabbed at his wife's cheeks as he put a smile on his face for her.

"I thought of a new name for our little girl that we haven't tried yet. Kylie. How does Kylie Hollister sound to you?"

Cassidy turned her face away. *Not now, Brady!* she wanted to scream at him. *How can we talk about something like this now?* She took deep breaths and demanded, "Why did he take her, Brady? Mom never did anything to him. What is he going to do to her?"

Brady gripped his wife's hands in his own as he told her everything he knew of the situation. "Edna and Beth met me at the door of the hospital. Jubel has been calling to tell Edna what's going on. She told me Higgins had gone to an outfitter named J.J. Stearns, got two horses and gear from him, then hit him over the head and tied him up before taking your mother into the mountains. Stearns was still in the emergency room getting his head stitched up, so I paid him a visit before I came to see you. Higgins told him he wanted the marshal to come alone to meet him. He took your mother hostage to get the marshal to chase him up into the mountains. The outfitter said your mother's hands were taped behind her back when Higgins pulled her out of his truck. He cut the tape, retaped her hands in front so she could hold onto the saddle horn, then he helped her up on a horse. He tied a lead rope on the horse, mounted up, and led the way up a trail through the trees."

Cassidy studied her husband's face with grief-ridden eyes. He seemed to be telling her everything as honestly and thoroughly as he could but she silently wondered if he was shielding her from some of the grim details.

"The fact that Higgins didn't kill Stearns is encouraging," Brady continued with confidence. "He isn't out on a killing rampage. He's not lashing out at everyone around him. He's only after the marshal."

"He wants to kill him?" Cassidy wondered aloud.

Brady took a deep breath before he answered quietly, "It looks that way."

"Why?"

"Revenge, probably. He was supposed to be in court today and Dad was the one who pushed to find evidence of the link between him and Trent Dominic."

"Is he going to hurt Mom?" Cassidy cried. She couldn't bear to say the awful things that came to mind.

Brady shrugged his shoulders in answer to his wife's question. He could not predict the outcome.

"Brady, you've got to stop him! You've got to try to get Mom back!"

“Cass, Dad’s already on the trail. He knows what he’s getting into. Higgins said the marshal had to come alone and your mother may be in more danger if he thinks his demands aren’t being met. And besides, I’m not leaving here until I know you and our little girl are safe.”

“We’re okay!” Cassidy assured her husband. “We’re both okay. They might even let me out of the hospital tomorrow. I didn’t really go into labor or anything. We just had a bad scare.”

“But you can’t go back to the ranch,” Brady pointed out.

“Edna said I could stay with her,” Cassidy argued. “She’s close to the hospital.”

“Are you sure you don’t need me to stay with you?”

“I want you here,” Cassidy admitted, then with a slightly teasing grin, she added, “but I don’t need you.” Tears suddenly overflowed once again as she added, “Not like Mom does.”

Brady kissed his wife tenderly before leaving the room. She nestled down into the pillows and pulled the covers up tight around her, feeling more at peace, knowing that Brady would do what he could to help rescue her mother. As she considered the information her husband had shared with her, Cassidy drifted into an exhausted sleep.

Higgins reined in his horse at the edge of the timber and dismounted. He looked up at the damp and chilled Elaine and offered her a hand to help her down from where she sat on the sorrel mare. She ignored the offered aid and tried to climb down by herself, but her cold, wet fingers were too numb to hold onto the saddle horn. Higgins was there to catch her when she fell. Elaine pulled defiantly out of his grasp.

“You remind me of my first wife,” the man said with a sarcastic smile. “When she was mad at me, she’d give me the silent treatment and pull away like that.”

Elaine glared at the man, but offered no comment.

“Are you mad ‘cause I kicked your little dog?”

“I’m angry about a lot of things,” Elaine retorted. “Would you please cut this tape off my hands? I would like to find a place where I can go to the bathroom.”

Higgins regarded the woman as he produced a pocket knife. "You're not gonna try to run away are you?" he asked before sawing the duct tape.

"Run?" Elaine questioned. "I can hardly walk. I've never been on a horse so long in my life."

With the tape removed, Elaine shuffled stiffly away, trying to ease the protesting muscles in her legs and restore feeling in a backside gone totally numb from spending hours in a saddle.

"You'd best hunker down under the pine trees where you won't get so wet," Higgins advised Elaine the moment she returned to stand by the horses. He handed her the sleeping bag he had untied from her mount.

Elaine picked a sheltered spot where generous pine boughs swept low over the rocky ground. Cradling the bedroll in her arms, she stooped to crawl into the little haven. While she unrolled the sleeping bag and draped it around her, Higgins tethered the horses in an open area where they could reach grass. After caring for the animals, the man carried the gear into the meager shelter to drop them under the pine boughs next to his captive.

In the failing light, Elaine watched in silence as Higgins extracted a flat bottle from inside his jacket, removed the cap, and took a long gulp of the liquid inside. He offered a drink to Elaine, who only frowned at the man.

"It'll warm you up," he informed her. "I ain't building a fire. This is the only warm drink you're gonna get."

So cold she was shaking, Elaine nevertheless refused the flask. She noted that Higgins was wearing a heavier coat than she was and seemed impervious to the chill dampness in the air. Her coat had been more than adequate for a trip to town in the valley in the middle of the day, but was not serving her well in the higher reaches of the mountains as evening approached. She curled deeper into the sleeping bag, clutching it tighter around her. Perishing because of hypothermia hardly fit into her plans to survive, yet she doubted she would benefit from the proffered beverage.

"Drink it, Lady!" Higgins hissed at her and thrust the flask under her nose. "I want you alive when that marshal shows up!"

Elaine grasped the container and hastily took a large gulp. As she choked on the vile tasting liquid and gasped for breath, Higgins laughingly retrieved the flask before the contents were spilled.

"Your first taste of whiskey?" he asked, baring his teeth with his arrogant grin.

"And the last," Elaine retorted with another cough, the awful taste still clinging venomously in her throat.

"It warmed you up, didn't it?"

"My insides are scorched, thank you," she complained. She jerked the fluffy down sleeping bag up over her head and pulled it tightly around her shoulders, hoping to prevent the escape of body heat that kept her shivering.

Higgins reached into the saddle bag and extracted a handful of beef jerky, offering some to Elaine. With her hands stiff and swollen from being bound, she could hardly grasp the dried meat and maneuver it toward her mouth.

"Why are you doing this?" Elaine asked with a glance at her captor. She asked in a kinder tone than she had before, as if she were sincerely interested in the ex-sheriff's motives.

"Why not?" he retorted. "If they're gonna send me to prison, it might as well be for wasting a U.S. Marshal as for that other pile of crap they're trying to pin on me."

"You're saying you didn't do the things you're being charged with?"

"I'm sayin' the marshal could have left well enough alone," Higgins snorted. "I resigned as sheriff but that wasn't good enough for him. He had to keep diggin' up dirt 'til now I'm lookin' at a whole lot of years in the big house."

Elaine recalled that the smug uniformed Higgins would have let Trent Dominic's men find Cassidy and dispose of her. Decades of imprisonment seemed less than adequate to punish an officer of the law who would look the other way as gangsters did what they pleased.

Besides praying for protection for everyone this man was coming into contact with, Elaine had spent hours while climbing the mountain reciting as many Bible verses as she could remember. She turned her attention back to meditating on the Word of God. *"He who dwells in the secret place of the Most High shall abide under the shadow of the Almighty. I will say of the Lord, He is my refuge and my fortress, my God, in Him will I trust. Surely He shall deliver you from the snare of the fowler…"*

"I hear tell in town the marshal wants you to marry him," Higgins commented, breaking Elaine's train of thought as he pulled a saddle up behind him to lean on it. "Why'd you turn him down?"

Elaine stared at the ground, keeping her lips tightly sealed. She wasn't about to discuss her personal life with her captor.

"You don't realize it, Lady, but I'm doin' you a big, big favor," the man continued as he lit a cigarette. "You're gonna have the rare chance to see the marshal in action and probably live to tell about it. You don't realize how many outlaws never live to stand trial once U.S. Marshal Bret Hollister goes after 'em. Folks think he's some great lawman that always gets the job done. But, I tell you what, he's nothin' but a cold-blooded killer with a big, fancy badge."

Elaine had been keeping her eyes averted from her captor. Now, she stole a glance his way and found that he was watching her closely, gauging her reaction to his words.

"You just remember when the shootin' starts tomorrow," Higgins informed the woman, "The marshal ain't comin' up this mountain after you. He's comin' after me." Higgins paused, letting his statement penetrate. "He's blood-thirsty. If he lives through this, you just keep that in mind if you get any bright ideas about marryin' that man."

Higgins pulled the other saddle closer to Elaine, resting it in a position on which she could use it as a pillow. She kicked off her shoes, which she put under the saddle to ward off the drizzling rain, and climbed completely inside the sleeping bag, pulling the zipper up to her neck. The man came toward her with the roll of duct tape. Elaine felt a moment of claustrophobic panic as he taped around her shoulders and arms, leaving little room to move and confining her in the blanket. The man then unfurled his own bedroll, spread it across his legs, and lay back on the saddle with his hat pulled down over his face.

As light showers subsided to a fine mist, Higgins relaxed. Just as Elaine wondered if he was asleep, the man issued a warning to his captive. "You keep cooperating, you'll get out of this alive. Don't make me hunt you down."

Curling up into a tight ball to stay as warm as she could, with the sleeping bag encased like a cocoon around her, Elaine laid on the ground, resting her head on the cool, damp leather of the saddle. Higgins' words echoed in her mind. *"The marshal ain't comin' up this mountain after you. He's comin' after me."* Had her captor put into words a suspicion Elaine had not been able to pinpoint before this? *He has a reputation for being tough and relentless,* she considered. *Is he also as ruthless as Higgins says he is?*

Marshal Hollister stripped the saddle and bridle from the buckskin horse and dropped them under the low-slung bows of a pine tree next to the trail. With a wave of his hand he signaled the animal to go on his own. Surely the horse knew how to find his way home and would probably be happy to do so, knowing a warm barn beckoned. The gelding turned to follow the track downhill, picking his way carefully along the rock-strewn stream of mud that made every step treacherous.

Removing his hat, the marshal fit his arms through an elastic harness that held a pair of binoculars tightly to his chest, then pulled his coat on over it. Removing clips of ammunition and the last of his sandwiches from the saddle bag, he filled the pockets of the coat. He grabbed up the canteen of water from where it lay on the sodden ground and strapped it to his waist, put on a pair of night vision goggles, and replaced his hat over his damp hair. Pulling his rifle from the case, he settled the attached sling over his shoulder before stepping from under the shelter of trees to start his climb.

Instinct told the marshal that Higgins would want to be at the top of the long slope first thing in the morning. In the light of day, the man would be able to watch the entire side of the mountain–the tree-covered slopes, the barren rock ledges, and the brushy upper reaches of the terrain. He would watch the marshal attempt to find the horses' tracks after rain obscured them. He would train his rifle on his enemy and wait for an opportune moment to pull the trigger.

As he urged the buckskin along the trail, the marshal studied the rock outcroppings that loomed above. While there was still light enough to see, he committed to memory as much about the terrain as he could, for he had already made up his mind to do the unexpected. Higgins would anticipate that the marshal would struggle through the mud on the same trail the ex-sheriff had taken. He would probably not consider that the man might climb on foot up the rockier side of the slope. The going would be slow, the marshal knew, but if he traveled most of the night, and if Higgins appeared on the ridge as he predicted, he might well have his enemy within the range of his rifle in the morning light.

Edna didn't agree with her husband's decision to ride up into the mountains with Brady, but she had already learned when Jubel's mind was made up, arguing was a waste of time. Instead of going home to worry and fret about how her spouse was faring, she stayed at the hospital long after her normal hours of volunteer work. She wanted to be available to sit with Cassidy and because she waited, Edna now had the opportunity to present a pleasant surprise. Putting on her usual cheery demeanor, she headed down the hall toward Cassidy's room.

Edna appeared in the door just as the patient was finishing a very late supper. Sporting a wide grin, she pushed a wheelchair through the door. Cassidy glanced at the seat of it. Pansy's beady little black eyes and mop of multi-colored hair peaked out from under a white towel with which Edna had made a bed. The little dog lay quietly, enjoying the attention she had been getting from Edna and a lenient night staff who overlooked the unauthorized visitor in their facility.

Cassidy couldn't help but laugh at the pup, which rolled slightly to her side, signaling that she wanted to be petted. The young woman reached over and tousled the furry head and scratched her tummy, noting quickly that if the little dog were in good health, she would have leaped out of the chair and onto her bed by now.

"Is something wrong with her?" Cassidy asked.

"A couple of Jubel's friends found her lying in the grocery store parking lot," Edna explained. "At first they thought she was dead, but she had only been knocked out, so they took her to the vet. She has some broken bones, but she's being a good patient. She understands she's got to rest in order to heal."

Pansy let out a muffled woof as if to remind the women she wasn't getting sufficient sympathy from them and put on her most woeful, irresistible look. Edna reached down and carefully lifted the forlorn pup, gently laying her next to Cassidy.

As they curled up with one another, the elderly woman lowered Cassidy's hospital bed to a comfortable sleeping level. Dimming the lights in the room, Edna quietly slipped out into the hallway to leave the pair alone while she got a cup of coffee. When she returned a short time later, they were both fast asleep.

Larry Higgins moved the horses further up the slope where they could forage for food. The wet grass would sustain them for a long time–long enough to finish the business at hand. In the predawn light, he watched the slumbering Elaine, surprised she had not attempted to flee during the night, for he had slept much harder and longer than he intended. Of course, had she been able to escape the sleeping bag, her tracks would have been easy to follow after the rain. And making her way over unfamiliar mountains in the dark of night could have been her death sentence. She had chosen the safer of two options–awaiting the outcome of the confrontation that was to come.

With a wary eye on the landscape that spread beneath him, Higgins studied the terrain, fresh-washed and anticipating the streaks of sunrays that slowly spilled over the distant ridge. He was more sober now than he had been in a long time. He didn't like the feeling, yet he was determined to follow through with the venture he had begun. He needed complete sobriety and concentration to fulfill his mission. Though he had breakfasted on beef jerky and large draughts of water from the canteen, there was a gnawing in the pit of Higgins' stomach. An excitement was rising within him. He smiled to himself. U.S. Marshal Bret Hollister was on his way. He could feel it.

"There's no tracks, Jubel," Brady spoke dejectedly as he sat down on a fallen log next to Jubel's bedroll. "The rain wiped 'em out. I can't find a clue as to which way to go."

We haven't been following tracks since sundown last night, Jubel thought to himself. *And it didn't rain hard enough to wipe out all tracks. I was only pretending we were on the trail.*

The old man lifted his hat from his face to peer at the sparse spears of sunlight that invaded the dark forest. He rose stiffly from his warm bed and reached for his boots. He didn't utter a word to the young man until he was dressed.

"I reckon I'll fix up a campfire and heat some coffee..."

"Jubel, I need your help finding the tracks!" Brady insisted. "Do you *have* to have coffee?"

"I ain't gonna break my neck tryin' to get up to the top of that ridge before the sun dries the ground!" Jubel spoke gruffly. "Up there is where we gotta be!"

"How do you know?" Brady challenged.

"'Cause we ain't got tracks to follow. We gotta go up high so we can take a look around."

Brady walked disgustedly toward the horses. He hesitated only a moment before grabbing up a saddle and bridle. As he readied his horse for the long trip up the slope, he spoke to his uncle. "No one will fault you, Jubel, if you go back home to Edna. There's probably nothing more you can do to help anyway."

"Prob'ly not," came the short, disgusted reply. As Brady was about to mount up, Jubel added, "No one would fault you either if you went home to your wife. No matter what she says, she needs you right now."

Brady turned to face his uncle. "I can't sit around in a hospital room, Jubel! I have to try!" Utter frustration showed on the young man's face.

"Try what?" Jubel challenged the young man. "Higgins gave orders for the marshal to come alone. If he sees there's other people around, it's hard tellin' what he'll do."

"I need to know where they are, Jubel...in case something goes wrong. I'm not going to interfere with the fight," Brady stated as he mounted the horse. "But afterwards, if Higgins is still alive...well, I want to make sure

Elaine is all right. I'm going to the top of the slope to look around. If I don't see or hear anything within a few hours, I'll head back down to the outfitter's."

As Brady turned the horse up the muddy trail, Jubel called behind him, "I'll mosey on up there. After I've had my coffee."

TWENTY-NINE

"Get up, Lady," Higgins ordered as he tapped Elaine with the toe of his boot.

Elaine had been feigning sleep for quite some time, listening as Higgins moved about the area. She had occasionally opened her eyes to study her surroundings in daylight, searching out the most likely avenue of escape should there be a chance to do so.

As she rose stiffly in her pine needle bed, Higgins removed enough of the tape to allow the woman to escape her confinement. He allowed his captive a few minutes of freedom before handing her a couple sticks of beef jerky and the canteen of water. She ate in silence as the man gazed through his binoculars at the terrain below them.

With the meager breakfast finished, Higgins tied a length of rope around Elaine's hands, then led his captive up the rocky game trail to a ridge that overlooked a vast slope of the mountainside. The bluff on which they stood had a rock face that dropped several feet to a long hillside created by centuries of avalanches. Rock that had tumbled from above piled onto the mountainside and soil filled large areas, giving scrubby plant life a place to take root. Elaine looked downward, judging the distance from the rocks under her feet to the brushy plane below. *Is he going to push me over the edge?* she wondered. *Or when the shooting starts, is that slope going to be my best chance of survival?* Elaine was certain she would survive the short drop to the dirt, but wondered if she would tumble all the way down the steep hillside to spill over the rim of rock far below.

The waiting seemed endless. Elaine sat quietly beside Higgins in a spot where he was partially hidden behind boulders, yet able to view the scenery. She watched in silence as the man methodically studied every tree and stone, checking for movement that would pinpoint the marshal's whereabouts. He concentrated most of his search on the trail that he and Elaine had ridden and noted the disposition of the horses where they grazed near the edge of the stand of trees below them, for they would be the first to sense a visitor in the area.

As Higgins slowly panned the landscape, he suddenly froze. Elaine noted the change in the man's demeanor. Looking down the mountainside, she saw the marshal standing on the lower edge of rimrock a few hundred feet below.

"Larry Higgins!" the marshal called. The words echoed against the high peaks. "Let the woman go and give yourself up!"

"Cut the crap, Hollister!" Higgins voice echoed back. "I ain't givin' up!"

"Let the woman go! This is between you and me!"

Higgins stood and jerked Elaine to her feet, then drew her close in front of him, using her as a shield. She watched nervously as he gripped the rifle in his fist. The gun was ready to fire and the barrel was pointing in the direction of the marshal.

"He's gonna try to kill me, Lady. And I'm gonna try to kill him." Higgins words were deliberately spoken close to Elaine's ear as he held her tight in an attempt to entice the marshal into a jealous rage.

"Because you're both barbarians!" Elaine retorted as she elbowed Higgins in the gut. She hurled her body sideways, momentarily breaking his one-armed hold on her. Elaine dropped to her knees. Higgins' strong hand pulled her upward by her hair just as she grabbed the loose end of the rope between her tightly clasped fists. She clenched the fibers with all her strength, praying Higgins would keep his feet planted where they were and that he wouldn't feel the noose that snaked around his boot.

"Your woman's a feisty one, Marshal!" Higgins called and pulled Elaine close once again.

"Don't bother callin' me 'Marshal'!" Bret returned. "I'm not wearin' my badge."

"Why aren't you wearin' your big fancy badge…Marshal?" the ex-sheriff taunted.

The reply was barely audible as the man's low, threatening voice echoed across the hills. "'Cause if you hurt that woman, what I do to you ain't gonna be legal and it ain't gonna be ethical."

Elaine glanced down at the rope she gripped. Sure that it was still encircling Higgins' foot, she made a sudden leap forward over the rock face. Higgins, thrown off-balance by the move, opted to grasp his rifle with both hands and let the woman fall. Excruciating pain shot through Elaine's shoulders as she hit the end of the rope, but the weight of her body was enough to jerk Higgins' foot out from under him. The blast of a rifle resounded through the mountains as Higgins tumbled over the lip of the ridge, bringing with him a spray of rock and dirt that gathered momentum and propelled the man down the slope. Elaine ducked her head as rocks skittered past her. Sliding downhill feet first, she rolled sideways as the path of debris widened and intensified. She finally managed to halt her descent in a meager patch of brush.

Within seconds, silence prevailed over the mountainside except for an occasional errant, unsettled stone that briskly hopped down the newly cleared landslide trail. Elaine breathlessly stayed where she was, praying that the remainder of the mountainside would stay intact. She slowly eased her body into a position where she could see down the slope. No where did she detect Higgins or Marshal Hollister in her range of view.

Piercing pain shot through her shoulders as Elaine moved cautiously across the rocky slope in search of sturdier ground. She would retreat to the haven under the pine boughs where the horses were tethered, she decided, for surely someone would find her there. *Lord,* she prayed as she gritted her teeth against the ache, *I need help! I don't think I can get down this mountain alone.*

Jubel joined Brady at the top of the ridge, arriving a half hour after his young nephew did. Brady had spent much of the time resting his horse as it worked hard to navigate the slippery trail. A couple of hours later, the soil had dried sufficiently to provide easier going for the older man's mount.

With his horse tethered several yards below the rim of the hill, Brady lay on his stomach, searching fervently through his binoculars. He ignored his uncle until Jubel stepped past him, still astride his horse, in plain view of anyone who happened to be watching from the direction Brady had been studying.

"Jubel!" Brady called in a hoarse whisper. "What are you doing?" He leaped from his prone position and tried to steer his elderly uncle away from the top of the ridge.

"What are you doin,' Boy?" Jubel asked as he stiffly dismounted. He dropped the horse's reins and pulled his own pair of binoculars from the saddle bag, then silently strode along the wind-swept ridge. Sitting on a large rock, facing the opposite side of the ridge Brady had been studying, Jubel pulled the glasses up to his face and methodically searched the rim above the trees.

"Sit down, Brady," he ordered softly, indicating a spot nearby. The younger man wordlessly did so, though he was impatient to return to his search on the other side of the knoll.

"You look off to the right," Jubel ordered. "See if you can find the game trail that leads up to the end of this rim and crosses to the other side of the canyon."

"Why?" Brady questioned as he lifted his glasses.

"Because that's the ridge Higgins is on."

Brady looked at Jubel with shock. "You lied to me? You led me up here when Higgins went the opposite way!?" Fury rose in the young man.

"Not opposite," Jubel corrected patiently. "Parallel. We're parallel to the ridge where Higgins goes hunting every year. And we can get there from here."

Brady lifted his binoculars and obediently studied the terrain. "Why didn't you tell me from the start?" he accused.

"You wouldn't a listened," Jubel pointed out. "The same way the marshal wouldn't a listened if I'd a told him we were gonna try to get close to his whereabouts to back him up if need be. He thinks I was deliberately leading you astray so you wouldn't get yourself killed, so don't go doin' nothin' stupid and gettin' yourself killed or I'll be in hot water for sure."

Brady contemplated his uncle's words as he mentally scouted the trail that would hopefully lead them to Elaine. *Wily old fox,* he thought to himself before venturing to ask a question. "Jubel, what else haven't you told me that I should know?"

"Well," the old man began, "I reckon you should know your Dad never took any communication device with him. His phone and everything else is still in his truck." After a pause of several seconds, Jubel added another bit of solemn information. "And he left his badge, too."

Brady turned with a start toward the old man. Why would his father leave his badge? The horrible truth dawned upon him. *Because he didn't go into the mountains as a U.S. Marshal. This is personal. He has no intention of bringing Larry Higgins back alive.*

The echo of the rifle shot on the far ridge took Brady and Jubel by surprise. Both silently remained on the high ground as they searched through binoculars for any sign of movement on the far-off mountainside.

Brady's stomach knotted tighter with each passing second. Though he knew in his heart Jubel had done the right thing by allowing the marshal to handle the situation alone as he needed to, the single rifle shot caused a feeling of dread to wash over him.

"What size rifle was Dad carrying?" the young man asked.

"I believe he's got his .243."

"That was Higgins' rifle that went off," Brady stated flatly.

"Yeah." Jubel lowered his binoculars and sat quietly.

Brady had learned from the outfitter the size of gun Higgins carried. The marshal was toting a lighter-weight, smaller caliber rifle that would have resounded with a sharper, higher-pitched report. With every second that waned, Brady's ache increased. *Why isn't the marshal returning fire?* he wondered.

Jubel rose from his perch on the rock and moved to a spot farther down the slope, then raised his binoculars once more.

"We'd better get going, Jubel," Brady advised his uncle.

Jubel didn't move, but silently pointed in the direction of the uppermost edge of the trees. Brady came to stand next to the older man and studied the area on the far side of the canyon. At first, he detected only the faintest swish of a horses' tail through the branches, but after moving further downhill, he realized there were two horses there.

"A bay and a sorrel. That's what J.J. gave Higgins and Elaine to ride," Jubel informed his nephew.

The men continued to search the opposite rim. Long minutes passed before a human figure stepped into view. Elaine! Both of them sighed with relief. They could see that the woman's hands were tied together and watched as she slumped down under the boughs of the trees to work at breaking free from her bonds. As she toiled it became apparent, even at the great distance between them, that she was injured. It was now time to take the trail. It was time to interfere, no matter what the marshal said.

Jubel climbed up the slope and mounted his horse. Brady fetched his horse from where it was tethered and did the same. Though he was anxious to rush to Elaine's aid, the younger man resolved to let his wise old uncle lead the way. *How many times have I bullied ahead and missed the clues right under my nose?* he wondered. *I thought I was pretty good at detective work, but I have to admit, Jubel can sure outsmart me.*

Brady suddenly recalled the biting remark he had made a few hours before. "Jubel?" he spoke from his position behind the older man's horse, "about what I said earlier…about you not being able to do anything more to help…well, I was way outta line to say a thing like that. And dead wrong about it, too. You've been more help to me than you'll ever know. And if Dad didn't live through this…well…"

"Apology accepted," Jubel tossed the remark over his shoulder and urged his horse along the rocky game trail.

Thank you, Lord, for giving me Jubel, Brady prayed in silence. *I tried to dismiss him and go my own way. Where would I be on this mountain if I'd gone on my own? Thank you for reining me it. And Lord, thank you for watching over us. Thank You ahead of time that everything is going to turn out right.*

Marshal Hollister climbed back up to the rimrock that he had hurriedly vacated when the rock slide began. Peeking over the edge, he found that Elaine was on her feet, making her way across the slope. Knowing she was alive and on safe ground, he quickly descended. He was not going to give his position away to his enemy by calling out to her. Slinging the rifle over his shoulder, he held his pistol at the ready while cautiously stepping across the fresh-laid pile of loose dirt and rock that had moments ago threatened to carry him down the mountainside.

It did not take long to locate Higgins. The man was half covered with dirt and unmoving as the marshal approached. Blood oozed from a laceration on the man's cheek and also trickled from a corner of his mouth.

"Come to watch me die, did ya?" Higgins muttered from his contorted position under the debris. "Or finish me off?"

The marshal holstered his pistol and laid down his rifle before kneeling at Higgins' side. He brushed away dirt and rock, then removed his coat to lay it behind Higgins' head, cushioning it from the hard stone on which it lay.

"I'll go get the horses and we'll get you out of here…" the marshal began.

Higgins shook his head slightly. "There's no gittin' me off this mountain alive, Marshal. I'm busted up inside." The injured man tried to smile, but winced with pain instead. "That woman, she done me in."

Higgins coughed weakly before he continued. "I guess I should have stuck with my plan to take her daughter…but I see she's in a family way…"

"Thank you, Larry, for not using Cassidy as your hostage," the marshal spoke sincerely.

"I figured her ma would be easier to handle, bein' older…" Higgins said between bouts of coughing. "Don't ever get her mad, Marshal," he warned.

Bret sat down on a nearby rock and eyed his enemy in silence.

"I think it's 'cause I punted her little dog…across the parking lot. That's probably what set her off…" Higgins added, coughing again and pausing frequently to catch his breath. "She's not real happy with you either.…She says we're both…barbarians."

"She said that?" the marshal asked with a smile teasing his lips. Higgins grinned, too. The animosity between the men was melting away, for there was no longer any point in fighting. The end result was already decided.

"I told her…you were a cold-blooded killer with a…big fancy badge…" Higgins confessed.

There was a long, awkward silence. The marshal clenched his jaw tightly and glared angrily at the fallen man beside him. It was bad enough the whole county seemed to know of his intentions toward Elaine. Now, she'd been told he was vicious. And yet, he wondered, how could he deny it?

The marshal changed the subject by asking Larry if there was anything he could do for him. Higgins ignored the question to ask one of his own.

"How'd we ever come to this?"

The marshal sighed. This was not the end he wanted or expected. It would have been far easier for him to have found Higgins' dead body than to watch a life ebbing away while being challenged with profound questions.

"Well, I figured you wanted to kill me and I was more than happy to return the favor," Bret answered cordially.

"I tried to blame you for ruining my life," Higgins confessed through clenched teeth. "If you wouldn't have dug up all those charges...maybe my wife wouldn't be divorcing me...maybe my boys would talk to me instead of...bein' ashamed..."

Bret watched Higgins in silence. He wouldn't argue with the man at this point. Higgins well knew that the source of his trouble was himself.

"Larry, is there anything you want me to tell your family?" the marshal offered.

Higgins nodded, the effort releasing another trickle of blood from his mouth. "Why does it take dyin' to get a man to say...what he shoulda been sayin' all his life?" the wounded man wondered aloud.

"Tell Linda...my first wife...I'm sorry," Higgins began, speaking slowly and deliberately. "She never deserved the way I treated her....She's got herself a good man now...and I'm happy for her....Tell the boys...I love 'em both. I'm right proud of 'em....Tell 'em to take good care of their mama....Tell my folks it wasn't their fault I turned out the way I did....They raised us kids in a fine Christian home....My brothers...and sister...they all turned out real good....Tell 'em all I'm sorry....Tell 'em, forgive me..."

The marshal swallowed hard. Life on earth was quickly ebbing away for Larry Higgins. His breathing was more labored with each passing minute and every word took increased effort. Bret knew he was about to witness a soul slip into eternity. He also knew there would come a judgment day for every man–including himself.

"While you're at it, Larry," the marshal suggested, "maybe you want to talk to the good Lord. Ask His forgiveness, too."

"What would you know about that?" Higgins gasped.

"I was raised in a fine Christian home," the marshal stated shamefacedly, repeating Larry's description of his upbringing.

"Then how'd we end up like this?" Higgins wondered, his voice barely above a whisper. "I don't know how…to talk to God any more, Marshal."

"I ain't good at it either," Bret admitted. "But I'll try to do the talkin' for you, if you'd like." Higgins nodded his assent. The marshal took Larry's hand in his own and gripped it tightly.

"Lord," Bret began haltingly, "I reckon I'm every bit as sinful as them outlaws I was always chasin'…"

Higgins managed a smile as his eyes fluttered shut. His lips moved as if he were repeating the solemn words. Rather than watch the dying man's face, Bret looked out over the distant valley as he continued.

"I tried to look real good for folks, but I didn't fool You. You know the heart of me. I'm askin' You to forgive me, Lord, for goin' my own way. For actin' like I knew better than You how I should live. I've been doin' wrong…"

Higgins' hand went limp in the marshal's own. Bret turned his attention to the man. His eyes were closed. His lips ceased to move. He laid quietly, each breath rasping with pent-up blood that he could not expel from his lungs. The sharp lines of pain and grief slowly eased from the man's face as Higgins slumped into what looked like a peaceful sleep. With the marshal sitting beside him, Larry Higgins breathed his last. Bret remained by the body in quiet contemplation for several minutes before folding the limp hands across Larry's chest.

Willing his stiff muscles to move, the marshal stood. He removed his vest, then his shirt, with which he covered Larry's face. Replacing his vest and pulling the coat from behind Larry's head, the marshal removed his hat in a gesture of silent final respect to the man whom he had called an enemy just a short time before.

As the marshal began his tedious climb up the mountainside, he considered what had transpired. He had long understood laws and boundaries, yet had stepped over the line and he knew it. Larry Higgins had spoken an undeniable truth. Being called a cold-blooded killer had struck the marshal like a physical blow, not only because the words were too close to reality, but also because they had been spoken to Elaine. *I thought I was falling in love with her, but how can a man have so much hate in him and love somebody at the same time?* the marshal wondered.

The words Bret had spoken for Larry were meant for himself as well. The decision to say them was not an emotional one, but it was sincere–an inward resolve to give up his current way of doing things to walk in obedience to God's Word. With only the imposing mountains to hear him, the marshal paused in his journey up the long slope. Turning to look back on the site where the body lay, the marshal spoke aloud. "I reckon, Sheriff Higgins, you brought one last man to justice. You didn't even know it."

THIRTY

"I don't want to hear it, Skeeter," Cassidy stated as the young pastor took a chair near Knowlton's couch where she was resting.

Skeeter regarded her in silence before speaking cautiously. "You don't want to hear that Toby has been fed and watered and Fancy has been put out to pasture and you have a hundred healthy calves running around the ranch, kicking up their heels?"

Cassidy turned away. "You know what I meant. I don't want to hear your reasoning for what Mom is going through. It seems like every problem that comes along, you have an explanation for it. 'God is testing you.' 'God is trying to teach you something.' 'He's building character'..."

"There's no explanation for this that I can think of," Skeeter confessed quietly, "other than, this is just the way life is sometimes."

Cassidy looked at the man and knew he shared her pain, for the sorrow in his eyes was unmistakable.

"I'm at a loss for words," Skeeter admitted. "That doesn't happen very often."

A hint of a smile played at Cassidy's lips as she apologized. "I'm sorry. I know you're trying to help. Thank you for taking care of things at the ranch. I really appreciate it."

"I wish there was more I could do," Skeeter said quietly. "All I can tell you is that there's a lot of people praying for her. The key to getting through this is to focus on our Source of Help and remember that God will bring good out of this. He promised good things to those who love Him and keep His commandments."

Bud Knowlton stepped through the front door of his house and led a visitor to the couch where Cassidy lay.

"Tom!" the young woman cried and lifted her arms for a hug from her older brother. "You made it!"

The two embraced briefly. Skeeter vacated his chair and offered it to the new arrival. Cassidy introduced the two men and they chatted briefly before Skeeter turned his attention to Bud and Beth, leaving brother and sister to talk in relative privacy.

"Jason is on his way," Tom informed Cassidy. "I know you told him not to come, but there's no use him trying to take his final tests with something like this going on. We've gotta stick together in this. Mr. Knowlton tells me no one has heard anything today–from the marshal or from Brady."

"They say, 'No news is good news,'" Cassidy reminded her brother. "I suppose cell phones don't work up in the mountains…"

The words were hardly out of Cassidy's mouth when the telephone rang. All conversation stopped as Beth grabbed the receiver.

"Hello? Yes, Edna." Beth listened intently for a time. "Thank you. I'll let her know right away."

Cassidy sat up on the couch, anticipating good news. Beth smiled at her as she laid down the phone. "Brady called Edna, thinking you were staying at her house," the older woman informed her guests. "He was able to get a call through when he was up on a high ridge. He and Jubel saw your mother. She was alone. They're on their way to get her now."

"I want to go to the outfitter's!" Cassidy announced. "I want to be there…"

"Nothin' doing, Young Lady!" Beth spoke firmly, placing her hands on her hips in her most formidable no-nonsense manner. "We did enough fast talking with that doctor to allow you to stay here instead of making you stay in the hospital or in town with Edna. I told him I was better able to keep you corralled than Edna was and believe you me, you're gonna rest and stay quiet for a few days like he says!"

Cassidy smiled at Tom's shocked reaction to their hostess. Beth had offered her roomy home as a quiet haven for Cassidy as soon as she learned that her brothers were coming to Wyoming. Cassidy quickly explained to her older brother that Edna was only five foot one inch tall, about 120 pounds, and seventy years old. Tom studied the imposing Beth, at six foot tall and twice the weight of Edna and agreed with a laugh that Cassidy wasn't going to get away with anything foolish around that woman.

There was mild celebration and lighthearted chatter in the room, yet uneasiness also. How far did Brady and Jubel have to go to reach Elaine? What would be her condition when they arrived? Where was the marshal? And where was Larry Higgins?

An exhausted Elaine slumped against the trunk of a tree. She closed her eyes and begged God once again to send help. The canteen of water lay at her side, too tightly capped for her to open it with her bruised and swollen hands. The rocks that felt so sharp as she searched for a place to lay down the evening before had barely frayed the tightly knotted rope around her wrists, though it seemed she had sawed at the fibers for hours. Her strength was spent. Her throat was parched. The intense sun had pushed the temperature up on the mountain face and Elaine perspired in the sweater and jacket that had been insufficient to keep her warm a few hours before.

"Elaine?" Bret's deep voice called from a point down the slope.

"Here! I'm here!" she called, tears of relief welling up in her eyes.

He walked steadily toward her, carrying his coat over a shoulder, hooked on one finger, and toting his rifle in the opposite hand. His white t-shirt was relatively clean, but vest and pants were mud caked. A full day's growth of dark beard shadowed the man's jaw. Fatigue etched every line of his face and slowed his every labored uphill step.

Tossing the coat to the ground, Bret lay his rifle down on it. Drawing a folded knife from his pants pocket, he dropped to his knees and sawed at the rope that bound Elaine's hands.

"He's gone," Bret said simply.

"He got away?" she wondered aloud.

"No. He died."

The marshal began to methodically rub each of Elaine's fingers in an effort to restore healthy circulation.

"He's nothin' but a cold-blooded killer," Higgins' words haunted Elaine as she silently watched the marshal massage her swollen hands. *I heard the*

shot when I leaped out of the way. A deadly shot. What are you feeling inside, Bret Hollister? Do you have any remorse?

"Aaahhhh!!" Elaine screamed as the marshal moved her right hand up out of her lap. "My shoulder! Don't move my shoulder!" She stiffened and gritted her teeth against the piercing pains that shot from her neck down the length of her arm.

Bret pulled her coat carefully down off her shoulder and cringed. Under the light-weight sweater Elaine wore, it was obvious the shoulder was badly dislocated or broken. Large beads of sweat ran down her face. She closed her eyes tight as she fought against the pain.

Reaching for the canteen, the marshal turned the cap open and offered the cool water to Elaine, who drank thirstily. He held the canteen, for it was quickly apparent that her left arm was not functioning at full capacity either.

"I'm sorry you had to go through a thing like this, Elaine," Bret said softly. He raised his eyes to study her face–that familiar uncomfortable stare that always made her look the other way. She dropped her eyes to look at the ground but he quickly placed his fingers gently under her chin, raising it, beckoning her to look directly at him.

"Did he hurt you?"

"No. I did this to myself," she was quick to answer. "When I jumped off those rocks…"

"Did he hurt you?" the marshal asked again, steadily.

Elaine knew the question was really whether Higgins had molested her. She was quick to shake her head. "He didn't touch me…not like that," she assured the man. Trying to make light of the matter, she added, "He just made me ride horse until my butt went numb…" She stopped speaking, noting that the marshal remained totally serious.

"Can you ride out of here?"

"I'll have to."

With the marshal's help, Elaine rose to her feet and scuttled out from under the pine boughs to stand erect. Once Bret had slipped her jacket from her arms, he retrieved the remainder of the duct tape. Folding her injured right arm across her stomach, he strapped the appendage tightly to prevent further injury from the jarring horseback ride.

After saddling the horses and gathering the supplies, the marshal helped Elaine into the saddle of the mild-mannered sorrel that she had ridden up the mountain. He mounted the bay to lead the way downhill. The pair had gone a few hundred yards when Bret stopped and turned to face Elaine.

"How are you doing?"

"Okay," she smiled weakly. Though the makeshift duct tape sling was uncomfortable, it held her arm tightly enough that the stabbing pains were replaced by a constant dull ache.

"I don't want to leave Larry's body up here," the marshal informed her.

Elaine noted that Bret called Higgins by his first name, as if he were well acquainted with the man.

"Do you have any strength at all in that left arm so you could help hold the horses? I'm gonna have an awful time getting his body up into a saddle, but I've gotta try."

Why do you have to be the one to remove his body? Elaine wondered in silence. *Isn't there someone else who can do that? Or do you intend to parade to the outfitter's place as if you were toting a trophy deer out of the mountains?*

The marshal noted Elaine's frown. "You don't have to look at the body, Elaine. I've covered his head with my shirt and I'm gonna throw one of the bedrolls over him once I get him on the horse."

Elaine remained silent and the marshal stated firmly, finally, "I'm not leavin' his body up here for the bears to tear apart!"

J.J. Stearns' son was the first to see them–a weary and bedraggled group of riders that emerged from the black specter of forest to plod across the twilight-darkened valley. By the time the quartet of horses arrived at the buildings, everyone inside had emerged to stand vigilantly, quietly awaiting the news they had feared or hoped for.

Brady led the way, carrying with one arm the extra saddle and gear that the marshal had left behind when he turned the buckskin loose. The large bay gelding plodded behind Brady's mount, carrying Elaine and the marshal. Jubel was the last to emerge from the dark forest into the pale light of the clearing, riding the horse he had rented from J.J. and leading the sorrel mare that carried the body of Larry Higgins.

The group who huddled on the porch of J.J.'s establishment watched quietly as the men dismounted. The marshal helped Elaine from the saddle. With her jacket buttoned awkwardly without her right arm in the sleeve, it was apparent she was injured.

"Did the buckskin come home?" the marshal asked as he approached the silent group.

"Yeah. He came back."

Bret eyed the people who stood behind J.J. The tear-stained face of a woman who sobbed quietly and the somber demeanor of two of the men led the marshal to suspect they were related to Larry Higgins. The outfitter confirmed his suspicion.

"Marshal, these are Larry Higgins' two brothers and his sister."

The marshal sighed deeply, audibly. "I'm sorry to tell you…"

"We heard the shot, Marshal," one of the men interrupted. "We figured Larry wouldn't be comin' home alive."

The woman wept aloud while her other brother enclosed her in his arms.

"The shot you heard was from Larry's rifle," the marshal quickly pointed out. "His gun accidentally went off when the ground gave way underneath him. A landslide carried him down over a rock ledge…" Bret stopped speaking, noting that Elaine was hurrying away from the group. Several others followed his gaze and Larry's brother spoke again.

"Did he hurt her, Marshal?"

"No. The landslide did." It was the only explanation the marshal offered them. "I've got to get her to a doctor."

"I've got some sandwiches made up," a woman announced. "You folks had best eat a bite before you go." Without waiting for Bret, Jubel, or Brady to come inside the building for food, J.J.'s wife asked her son to help bring it out to them.

"Thanks for bringing his body back," one of the Higgins men said.

The marshal nodded wearily as he wolfed down a sandwich. "Thank those two," he said, indicating Brady and Jubel. "If they wouldn't have come along when they did, Larry would still be up there. I couldn't get him on that horse by myself."

Weariness lay on the marshal like a heavy weight. He wanted nothing more than to get cleaned up and lie down on a nice, soft bed. Yet the grief in the eyes of Larry's family compelled him to stay a moment longer and speak with them.

"Larry didn't die right away," he said softly. "I talked to him awhile before he did. He wanted me to give messages to your folks and his kids and his first wife. If it's okay with you, I think we should all get together so we can talk."

After exchanging phone numbers and designating contacts, the marshal went in search of Elaine. He found her leaning against the far side of his vehicle, out of sight of everyone. Tears streamed down her face as she tried to control the deep sobs that racked her body. As Bret came around the back of the truck, Elaine couldn't gain her composure fast enough to conceal her hurt when he approached. She turned away from him, as she so often did. Instead of making her face him, Bret simply stepped close and stroked her tangled hair. When her grief seemed most unbearable, he loosely encircled her with his arms and held her quietly.

"I killed him," Elaine sobbed. "It was my fault."

"Elaine, there was no way you could have known there'd been enough rain on that slope to loosen the rocks..."

"I thought you shot him...but the shot came from above me...from up the slope, didn't it?"

"Yes, it did."

Bret said no more. He was too bone-tired to fight an emotional battle in trying to convince Elaine she was not at fault. He could only hope reason would return to her after a night of rest. But rest was not going to come soon. Her injuries still had to be dealt with.

Brady came around the vehicle, bearing a cup of coffee and a sandwich in his hands for Elaine.

"I'd better get going," Bret muttered.

Brady intervened when his father moved toward the driver's seat. "Dad, you're not driving! You can hardly keep your eyes open, you're so tired!"

Bret didn't argue. He meekly allowed his son to open the back door of the vehicle and climbed inside, holding the sandwich and coffee while Brady helped Elaine in. Once she was settled, Brady ordered her to eat something. At first she refused, but he stood his ground until Elaine took the sandwich and feebly lifted it to her mouth with her left hand.

Brady returned to the somber group standing next to the horse that bore Larry Higgins' body and explained that he was going to head for town. He offered his condolences to the family. Thanking Mrs. Stearns for the sandwiches, he grabbed three more as he retreated toward the marshal's truck. Jubel followed.

"I'll call the hospital and give 'em the heads up that you're comin' in," Jubel informed the group in the vehicle. "I'll help take care of Larry's body and tend to the horses before I mosey on down the mountain."

THIRTY-ONE

"I want her to come with me," the marshal insisted.

"Mom is just getting out of the hospital!" Cassidy argued. "We're taking her to Knowlton's where she can rest…"

"This won't take long!" Bret interrupted his daughter-in-law. He eyed Cassidy and her brothers sternly. "You're all concerned about your mother's physical health, but she needs to heal emotionally, too! She's been through a lot and so has Larry Higgins' family and everybody needs to hear what went on the day Larry died! I'm taking your ma with me and after I've said my piece, you go ahead and take her to Knowlton's!"

"She's been through enough!" Cassidy hissed and stood her ground between the marshal and her mother, who sat rigidly in the chair in her hospital room.

"Please stop!" Elaine begged weakly. "Bret, I can't do it. I can't face that family."

The marshal pushed past Cassidy and knelt down so he was eye level with Elaine, bringing his face close to hers. "Elaine, you look me straight in the eye," he commanded in a soft, yet firm tone. "You tell me you aren't still blaming yourself for Larry's death. You tell me you're not gonna start bawling every time you hear his name…or that you can look at the Big Horn Mountains without having nightmares about 'em. You tell me you're not bottling up a bunch of hurt inside. If you can do that, I'll let you go to the K Bar B right now and we won't say another word about it."

Elaine shut her eyes tightly in an attempt to stem the tears that stung. Her chin quivered and a painful sob racked her body. The marshal stood and wordlessly motioned for the nurse who waited nearby with a wheelchair, ready to escort the discharged patient from the hospital.

"You'd better come, too," the marshal suggested to Elaine's children, though it sounded more like an order. A quiet parade left the hospital room behind.

The atmosphere was somber yet expectant as the marshal led the way into the church that had been kindly offered as a meeting place for the Higgins family during their time of crisis. He made no attempts at introductions as he moved to a spot in the aisle and turned to face the back of the room. The little audience eyed one another as they quietly selected seats in various pews. Scarcely were they settled when the marshal began to speak.

"Larry died as the result of a rock slide that carried him down the mountain about 200 yards and dropped him over a ledge," Bret spoke unceremoniously to a still audience. "As all of you know, he had taken Mrs. Henderson up into the mountains against her will. She saw a possible chance to escape and tripped him. When Larry fell, the weight of him dislodged some rock. Because of all the rain on the slope in the past few weeks, the ground was unstable and it let loose. Mrs. Henderson was injured in the fall, but was able to roll out of the path of the rock slide. I found Larry within a few minutes after his fall. He knew he wasn't going to get off the mountain alive. We had several minutes together before he passed away."

As the marshal relayed the messages Larry had given for his sons, his parents and his first wife, tears of grief began anew among his relatives–especially when Bret reiterated Larry's regrets at not having said the words personally as he should have. Bret then relayed Larry's final moments–the prayer Bret had spoken and the dying man's struggle to repeat the words and maybe add some of his own. The description of the peace that encompassed Larry's passing brought a notable sense of relief to his family.

When Bret finished speaking, he moved toward the pews that held the mourning family to offer his condolences. Larry Higgins' mother and father rose from their seats to thank the marshal for sharing their son's final moments. After speaking to the parents, Bret moved among the relatives, making it a point to speak to each of Larry's sons. After greeting Larry's brothers, Bret glanced around the small crowd. Larry's mother had sat down next to Elaine and was tearfully hugging the wounded woman. The gesture assured everyone that the Higgins family found no reason to blame Elaine for what happened to their loved one. With her children and strangers surrounding her, Elaine wept deeply and mournfully.

Nearly unnoticed, the marshal slipped out of the church and hastened toward his vehicle. Brady hailed him before he climbed inside.

"You headin' up to the cabin?" he guessed as he approached his father.

The marshal shook his head. "Back to Cheyenne," he corrected.

"Dad, you've been through a lot, too. Can't you take a day or two off and get some rest?"

"I've got too much to do to take time off. I'll be back up here as soon as I can."

"Gladys Cole will cover for you," Brady argued.

"She can do most everything that needs to be done," the marshal agreed. "But she can't resign my position for me."

Brady was stunned. He wondered if he'd heard his father correctly. "What?"

"I'm resigning as a U.S. Marshal," Bret repeated, making sure his son understood him.

Brady could only stare at his father. For nearly all of the young man's life, his father had worked for the Marshals Service. But the familiar stern look said without further words that his father's mind was made up.

"When did you decide this?" Brady wondered aloud.

"The day Larry died."

"Is it because of Elaine?" Brady asked.

The marshal didn't answer directly. "I reckon if I'm gonna underestimate my enemies so badly, it's time to call it quits. I don't want to see my loved ones hurt. He was stalking Cassidy first, you know."

"Oh, Lord," Brady whispered. He pulled his hat off and ran his fingers through his coarse hair as he contemplated the horrors of what could have happened had Cassidy been the hostage. He walked several yards around the parking lot, taking deep breaths to calm the distress that rose within him.

When he returned to stand before his father, the young man questioned, "You intended to kill him, didn't you, Dad?"

The marshal eyed his son. "You knew I wasn't out to arrest him?"

"Jubel told me you left your badge in the truck," Brady acknowledged. "We figured you were taking this as a personal fight. It had nothing to do with the law anymore."

Bret sighed deeply as he confessed, "That's the reason I'm leaving the Service. Higgins called me a cold-blooded killer with a badge. I reckon he knew how to call a spade a spade. I didn't really care much about human life anymore. Not 'til I had to watch a man die slow…and think about a soul going to eternity."

Father and son regarded one another in silence for several awkward moments until Bret spoke again.

"That prayer…that was mine. It wasn't just for Larry."

Brady smiled as he recalled the words his father had recited a short time before.

"There's something else I learned from Larry Higgins," the marshal added. "You'd best tell people you love 'em while you've got the chance."

The father studied his son for several sober moments before he asked, "Have I ever told you that I love you? That I'm proud of you? That I'm sorry I wasn't a good dad, but you turned out to be a wonderful man anyway?"

Brady swallowed hard. "You tryin' to make me cry?" he asked hoarsely.

"I didn't do right by you, Brady," the marshal confessed. "We should have talked together and cried together when your ma left instead of bottling everything up inside. I reckon its okay to do it now."

Bret gave his son a big hug. Brady returned the gesture.

The two men were in intense conversation, standing side by side with arms over one another's shoulders when Cassidy, Tom, and Jason emerged from the church, followed by Elaine and Mrs. Higgins.

"Keep my resignation under your hat until after I've told my staff, will you?" Bret asked his son.

"I won't say a word," Brady promised, then quickly asked before the approaching Cassidy could overhear their conversation. "By the way, what are you going to do with all your new free time?"

Bret grinned broadly as he eyed his daughter-in-law's protruding belly. "I'm gonna learn to be a really good grandpa."

Bud and Beth Knowlton invited Elaine to stay with them after the surgery that realigned her shoulder and repaired torn ligaments, citing the fact that Cassidy and Brady should be preparing for the baby that was due in less than a month. Elaine had gladly accepted the offer, for she and Beth had become fast friends.

With a right arm still useless and the left hampered also, Elaine was little help to Beth with the daily household chores. Yet the normally active and self-reliant woman needed to do something physical, so Beth didn't deter her when she opted to go for a long walk each day after breakfast. Elaine would return to the house in time for lunch so the women could spend the afternoon together.

Feeling especially restless, Elaine opted to hike to the top of Black Mesa instead of strolling around the ranch grounds or pacing the long length of a hay field as she had been doing for nearly a week. Why the hill beckoned her, she didn't know, and scarcely paid attention to her surroundings as she slowly made her way up the rough truck track that led to the top.

Though the painful events of the previous week were slowly subsiding, some of Larry Higgins' words still kept resurfacing in Elaine's mind. She found it difficult not to dwell on them. "*...a cold-blooded killer with a big fancy badge...I'm doin' you a big, big favor...the marshal ain't comin' up this mountain after you. He's comin' after me...*"

The words wouldn't have so much effect on her if they weren't so heartbreaking, Elaine confessed to herself. She had to admit that she was physically attracted to Bret and she also found him intriguing, for he had mysterious contrasts. She had been at the receiving end of his harshness, yet she had felt the gentleness of his touch. He could be rash, yet caring. She recalled the way he had methodically rubbed circulation back into her swollen hands and secured her injured arm; the way he held her close to keep her warm on the long horseback ride down the mountain; the way he softly stroked her hair when she was crying. Yet he had climbed a mountain to kill a man…

Wind swept through the woman's hair as she topped the rise, the same way it swirled little clouds of dust as she stepped across the sparsely-grassed ground. Blood had been shed here, she reflected–at the hand of Bret Hollister and his deputies.

Lord, should I confront the marshal about Larry Higgins' accusations? Elaine prayed. *Will I drive a wedge once again between him and Brady? Yet how can I keep silent if the marshal really is as ruthless as Higgins said he is?*

Deep in thought, Elaine was startled to hear the sound of a vehicle that approached the top of the hill. She hoped Beth hadn't become worried and come looking for her. *Maybe it's Bud, coming to check on the cattle,* she reasoned. When the truck topped the rise and the engine was shut off, Elaine turned to find the familiar silver and black SUV parked behind her. She swallowed hard to clear the lump in her throat. She didn't want to face the man. Not now. Yet he was the person she most needed to see.

Bret didn't move from the driver's seat for some time, but quietly stared at her through the dusty windshield. Elaine watched him sitting there before slowly looking away. The door of the vehicle finally opened and he stepped out.

"Nice, quiet place to ponder things," the marshal observed.

Elaine simply nodded.

"So what are you thinking about?" he wondered aloud.

"You," she answered without glancing up at him.

"Is that good or bad?"

She kept her eyes averted as she said, "Both."

"Are you thinking about my little speech in front of Larry Higgins' family?"

"That, and other things. Why?"

"I was hoping you were feeling better, knowing Larry is in a better place."

"Is he?"

The marshal frowned. "Don't you think so?"

Elaine finally faced the man squarely. Last week, he wanted her to vent her pent-up feelings and she totally lost her composure before her family and a roomful of strangers. Now that they were alone, she was determined to finish what he had started and do a thorough job of it as she had rehearsed countless times in her mind.

"I'm not so sure you didn't make the whole story up to make everyone feel good. Or to smooth things over so no one would know you intended to kill him. I'm not so sure you really talked to Larry Higgins at all!" she challenged.

Bret was obviously startled. "How would I have known about his boys and his first wife if I hadn't talked to him?" he argued.

"You investigated the man! You could easily find that information," she retorted.

Bret pulled up to his full height and issued his most stern look.

"What I told Larry's family was the truth. And he said other things, too, that I didn't tell. He warned me to never make you mad," the marshal said. "And I'm sorry to hear about your little dog. Larry told me he punted it across the parking lot."

Elaine eyed the man suspiciously. "Pansy's doing pretty good," she remarked. "Pete's daughter, Emily, offered to take care of her, since she wants to be a veterinarian when she grows up."

"I didn't know the dog survived," the marshal stated flatly.

Elaine nearly laughed aloud at the obvious disappointment in the man's voice. "I don't blame you for not liking Pansy. She's never been nice to you."

"I'm not sayin' I don't like her!" Bret defended. "She's a nice dog… when she's sleepin'."

The marshal paused a moment before he said anything more. He folded his arms across his chest in his most intimidating manner, yet a slight smile curled his lips as he spoke. "If I didn't talk to Larry, how would I know you called me a barbarian? In fact, you called both me and Larry barbarians."

Rosy color crept into the woman's cheeks as she remembered the accusation she had made. It was hardly possible the marshal had overheard the comment as she wrestled free from her captor's grip. Elaine dropped her eyes to the ground and nodded. Obviously, her assumption had been incorrect. The two men certainly must have spoken to one another.

"I also found out Larry told you I was a cold-blooded killer with a badge."

Elaine looked directly into Bret's eyes as he confessed the truth.

"I can't deny it, Elaine. I had enough hate and anger bottled up in me, I intended to kill that man the first chance I got."

The marshal studied the far-off hills as he continued to speak. "I don't blame you for not trusting me. You must have sensed I didn't care anymore whether certain folks lived or died. That outlaws were becoming personal enemies. That I enjoyed dealing out my own brand of justice…"

The marshal walked in a large circle at the top of Black Mesa, occasionally kicking at clumps of grass or stopping to study the terrain around him. Elaine considered what she had learned of the gun battle that had taken place here nearly two years ago and wondered if the man was reliving it in his mind. She also wondered if the memory caused excitement or remorse.

Bret eventually turned his attention back to the woman who watched him in silence. "I suppose you're planning on moving back to Wisconsin," the marshal ventured.

"I'm going home for a visit as soon as I feel comfortable driving that far," Elaine explained. "Brady and Cassidy have asked me to stay at the ranch. I'll watch the baby for them while they're working."

"If you need someone to take you back to Wisconsin, I could do it."

Elaine eyed the marshal. "Do you have some vacation time to use up?"

The man smiled mischievously. "A long vacation. I'm taking early retirement. I'm through with the Marshals Service in a few more weeks."

The announcement stunned Elaine. It took several seconds for her to ask, "Why?"

"I've been taking a good hard look at myself. I need to know there's more in me than just bein' a U.S. Marshal."

Bret reached down and lifted Elaine's left hand. Her heart pounded as she averted her eyes from the man's face to watch him caress her fingers with his own warm palms. Fearing that a marriage proposal was coming, she silently prayed, *Lord, give me strength and give me wisdom to say the right thing…*

"Elaine, I tried to convince you before that I was falling in love with you," the marshal said softly. "Maybe I was trying to convince myself. I thought I was capable of it, but I wasn't. Not with the kind of love you had with Keith, anyway."

Tears sprang to Elaine's eyes at the mention of her precious husband and the deep affection they had for one another.

"There was something missing in my own life and I thought someone like you was what I needed. I know now that what I needed was the Savior. The hatred is finally gone, Elaine. It went away the day Larry Higgins died. Those were my own words in that prayer."

Excitement welled up in Elaine. *Lord, can it really be true?* she wondered as she intently studied the man's face.

"I do love you, Elaine…as a friend. I hope you'll feel the same way about me. Someday, that right person will come along for both of us. The good Lord will give us the kind of love we really need, right?"

Elated by the man's words, Elaine's heart skipped as she spoke. "Yes, He will," she agreed. "And I am so happy for you; if I could, I would give you a big hug!"

Bret took the initiative and gently encircled the woman in his arms, giving her a light kiss on the top of her head as he held her briefly.

Elaine stepped back to gaze up at the man and affected her most mischievous grin. "I have a question for you," she said.

"What do you want to know?"

"What were you planning to do to Larry Higgins that was illegal and unethical if he hurt me?"

Bret laughed aloud, the joyous ring of it echoing across the surrounding hillsides. "I suppose you've been worrying about that all week, wondering how mean I could get. I tell you what, Elaine, I had no plans. I was just talkin' smart."

"Trying to intimidate him?"

"Yeah. Us barbarians are pretty good at that, don't you think?"

"You're never going to let me forget that I called you a barbarian, are you?"

"No. Never," he stated emphatically.

"So, what do barbarians do with themselves when they retire?" Elaine teased.

"Don't worry. I have plans," the marshal assured her. "What I'm thinking is that I'll put the house in Cheyenne up for sale. I'll keep my fancy cabin up here for when I come to visit my grandkids. Then I'm thinkin' about getting into search and rescue, maybe in one of the national parks. And I'm even thinking maybe I could learn to be a chaplain."

"A chaplain!"

"I know I'm rough at it," Bret confessed. "But you have to admit, I got things out in the open with you and Larry's family. I'd like to be there for the families of people who are missing or have died up in the mountains."

Elaine was incredulous as she noted the change in the marshal's demeanor that had taken place in the past few days. She remarked with wonder, "My friend, the chaplain. I honestly never expected to say that about you!"

"Brady! Give back the binoculars!" Cassidy ordered. Brady merely held them out of his wife's reach, teasing her with them. "Fine!" she pouted and headed out the front door of Knowlton's house.

Brady knew she was heading for the barn loft. "Cassidy, don't you go climbing up that ladder!" he warned as he bolted out the door after her.

"Don't worry! I can still get up there!" she argued as she hurried toward the building.

"I'm not worried about you getting up there! What if you can't get down? We'll be in an awful mess! And you can't see much better from up there than you can from the house anyway!"

Bud and Beth Knowlton followed their visitors to the ranch house porch and laughed at the young couple who made their way toward the barn.

"Your folks should have called you Calamity Jane instead of Cassidy Jane!" Brady complained. "You get the worst notions in your head sometimes...."

"She's the perfect match for you, Brady Hollister!" Bud called. "And I can hardly wait to see what kind of problem child you two are gonna have!"

Brady paused in his pursuit of Cassidy long enough to turn and shout at the Knowltons, "This is not funny!"

The laughter of Bud and Beth could still be heard as Brady entered the barn. Before Cassidy could ascend the ladder to the hay loft, her husband grabbed her.

"Brady, something serious is happening with our folks! It looks like they're arguing, then they turn their backs on each other, then they're holding hands....I want to know what's going on!"

"I'll tell you what's going on! I promised Dad I wouldn't tell anyone, but I'll tell you."

"You've been talking with your dad on the phone every day this week. Is he asking Mom to marry him?"

"No," Brady assured his wife. "He's probably telling her he's quitting his job with the Marshals Service."

"What!?" Cassidy questioned, eyeing her husband to detect whether or not he was teasing her. "Are you sure?"

"He announced it Monday morning to his staff."

"That's unbelievable! It's like...that was his whole life!" Cassidy exclaimed. "Is he doing it because of what happened to Mom?"

"He's doing it for his own good," Brady corrected. "I shouldn't tell you the rest of it because I wanted it to be a surprise. He finally gave his heart to the Lord, up on the mountain, when Larry died. You'll really see a difference in him. He's more calm and relaxed. And when I talked to him over the phone last night, he had finished reading the Gospel of John and now he's studying the book of Romans."

"He hardly ever read the Bible before, did he?" Cassidy wondered aloud.

"It showed, didn't it?" Brady reminded her. "Jesus said, 'You will know them by their fruits.' When I was a little kid, Dad was enthusiastic about going to church. I think until Mom left, he really was living for the Lord. But in recent years, he's just been going through the motions. He'd been withdrawing more and more from Christian friends like the Knowltons and wasn't having a lot to do with me or Jubel anymore 'til you came along."

"So, I started something?"

"I think that ornery little dog of your ma's started something," Brady teased as he pulled Cassidy into his arms for a passionate kiss.

The ringing of the steel triangle announced that lunch was ready in the Knowlton house. The young couple didn't immediately evacuate the barn, but stood together for several moments longer, looking into one another's eyes.

"What are you thinking?" Cassidy asked.

"I'm thinking about you and me. Can you believe this summer we'll be married two years already?"

"They say, 'Time flies when you're having fun.'"

"It hasn't been all fun, Cass. We've had some hard times, you and me. I'm sure glad I had you to help me get through 'em. I know one thing–I love you more than I ever thought I could love anyone. And I need you more than I've ever needed anyone."

Cassidy blushed at her husband's tender words. She reached up to kiss him and hold him tight one last time before they headed toward the house.

"Do you remember the day after we got married?" Brady asked as the pair walked arm in arm across the yard. "I promised you someday we'd have a nice, quiet, normal life."

"With kids," Cassidy recalled with a laugh. "And a dog. A *big* dog."